A BRAID OF LOVE

A Novel

By

Alexandra Y. Caluen

A BRAID OF LOVE
Copyright 2019 by Alexandra Y. Caluen

Cover image & design by RK Young

A BRAID OF LOVE

The Tango à Trois Playlist

Bird on a Wire – k.d. lang

Possession – Sarah MacLachlan

I'm a Fool to Want You – Freddy Cole

Angel Eyes – Michael Andrew

Temptation – Diana Krall

Night and Day – U2

You Go to My Head – Royal Crown Revue

Until it's Time for You to Go – Freddy Cole

If We Never Meet Again – Tony Bennett & k.d. lang

In the Wee Small Hours of the Morning – Frank Sinatra

Maybe You'll be There – Diana Krall

Promise Me You'll Remember – Harry Connick Jr.
(music & lyrics by Carmine Coppola & John Bettis)

Un Beso - Quintango

A BRAID OF LOVE

Chapter 1
June 2018

It wasn't unusual for Geoffrey to wander into his cousin's restaurant, not too far from the Abbey Road recording studio. His parents' house was an easy distance, and a favorite coffee shop with good WiFi was nearby. He considered it 'his' neighborhood, even though most of his friends and both of his lovers lived elsewhere.

Recording artists stumbled into the restaurant with some regularity. Geoffrey didn't generally write about celebrities or about music – travel articles were his thing, the thing that kept him earning in between novels – but he loved to hear the musicians talk about their experiences. He rarely participated in the discussions, because they didn't know him and he wasn't the sort who would walk up and introduce himself to someone simply because they'd landed in the same curry shop. But they tended to be either excited or frustrated after working on a recording, and he never failed to pick up some snippet of conversation that gave him an idea for a scene in a book.

On that particular rainy afternoon, he was sitting at his usual table in the corner of the otherwise-empty restaurant, frowning at his laptop, picking away at a scene that was causing him considerable irritation. Then the door opened and two people came in, and Geoffrey forgot where he was for a moment.

He recognized both of them, though they'd never met. One was Janis Vaughn, a favorite recording artist, an American jazz singer and pianist. He'd known she was in England; he'd gone to her concert at Cambridge. She was – as she almost always seemed to be – with her tour manager Niall Phelps. Geoffrey had that internet-age feeling that he knew them, because he followed Janis' social media. She and Niall had been working together on tours for nearly four years.

Janis' life wasn't precisely an open book, but she posted with sufficient frequency and transparency that Geoffrey knew she was straight and single, having recently ended a long-term relationship back in California. Niall on the other hand was gay and single, having lost his fiancé – the actor Oliver Dunn – to a massive aneurysm in 2013. He'd spoken about it publicly for the first time only that spring. He and Janis were both even more attractive in person than they were on the internet. Geoffrey had always thought she was lovely, and Niall was most definitely his type.

All the same, he was unprepared for the physical sensation he felt, being in the same room with the two of them. It was something close to the delicious shock of being out for a winter hike and having a tree dump snow down one's collar. He shivered, realized he was staring, blinked, and realized that Niall was staring back at him. *Oh my heavens. Of all the curry shops in all the world, you walked into mine.* There was no mistaking Niall's expression. Geoffrey blinked again and dropped his gaze, reminding himself to breathe.

You beauty, Niall was thinking, gazing at the handsome young Indian man in the corner. His mind was otherwise blank for a moment until Janis nudged him, told him not to stare, and said something about Iceland. Niall caught up, managed to reply somewhat normally, and utterly failed at not flirting with the young man for the entire time they were in the restaurant. How could he not, when the expression in those startled eyes had been so clear.

Geoffrey had to remind himself to breathe again and again over the next hour. Every time he started to feel he knew what he was about, he'd focus in on that face again and lose track of the conversation. Niall flirted with him continuously, shamelessly, thrillingly. Before he and Janis – who was a complete darling about it, Geoffrey could tell that she was amused, her affection for Niall plain to see – finished their meal, he'd convinced Geoffrey to join them. They all talked together for a while, and then Janis said, "I'm going back to the flat now. Let me know if you'll be out late." She stood; Geoffrey stood as well, wondering if they'd passed some sort of signal that he'd missed.

Niall stood too, to give her a hug. "I'll send you a text," he said, then added, "Don't forget to stretch," because he had the fullest intention of propositioning their new acquaintance, every intention of making that encounter – should it come to pass – last as long as humanly possible, and thus no intention of being home that night to remind her.

Janis might have read his mind. "I promise. Geoffrey, it was very nice to meet you."

"You as well, Ms. Vaughn. A pleasure." He thought for a moment she might be about to say 'call me Janis,' but instead she nodded again and smiled. She let Niall help her into her raincoat, picked up the umbrella he'd left by the door, and went out.

"Well I hope the bloody rain lets up before I have to walk back," Niall remarked, turning to Geoffrey. "Or ought I have gone with her?" The other man seemed to be still processing the fact that he hadn't.

They kept eye contact for a long moment. Geoffrey didn't want to make any assumptions, but the energy between them was undeniable. There were other people in the restaurant now, and the next thing he really wanted to say was something he didn't much want his cousin's regular customers to hear. "I have an umbrella," he said eventually. "Would you care to walk out with me?"

"Yes, thanks. Let me settle up." Niall did that while Geoffrey retrieved the laptop bag he'd left behind the counter before moving to Niall's table, then said goodbye to his cousin. He went to the door, shrugging into his own raincoat. Niall was there a minute later. Neither of them said anything else until they were outside. Halfway down the block Niall glanced over at Geoffrey and said, "Was I mistaken or might you be interested in spending the evening with me?"

Geoffrey's heart rejoiced. "You were not mistaken. I know where we could go. It's not my own, but it is discreet."

"I'm at your disposal. Lead on, Mr. Anand." They walked a block without saying anything else. "Forgive me if I go silent. I'm a bit nervy."

"Do call me Geoffrey. I read your interview, from York. I'm very sorry for your loss."

"It was a long time ago." Niall glanced over at him again. "But thank you. I haven't been … living a full life, one might say, until quite recently. I'm not used to it yet."

There was so much Geoffrey wanted to say to that. The other man – taller, older, and in Geoffrey's opinion quite devastatingly handsome – could have taken him against an alley wall and he would have called the day good. The thought startled him; it was a thought he'd never had before. *You don't really know him*, he reminded himself. But that Niall was nervous, perhaps in need of comfort, and capable of saying so made Geoffrey feel ... important, he realized. Trusted. Valued. Eventually he said, "Mr. Phelps, I should consider it an honor to provide any comfort you require."

"Do call me Niall." His voice – a marvelous voice, he might have been an actor, one could quite easily imagine him on stage - was warm. They walked on. Geoffrey didn't want to hail a cab. It was more discreet to arrive on foot, the place he had in mind wasn't that far away, and the rhythm of their steps was hypnotic. Niall moved like a racehorse. It was the effortless, almost lazy grace that went with power. Geoffrey couldn't help imagining the body under the raincoat, under the jeans and the cashmere pullover. The rain had let up, and the sky was still light when they reached their destination. It looked like any other townhouse. Niall didn't say anything as they went in, as Geoffrey addressed the well-dressed person in the small office inside, or as they went upstairs. The room they went into was a bed-sit, with a sizable bed occupying most of the space and a small couch defining the sitting area. The couch faced a TV screen; on one side of it was a well-stocked bar cart and on the other, the door to a private washroom. "A well-appointed room, Geoffrey. I didn't know such things existed."

"They charge by the tot," Geoffrey said, smiling. "One generally brings a bottle of one's own."

Niall laughed. "I'd like a drink. And I'll pay for it." The phrase landed between them with a thud. He suddenly wondered if he'd misunderstood. Geoffrey

5

clearly saw that hesitation, that uncertainty. He moved his head a few degrees, smile fading, inviting clarification. Niall quickly reviewed the encounter so far. The other man was dressed much as he was. He'd been working, not soliciting. But this couldn't be left unsaid; there was Janis to consider. "I've not thoroughly misread this, have I?"

"I'm not a prostitute," Geoffrey said neutrally. "And I don't generally pick up men at my cousin's restaurant. I felt I knew you, so I've taken the chance of bringing you here. It didn't occur to me you might think I expected payment."

"I didn't. I don't. I beg your pardon, I'm doing this so badly." Niall took a step backward, toward the entry door. He didn't go out, though.

Geoffrey saw the anxiety on his face, along with the wish for reassurance. He'd had a moment like this before. It was almost to be expected when one was open – within reason, though there was little enough reason behind his present feeling of 'I must' - to chance encounters. He held up a hand as if to say 'wait,' and went to the bar cart. "Gin, whisky, or port?"

"Whisky, please."

That was Geoffrey's drink too. He poured into two glasses, took them over to Niall – still standing by the door – and held one out to him. He took it, studying Geoffrey's face with an intensity that was almost unnerving. "Niall. Shall we drink to understanding?"

"To understanding." Niall's voice was slightly hoarse. They clinked glasses, and drank. Niall never took his gaze from Geoffrey's face. "Christ, you're beautiful."

"I'd the same thought a moment ago." Geoffrey leaned in a little, lifting his face. Niall closed the distance and kissed him. It would have been so easy to simply ravish each other. The desire – indeed, the intention – was there. But perhaps the understanding that they drank to was already growing. While each put an arm around the other, and each opened his mouth for that enchanting kiss, neither of them pushed or pulled or did anything else to disturb the balance that both felt was delicately held. When Niall lifted his head and they each took a breath, Geoffrey stepped back. "Will you stay?"

"Need you ask?" Niall stepped past him, going to the couch and collapsing onto it. "What a lovely mouth you have." Geoffrey smiled. He'd actually been told that before. "Why are you single? Or are you?"

"I am." Geoffrey sat beside him, wishing they were ready to go to bed and knowing they weren't, quite. "I have lovers, people I've known who know me and appreciate my … difficulties. We see each other as needed. We all prefer it to the club scene. We're all on rather an extended hiatus from dating."

He gave 'dating' such a revolted emphasis that Niall couldn't help smiling. He focused on something else. "What difficulties?"

"I live with my parents, for one." Niall laughed. Geoffrey was still smiling. "London is expensive, my parents have room, and while they can be relied on to present me periodically with a prospective bride, they have yet to present me with an ultimatum."

"For one," Niall said. "Mine would be my very minor celebrity. And my connection with Janis. We're very close."

"So I've gathered, from her social media." There was a hint of a question in his voice. Niall certainly heard it. "May I inquire?"

"You may." Niall had been thinking about it - how much to say, because something had to be said - on the way to the hotel. "We are not lovers." There was more he wanted to say. He stifled the urge. It was far too early for that. He did add, "Her well-being is essential to my own happiness," because that was true. It also went quite a way toward explaining why he was, himself, still single.

Geoffrey nodded. That might not have been all Niall meant to say, but it was all Geoffrey needed to hear. He was having a rather fantastical thought, and it was far too early to share it. Perhaps after he and Niall made love, after they knew if this was to be a one-time affair or if they might make more of it. Except Geoffrey had to leave the next day. He was going to Wales to work on an article, and would be gone for the better part of a week. So, recklessly, he said, "My other difficulty is that I like to be made love to by men, and I also like to make love to women. When I say 'lovers' I actually mean two people, the same people, a man and a woman. I've known them for years. They know about each other. We're all friends, in fact." He stopped talking, because Niall's face had gone blank and Geoffrey didn't know him well enough to know what that might portend. *Hell*, he thought. *Hell and shit and bloody damnation.* "I'm sorry," he said, and gulped some whisky. "I can't imagine that's what you wanted to hear."

You have no idea, Niall thought. He set down his own glass, took Geoffrey's out of his hand and set it aside, and pulled the other man to him. The next time they separated, it was only to move over to the bed.

"How do you stay so fit," Niall said absently, some time later. They were both naked, both thoroughly aroused. Taking a moment to see, and to touch, the entirety of each other. Geoffrey had seen and enjoyed those long limbs, the pale skin contrasting deliciously with his own. Now Niall ran both hands down Geoffrey's back, then his legs, caressing a calf, bending to kiss the back of a knee. He lingered there. Geoffrey made a sound that said he wanted more. "Your answer, if you please, sir."

Geoffrey laughed into the pillow. "An answer for every kiss. I write adventure stories." His reward was another lingering kiss, behind the other knee. "I have to do research. One can't write about a person skiing the Alps without at least attempting to ski the Alps." Another kiss, ascending the back of a thigh.

"One actually could," Niall pointed out. "If one assumed that one's reader had never skied the Alps." He kissed the other thigh, apparently a bonus.

"Most people haven't," Geoffrey agreed. "I like to know that of which I speak. It's led me up mountains and down rivers." Another kiss, higher up the back of his leg. Tongue and teeth and hot breath. *God*, he thought, feeling his cock twitch against the sheet. "Across glaciers and deserts. I don't care for deserts." Another kiss, on the other leg, accompanied by a soft laugh. Geoffrey was losing his mind. "I like beaches. Ocean or lake. Perhaps it's water I like. God, Niall, I can't think when you do that." Niall's mouth was at the top of his thigh, open as if about to take a bite of his arse, and then he did. Geoffrey uttered a sound that wasn't a word, hips jerking against the bed.

"Oh, you like that, my lovely. So do I." Niall was on him then, hips pressed to Geoffrey's, erection thrust between his thighs. He had his teeth in

9

Geoffrey's trapezius a moment later, not too hard. Enough to remind them both what animals they were. Geoffrey pushed up against him, getting his hips right up off the bed so that Niall's cock slid against his own. "Holy mother of *God*."

Geoffrey laughed out loud. "I want you in."

"I shouldn't. I didn't plan. I don't want to hurt you."

"You won't. On the nightstand." Lube, next to a condom.

"Where'd that come from?" Niall hadn't been noticing much in his haste to get his kit off. "Travel with it, do you?" He reached over to get both things, prayerfully glad to see them since he hadn't even thought of it. Of course, he hadn't been expecting anything like this today. "Thank God for you."

Geoffrey pushed up again, hearing the condom wrapper rip. *Get in me, you beautiful man.* "Had a thought I'd visit my friend later."

"He'll miss you." Niall had the lube now. A little in his hand, and then his hand around Geoffrey's cock. Slowly, as if he really liked the way it felt. Brushing his thumb across the tip. Geoffrey bucked underneath him, gasping into the pillow. "Will you spend in my hand, love?"

"Yes, but after. After. Now. Niall." Geoffrey knew he sounded desperate, and perhaps senseless. Evidently Niall got the sense of it. He took his hand away, and then it was at Geoffrey's arse. First the lube alone, then a thumb. Geoffrey's head went back, neck arching.

"Choirs of angels, you're a lovely creature. Shall I have you?" Another caress with the lube, then a push. Slow. Killingly slow. "Your back, love. You're

10

like a gazelle." Niall braced himself on one hand, swept the other up into Geoffrey's hair, then down his spine. "Arch for me, sweetheart." Geoffrey made an animal sound and complied. Niall pushed further in, leaning forward to get one arm around Geoffrey's ribs, pulling him up to hands and knees in a surge of unexpected strength. Niall was breathing harshly, past speaking, and Geoffrey was past thinking. Only wanting. He pushed back, wanting it deeper, spreading his legs to accept Niall's strokes. He was close to climax himself, but he wanted that first, he wanted all of it. Niall was gripping his hips, holding him steady. Suddenly he said "Jesus!" and Geoffrey felt him go, the pulse of him, the curve of his body against Geoffrey's backside. He was motionless for a moment, panting. Then, still inside, he reached around and took Geoffrey in hand again. "You utter beauty. Let's have you. There, my lovely. Holy Christ, give it to me, there, *now*." Geoffrey convulsed, coming hard. He might have collapsed if not for Niall's arm around his ribs again, holding him up. Another moment without moving. "All right, sweetheart?"

"I'm all right." He had his balance. Niall took his hand away, then his arm, withdrawing with care and stepping off the bed. Geoffrey slid down, letting his mind go blank for a minute. He felt rather than saw Niall return, placing the whisky glasses on the nightstand. Then he was gone again. Geoffrey heard water running. A minute later Niall was there with a warm damp cloth, tending to him.

Not too much later they were lying together, holding each other loosely, gazing at each other. "This is not what I expected from this day," Niall said. "How old are you?"

11

"Thirty-four." He knew Niall was five years older. "When were you last in London?"

"Before this tour, not since December of 2014. One year after I lost Oliver. That was not a good year." An understatement, avoiding the confession of just how seductive the Thames had seemed, cold and gray and blessedly final. "If I had not had Janis waiting for me, relying on me, I'm not entirely sure I'd have survived."

"Poor darling." Geoffrey brushed a hand up his cheek. "I'm glad you had her. You had each other. Did you know her music before?"

"I didn't. I went to America on impulse. It was either America or Russia. The people I worked with said, don't go to Russia unless you want to come home an alcoholic. Of course, they hadn't seen Janis in a bar." That got the intended laugh. "You recognized her. Us."

"I have all her records. I'm mad about her. Went to the concert at Cambridge." They talked about that, about the tour, about Janis for quite a while. Then Geoffrey said, "Do you always talk like that in bed? I liked it."

"I've never talked so much in my life." Now that he thought about it, he wasn't sure why. "You liked the blasphemy?" Geoffrey laughed, closing his eyes and shaking his head as if to say 'the other things, you ninny.' So Niall said, "You liked being called sweetheart, and lovely, and beauty. You're all of those." He was about to say something else, something needy like 'can I see you again,' but managed to stop himself.

Geoffrey was studying him. *What did you not say*. "I have to go to Wales tomorrow. I've made

12

arrangements, I have appointments. I'll be gone most of a week. Research for an article. It's due in three weeks so I can't put it off. But could I see you when I'm back in town? Will you still be here?"

Niall knew that if he told Janis he needed more time in London, she wouldn't even ask why. He also knew that if he woke up the next day feeling the same way he did in this moment, he and Janis might be in deep trouble. It might have been wiser to say 'maybe,' and wave it off. Instead he said, "We'll be here. I'd be delighted to see you again. Do you have to go home tonight?"

"No." Geoffrey leaned in and kissed him. "How did you come by these?" He traced a finger under Niall's hazel eyes, golden brown mixed with mossy green, fringed with brown lashes and gazing back at him with concentration. "I've never met a red-haired person with dark eyes. Tiger eyes. They're beautiful."

"I prefer the term 'auburn,' but in view of the compliment I'll accept 'red.' My father's the same. His hair's gone sandy now at sixty." *And a bit thin*, Niall thought. But the eyes were still the same, and his mother didn't seem to mind the hair.

"Only twenty-one when you were born?"

"And married with my mother's father's foot on his neck." Geoffrey laughed again. "She was eighteen. They managed, though. Once they got over the shock of being married, they realized they rather liked it. He works in a brewery, and she as a bookkeeper. I have a brother and a sister, Allan and Marianne. He works in Aberdeen. She's a veterinary nurse in Newmarket." It was a lot of detail. He'd never told a lover so much at all, let alone so much so early. Except for Oliver.

Geoffrey didn't know if Niall usually spoke so openly. He doubted it, and therefore appreciated it. The confidences added to his feeling of being trusted, of being important. "I have a brother as well, he's two years older. His name is Wellington, poor bastard." It was Niall's turn to laugh, imagining the nicknames. "He's a banker like my father, he's married and has two children."

"Your parents must be happy. Mine were ecstatic when Allan and his wife hatched a chick." That was enough about his family. He wanted – maybe needed – to see if there were points where he and this mysterious man might converge. "They've never quite grasped what it is I do. Neither of them has the slightest inclination to travel."

"My parents have been home to India twice since coming to England. They don't go anywhere else. They think I'm mad to travel all over, alone. My mother does a lot of volunteer work with immigrants, she hears such terrible things. She says, why can't you write poetry, you can do that at home. My father likes my books, though."

"I shall have to look them up." There were so many things Niall wanted to say. He could lie here all night gazing at Geoffrey. The man was stunningly beautiful, temple art made flesh. It was almost unfair that he was also intelligent, well-spoken, charming. Niall realized his fingers were twined with Geoffrey's. He never wanted to let go. He needed to talk to Janis.

Geoffrey could tell Niall was thinking hard. He knew the nature of the other man's work must make any kind of relationship difficult. And then there was Janis. *What's the absolute least of him I could live with*, he asked himself, not even wondering why. He felt he could spend the rest of his life in this room, in

14

this bed, with this man, and be happy. They were touching only at the hand now; that alone was enough. "Are you hungry at all, darling?"

"Not enough to matter. I don't want to go out." Niall wasn't sure if that was what Geoffrey had been getting at. He wasn't sure what 'darling' meant. It didn't seem the casual, almost careless name-substitute one commonly heard from actors, or musicians, or those who traveled with them. He wasn't sure what he'd meant when he called the younger man 'love,' either. That was an endearment previously applied only to two people: Oliver and Janis. He suddenly felt the need to say that. *This is not what I usually do, this is not how I usually am, if this is what I believe – what I fear – it is, he has to know*. "You asked a question earlier. I didn't fully answer. No, I don't usually talk in bed. And I haven't called anyone sweetheart, or love, since Oliver. Except Janis," he added, because he wanted to be honest.

"I don't call anyone darling, either." Geoffrey pressed close, tucking his face into the curve of Niall's neck. "I'm feeling rather overwhelmed."

"So am I."

They slept for a while. When they woke, they kissed again for quite a while. There was no urgency. They made love in a different way, a way that again suited them both right down to the ground. They talked again, and slept again. When the window was pale with dawn light, Niall turned his head to see Geoffrey gazing at him, those soft dark eyes full of contentment, and worry, and something painfully close to love. "There's something you should know," he said. Geoffrey closed his eyes for a moment, as if he were afraid this was going to be 'I can't stay,' or 'I

15

won't come back,' or perhaps simply 'once more, then goodbye.' Niall couldn't have said any of those things under torture. "Janis and I. I told you we are not lovers. But we are in love. It's a frightful situation and neither of us knows what to do."

I do, Geoffrey thought on a flood of sudden hope. He couldn't say it. Not until – or unless – by some miracle Niall invited him to meet Janis again.

It was still early when they left the hotel and began the walk back to St. John's Wood. Niall tried to watch Geoffrey without watching, dreading the moment they'd part. He would miss that feeling of rightness, of fitting together, of ease. And, of course, his beauty. *He really is like a gazelle*, he thought. Taller than average, though not as tall as Niall. Light-framed and graceful, with an alertness that promised a quick escape from the wrong approach. He must have left countless frustrated pursuers in his wake. Yet he'd yielded to Niall, in every sense, with complete and irresistible abandon.

Geoffrey wanted to hold Niall's hand. He wanted to cancel his trip. He wanted to say 'run away with me.' He did none of those things. Then they were at a corner, and Niall stopped walking. "I'm this way," he said, indicating a change of direction. "Shall I call you later?"

"I wish you would." They'd exchanged numbers. Geoffrey would have asked, if Niall hadn't. "I'll be on the train to Cardiff. Nothing to do but think of you." That was too much, too desperate; he almost said something else to wave it away.

But Niall leaned close and kissed him, the merest brush of his mouth across Geoffrey's. "May I speak to

16

Janis about you? I want her to know." Geoffrey's smile was all the answer he needed. Throwing caution to the winds, Niall took the other man's head between his hands, stroking his thumbs up Geoffrey's cheekbones, kissing his eyebrows and his nose and then his mouth. "If I don't back away now we'll be nicked for indecency. I'll call you." He let go, stood away, took another step back. Geoffrey couldn't speak. Niall sketched a wave, walked backward for a few steps, may have seen from Geoffrey's expression that he was about to collide with a signpost. He stopped, said "Be off with you or you'll miss your train," with almost visible effort turned around, and walked away.

Geoffrey let himself into his parents' house, hoping to achieve his room before they saw him – he was in a state clearly indicative of the manner in which he'd spent the night, a manner which his parents both preferred to pretend he never indulged – but walked straight into the pair of them coming through the hall. "Good morning," he said, dodging all questions, and fled up the stairs. By the time he was showered, dressed, and packed his father had left for work and his mother was on the phone with an embassy. Geoffrey leaned in to kiss her, mimed 'I'll call you,' and made his escape.

All the way to the station Geoffrey knew he wanted to write, something in verse, as soon as the train was away. He hadn't written about a relationship for years. He wasn't even sure this was a relationship, but he generally went where the writing impulse took him. The only problem was that as soon as they were off, he realized the words coming to him weren't his own. *'Whoever loved that loved not at first sight.'*

17

Meanwhile Niall had texted Janis to let her know he was en route. His mind was racing. He was nearly certain that Geoffrey felt the same way he did, nearly certain that there was a way they could make this work. 'Nearly certain' wasn't enough. *Thank God we don't have to travel right now.* They had no commitments. They had time to sort it out, if by some miracle Janis was willing to try. He was nearly certain that Geoffrey would be.

She was waiting for him, failing to hide her anxiety. They had coffee and breakfast. Niall told her a lot about the night, without telling her everything about his night's companion. Then she said, "Would you please stop dodging and tell me what's going on? I'm in a panic that you're about to run off and leave me."

"I know you are." Niall turned away from the basin, drying his hands. He leaned against the counter. "I'll remind you his name is Geoffrey Anand. He's thirty-four, he's a writer. A novelist, and writes travel pieces for the glossies. He owns every one of your records, he's bi, and he thinks you're lovely. We talked about you half the night."

Janis stared at him. "What are you telling me?"

"Well it's everything but the effing guitar, isn't it?" He saw her remember the not-even-half-serious conversation they'd had eighteen months ago, the first time they openly acknowledged that they loved each other, and not simply in the way of friends. The conversation in which they had each articulated the wish for a third person, someone whose love they could share, someone who might make it possible for them to stay together. They had never spoken of it since. It had never seemed truly possible. He waited

18

half a minute for her to say something. "Would you meet him again?"

Janis closed her eyes for a moment as if she were reconnecting with reality. She inhaled audibly and looked back up at Niall. "Are you proposing that we … ménage?"

He crossed the room in a rush and knelt at her feet. "Could we perhaps start with a proper *dîner à trois*? Would you consider it? I do love you so."

"I love you too." She bent to kiss his forehead, then his mouth. He took her hands in his, lifted them to his lips for kisses. He knew she saw the hope in his heart. "Call him, sweetheart. Let's have dinner."

Chapter 2

Geoffrey was on the platform at Cardiff before his phone buzzed with a text notification. He'd begun to think that Niall had had second thoughts, that 'I'll call you' had meant the opposite. He should have known better. *Hello sweetheart, Janis and I had a chat this morning. She'd like to invite you to dine with us when you're back in town. Might you be willing?*

Geoffrey texted back immediately: *I'd be delighted. What does one bring to dinner with one's favorite musician?*

Only your lovely person. How is Wales today? We've bloody rain a-bloody-gain

Geoffrey laughed. *Sunny today. It won't last. Console yourself with the vision of me on a motorbike in the inevitable downpour*

A motorbike?! Are you mad? You've managed to derail my thoughts of joining you with a single word

I could rent a car instead

Niall was all too tempted to say 'do.' *Get on with you. Hurry up and write.* He almost added 'come back to me' but settled for *Be safe, my dear sir.*

Geoffrey replied with *I will, talk to you soon*, did not add 'I'll miss you,' and went to see about his transport.

Wales was one of his favorite places, and he knew it well. Which was a good thing, because his attention to his itinerary was continually interrupted by memories of his night with Niall, and speculation about meeting Janis again. She called, on his second night away. Niall had given Geoffrey her number, a mark of profound trust. He picked up as soon as he saw the caller ID. "Good evening, Ms. Vaughn. I hope you're well."

"I'm great," she said. "How's Wales?"

"Tell Mr. Phelps if it rains any harder I'll need a snorkel."

She laughed. "He'll be so happy to hear that. We've been underwater all week. Listen, I think he mentioned to you that I'd like to meet you again. Could you come to dinner next week?" She mentioned a day and a time. "I do not cook and you really don't want him to, so we'll have it catered at our flat."

"I'd be delighted," he told her, as he'd told Niall. It was all the more true now that he knew it would be a dinner at home. That made him wonder if Niall might have had the same thought he'd had himself. If the three of them might find things to discuss that were best discussed in private. "Can I contribute?"

"You can tell me all about Wales. I've never been there, or Ireland. But don't let me take up all your time, I know you're working. We'll see you next week. Oh, and I'll call you to re-confirm."

No need, he thought. Nothing would get between him and this meeting. But he said, "I look forward to speaking with you again." They ended the call, and he went straight to the bar, downstairs from his room, for a whisky. All he wanted to do was call Niall and ask what this really meant. Instead he had his drink, then went back upstairs to write. He was working on three separate things. One was the article for the travel magazine. The second was a draft of a new novel. The third was a journal of his thoughts about Niall, and about Janis, and about the future.

On Geoffrey's last day in Wales, Janis called again and they confirmed the dinner date. An hour later, Niall called. "Hello love. Will you make your deadline?"

"The article's nearly finished," Geoffrey said. They'd spoken every day. Each time, he knew, they had come closer to saying things that were probably premature. Talking about work was their so-far-successful strategy to avoid toppling off a cliff together before they knew they had a safe place to land. "These things never take long once I've done the legwork. This new novel is a blooming nightmare, though."

"Why, what's happening?" Niall couldn't keep the laugh out of his voice.

"This hero of mine. He was meant to be one sort of person, and now he's said no, sorry, I'm buggering off this direction instead and you'll come along and like it." He sighed, but he was smiling, because Niall was laughing. "I've all this research for his back story and now the bastard's simply sauntered away from it, two fingers up, laughing in my face. I'll have a hell of a time rewriting."

"You can't give him a good shake and put him back where he belongs?"

"I really can't. Once a character comes to life I know I've got something. So I have to make the story fit him, not the other way round. I tried, you know, once before."

"Had another who was noncompliant?"

"Like trying to put a sodding squid in a box," Geoffrey said, with feeling. "Tentacles flailing about taking hold of everything he oughtn't. Anyway I forced the issue, and it was an abject failure. I learned that my readers don't give a toss about plot if they love a character. The comments were instructive. So, since I did love the squid, I rewrote the thing to suit him, and now it's one of my best-reviewed."

Niall had been trying to stifle more laughter since 'squid,' and failed at its second occurrence. He got himself in order. "Which one was that?" Geoffrey told him. "I'll read it again, see if I can tell where he took over."

"You've read it?"

"Angel eyes, I've read them all. What else was I to do?"

God, you piece of utter perfection. It was all Geoffrey could do not to say 'love me forever.' Instead he said, "Back in town tomorrow. See you the day after."

"I look forward to it." Niall's voice was low, warm, caressing. "Travel safe home." He disconnected without another word. He'd heard 'love me' in Geoffrey's voice, and it was all he could do not to say 'I will.'

It was Niall, not Janis, who met Geoffrey at the door. So after a civil greeting, and after the door was closed, it was possible that they could kiss hello. "I've missed your mouth," Niall said a minute later, very softly, as if he knew they might be overheard.

"The same." Geoffrey stood away.

"Come through to the parlor." Then there was Janis, and she was gracious. Better than gracious: she was friendly, introducing the subject of her tours with Niall without delay, almost as if to say 'he is essential to me.' Geoffrey had the distinct impression that the subtext was 'and thus you are of interest to me.' He did wonder what she already knew. Niall was telling road stories, managing the conversation as well as he must manage the tours. Geoffrey listened to everything that was unsaid.

After a while Janis suggested dinner, so they all went through to the dining room where they were served by a polite helper. Now Janis asked questions about Geoffrey and his history, which somehow led to talk of marriage. He told her about his parents and their gentle but inexorable pressure. "You haven't wanted to?" she asked.

"Well," he said, with a glance at Niall, "there are reasons a traditional marriage would be difficult for me." He paused for a sip of champagne. Then he went for it. "A partner such as, for example, Mr. Phelps would not be the partner my parents would choose."

"Do call me Niall, pet." Niall appreciated the implication that he might be the partner Geoffrey would choose. He didn't intentionally make his voice sound that way, the way it had when his mouth was on Geoffrey's skin. Janis glanced over at him, though, with an expression between merriment and apprehension.

Geoffrey smiled. "And the partner of my parents' choice would most likely not welcome the presence of Niall in my life. But having met Niall, I'm not at all sure I could do without him." Geoffrey's hand was on the table. Niall's hand covered it.

"Holy wow," Janis said. "Geoffrey, have you been in love before? Oh my God, I'm sorry, that's so much none of my business." She buried her nose in her glass.

"It is your business though," he said. "I've an idea how important Niall is to you. I've spoken with touring artists before, I know how difficult that life is. And the answer is yes. I had my heart broken at university. It was a good experience." In the sense of 'instructive.'

"I had one of those too," she said. "And it was good experience. I recently got out of a long-term off-and-on thing with a man back in California, another musician, a teacher."

Geoffrey nodded. "Mr. Goldman." She looked surprised. "I read the liner notes. I understand you're in England indefinitely?"

"I just started discussing the possibility of a USO tour. Niall and I spoke about that this week, while you were away. Not even close to deciding when, or for how long, or where we would be going. There is some unfinished business for us both here, and frankly, Geoffrey, you're part of that." He was startled; it surely showed on his face. "Because I am relatively certain that Niall couldn't do without you, either."

"Janis!" It was as close to a yelp as Niall had ever heard come out of his mouth. *Oh my Christ what are you doing Janis not yet -*

"I'm sorry, precious, I know I'm overstepping. Forget I said that," she told Geoffrey.

"How could I?" He was looking at Niall. "The thing about having been in love," he said slowly, "is that one knows what it feels like. I haven't gone looking for it. It came to me before as a surprise. Not unlike being in a curry shop on a rainy day, and seeing the sun come in."

After a moment in which none of them moved or spoke, Janis said, "Do you write romance novels? Because you totally should."

Geoffrey gazed at Niall, who seemed on the verge of tears. "I write about overcoming obstacles. Adventure stories. But I think my next will have a romance."

Niall stood up and said to Janis, while looking at Geoffrey, "Darling, would you excuse us for a moment?" She said something that appeared to be affirmative, but neither man really heard her. Niall took hold of Geoffrey's hand as soon as they were through the dining-room door. A few seconds later they were through another door, and then the door was closed. Geoffrey's back was against the wall. Niall's hands were in his hair and they were kissing, open-mouthed and desperate.

Geoffrey's hands were on Niall's face and he could feel that yes, there were tears. "Don't cry," he managed. "I love you. I know it's too soon. I love you."

"I love you too. Oh God, what are we to do." It sounded like a genuine prayer. More kisses. "I need you."

"I need you too." They were both fiercely aroused. The idea of having each other while Janis waited two rooms away made it worse. Going back in this condition was unthinkable. Not touching each other was impossible. Niall dropped to his knees and a moment later had Geoffrey free, in his hand, and then in his mouth. Geoffrey made some kind of muffled sound, one hand in Niall's hair and the other arm over his own mouth. It took no time. He'd spent the last week dreaming of this. He was breathing hard, head resting on the wall, when Niall stood up and kissed him again, pressing against him. His urgency was unmistakable. Geoffrey laid a hand on his face, brushed his hair back and said, "Darling. May I?" He had his other hand on Niall now and couldn't remember undoing his trousers. Perhaps they'd done it together. "In my mouth?" God, he wanted that again, and naked this time, as Niall had done it.

Niall's own mouth was on Geoffrey's neck. "I think you could bring me off just saying that." His voice was a vibration, a shiver, the breeze that lifted a single fallen leaf from the pavement.

"In my mouth," Geoffrey said again, lingering over the words as he meant to linger over the act, feeling Niall's cock jump in his hand. He moved, took half a step, putting Niall's back against the wall now. "I'll have you *in my mouth*." Another reaction, and a sound that was close to a whimper. Geoffrey knelt down and put his mouth to that cock. Slow, tantalizing, not wanting to miss a single twitch or shudder or choked breath from the man who was on fire under his touch. He could have taken all night for this, but Janis waited. He bit down gently, heard the gasp from above, then drew away enough to say, "Fuck my mouth, you tiger." Niall growled as if he'd transform into that very thing, and did what Geoffrey asked. Geoffrey gripped Niall's hips, Niall held his head, and a minute later it was all over.

"Christ," Niall said faintly. His knees felt weak; only the wall kept him upright. "How long?" Then, "Shit, I'm sorry, I should have –"

"We'll deal with it." A distressed sound. Geoffrey got to his feet, none too steadily. "Darling. To the best of my knowledge I'm clean as a china plate and I'm not afraid of you. We'll make certain soon. I couldn't have waited another second. All right?" Eye contact, a nod. "We'd better go back. Have you a washroom?"

"I do, thank God." They both giggled then, trying to stifle it, hoping they'd been as quiet as they'd tried

27

to be. They tidied up, settled themselves, and went back to the dining room. There was no concealing what they'd been up to, though they hoped the full extent of it wasn't clear. Janis didn't mention it.

As proper as a trio of diplomats, they carried on through dessert and coffee, genteel conversation, and then the suggestion of brandy and music. The helper went away. They went back to the parlor and Janis played the piano, a waltz. Geoffrey mentioned dancing; Janis got excited; Niall denied all knowledge and Geoffrey nearly said 'I'll teach you' to both of them. Then the conversation shifted to what she'd been recording that day at Abbey Road. One of the pieces was a tango, a not-well-known instrumental piece called 'Un Beso.' Geoffrey knew it. Janis got excited all over again, and offered to play her version of it. "I mean, if you'd like to hear it. And crap, I hope we're talking about the same thing."

He was smiling, one hand on Niall's leg. "I think we must be, don't you? Do you have that record?" She nodded. "After you play, would you like me to teach you some tango?" Her face was answer enough. "Niall, I do see why you love her so."

Janis turned to the piano without another word. She didn't begin to play immediately. It seemed she was in communion with the instrument. After a minute she turned her head and made eye contact with Niall. He couldn't help reacting, because in her eyes he saw 'Is it possible?' And in his heart was only 'Please let it be so.' She began to play, and for the first time Niall was conscious of the song's title and what it meant: a kiss. Eight minutes later, she stopped playing and looked at Geoffrey. "Oh my *Christ*," he said. "If you played that at a milonga, people would *weep*." He had nearly wept himself.

28

Not much later, they were dancing. Niall sorted out the music, leaving the room at some point. Geoffrey knew it wasn't because he couldn't bear to watch. They'd made eye contact, confirming the few words they'd shared while Janis was out of the room. Events were moving faster than Geoffrey had dared dream. He and Niall had not explicitly discussed Geoffrey's genuine attraction to Janis, but he was now confident that she was also attracted to him. And she liked him. Two out of three factors essential to a possible future for all of them. *Does she want this*, he wondered, holding her close. Hoping his body spoke to hers as clearly as her music had spoken to him.

He tuned in to the music again and stopped dancing. They stood still. Geoffrey listened to 'Un Beso' and to Janis breathing, slightly shallow, slightly fast. He turned his head a few degrees and kissed her cheek. "You're a lovely dancer. Should I stand away?" He was aroused too, she had to be aware, and he didn't want to offend.

"What did Niall tell you?" she asked, very softly.

"He told me that he hoped to stay with you forever. He told me that he loved you very much, and hoped I'd love you too. Then he said he wouldn't mind if I kissed you, or if you kissed me. Would you mind?"

"God, no." She turned her head, and he kissed her. She was glorious, passionate, uninhibited. It had been a long time since Geoffrey kissed a woman who cared for another man, who needed him to care for that other man too. If he hadn't already begun to care for Janis he would still have tried to make this kiss reassure her, not only entice her. This kiss had to tell her that he wouldn't try to take Niall away from her,

29

that he was there for her too, if she'd have him. They were both trembling when he lifted his head, long minutes later. "Geoffrey."

"Yes, love."

"Is Niall here?"

"No."

"I am inclined to care about you, because he cares about you. And I am inclined to trust you, because he trusts you." She stopped.

Geoffrey thought he knew what she was trying to say. His hand stroked down her back, then up into her hair. "Likewise." But he waited. The stakes were too high for guesswork.

She made eye contact. "Would you please go find him, and ask him if it's all right if I take you to bed?" He didn't say anything, only kissed her again, and left the room. She was standing there with her eyes closed, arms wrapped around herself, when Niall came in again. He didn't have to speak. "Precious."

"You blooming miracle." He put his arm around her and walked her out of the room. She kept her eyes closed until they were in her room, where Geoffrey waited. Niall wasn't sure what to do now. "Do you want me to stay?"

"Would you? Could you?" Her voice held the same uncertainty he was feeling.

Niall was relieved that she wanted him there. "Of course. You realize I've never done this before either." Janis leaned back against him, Geoffrey leaned in against her, and both men put their arms around her. Geoffrey kissed Niall, and then he kissed Janis. Between the pair of them they got her clothes off, and then their own. They arranged themselves in bed, all three of them offering soft words and kisses.

All of them were aware this was potentially life-changing. It was profound, and frightening. A shining dream to be reached for with open hearts and gentle hands. Before long she asked for more. Geoffrey reached for a condom.

Niall lay close to Janis as Geoffrey began to make love to her. Watching his lover kiss his love. Watching her respond in a way that told him just how hungry she'd been since she was last in Los Angeles, seven months ago. He'd offered, and she'd told him she wouldn't use him so. He'd been grateful. Now he was aflame from the sight of Geoffrey's lovely brown body working in her, and the sounds they made. They climaxed within seconds of each other, a thing Janis had told Niall was rare. He was half-blind with arousal when Geoffrey landed between them, saying with a happy sigh, "This is unreal. Christ, this is *perfect*."

"It kind of is, isn't it?" Janis sounded breathless, and satisfied, and amazed. The room was quiet for a few minutes. Niall was stroking Geoffrey's chest and flank and hip, kissing the side of his neck. He thought Janis might have noticed, and knew she had when she said, "If you want to, you know, go ahead."

It was Geoffrey who answered. "There are lots of ways for us to make love. Tonight I'd like to take it." Niall's arm tightened around his chest. Geoffrey arched his neck back, eyes closed, faintly smiling. "Have you ever seen that?"

"No."

"It can seem a bit rough."

"Geoffrey, I have your skin under my fingernails. Don't mind me. Niall?"

"Yes, love."

31

"Are we going to kidnap Geoffrey and take him on a USO tour?"

"Christ, I hope so," he said fervently. She laughed under her breath and made some space for them. Niall took his time, letting her see and comprehend the care he took with Geoffrey, and the way the other man enjoyed it. The lube, the condom, the preparation. He was afraid, for a moment, that being watched would make him nervous. Or that the act would disgust her. But he knew she loved him, and he was beginning to think this love really could conquer all. So he bent to his work, forgetting everything else in the heat of Geoffrey's body. After he finished, culminating with something close to a roar, he raised his head from Geoffrey's shoulder and looked at her. What he saw on her face was joy.

The three of them didn't leave the flat for thirty-six hours. They experimented with love play of various types. They ordered in when the leftovers ran out, got through two more bottles of champagne, talked music and writing and travel, and slept all together in Janis' big bed.

Geoffrey reluctantly composed himself for departure on the second morning after he'd arrived for dinner. The domestic was due, he didn't want to make things awkward for Janis, and they all needed some time to breathe. "I mean to speak with my parents," he said. "And with the people I used to see."

"You won't see them anymore?" Janis sounded surprised.

"It wouldn't be fair. It's one thing to have a lover who's a friend, when you both feel free to see other people. As many other people as you might like. But

32

I'm for you now." He watched them both, Janis and Niall, sitting close together at the kitchen table. "Both of you. And only you." He could see tears in both pairs of eyes. Janis turned to Niall, tipping her forehead against his cheek, murmuring something to him that Geoffrey couldn't hear.

"Then will you live with us, and be our love?" Niall's voice was quiet. It felt like an embrace.

Geoffrey answered without hesitation. "I will." It felt like a vow. He didn't kiss either of them again, not then. He didn't tell them when he'd be back, because he wasn't sure when that would be. Instead he said, "Get some rest," with a smile he couldn't help knowing was a bit wicked, and went out listening to them laugh.

Niall and Janis spent a quiet evening alone together, as they had so many times before. Only it would never be the same again. She played the piano for a while; he reclined on the couch, eyes closed, listening. When she lifted her hands and the room went silent, he looked over at her. "Janis. Thank you."

"It seems so obvious now." She sounded puzzled. Niall almost laughed. "You want a drink?"

He didn't reply, simply stood up and went to fetch two glasses of whisky. He handed one to her. They each sipped. "He pleased you."

She snorted. "Um, yeah. He's gorgeous. And he's adorable. What were the fucking odds." Another mouthful of liquor. "I mean seriously, what *were* the odds? Like eleventy million to one?"

"Approximately," Niall agreed. He leaned on the piano, studying her. She looked so much more relaxed than she had a week ago. No doubt he did too. "He'll live with us, then. You're sure?"

"There's always the chance it won't work out. None of my love affairs have before. But it has to be worth a good solid try, because you've never been part of one of my love affairs before, and you make everything else work."

"Darling." He bent close and kissed her.

"When you, you know. Went all the way. Would he have come from that, if he hadn't just been with me?"

Only Janis, he thought, appreciating her. "Yes."

"I thought so. Was that a test?"

"We certainly didn't discuss it in advance. If he'd asked for something else, I'd've done what he asked. Perhaps it was."

"He might have thought, she needs to see this, if she can't take it then this won't work." Niall nodded. "He's done this before."

"Once. With another couple."

Janis smiled. "So we're a couple."

"Well of course we are, darling."

"Niall, I am so fucking happy right now." Tears spilled down her face. She set her glass on the piano with a shaking hand. Niall sat beside her on the bench and held her tight.

He texted Geoffrey a day later, because so much was still unsaid: *Angel eyes. We missed you last night*

The reply came so fast Geoffrey might have had his phone in his hand: *I missed you too. I've told my parents that I've fallen in love*

34

What did they say?

'When can we meet her'

Oh dear

Geoffrey laughed. *I said, very respectfully and with love, his name is Niall and he's asked me to live with him*

Long discussion?

Very long

Niall took a moment to indulge some mild hysterics; he could imagine Geoffrey's expression. *You'll tell us all when next we see you?*

Indeed I will

When will that be?

Very soon, I promise. Some arrangements to make

Some hearts to break

My friends will be sad but not, I trust, heartbroken. I'll be in touch as soon as I've something approaching a plan. How is Janis?

Niall looked across the parlor at Janis, who was at the piano playing 'Un Beso.' *She's thinking of you. I'll let you go. I love you*

I love you too. It was still too soon. Geoffrey didn't care. He wanted to be with Niall again, immediately, forever.

Three weeks after they all met, two weeks after that first dinner, and one week after Geoffrey returned from his parents' house for what might be the last time, Niall lay an arm's length from Janis in bed and said, "I hardly know myself anymore."

She was laughing under her breath. "It's because of Geoffrey. I get turned on from watching him with you, why shouldn't you get turned on from watching him with me?" She still had her hand on Geoffrey's leg. Her head was resting on his hip. She looked across him at Niall.

"I'm temporarily retired from certain services," Geoffrey said, amused. "Whatever shall we do?" He had one hand in Janis' hair. The other went to Niall's body, stroking from his chest down to his erection. "Do you want this?" He meant his own hand on Niall.

"I want that," Janis said, clearly meaning something different and trying to make it sound funny. This had been the first time she'd brought Geoffrey off with her mouth. If he'd been thinking clearly he would have gone for her with his own, so she wouldn't be left hungry. He still could, but something made him wait to offer, or to make that move. Because she and Niall both were in need, and that was a combination they hadn't yet tried. He kept one hand on each of them, a human bridge.

Niall was having a slight anxiety attack. Through all their long and tangled history, he and Janis had kissed many times, but with affection, not passion. They had climaxed many times in each other's company, but not at each other's hands. He had never been aroused by her. Now he was aroused, and he knew it was because of Geoffrey. He didn't know if she would mind. But he loved her so much he wanted to try. "Geoffrey, darling, would you mind?" They made eye contact for a possibly telepathic moment. Geoffrey moved, Janis moved, Niall moved. A condom wrapper ripped. And then Niall was against Janis, still aroused, kissing her neck with his arm around her back. "May I kiss you, love?"

36

"I wish you would." Her voice was shaky. Niall kissed her, and for the first time ever his mouth opened over hers. She made a desperate sound and pressed against him. He was hard against her; she was soft, and small. It was so unfamiliar and so odd that he was afraid he would fail. He felt oversized and clumsy. He'd managed the act with women before, but long ago, with the aid of adolescent excitability and a colossal amount of alcohol. Now he was sober, and this was not the time to fail.

Before he could completely panic, he felt Geoffrey. Geoffrey's mouth on the back of his neck, teeth ever so lightly dragging across his skin. Geoffrey's hand on his side, stroking hard down to his hip and between his legs. Then Geoffrey's thumb at his arse, slippery with lube, probing, pushing. "Get in," Geoffrey said against his skin. "I'll drive."

Blindly trusting, Niall mounted, kissing Janis with all the love she inspired and all the passion the three of them shared in that room night after night. Her knees came up around him and she hummed into his mouth as he sank into her. Then the heat of her captured him, and Geoffrey's hand drove him on. The dual stimulation was mind-blowing. He lost track of time entirely. If it hadn't been for Janis clutching at him, her hips rising to meet his and then her head falling back with a scream, he might have had to wonder if it was anything close to as good for her as it was for him.

"There you are," Geoffrey said. He did something with his hand.

"Jesus Christ!" It happened. Niall came so hard he could barely see. Inside Janis. He felt her contract around him again, a different feeling than he was used to, a wonderful feeling. She was holding him tight.

37

They were both breathing fast. Geoffrey kissed his shoulder, taking his hand away. Niall kissed her again. "Janis, my God. What did that feel like for you?"

"Like heaven," she said faintly. "But you are heavier than Geoffrey."

"Oh." He was indeed. "Sorry, love." She was giggling as he disengaged, propping himself up, taking his weight off her chest. "Would you like to say something to your chauffeur?" Geoffrey was lying close. They were all within kissing distance of each other. Unsurprisingly, there were kisses.

"I don't know," she said. "What the fuck would I say?"

"Say anything." Geoffrey's voice was gentle. "That was a first. Do you mind that I helped?"

Janis being Janis, she told the truth. "I'm grateful. I know that wouldn't have happened without you. And Niall, don't you dare apologize," she said, as he opened his mouth to speak. "We've had that conversation."

"Sometimes I think we've had *every* conversation."

She giggled again. "Thank God for that. Anyway. Don't feel like I expect that. That does not have to happen every time, or often, or ever again. I really appreciate that it happened, okay? I will treasure that. If you ever want to, you know, yay. But I will love you just as much as ever, forever, regardless." Niall slid to the side, pressing his face against hers, knowing she'd feel his tears. He couldn't seem to summon a word. Geoffrey stretched an arm across her and rested his hand on Niall's ribs. Janis kissed Niall's forehead, wrapping one strong hand around his wrist and the other around Geoffrey's. After a while she

38

said, "So are you guys both going to come to L.A. with me for the holidays? Because I hope so, but if so, I really need to start planning now for the whole hi-mom-and-dad-guess-what thing." They all started to laugh.

Chapter 3

Many times over that summer, Niall wondered if there really were such a thing as fate. That he and Janis had walked down that particular street after her recording session; that she had then expressed the wish for a nice hot curry on a rainy day; that Geoffrey had been there, and that he had been so exactly the man they needed, and that he had been drawn to them too: all were such impossible-to-define variables in creating their new sum, three become one. *Solve for X*, he thought once, watching her laugh with Geoffrey as they danced in the parlor. *Where X equals love.* He had never seen her so happy, and he knew he'd not been so happy himself for a very long time. Since Oliver. Every day of this new life knit that mostly-healed wound more painlessly closed.

They all had time alone. They all needed it. Geoffrey went out, often enough, with his laptop to find a place where he could sit and write, where ignoring everything around him wouldn't feel rude. Sometimes he went for dinner with his parents, who were coming to terms with the fact that no, he wouldn't be marrying a nice Indian girl. Twice he left for days at a stretch to do research. Niall and Janis were different now, alone together. There was a closeness surpassing even their long-standing friendship. They still slept together when Geoffrey was away. While they didn't make love again, they did sometimes whisper fantasies of what they'd do when their lover returned, and bring themselves off together as they used to do on tour.

Janis went out, often enough, to meet with press or promoters, or other musicians, or representatives from her record company or the tour organizers. At home, she practiced every day, whether exercises or actual songs. She let Niall manage the household. Occasionally she asked that he and Geoffrey do whatever they meant to do in Niall's room and join her later to sleep. He suspected it was for his benefit as much as hers. Her own appetite, while vigorous, wasn't inexhaustible. He'd not yet begun to get anything close to enough of Geoffrey, whose response to him continued to be the stuff of dreams.

Niall went out himself, to museums or plays or movies, catching up on culture as he'd always done during the summers between tours. He also went to the fencing club that the others didn't know about. It wasn't a secret so much as a thing that was his alone, the way writing belonged to Geoffrey and music to Janis. She was in a phase he hadn't seen before, on the edge of inspiration. He knew she wasn't ready to start working on a new album yet. Neither of them was ready to let recording or touring break up their summer of love.

Early on, Janis pulled some strings and flashed some cash, and arranged for a concierge physician to come to the flat. Niall and Geoffrey were both nervous about this and couldn't have really said why. After listening to them fret on the morning of the appointment, Janis said, "This is because if we're all her patients we all have privilege. It's one person who will know us and whatever our issues are, who's legally obliged to keep her mouth fucking *shut*, and can take care of us in the context of our whole relationship. Okay?"

Niall stared at her for a moment. "And because you are who you are, no one will think anything of the fact that you've a private physician."

"Or of the fact that you'll travel to London to see said private physician in case of need." Geoffrey was impressed. He hadn't considered all the potential complications of their relationship. The need for discretion, yes; Janis was a public figure. He admired her clear thinking.

"Yes!" she said. "Good! I guarantee the only thing that will be weird about this is she's going to try to keep us separate for the talking part." This proved to be the case. The doctor had to be convinced that they all wanted to hear every part of the joint history, and assured that they wouldn't then blame her for allowing it. "Look, Doctor, we know this is not the norm. That's the whole reason you're here. We'll sign anything you need us to sign. But I have to get back to the piano, so can we get this rolling?"

So the doctor gave in, and from that point the only thing that troubled the men was a piece of Janis' history that even Niall hadn't known. They were all in their thirties, they'd all had other partners; it was statistically unlikely that none of them had ever contracted an STD. Niall and Geoffrey had made it through unscathed. They were both neat as cats by nature, and had both been as careful as it was possible to be while still having a sex life. Janis would have been the first to admit that neither description applied to her. "Thus the hysterectomy," the doctor said. "I knew there had to be some clinical reason for them to have done it when you're so young."

"Between the IUD perforation and the chlamydia and the PID, the thing was fucked. I didn't want children anyway. So I said let's get rid of it." Janis glanced over at her men. Geoffrey's face was carefully neutral but Niall was appalled. "You didn't notice I never had a period?"

"I ought to have done. I was always more concerned with what was going on in there," he indicated her head, "than in there." He made a gesture toward her midsection. "I'm sorry to have been so unobservant."

Janis set her hand on his arm. "You had plenty of things to think about besides the mysterious absence of tampons."

"Well," said the doctor, "once these test results are in I'll let you know if you should carry on the way you've been, or if you can dispense with barriers."

"Thanks. Fingers crossed. We're keeping the corner chemist in business." Janis must have noticed Geoffrey's abstraction. When the doctor had gone she said, "Precious, don't you think we've earned a whisky?"

"It's only half past three," he said, but he'd also noticed that Geoffrey wasn't quite right. He went to the drinks cart.

"What's the matter, sweetheart," Janis said quietly.

Geoffrey looked at her, then at Niall, then back. *Must be honest.* "I would have loved to have a child with you. We hadn't got to the point of discussing that. I didn't even know you never wanted children."

"Nor did I," Niall said, "until I overheard an argument with Stefan last winter."

"You overheard a lot of those last winter." Janis went to sit beside Geoffrey. "We're having to pack a lot of learning-about-each-other into a very short time. How much of a problem is this? Are you going to feel you've missed out on something important?"

"I don't know," he said. "It might have been simply an impulse, a wish, based on how lovely you

43

are and how lovely this is." 'This' was indicated by a gesture encompassing the flat, and everything in it.

Niall leaned over to kiss Janis' cheek, then Geoffrey's, and handed each of them a glass. "There are ways. Let's give it some time. We'll keep talking. We haven't even settled on … well, you know."

"Yeah, about that," Janis said into her glass.

Niall laughed under his breath, retrieving his own drink. There really wasn't any doubt in his mind, and he thought not in Geoffrey's. Maybe this was the time, even though it was so soon. At the very least, it would show the younger man that he wasn't simply a convenience. That this mattered, that *he* mattered. He knelt in front of Geoffrey. "Angel eyes. I love you. It's too soon, but you must know I'd be so very happy if we could be married. Might I ask you someday?"

Geoffrey was flattened, swamped, ravished with love. There had been Janis on the phone with her friend - the one friend who knew about them - on their second night, joking about whether he was Niall's boyfriend or his fiancé. They'd shared a glance, more question than agreement; then nothing. He leaned forward, blinking away tears, and touched his lips to Niall's. "Ask me any day. Ask me every day. I'll say yes. I love you."

Niall felt Janis take his whisky out of his hand, not a moment too soon.

Being engaged was, Niall decided, a wonderful thing. His parents were delighted; his siblings alleged the same; a dinner with Geoffrey's parents was unexpectedly joyous. Seeing Geoffrey's old room was, on the other hand, almost troubling. Not the books, or the maps, or the few tangible souvenirs of his travels. None of those things taken alone. Simply the mass of them, and the inescapable realization that being away from England – or at least, away from the city - was more than work, more than entertainment. It was something Geoffrey needed. Niall had always enjoyed travel but he couldn't recall ever feeling 'I must get away' except during the awful, tearing grief after Oliver. He liked the outdoors, but he didn't feel stifled by walls.

There was also the rather abrupt understanding of what 'adventure' meant. Geoffrey didn't go only to the Camargue, or the Pyrenees, or even the Alps. He went to hazardous places. On the wall were belts for krav maga, photos from mountains so high one could look down on the tops of clouds, or from the decks of sailing ships on waves that obscured the sky. On the shelf next to 'The Devil Drives' and 'The Seven Pillars of Wisdom' were texts in Russian and Arabic.

He saw that room after dinner, so Niall didn't have the opportunity to ask the senior Anands for their views on their younger son's peripatetic ways. He had, quite clearly, understood they were happy that Geoffrey was to marry, and to marry an Englishman if not an Indian woman. Perhaps they thought Geoffrey would be safer now. "I never quite grasped the extent of your adventures," he said as they walked home. "Even having read your books."

"The research mustn't take over," Geoffrey said, with a sideways glance. "A genre novel wants story and character, not a dissertation on the history of the opium trade. My father provided me the means to go places many can't, because he understood I wanted to write about them. And I have, for the most part, paid my own way the past eight years."

"He loves you very much."

"Yes. It's his own fault really, he's the one who brought me up on Haggard and Kipling, and Edgar Rice Burroughs. I suspect that if I were the firstborn, I shouldn't have had such freedom." They walked on for a while. Niall seemed thoughtful. "My mother used to lament me. She was certain one day I'd simply disappear. Every time I went somewhere, it was days of protest."

"When did that stop?"

"When Wellington and Parris had their first child." Geoffrey heard a soft laugh. "Yes, I'm no longer the spare."

"Oh darling, that's horrid." Niall remembered something Geoffrey had said on their first night. "Do you ever write poetry for her?"

"Yes. I write her something after any journey. One day maybe I'll publish those."

"Are they Kiplingish?"

Geoffrey laughed. "They are."

Niall was in his room with Geoffrey about two months after their cohabitation was finalized, one hand in that glossy black hair and the other holding a cup of tea. They sat up against the headboard, warm and drowsy from the encounter following their retreat from Janis' room. They'd been lying close together when they awoke, and naturally started kissing. Janis had said "Aroint thee, varlets" with something between a laugh and a yawn. They had obediently exited, snickering.

Niall was still inclined to snicker. "Do you ever think, Christ, not again?"

Geoffrey laughed. "Not yet. You're so right for me."

46

"And you for me." Niall kissed him, lightly, so as not to disturb the delicate balance of their teacups. "How goes your bastard of a hero?"

"He's still a bastard." Niall snorted. Geoffrey sipped some tea. "I'll tell you the truth. Practically the minute you and I were engaged, the envious twat demanded his own romance. Then I had to have a serious chat with him about what sort of romance. Because in the past my heroes have had relations, as you know. Mostly off the page, and always with women. I assumed most of my readers would find that more palatable. However, and perhaps not surprisingly, this bugger demands buggery." Niall had to set his cup down, he was giggling so hard. "And he wants it out in the open. I may find myself with a new readership, or with none at all. But clearly I shan't get anywhere with the book until I give him what he wants, so off the plank I go."

"God," Niall said, recovering. "What will your father think?"

"I'm beginning to wonder about dear old Dad. He's asked some interesting questions of late." Niall was off again, sliding down in the bed, giggling helplessly. Geoffrey finished his tea and set down his cup, smiling. "I adore you."

"Likewise. Heavens above." Niall took a breath. "I can't wait to read the thing."

Geoffrey leaned over to kiss his forehead. "Tell me something."

"Anything, love."

"The day we met, I thought, why is this man not the new Peter O'Toole? You've the height, the presence, and God knows you've the looks for it. Your voice, well, you know what it does to me." Niall had brought him off once with nothing but words and a single touch. Granted, that touch had been with his mouth. "Were you ever an actor? Is that how you and Oliver met?"

"We met when I was at Oxford," Niall said. "I was with the OUDS and he came in to play Prospero, show us how it was done, you know, though he was nowhere near old enough for the part. So *he* said. Nothing happened then because he was a Royal Shakespearean and I a bosky undergraduate. I was too overawed to make an approach, and he was much too proper."

"Had you a part in that? In Tempest?"

"Ariel. A part for which you are better suited, though I didn't entirely fail it. Anyway, soon after that I woke up to the fact that my true talent lies in management. Started running things around the dramatics, and then in other theatres. Not long after I left university I was working at a theatre in London and the tour management people came across me. And shortly after that, I met Oliver again."

"Did he remember you?" Geoffrey couldn't imagine that he hadn't. He'd seen photos of Niall at twenty. 'Breathtaking' was the best word to describe him.

"He did. It was quite a magical evening, or rather weekend. Never felt that way before or since, until I met you."

Thank you for saying that. "Did you ever again play Ariel to his Prospero?"

"No." Niall gave him a speculative look. "I'd play Prospero to your Ariel, though."

"Shall I amend the text?" Geoffrey leaned down for another kiss, then another. "Shall you bind me?" Niall pulled him close.

September 2018

Geoffrey was in the parlor, where he generally wrote now when at home. Janis played and sang in there for hours some days. The music didn't distract him. Sometimes it inspired him. But on this day he wasn't writing, and she wasn't playing. She was on the phone with her friend Valerie. Niall was standing in the doorway, leaning on the frame, watching and listening with the same concern they heard in her voice. "Val, I saw it on the news. He's really all right? Well, obviously, okay. I couldn't believe it. All this time, I know, they were being threatened. When we saw them in Miami some asshole had just destroyed their cars with a chainsaw. You didn't hear about that? They were passing it off, oh well, we never drive anywhere anyway. He is not. Seriously no. That is bananas, and feel free to pass that on. What did Andy say about it?" She laughed. Niall and Geoffrey both relaxed. "Have you seen them? Yeah, no, not surprising. I left them a message and sent a couple of texts. I'll pester them some more soon. How are you and Russell? Any trips planned? Great. Oh yeah, it's amazing. Yes, they're officially engaged. I forget what that means in terms of which one of us is buying dinner at Morton's. Oh, I am? Okay. I still don't know what the fuck I'm going to tell Mom and Dad. We should probably rent an apartment because otherwise we're going to need to install a traffic signal in their hall." Niall turned away from the parlor door, shoulders shaking. Geoffrey had a hand over his mouth. Janis grinned at him. "Okay, I'll let you go. Ping me anytime. We still don't have anything resembling a plan, the whole USO thing looks like a no-go so I'm just working on new stuff, it's time to get a new album together. Oops sorry yeah hanging up now. Love you too." She ended the call and said, "You can laugh out loud, you know."

"That's all right." Geoffrey took a breath. "Niall, where are you?"

"In the kitchen. Do you need me?"

"Always. Janis, your friend is all right?"

"As all right as a person can be who got shot in the back. He's out of the hospital and reportedly determined to attend the Emmy awards on Sunday. He's nominated, and there's some buzz. Valerie heard via Tanith that Andy agreed to attend in a moment of blazing rage, like we'll show you motherfuckers, and has been regretting it ever since because now Victor thinks he can get away with anything."

Geoffrey hadn't quite sorted out all the names. Fortunately Niall was there again, delivering tea. He sat down next to Geoffrey. "That's Victor Garcia and his husband Andy Martin, they've been kicking up dust on a police drama for years. First gay couple played by a gay couple, first to do a proper kiss in a primetime broadcast, first major love scene. Death threats galore from day one. Tanith Salazar wrote and directed the movie they were shooting this summer. And our lovely Janis knows Tanith, and Valerie as well, from a play Tanith wrote and directed, six years ago, for which Victor played a villain and Andy did photography."

"Thank you, darling." Geoffrey added all that to the mental timeline and family tree.

"I worked for Valerie on the backing tracks and the cast album for Tanith's play," Janis said. "And we hit it off. She helped me make all my albums."

"Do you have the cast album?" Geoffrey was curious.

"Better," she said. "I have a DVD of the video recording they made at the dress rehearsal. Unfortunately it is not here in London. But I can get Mom to send it."

"We can see it when we go to California." That led into a discussion of the trip: when to go, how long to stay, whether Janis would try to record her next album while they were there.

She was semi-inclined to do that. "I know that studio. It has a wonderful piano. And Valerie would be there."

"Would you call Stefan to help you build the material again?" Niall's voice was neutral. Janis' ex was a talented musician in his own right, but had never dealt well with Niall's place in her life. Geoffrey knew that much. He didn't actually know how Niall felt about it.

Nor, apparently, did Janis. "Would you hate that?"

Niall was surprised. "It's irrelevant, isn't it? If he's what you need, then he's what you should have. But no. I've no quarrel with him." *Not anymore*, he added silently. Then, as much for Geoffrey's benefit as his own, said, "Not now that he isn't making you miserable."

She nodded. She was sitting on the piano bench, noodling. After a minute she gave the men a sideways glance. "I've kind of been getting obsessed with tango music. You might have noticed."

Geoffrey smiled. They danced almost every day, though often for only ten or fifteen minutes. Niall was reliably in the room, and reliably declined to

51

participate. He'd told Geoffrey once that watching him dance reminded him of a day he'd seen a fox playing in a meadow. Running and jumping in the long grass for no apparent reason, joyously beautiful. Now Geoffrey thought of that every time he danced. He heard the piano again, and realized he'd been gazing at Niall. Fortunately Janis seemed absorbed by what she was doing. But her shoulders were hunched. Geoffrey stood up and went to her, drawing those shoulders gently back, correcting her posture. The sides of her neck felt like rock. "Is your neck bothering you?"

"It's been better," she admitted.

Niall asked, "Do you want me to call Bruno? Or a local person?" Bruno Zidane was the Liverpool-based massage therapist who'd kept her functional for the last six dates of her U.K. tour after a whiplash injury in April. "We ought to have kept you seeing someone regularly. I'm sorry I didn't think of it."

"We've all had other things on our minds." Janis leaned back against Geoffrey. "If Bruno wouldn't mind coming down, maybe he could sort me out again and then we'll see about a local person."

"I'll fix it." Niall came to kiss her, touched Geoffrey's shoulder, and went out.

"It's probably my fault," Janis told Geoffrey. "You know I skive off yoga every chance I get. I feel like with all the gymnastics we do in bed, yoga is a waste of time." He laughed under his breath. "But maybe not."

"No, maybe not." He bent to kiss the side of her face. "I'm not a qualified therapist, but why don't you lie down and let's see if I can help." She seemed amenable, so they left the parlor, going to Niall's room. He found them there a half-hour later. Janis was face-down with her head resting on her folded arms at the foot of the bed. Geoffrey was kneeling in front of her, frowning as he pressed his thumbs into the muscles of her upper back. "This is properly buggered," he said, and she snorted. "Why haven't you said something?"

"I've been so happy I couldn't care about a stiff neck."

"Daft wench. How d'you propose to make a new record if you can't turn your head?" Geoffrey glanced up at Niall.

"Bruno's on his way. He said something rude about people who don't do their yoga. He'll be here tonight, stay over, work on you before bed and again tomorrow morning. Then we'll see how you go. All right?"

"Sounds fine," Janis mumbled. "Ow." Geoffrey and Niall looked at each other again. This would be the first time anyone who knew any of them came into their home for longer than an evening. They were both at a loss. "Guys?" They looked at Janis, who still had her head down. "This is us. Bruno of all people is not going to make a scene about it. Put clean sheets on this bed, park him in here, and you sleep with me as usual. Right?"

"Right," Niall said after a moment. "I'll lay on some dinner." He went out again.

"Geoffrey?"

"Yes, love."

"Last time we saw him, Bruno smoked. Constantly. Everything in here is going to require decontamination."

"Don't worry. I'll see to it."

53

But much to their mutual astonishment, that wasn't necessary. After a hug hello, Janis stood back and said, "Okay, what happened to my Liverpudlian smokestack?"

Bruno laughed, saying, "Siobhan's determined to start a nipper as soon as we've married. She says, let's do it while we're young, get it over with while we have the energy, and have someone to look after us when we're old. Then she says, but you mustn't smoke while I'm gravid, or with a baby in the house. So I've given it up."

"Well done," Niall said. "When's the wedding?"

"It's a mystery. Letting her do it all, aren't I? She'll tell me the day and I'll be there." That led into a discussion of Niall and Geoffrey's complete lack of plans. Bruno didn't seem to require any clarification about their living arrangements. He exhibited no surprise or puzzlement over the fact that the two-bedroom flat had a conveniently-available bedroom. All he said to Janis before they went to bed was, "You seem much happier now. That's good."

"And yet, my neck is still fucked. So thanks for coming down."

"Had to fling a few off the schedule, but I wouldn't let you go without care. They'll take the next available and be grateful."

"I'll puff you up on Facebook again."

"Too right." He kissed her cheek and went down the hall. Janis washed up and joined her gentlemen.

Bruno worked on her for the better part of two hours the next morning, read her a lecture about skiving off yoga, handed Niall a referral for a local therapist and said, "This one's from the same school as me, he'll do. You ring him. She won't."

"She forgets," Niall said. "Too much music in her head for trivial concerns such as healthcare."

"Thanks for not saying I'm an airhead," Janis muttered, now lying face-up on the guest bed and strictly forbidden from playing piano for the day. "What am I supposed to do with myself all day?" Nobody said anything for a moment. Niall might have snickered. "Well come on, guys, I'm not supposed to do *that* either."

"I know," Geoffrey said. "Let's go to Regent's Park. It's a fine day and the walk will do you good. Right, Bruno?"

"That'll do. Now I'm off. You call if anything goes awry." He leaned down to kiss Janis again.

She patted his arm. "And you call when you know the wedding date." All the men went out.

After Bruno had gone, Geoffrey joined Niall in the kitchen to finish the tidying-up. "I'm glad Janis has a domestic, and that's a fact," Niall remarked, drying his hands. "At first I said let me handle it, she flatly refused, we had a bit of a wrangle about it. We'd always lived separate between tours, didn't have a plan. She won, of course." Geoffrey laughed. "What did you think of Bruno?"

"Seems eminently competent. It was lovely to see the care he took with Janis. Looks a bit like me, doesn't he?" He watched Niall's face, the quick and reminiscent smile. "Fancied him, did you?"

"Fancied him rotten. Had a go, he laughed it off, we've been mates ever since. A good thing," he added. "Because Janis needed a lot of care. Did you see the social media from that time?"

55

"I did, yes. I wondered about what they got up to."

"The world and you. No doubt she'll tell you one day."

Geoffrey understood this to mean that Niall wouldn't, which was fair. He got himself a cup of coffee and went to write for a while.

Niall returned to his bedroom about a half-hour later and dropped her phone by Janis' hand. "What's this for?"

"Bruno texted. He said there were some paparazzi outside, he apologized."

"It's not *his* fault. Someone must have recognized him from the stuff this spring." Janis picked up the phone and read the text, sending back a quick *No worries mate, it is what it is, drive safe*. "Eh. I suppose it'll show up on the internet later. Whatever."

"I'll have an eye out. See if there's anything we should respond to. And we'll go out the back for the park." They'd all known it was only a matter of time before the tabloid press started on them. Niall and Janis had been subjected to some offensive speculation in the past. It was possible that the presence of Geoffrey might be seen as normalizing the relationship, because the whole world knew Niall was gay. On the other hand, the world had a prurient imagination, and it wasn't impossible that someone would accidentally hit on the truth of the matter. Or that someone who knew Geoffrey would talk. "I'll let your management know, too."

"Oh shit, yeah, I haven't talked to Randa since the USO thing fell apart. Could you tell her we're planning to be in Los Angeles at the end of the year? We should try to get a meeting."

"And you should talk some more with Valerie about the next album."

Janis sent a text, which included some major squee about Victor's Emmy award, to set up a call. The first result of the call came a week later in the form of a package from L.A. Niall brought it into the parlor with the rest of the morning mail. "Were you expecting something from Ms. Benton?"

"No, what is it?"

"Well I haven't opened it, love, it might be personal." He handed it to her. "And here's a card from Bruno and Siobhan. They're getting married on Guy Fawkes Day." Janis laughed for a solid minute. "He says, that way we'll never forget the anniversary. Will we go?"

"Oh, of course!" Janis was still giggling as she opened the package from Valerie. "Hey, she sent a copy of that cast recording, Tanith's play. And this is another one. From the movie this summer. Oh, how *cool*." She got up and fed the disc (which looked distinctly homemade) into the music system. "I knew she worked on this, she said it was a marathon day. One day! Geoffrey?"

He was in the kitchen, taking out his frustration with his still-noncompliant hero on a batch of bread dough. "Yes, darling?"

"I have a new CD from that movie Victor and Andy shot this summer, Valerie says it's all tango."

"Oh smashing!"

"I'll turn it up."

Two hours later, Geoffrey's bread was in the oven, he and Niall were sitting on the couch, and Janis was lying on the parlor floor listening to the movie soundtrack for the third time. Niall was reading and Geoffrey was writing, but they were both aware that she was In It. They didn't speak until the bread was out of the oven and she'd finally turned off the music system. "I want that cello," she said. "And I want to know who the fuck was playing piano."

"There's no credits? Let's have it." Niall held out his hand. She gave him the CD case and everything else from Valerie. The case didn't have liner notes, and Valerie's enclosed letter was uninformative. "Well, my love, you'll simply have to call her. Not right now!" She'd made a move toward her phone, resting on top of the piano. "It's four in the morning for her."

"Fuck."

"In a bit, love," Geoffrey said absently. "I've finally got this bugger doing what I want." Then he looked up because Niall and Janis were both laughing. After a moment he realized what he'd said, and in what context, and made an apologetic move.

"Sweetheart, if I *ever* say that by way of a demand, I sincerely hope you will say 'fuck yourself,'" Janis said, still laughing. She'd said 'fuck me now' more than once, but never while they were all decorously in the parlor and never while he was working. "I'm going to go eat some bread. You make that bugger do what you want." She kissed the top of his head and left the room.

Geoffrey turned his head and regarded Niall. "The irony of course is that now I'd quite like to." Niall laughed again, kissed him, and went to join Janis in the kitchen. Geoffrey wrote a filthily-explicit and entirely-out-of-context sex scene; laughed at himself;

58

then got on with finishing the suspenseful action scene he'd finally made sense of. Then he went to find Janis, and had her bent over the dining table not much later. Niall was nearby, clothes off and eyes dark with desire, because what Geoffrey said was, "I'll bring you off, love, and then I want your mouth on me while Niall's in me. I've written it and now I want to feel it. Shall we?" He had his hand between her legs, and felt the slickening rush of her hunger. *Altogether*, he thought afterward, *a success*.

"Did you really write that?" she said later, when they were back in the parlor waiting for a good time for her to call Valerie.

"I did. I often do. I always delete the scenes later," he assured her, "because that laptop does leave the house, and passwords are not unbreakable. But I'll have the occasional idea, so I'll write it out. To figure out the … mechanics." Niall and Janis both laughed. "And then sometimes we try it."

They spoke over each other. "Sometimes?! Not every time?"

"The two of you are not bereft of invention," he pointed out.

Janis said, "Don't delete that one till tomorrow," and left the room for about twenty minutes. When she came back in she said, "Amazon will be delivering a new laptop that can live here. Not connected to the internet. Cable-locked to the piano leg if you prefer. I want to see all this crazy fuckery you're writing."

"As do I," Niall said. Then it was finally late enough for Janis to call Valerie. She sent a text first, to make sure it was a good time. The men sat and listened, sipping sherry and contemplating dinner, while she talked.

"Yeah so who? Who the hell is that? From Argentina? Okay, well, that makes sense. Do you think he'd be amenable to working with me?" She made a note, muttering to herself. "And the cello. Must have cello. No, I don't have a clue what music yet. It's like I'm craving the tango style applied to non-tango things, which fuck knows if that will even work. Well, okay, when I was spitballing the USO thing with Randa I had a few things on my list, like to workshop a proper tour. Some of those might work. I need to study this music a lot more because there is definitely a flavor, it's not going to work with any old pop song, and I don't want my regular audience to think what the fuck. Yeah. Well, yeah, ideally the tango audience would pick it up too and would not think what the fuck. Say what? Well, shit, why didn't I think of that." She laughed. "Yeah, okay, it's just I haven't really worked with anyone but you and Stefan and we were going mostly for theme, not for flavor. So can you ping this guy, see what he thinks? And if he's not averse put him in touch with me? Best case scenario, we're in L.A. through March and get this thing laid down, and get the record company revved up for a new tour. Yeah, we'll be there mid-December at the latest, and oh by the way my two men will be married by then. Oh, totally, I can't wait. Thanks Val. Give my regards to Russell." She disconnected looking satisfied.

The next day, after setting up the new computer, Geoffrey began writing down some of their particularly-memorable encounters (first transcribing the scene that had ended up in his fictional work-in-progress and then deleting it from that file). Then he thought of writing about their day at the races in

Newmarket, when they'd had dinner with Niall's sister. And then there was that windy weekend in Scotland, meeting Niall's brother and his wife in Aberdeen.

One day, opening the file that was now as much memoir as pornography, he found a page he hadn't written. It was about the day of the accident on the road to Liverpool, when Janis and Niall had met Bruno. Another day, he found a paragraph briefly recounting Niall's first Christmas after losing Oliver, including a rather wrenching reference to the Thames. Before long, without discussion, they were all writing regularly. Passages appeared about family history, growing up, other partners. When it came to the bits about their life together, none of them made notes as to who'd written what, but they each had their own style; everyone knew. Some of the sexual fantasies made them all laugh; some sent them straight to bed (they all quickly began using comments in the text to rate these sections).

Then the fencing club made an appearance in the journal. Geoffrey and Janis cornered Niall the next time they were all together. "Okay," she said, "what the actual fuck. Fencing? *Swordplay?* Of a non-euphemistic variety?" Geoffrey was giggling. "How long have you been doing that?"

"Since university," Niall said, pulling Geoffrey down onto his lap. "Off and on. Only during the summers, the past few years, for obvious reasons. At first I kept it up because of a friend from the OUDS, then because of Oliver. We used to go together. I almost gave it up, after. But I missed it, so I went back."

"Do they ever let people come and watch?"

Niall gazed at her fondly. "Yes, they do. I'll arrange it, shall I?"

"You realize you're bound to become a model for one of my heroes now." Geoffrey's expression said he'd like to engage in some euphemistic swordplay.

Niall pretended to frown. "You mean I haven't been already? Darling," he said to Janis, "I'm afraid I need to have a private word with the writer."

"Yeah," she said, rolling her eyes. "I expect you do." She went to the piano.

Niall escorted Geoffrey to his bedroom. "So," he said a few minutes later, when they were naked. "I don't recall that I've ever seen you so obviously inspired. Tell me your inspiration."

"Well first of all I thought how knightly you must look wielding a blade." Geoffrey had his mouth on the back of Niall's neck, and a hand around his front, brushing lightly up and down. Then further down. "And I did at first see a sabre. But then I saw this." Caressing Niall, whose breath grew short. "As I always do." Niall laughed softly. "Have you ever read a romance novel?"

"If 'Pride and Prejudice' counts, then yes."

"Good Lord, of course it does. Well, in the great days of the bodice-ripper, there were many euphemistic descriptions of equipment like yours. Velvet sword, for example." His hand had a rhythm now.

"Recommend me a classic and I shall read it," Niall said tightly, wishing Geoffrey was in front of him, or under him, or somewhere he could get his hands full. "Do you mean to deprive me of your own equipment?"

"You feel it, do you?" Geoffrey pressed his hips against Niall's. "You feel how I want you."

"Christ, Geoffrey. Let me touch you. Let me at least kiss you." Niall arched his neck, turning his head, trusting Geoffrey to give him that. And he did, though only for a moment. Then he let go of Niall, turning and moving, going for another upside-down kiss before lunging for Niall's cock, getting it in his mouth with a ravenous sound. Niall was on his back then, with his hands on Geoffrey's hips and his mouth full of Geoffrey's cock. He went off sooner than he'd have liked, feeling the vibration of the sound Geoffrey made, an echo of his own harsher sound, which became a low voluptuous hum now that he could concentrate.

"Christ almighty," Geoffrey said not much later. He was breathless, his head resting on Niall's hip, almost motionless, tense with imminent rapture. Then he bucked against Niall's mouth. "Jesus!" Niall rolled them both over, going for the best angle to take all of Geoffrey in that final moment, one hand behind a knee and the other pinning the opposite thigh. "You glorious brute." It was faint. Geoffrey was limp underneath him, breathing hard.

"A brute, am I?" Niall kissed him, then bit gently. Wrapped a hand around him and licked the tip.

Geoffrey jerked again, making a sound that was something between a squeak and a whimper. He felt Niall smiling against the tender skin of his groin. "My tiger. I love you so."

"I love you too," Niall said, still smiling. "It's a good thing we're getting married."

"It's the best thing in the world."

They'd finally gotten down to planning for their wedding. Janis had said, "Trust me, you want to be married before we go to the U.S.," and they both suspected she was correct. They booked a ceremony with a registrar not far from Oxford, and then gave notice at the registry office. They booked a suite for Niall's parents at a hotel close to the flat; Geoffrey's parents of course lived nearby. All the siblings were invited. Niall's sister Marianne promised to come down for the day. Geoffrey's brother and his family would be there. Geoffrey and Niall were excited to the point of delirium.

"I am going to cry at Bruno and Siobhan's wedding," Janis said, the week before that event. "Things might get ugly at yours. Like, complete meltdown ugly."

"That won't be ugly," Niall said, taking her hand. "Quite the opposite."

There was one thing Niall thought he needed to do before they married. Something Geoffrey needed to know. He'd told the story to Janis years ago, in a spasm of desperate grief. Now he had enough distance to set it down calmly. All the same, he waited until Geoffrey and Janis were both out of the flat, and then opened up the journal and wrote.

Oliver died on the night of his birthday party in 2013. He was thirty-eight. We were at a pub in our neighborhood; we'd had a few drinks, some friends were with us. There was no warning. He stood up complaining of a sudden headache, put a hand to his head, and went down. There was nothing to be done. For a long time I couldn't speak of it. For a long time all I could see was his face, his eyes as the life went out of them. For a long time I thought I could never love again. I was mistaken.

64

Neither Geoffrey nor Janis referred to that paragraph, though he knew they both read it. He knew because the next day, after breakfast, they took him back to bed and cuddled close, saying nothing, initiating nothing. Simply being together and loving each other in the way that had gradually, and at last completely, washed away the residue of pain.

Chapter 4

Niall and Janis kissed Geoffrey goodbye, wishing him joy of a no-doubt-frigid expedition to the Hebrides. "Why in October?" Niall had asked; Geoffrey had given some answer regarding a proposed article on island Scotches. Since that was a topic of interest to Niall, and he had no idea how these travel glossies queued their work, he didn't make much of it. It was only, he told himself, that he had no urgent business of his own; Janis was thoroughly occupied with her tango obsession; and he'd read a bit too clearly for comfort that Geoffrey needed to get away. *Mustn't cling, he isn't leaving us, it's nothing.* He booked extra time at the fencing club, arranged to meet some old friends, and tried very hard not to check his phone every hour on the hour.

Meanwhile, with every mile away from London Geoffrey felt less fettered. Complete sexual satisfaction went a long way, but he'd never before felt so accountable to his partners. He thought he'd accepted it; that was what commitment meant, after all, and he'd committed of his own free will. Before they'd even asked. *Because of Niall*, he admitted to himself, finally at rest in the fire-lit bar of a pub motel near the coast.

Janis was wonderful. He loved her body and her music, her quick intelligence and her bright spirit. He loved the way she loved Niall; it was a love that left plenty of space for his own. Nothing about their life since June made him regret his choice. *It was a change, that's all.* No longer a single man. Bound to London more than ever, and more than he liked. Perhaps if he said that, they'd understand. They

66

wouldn't look so worried when he left, as he always would. *But I'll always come back, loves*.

All the same, finding that his mobile lost signal as soon as he was over the water caused him no pain. Knowing that Niall and Janis would wonder where he was, and how he was, provoked only modest guilt. When at the end of four days he returned to that pub motel with a crate full of superlative whisky and a near-complete draft article, it was to find a dozen texts and as many missed calls. He sighed, thought *they'll have to learn to trust me*, and waited until after dinner to call back. A call was easiest. Niall could put Janis on speaker, they'd get all the news at once, and then he could go to bed.

At what Geoffrey thought was the end of the call, Niall said, "It's only me now, love. Was that enough of a break for you?"

Oh hell, Geoffrey thought guiltily. "It's not that I want to be away from you. Not per se. It's the city."

"Not the gilded cage?" A reference to their second night, when Janis had been on the phone with Valerie. "You know the door is wide open. We need you, but only as much of you as you can spare." It cost Niall to say that. No doubt Geoffrey could hear it in his voice. Then, because he had to be honest, he added, "I need you rather more than that. All I ask is that if it's too much, you'll say so. Don't make me wonder, if you please, sir."

"An answer for every kiss," Geoffrey said slowly. "I'm still in your debt. I shall try to anticipate your questions, sweetheart. I am looking for a balance between freedom and commitment. I am not looking for a way out."

Niall was awash with disproportionate relief. It was too soon for this, but then, everything was too soon. After a moment to breathe, he said, "Thank you. I forgot to ask. Which did you prefer, Skye or Harris?"

How could I ever want to leave you. "Islay," Geoffrey said. "And I'm bound to give this bottle of Laphroaig to sodding Wellington." He heard Niall laugh. "I love you."

"I love you. See you tomorrow."

November 2018

A week after Bruno's wedding and two weeks before his own, Niall was enjoying a day in the country. Geoffrey was in London meeting with a publisher who'd seen his new e-book and proposed a series of male-male romantic suspense novels. Janis was inside a vast country house with a very prominent theatrical composer, talking about anything and everything, but mostly music. Niall strolled in the garden, having sent a text to Valerie in response to hers, waiting for her call. When his phone rang he connected immediately. "Valerie, hello. How are you?"

"I'm doing great. How about you?"

"Freezing my knickers off while Janis talks music with his worship." It wasn't actually that cold, and Niall had a proper coat on, but he happened to know it was seventy-five degrees in Los Angeles.

"She was so excited." Valerie snickered. "She said guess who I'm going to meet! Oh Em Gee ponies! She literally said that."

Niall laughed. "He looked pleased to meet her as well. I was made welcome, but they were off to the races and I'd nothing to contribute. I'll go in and beg shelter from the housekeeper presently. Have you something to tell me?"

"I do. Tanith sold her movie, they're doing a premiere event next month in downtown L.A. Want me to get you some tickets?"

"I'm sure we'd all love to see it. Janis has hardly taken the disc out since you sent it."

"Okay, cool. Well, in other news, Victor and Andy are being sent on a promotional tour. International, late January to March. Their co-star the piano player is going to the Buenos Aires gig too. The advance press in Argentina is already bananas." The movie was about Carlos Gardel, an early and eternal star of Argentine tango. "But otherwise, Tomás is definitely in L.A. He teaches Argentine tango and he has a few piano students, he's based in West Hollywood. And he's interested. I emailed Janis the list of songs he suggested, with his contact information so I can get out of the middle of this until she wants to get into the studio. You're copied on that."

He'd seen the message come in but hadn't read it yet. "You're wonderful, thank you so much. Did she tell you the title she had in mind?"

"No. She's never chosen one before the recording was finished. I mean, they haven't even finalized the set list."

"She said she wants to call it Tango À Trois. For the world, that's the two pianos and the cello." He knew Valerie didn't need to ask what it really meant.

"Could be risky. I saw there was a little tabloid skirmish after Bruno came down."

"We're all hoping our wedding will smooth that out a bit. Janis had more to say to the comment on me than to the speculation about Geoffrey." Valerie made a sound of comprehension. "In a sense it's true of course; she *is* keeping me. Until we're actually on tour, I've quite an easy life." He had plenty to do; he'd become Janis' all-purpose organizer, facilitator, and logistical manager. He even answered much of her fan mail. But compared to life on tour, it felt like next to nothing. He was uncomfortably aware that he'd have been finding it dull, were it not for London, and Geoffrey.

Valerie made a *pfft* sound. "Janis is a terrific girl, but she would be the first to admit that she can wear a person out. She told me how much of her stuff you get done. And once you're on tour, you're working every damn minute. Maybe you should arrange another interview. Go through a day in the life."

It wasn't a bad idea. Niall filed it away. "It's no great matter. For now, a kept man I am and will be until the company approves a tour for the new record, which of course can't be until the bloody thing's done. Geoffrey's planning to get out into the mountains and do some research while we're in California. I've no idea what I'll do with the time."

"You're not going to the mountains with him?"

"I, my dear, like my comforts. I shall accompany him to a given destination, observe the conditions, determine whether or not I should expire from lack of Scotch while he is tramping in the snow or dangling from cliffs, and dispose of myself accordingly." Valerie was laughing. "I've read two hundred books this year and am beginning to think I need a hobby."

"Hang out in L.A. and teach people how to speak," she suggested. "Tanith could set you up with that in about a minute and a half."

It was another good suggestion. "I'll consider it."

70

"Do. Anyway, that's the sum of it and I guess I'll see you in about three weeks. Oh hey! Are you and Geoffrey doing a honeymoon?"

Niall laughed. "Wouldn't you say that's what we've been doing since we met?"

"You have a point. Give him my regards."

"I'll do that thing. And ours to Russell." They ended the call and Niall looked around, observing that the sky was now leaden and his legs were cold. He slid the phone into his pocket and headed for the house. There he found that the luminary had disappeared with Janis into a room with a piano, leaving word that they would all meet for tea shortly. Niall accepted a glass of whisky and a chair by a fireplace, where he got his phone back out to check in with Geoffrey: *Hello my love, I've been abandoned in favor of a piano once again. Does that publisher propose to make you rich?*

An answer came promptly: *I'm in a posh pub down the street from their office having a Laphroaig to celebrate. They practically wet themselves when I told them my ideas. They are writing a contract*

Well done! There shall be champagne tonight. Valerie sends her regards and suggests I could, quote, teach people how to speak while in Los Angeles. That is, while you're off being frightfully sporty in the mountains

You're sporty enough, you gorgeous brute. The publisher blushingly asked about a certain scene in the last, and I had to assure her with a straight face that yes, that was possible. Verified, in fact

Niall laughed. *Which scene would that be?*

You might guess. I shan't tell you. You're in Sir Whatsit's house and he mustn't find you with your cock out

71

Vicious sod. Niall, still laughing, was definitely feeling a bit warm. Geoffrey probably had the right of it. *It'll be out, and in, later. I love you*

I love you too. Geoffrey put away his phone, all too aware that he was somewhat tumescent himself. He tried to concentrate on the excellent Scotch, on the contract, and on the three books for which he'd need to devise suspenseful plots and thrilling adventures … as well as verifiable frolics, about which the least imagined (at the moment), the better. He glanced up at the bartender, a tall blond with a substantial mustache, who'd given him the once-over when he came in. "My fiancé's rendered me unfit to travel. Could I have a glass of ice water?"

Geoffrey was home before Niall and Janis, and used the time to make some notes about the three new books. Each would have an ex-military hero now working as some sort of investigator. Each would have a male love interest with some type of globe-trotting profession. A great deal of research would be necessary. He made a start on it until his fiancé and his lover were home. Then Niall opened the champagne, very deliberately holding Geoffrey's gaze as he eased out the cork, with his long fingers wrapped around the neck of the bottle. That had Geoffrey every bit as disabled as he'd been at the bar, but there was dinner to be got through. Janis talked about the luminary for two hours straight. Niall had mentioned to her that he had a specific agenda for the evening, and once they'd had coffee he made sure to remind her. She said something about going to play the piano for a while. Geoffrey didn't quite get the sense of it, because Niall was looking at him in the way that said 'I'll have you' and Geoffrey couldn't wait.

"Was this the scene?" Niall murmured not too much later, when he had Geoffrey pinned to the wall beside his bed. They were face to face and Niall was in, holding Geoffrey off the floor. Geoffrey had his legs wrapped around Niall, one hand clutching the top of the headboard and the other arm around Niall's neck.

"Yes. God, Niall. Yes." They barely moved. It was the pressure, the strained-for kisses, and the lovingly filthy things they whispered to each other that finally brought Niall off. And his convulsion that sent Geoffrey over the cliff after him. "Christ!" Seconds later he was on his back on the bed.

They lay still for a moment. Then Niall withdrew, careful as always, seeing to Geoffrey to ensure he'd taken no harm. "You're all right, sweetheart?"

"I'm all right. I love you."

"I love you. I could do nothing but kiss you till our wedding night, and be satisfied." *Kiss you when it's easy*, he thought.

"You may kiss me as much as you like, sir." Geoffrey was smiling, eyes closed, sore and shaky and blissful. "Will Janis mind if I excuse myself from further frolics this night?"

"I warned her I meant to use you ill." Niall watched Geoffrey laugh. "She said, I'll cuddle him like a teddy bear, and he can cuddle me tomorrow if he's up to it."

"Done."

Niall kissed him again – easily, leisurely, brushing his face against Geoffrey's like a cat – and stretched out on his back, sighing with contentment. Then, "Ow! Shit, shit, *shit*!" He drew a knee up to his chest, hissing.

"Cramp, have you? You earned it." Geoffrey was laughing.

"Bleeding hell!"

"Bruno would say it's no more than you deserve for not stretching."

"Bugger Bruno! I'm stretching now, aren't I? Christ, leave *go* you effing bastard!" Geoffrey had a hand around his shin, forcing the leg straighter. "Will you snap it right off?" More laughter. "Stop bloody giggling, you merciless swine." After a minute the cramp eased. Niall took a breath, not trusting it, foot still in the air. "Your hero never had a cramp." He looked over at Geoffrey. "Perhaps you should put that in next time. So your readers know what you're letting them in for."

Geoffrey said, "That would throw a spanner in the works, wouldn't it? The hero's engaged in some thrilling action with clothes off, then he's after some thrilling action with clothes on, and finds himself bound up with a cramp." Niall made another suggestion. Geoffrey laughed again, and lobbed one back. Before long he said, "I'll need to write that out promptly or I'll forget the best bits."

"No you won't. You never do." They rested until there was no more music from the parlor. Then they hauled each other off the bed, washed up, and went down the hall to Janis.

She wrapped herself around Geoffrey's back. "It was *that* scene, wasn't it?"

"It was indeed," he said drowsily. "The publisher asked about it." Janis giggled.

"And angel eyes made the mistake of mentioning that to me," Niall said, his tone regrettably devoid of regret. Janis giggled some more. Niall kissed her

74

cheek, then turned to his side with his back against hers, counting the days until their wedding and wishing it were possible for all three to join in law the way they had in love. *Don't be greedy*, he thought. *This is so close to everything.*

Niall woke to soft laughter in the dim light of dawn. "You're sure you're up for this?" Janis' voice.

"Can't you see for yourself?" And Geoffrey. Niall smiled. There was no point pretending to be asleep. He rolled over to watch. Geoffrey was on his back, definitely up for it. Janis was on her hands and knees above him, and they were kissing. Geoffrey's hands went to her breasts, and her flanks, and her hips. Then one dipped between her legs and she made a hungry sound. "That's for me, love? Let me feel it." She slid across him and his head went back, eyes closing on a sharp inhalation. Niall had a hand on himself. "Will you then. Janis. Will you."

"Will I ever." She slid across him again and then took him in. Deep, arching her back, flinging her own head up with her eyes closed. "Fucking amazing, this is just always fucking amazing, goddamn Geoffrey, always, always." Geoffrey turned his head slightly as if he knew Niall was watching. He glanced down to see what else Niall was doing, his teeth sunk in his lower lip, and then those lips parted. Niall leaned close and kissed him. That was all it took, and he was coming. His breath went out with a low sound, he felt Geoffrey's mouth curve against his, and then Janis had her hand in his hair, none too gently. "I want to kiss him too." Neither was quite sure which of them she meant. She bent down, still working, and pulled Niall's head up. She kissed him hard, then let him go and went for Geoffrey's mouth. Niall lay there and watched for the few seconds more before she pushed back and arched again. "Jesus!"

"God, Janis!" Geoffrey had an arm around her. He took them over, mounting for a few hard swift strokes with her arms and legs locked tight around him until he finished. "Christ!" Slowly she let go of him. Slowly their breath evened out. Then Geoffrey slid off to the side between Janis and Niall. They all held hands. And before long they all went back to sleep.

Their wedding day barely dawned. It was cold, it was dark, it was raining. As far as Niall and Geoffrey were concerned, it was the most beautiful day since the sun first shone on the earth.

They arrived at the registry office early and found most of their guests already there, crowded into a lobby out of the rain. Niall's sister arrived mere minutes before the stated time, apologizing for traffic. Nobody minded. Everyone was excited. They all went into the room designated for the ceremony.

Geoffrey and Niall had taken to heart the registrar's permission to write their own vows. "We've a professional in the house, after all," Niall said to Janis when she asked. He didn't let her read what they'd written, though. He knew that the prophesied meltdown was highly likely whatever they did. So they got through the formalities of the ceremony – including some of the traditional text, only slightly modified - with both aplomb and dispatch, then went for the throat.

They stood face to face and hand in hand in front of the registrar. Niall said, "Let my love be a river, flowing and never failing, ever refreshing."

Geoffrey said, "Let my love be a willow, bending and never breaking, ever renewing."

Niall again: "Let my love be your strength when you're weary."

And Geoffrey: "Let my love be your comfort when you're hurt."

Then together. They'd practiced this, Niall dredging up his long-ago theatrical training to share with Geoffrey, to perfect their cadence and diction. They wanted everyone to hear the words. "Let our love be as ceaseless as the tides and as warm as the sun. Let our love be a shelter for our friends and a delight to our families. Let us vow to love till our last breath." They had to take a breath themselves then. Niall was vaguely aware of the sounds of meltdown. He smiled down at Geoffrey's tear-streaked face. "I'll have you," he said almost soundlessly. They both knew that to those watching, it would seem he said 'I love you.'

"And I'll have you," Geoffrey said just as quietly. Then, more distinctly, "With this ring I thee wed." He had it in his hand. The plain gold band was warm when he slid it onto Niall's finger. He held Niall's hand in both of his for a moment.

Niall fished in his pocket for the other gold band. "With this ring I thee wed." When the ring was in place he lifted Geoffrey's hand to his lips.

"Then seal these vows with a kiss," said the registrar, and they did.

The reception was in the same room, a simple and fleet-footed affair involving champagne, cake, and a lot of hugs, kisses, and pictures. Then Niall and Geoffrey were bound for the Old Bank Hotel in

Oxford. Everyone else returned to London for a catered dinner at the flat. Niall's sister would stay the night with Janis before returning to Newmarket.

The chauffeured car delivered them safely, the hotel was ready for them, and locking themselves in felt wicked even though they'd be going straight back to London the next day. "Well, my beauty. Five months from there to here; are we quite, *quite* mad?" Niall was smiling, opening another bottle of champagne.

Geoffrey was stripping off his morning coat. "Mad about you. I would have married you the day after we met."

"The same. What a chance that we stepped into that curry shop. Pour, would you darling, while I shed this confining garment."

"Shed any and all of them. I must say, you look like a prince. A duke, at the very least."

"Duke of Milan, is it? Janis wants us to wear these to the premiere in Los Angeles." They both laughed. "Had to decline for us, of course. It simply isn't done."

"Would anyone care, in Los Angeles? I'm inclined to wear mine back to London." Geoffrey handed a glass to his husband.

Niall took it. "Oh? I thought that was the plan all along. A toast to us, sweetheart." They clinked glasses and drank, gazing at each other. "My darling, my precious, my angel, my love. My husband."

"You're all of those," Geoffrey said softly. "My husband. I don't quite believe it. I love you."

"I love you." A kiss, then another, then a hundred. Some time later Niall's phone buzzed. "That will be Janis, I've no doubt."

"Tell her I wish we could have married her too."

"I had the same thought. If I tell her that, she'll be in floods again." He read Janis' text: *Congratulations my dear darling men. Those vows were OMG EPIC major fail from allegedly waterproof mascara. I love you both and wish you happy.*

Geoffrey read it over his shoulder. "Here." He took the phone and composed a reply: *Darling Janis, we owe all this blazing happiness to you. We wish we could have married you too. We love you. Niall & Geoffrey.* He looked up at Niall for confirmation before sending it.

The reply came quickly: *Crap there goes the mascara again. See you tomorrow OXO*

A week before their flight to California, Janis flopped down on the armchair in the parlor and said, "I'm out of time, aren't I."

"Yes, you are." Niall set down his e-reader and regarded her with amusement. "You needn't tell them, you know. We could stay somewhere else."

"I don't *want* to stay somewhere else. Their place is perfect. It's big, it's private, it's secure, and Dad said he could get in a second piano so Tomás and Isabelle and I can work on shit." She stared back at him. "What does Geoffrey say?"

Their husband and lover was across town, meeting with an expert in the gem trade; research for a new idea he'd had. "He says he's at your service regardless and not to take his feelings into account."

"That's not helpful. Actually that's a little insulting. He can't possibly think I *wouldn't*, can he?" Niall shook his head. Janis looked somewhat appeased. "What *are* his feelings?"

"Darling, he wants the world to know. If we were free to be open with your parents he'd be delighted." Niall let that sit for a moment, then, "His parents figured it out, you know."

"Shit."

"No, it's all right. I'm quite sure he's been as discreet as he could possibly be, but you realize they've been aware of his tastes for twenty years."

"Argh." She let her head fall back against the chair. After a minute she said, "What about your parents?"

"They haven't a clue." She laughed. Niall said, "I think it hasn't occurred to them that such a thing is possible. They've seen a lot less of us than Gyan and Vidya have."

"I looked up those names, you know," she said. "They mean knowledge and wisdom. I asked Vidya if that was why they married each other and she said no, they never met till their wedding day. Isn't that wild? They're so great together."

"Yes, they are. They made a commitment, and they've held to it. Like your parents and mine."

"Okay." It sounded like she was agreeing with something he'd asked her to do. Then she said, "What do you want me to do?"

"Janis. My dear love. I want you to do what's best for you."

"Well, what's best for me is hanging out with my parents with my two men, so let's get this fucking show on the road." She lifted her phone off the side table and checked the time. "Might as well be now." She hit the third number on her speed dial. Niall heard the receiving phone ring twice, and then the call connected. "Hi Mom. Ready to be driven crazy by tango-ish music for several months? Oh he is, is he?" She laughed. "Well, the first thing is making a new arrangement of the one from the EP. The lawyers are clearing the rest of the list as we speak. Twelve more tracks. All the others are going to be vocals but with variations. Yeah, with the big one it'll be a nice full album. But listen. There's something we need to talk about. Oh no, they're doing great. Yeah, they'd love to stay with you too if that's okay." She made an 'eek' face at Niall; he almost laughed. "But Mom here's the thing. We still sleep together. Yeah, all three of us now. Um, not exactly. Actually no. Actually yeah. There is that. Sometimes a lot of that. It's amazing but I know it sounds a little freaky and if – okay. No, I love him like crazy. I love them both like crazy. Yeah, they both love me too. I have never felt so safe and accepted and cherished in my entire life except with you and Dad." She wiped her eyes. Niall looked away, swallowing, blinking. "So that's okay? You still have a week to soundproof the room." A shaky laugh. "Geoffrey learned how to bake bread. You two can have a bake-off. I love you too. I love Dad. We'll see you in a week." She ended the call, said, "Oh God," and sobbed for a minute.

Niall kept his hand on her shoulder until she raised her head again. "Come here, sweetheart." She threw herself onto the couch and into his arms.

Janis' manager Randa and her local press agent had talked her into doing a television interview before leaving London. One reason was that it might be a long while before she was back in the U.K.; the other was that with a new album in the works, it was time to get the word out. Geoffrey and Niall planned to go with her to the taping. They were all surprised when they got an email from the producer suggesting that Niall participate in the interview. "Do you think that's wise?" he asked Janis. "Of course I'll do my best bastard, if necessary, to stay on topic." Niall had a nice line in extremely civil abuse. He hadn't had a chance to exercise it for a while.

"Your best is quite a bastard. They probably want to get the human-interest side. You and Geoffrey, loverboys." Geoffrey laughed. "And of course the book contract might come up."

"I'll confirm but that's all," Niall told his husband. "If they want an interview about your work, they can bloody well set one up properly."

"Say what you like. I'll be in the wings if they want any clarification about the buggery." Geoffrey's last e-book had been acquired for a paperback launch by his new publisher; they were already promoting it with terms including 'hot,' 'adventurous,' and 'daring.' The e-book sales had taken off as a result. So far, the only interview request he'd received had come from a gay porn site, to which he'd responded with a polite 'thanks, perhaps later.' He and Niall had both then had a fit of screaming giggles.

"Could we have an interview about my new album that does not turn into a circle jerk?" Janis regarded them both with exasperation. "I'll tell them you'll be there but we're talking about the goddamned record and what we hope will be a tour. What kind of tour? What haven't we done? Oh shit! We have to go to Argentina!"

"Right then. A world tour. I'll do a bit of research on the cities with strong tango communities. And I'll go see about a serious tour manager's costume." Niall went down the hall to consult his closet.

He was still there a half hour later when Geoffrey came to find him for dinner. "What's the matter, darling?"

"The matter appears to be that, I belatedly realize, I haven't done a genuine job interview ever in my life, the last press interview I did was at the end of a tour when looking shabby and knackered was to be expected, and I haven't a thing to wear." He glanced at Geoffrey. "I don't suppose I could wear the morning coat. No? Then it's off to Savile Row tomorrow."

When they arrived at the television studio, Janis was polished and professional in a tailored, wine-colored jersey dress; Geoffrey was comfortable in jeans and a cashmere pullover; and Niall was splendid in a dark-gray silk blend suit with a crisp white shirt and lavender paisley tie. "You look perfect," Janis remarked while they were in makeup. "You look like someone not to be trifled with."

The makeup artist snorted agreement. "Looks like an ambassador." She smudged a tiny bit of brown eyeliner at the base of Niall's lashes.

"Is that absolutely necessary?"

"No, but you look smashing. Let's have these brows a bit more defined, it's all about the eyebrows these days. There you go. Crikey! Why aren't you on the telly?"

"I'm about to be," he pointed out, flattered but amused. Geoffrey was giggling, over in the corner.

"A proper eyeful. And as to you, miss, you look smashing too. That's a perfect color for you." The artist turned to Janis.

"He picked it out for me," she said dryly.

"Well, we can't all be good at everything, now can we?" The artist worked quickly, doing a few simple things with hair and makeup so Janis would look her best under the lights. "I was delighted to hear you've a new record in the works. There. How's that?" Janis checked herself out in the mirror and nodded approval. "Off to the ready room, then."

Forty minutes later Niall and Janis were officially tired of this interview and this host. There had been far too many questions about their personal lives. Niall had defaulted to bastard mode about halfway through, watching with increasing vexation as Janis gritted her teeth and tried to be charming. It was a live interview and the viewers weren't to blame; she clearly wanted to Give Good Show. He knew she believed that most of her fans were more interested in the music than in her private life. And she still posted regularly, she'd been telling the world about the evolution of this next project from the moment the notion struck. So it was all the more annoying that the host didn't mention any of that.

Niall had stopped paying attention – he was watching Janis and calculating the correct amount of alcohol for later application – until he realized she wasn't answering a question. She was looking at him with an expression that said 'kill this guy now.' "I beg your pardon," he said, with the merest glance at the host. "Could you repeat the question?"

"Certainly. It was concerning, in view of the special relationship you have with Ms. Vaughn, what arrangements you and your husband have made for the next tour?" He gave 'special' and 'husband' such insinuating emphasis that Niall instantly lost his temper.

His posture became almost offensively relaxed, in the manner of a predator stretching before gathering itself for an attack. He stared at the host for a moment. When he spoke, his tone was frigid. "As I believe we've said, no arrangements for a tour have yet been made. Should Ms. Vaughn's record company choose to support a tour, my husband may not accompany us. He has his own work." Now he looked straight at the camera. "Ms. Vaughn and I do have a special relationship. She is my best friend, and has been for four years. On the first anniversary of Oliver Dunn's death, only my commitment to Janis kept me from walking into the Thames." He glanced at Janis, silently inquiring whether she wanted to add something. She shook her head slightly and made a 'keep going' face. He looked back at the host. "Ms. Vaughn does not care to live alone. Moreover, it is not safe for her to live alone. She cannot advertise for a roommate." The host's head went back at Niall's scathing tone. He opened his mouth but Niall steamrollered on. "Nor should she be expected to hire a stranger, however well-vetted, to maintain the security of her home when she has a friend willing to serve. Further, Ms. Vaughn finds my presence helpful to the operation of her business, in which she has been very much engaged while here in London. Therefore, she has housed me here in London. And because she has a generous heart, she has housed my husband. Is that sufficiently clear?"

A producer was making frantic 'wrap it up' motions behind the cameras. The host cleared his throat. "Ah, thank you Mr. Phelps, I believe we're out of time. Thank you Ms. Vaughn, it was a pleasure to speak with you today. We'll be looking forward to more news of your next record. I'm sure it will be a tremendous success." There were a few more words, then the end music ran and the camera lights went off.

Niall was on his feet immediately. He pulled off his microphone and went over to Janis. "All right?" She took his hand and stood.

"I'm fine. Thanks. That was good." She turned to the host. "Nice job wrapping up. If the station wants any follow-up, please have them contact my press agent." He was trying to say something, but Janis ignored him. She dropped her microphone on a chair and followed Niall back to the makeup room, collecting Geoffrey on the way.

"Left him in ribbons, my tiger," Geoffrey said with quiet satisfaction as the door closed behind them.

The makeup artist was there, with a gleeful face. "Saw it on the monitor! Coo!" She and Janis both giggled. "Let's get this muck off you, miss." She started removing the makeup, glanced over at the door as if to make certain it was closed, then said, "There's a few on the crew would like to stand you three a round. Thought he'd wet himself." Janis giggled again.

Niall wasn't wasting time; he was helping himself to supplies to get his own makeup off. "A whisky would go down nicely." He glanced at Geoffrey. "I'm sorry, love."

"Why, for heaven's sake?"

"He turned you into a dirty joke."

"He might have tried. I thought you pitched it right. He meant to make you look a gigolo, of course."

"He does look like a gigolo," Janis said. "The kind you hire when you want somebody dead. Oh wait that's an assassin." The makeup artist laughed out loud. "The way you said I beg your pardon. And you so clearly meant, are you still here." Geoffrey snorted. A few minutes later they were ready to go. "Where's the pub?"

Facebook and Twitter blew up. Janis pointed out a few posts where a screenshot of Niall's face was captioned 'knight in shining paisley,' but he was still too upset to be amused. They'd gone for a round with the TV crew, then straight home for another. Geoffrey ordered some dinner; Janis played piano for a while; Niall did his best not to rehearse things he wished he'd said instead, or in addition. Or things he wished he *could* have said, such as 'Get stuffed you parasitic swine.' "I'm sorry," he said after a while. "I'm poor company."

"Sweetheart, you are always perfect. If you want to go have some me time, please do." Janis swiveled around on the piano bench.

Geoffrey nodded. "You were ambushed, darling. He's wishing he hadn't done it now, I expect, but it's only natural you'd be upset."

Niall sighed. "Could have been worse, I suppose. I don't want to be alone. Might there be a spare pair of arms about?" Then he thought *I should have asked earlier*, because they were both on the couch hugging him a moment later.

He was feeling quite thoroughly comforted by the time Geoffrey sat back and said, "Now there's one thing we've to get straight, loves. I can write anywhere. Whither thou goest I will go. Right?" Niall hugged him again, hauling him bodily across his lap so he and Janis could both kiss his laughing face.

Part II

Chapter 5
December 2018

"Yes, I'm an English citizen. Yes, I was born in England. Yes, I've been to the United States before. I am self-employed. I am a writer." Geoffrey named a few of the magazines he contributed to, and his publisher. He was in a room somewhere in the bowels of the airport, having been separated from Niall and Janis almost immediately after disembarking from their plane, as they were all heading for Customs. There was no clock in the room. There was a window, but it only looked out onto a corridor. A suit-wearing official sat at the desk across from Geoffrey; a uniformed, armed officer stood behind him. "Yes, I'm here on a tourist visa. My husband is here with his employer. Yes, he has a work visa." The official had his passport, his ticket for the next leg of the trip, and his boarding pass, as well as a copy of Geoffrey and Niall's marriage certificate. The visa was right there with the passport. He continued answering questions, keeping his voice steady, though his anxiety was mounting. "His employer is Janis Vaughn, the musician. She is an American citizen. She is going to Los Angeles to develop and record her next album. We will all stay with her parents, the composer Ed Vaughn and his wife Deborah. Yes, I plan to travel separately while we're in California. Yes, I've been to California before." He knew better than to ask why they'd cut him out of the herd, why they were questioning him. He'd heard how awful it could be for people of color trying to enter the United States now. He'd hoped some of those stories had been exaggerated. More questions. "I'll be doing research for the books that are under contract. Novels. Romantic suspense. That's romance and adventure. No, nothing to do with espionage." *Bleeding Christ*.

The suited official's cell phone buzzed. He glanced down at it, then back at Geoffrey. He picked up the phone without a word and left the room. The uniformed officer remained. *Hell,* Geoffrey thought. *Hell and bloody damnation, what now.* He knew he shouldn't be denied entry. His paperwork was in order. He had a legitimate reason to be traveling to the U.S., he had a history of compliance with his length of stay, he wasn't traveling alone, he didn't fit the profile. Except he did, of course. He concentrated on breathing. *Stay calm.*

The official came back in, scooped all Geoffrey's documents off the desk, and held the door open. "This way, please." He'd been polite throughout. As polite as Geoffrey supposed it was possible to be when carrying out the orders of a fascist regime. *Don't be bitter, surely we're going back now.* And they were. The official never said so, but they proceeded to the end of that corridor, and another, and then through a pair of guarded doors he saw Niall. Visibly tense, sagging with relief as they made eye contact. Geoffrey nearly cried. Twenty feet from his husband, the official handed over the papers, said, "Thank you for your cooperation," and stood away. Geoffrey stared at him for a moment to confirm that he was free to go, received an infinitesimal nod, and walked over to Niall.

Niall wrapped him in his arms. "We were bloody terrified. Are you all right?" Geoffrey nodded. "Let's get to the gate. Janis is there. She said if they held you too long she'd re-book us, before calling every

journalist she knows. Even that blighter in London."
Geoffrey laughed shakily. They checked to make sure
all the documents were there, then started walking
fast.

They made it to the gate approximately ten
seconds before the doors were closed. The airline
clerk was apologetic about hustling them through.
Janis was very polite, brightly friendly in the way that
meant she was in a blistering fury. Niall and Geoffrey
said next to nothing until they were seated. The first-
class cabin had large, semi-private seats. Janis was on
one side of the center aisle, with a stranger as her
neighbor; the men were together on the other. Niall
said quietly, "As soon as we're properly aloft you'll
be with me, my love." Geoffrey didn't ask what he
meant. Now that it was over and they were taxiing,
he'd started to shake. It seemed forever until they
were in the air and the seatbelt light went off. An
attendant was there a moment later to ask if they'd
like a drink. Niall said, "A pair of double Scotches,
please and thank you."

Janis said, "Another of those over here, please."
Geoffrey heard her neighbor ask if she was afraid of
flying. "No, I fly all the time," Janis said. "My friend
got hauled off by a storm trooper and we're all about
ten seconds from screaming." The neighbor wanted to
hear everything about it. Geoffrey listened without
listening until the drinks arrived. He and Niall both
disposed of theirs with indecent haste.

Then Niall said, "Over here now, sweetheart,"
and reclined his seat. Geoffrey made the move,
cuddling onto Niall's lap, tucking his face into the
curve of his husband's neck and feeling his arms wrap
tight. "There, darling." They stayed like that for a long
time.

Everyone had settled down when they landed at LAX. Then there was baggage claim, and the drive to Glendale. It was a long day of travel even without drama; they were all well and truly exhausted by the time they arrived at the Vaughn house. Janis said, "There they are. Holy shit am I nervous."

"Why, love? You're well over the first hurdle." Niall squeezed her hand as the limousine pulled up to the house.

"I don't know. It's been a long time since we were here. I haven't seen them for a year." And that had been only for a meal, not even at home, before she'd flown back to Rome from that last visit to Stefan.

"Don't worry." The driver was opening the doors, giving Janis a hand, then going to open the trunk for their luggage. Niall and Geoffrey got themselves out of the vehicle.

"Sweetie!" Janis' mother was there, hugging her. "God it's good to see you. Niall, you look great. Geoffrey? Hi, I'm Deborah, I'm so glad to meet you. Welcome to California." Her smile was warm.

"Thank you," Geoffrey said. "I'm delighted to meet you too. What a marvelous house." It was a sprawling ranch-style structure on a large fenced lot. The gated driveway was a leisurely U-shape bent around a rock-bordered pond with an artificial waterfall.

"We were lucky to get it before prices went completely nuts. This is my husband Ed." They were in their late sixties, both still fit and attractive.

"Hi Geoffrey," said Janis' father, holding out a hand. Geoffrey shook it. "We heard about your book contract, good for you. Janis said you'd be doing some research out here?"

"My publisher heard 'California' and said 'surfer?' with such a pathetically eager look that I'm afraid I'll have to learn. How cold is the water?"

"Bloody cold," Niall said. "You'll want a wetsuit. Ed, you look well. Thanks so much for having us."

"It's good to see you again, son. And by the way, that interview? We call that ripping him a new one." Deborah and Janis laughed. There was even a snort from the limo driver. "How was the trip?"

"The flights were fine," Janis said, "but I want to skywrite Fuck Trump from here back to New York." Both parents had an idea what had happened; they'd seen Janis' post, a phone picture she took on the plane of Geoffrey and Niall, captioned 'how he felt after half an hour with DHS.' They told the story while they got into the house. Deborah fed them a snack. There was another round of Scotch, and then they retreated to the room they would share. "This bed is a little small for three." Janis looked them over. "But I have a feeling that's a good thing tonight. I need approximately all the hugs."

"As do I," said Geoffrey. "Have I mentioned I love you both?"

"We love you too," Janis and Niall said together. The hugs went a long way toward making them all feel better.

Quite a while later, though, Geoffrey was aware that he wasn't the only one who wasn't sleeping. "I don't know why it was so upsetting," he said softly, to whomever was awake. "I wasn't arrested. I wasn't abused. I wasn't effing renditioned."

"Because you were separated from us, I suspect," Niall said. "Rationally I knew they couldn't do anything to you beyond send you back to England. But the thought of being without you while we're here was, frankly, gut-wrenching."

After a moment's consideration Geoffrey said, "That's it, I think. We'd just come off the flight from London and were laughing about how dozy we all were, and then I was in their hands."

"Exactly," Janis said. "One second you were right there with us and the next you weren't. We couldn't even see where you were for a minute, it was awful. Put that with being treated like a type, instead of like a person. A type made up of words that mean hideous things. I would have been screaming continuously."

"No you wouldn't." Geoffrey was amused. "Shouting for your lawyer, perhaps, but not screaming."

"Screaming curses." Janis snickered at Niall's suggestion. He put his hand unerringly on Geoffrey's, twining their fingers together.

Their first week in California, everyone was careful. Polite, friendly, not going too deeply into the personal. Niall and Geoffrey slept with Janis every night, but they were all mindful of being in someone else's house. While they did not withhold themselves from each other, they did keep things to the minimum. Deborah must have guessed; she finally put a stop to that, when Ed was in the study working on the piano and the rest of them were in the kitchen after breakfast. "You don't need to tiptoe around this," she said. "Ed and I have sex too."

"Eww, Mom!"

Deborah laughed. "Look, we know what men do together, and we know what men and women do together. We had a week to think about it before you got here. We appreciate that you've been respectful of our home. But if we're all going to be a family, you need to feel free to do … what you do."

Niall and Geoffrey left this one to Janis. After waiting half a minute for one of them to say something, she gave them a 'thanks for nothing' look that made them both snicker. "Okay. Well. Thanks, Mom. We'll try to keep it down to a dull roar. Did you soundproof the room?"

"We replaced the door, didn't you notice? We replaced the door to our room, too. Solid wood now."

"I did not notice that," Janis said. "I did notice that the bookshelves in the adjacent room mysteriously migrated to the wall behind my bed." Niall, who had *not* noticed that, laughed.

Their first night out was the premiere of 'The Ghost of Carlos Gardel.' When Janis, Niall, and Geoffrey were decanted by their driver in front of the Million Dollar Theater, Valerie wasn't waiting in the queue for admission. She'd come down the red carpet with the rest of the cast and crew. Janis got a text from her while they were waiting to go in, which she then showed to the men: *There are some excited people in here, most of us haven't been in the main credits of a feature before. Prepare yourselves for unintelligible squee.* "Well, what the hell do I say to that? I'd be squealing too."

"You've been squealing and we're only guests," Niall pointed out, which earned him a swat.

"Okay, so Geoffrey, Victor in real life looks like Rudolph Valentino. This poster does not fully do him justice." The barricade between the street and the theater was plastered with giant posters of the six co-stars. "The rest of them look great."

Niall was looking forward to seeing Victor and Andy in the film, but he was mostly enjoying being out with Janis and Geoffrey. The movie-premiere ticketholders included plenty of people on various rungs of the celebrity ladder, which explained the police cars stationed at each end of the block and the half-dozen private security people roaming alertly up and down the queue. Janis was thrilled to be going out to such a high-profile affair with no obligation to perform or to talk to the press. She was wearing a long slinky dress of dark purple velvet, with a long silver-gray fake-fur coat over it and purple satin shoes peeping out from under the hem. "You're particularly beautiful tonight," Niall told her. "It's an honor to be your escort."

"My escorts are both showstoppers," she said. "If you weren't going to wear the morning coats, the white dinner jackets were an excellent alternative. It doesn't look like anybody else did that."

"I don't suppose the audience will have an opportunity to dance," Geoffrey said, a bit wistfully. Tango music was being piped out the front of the theater. "We still haven't been to a milonga."

"Maybe tonight," Niall said. "We're out already. You say they always start late. Surely someone here will know of one." Janis looked excited. "You could dance in those shoes, couldn't you, pet?"

"I could, couldn't I, Geoffrey?"

"That's an excellent idea, sir." Geoffrey was smiling at Niall. "Might I convince you to dance with me once?"

"You could convince me of nearly anything, darling." Then, finally, the line was moving. When they reached the theater lobby, three things caught Niall's eye: a wall of behind-the-scenes photographs; a beautiful 1:12 scale ballroom used to create a digital set for the movie; and a sheaf of glossy two-fold guides to Argentine tango in Los Angeles. Niall picked one up, showed it to Janis, and tucked it in his jacket pocket.

After the movie, the Q&A, and an impromptu dance performance by the co-stars, people began streaming out of the theater. Many stopped to greet one or another of the performers; the event staff saw to it that few stayed for long. Janis and her men were spared being ushered out because of their connection to Valerie, Victor, and Andy. They waited their turn to talk to their friends. "Thank you for not bailing the second the Q&A was over," Janis told Victor. "How are you? You look kind of great. That tattoo looks kind of new. Are you supposed to do that so soon after getting shot?"

He was laughing. "It is new, and my doctor said it was okay. My employers threw a fit, but," he shrugged. "I'm good. It's been a crazy few months, but I'm good."

"You were fucking *fantastic* in this movie. And your husband, oh my God." She made a 'wow' face.

"I know!" Victor looked pleased.

"Where is he, anyway?"

"He's probably over in a corner coming up with a strategy for stalking Niall and Geoffrey. He had things to say about Niall after Miami."

Janis laughed; Niall was mildly embarrassed. "He still does photography, I know," he said. "I trust that's what you mean."

"Not entirely, or exclusively," Victor said, "but we'll go with that. Oh, here he is."

"Hi catnip. Hi Janis, good to see you again. Niall, there are rules about showing up at a premiere looking better than the stars." Andy was eyeing him with clear approval. He himself was tall – between Geoffrey and Niall in height - and handsome, with graying dark hair. He had a James-Bond-at-a-disco look to him in a black suit and red shirt, open at the neck to show a tattoo very like Victor's. "And this is Mr. Anand? The novelist?" They shook hands. "I read that last one." Andy fanned himself.

"Call me Geoffrey," he said with a smile. "Brilliant performance in the film. And it was a great pleasure to see you all dance tonight."

"Thanks. This was a labor of love. How long are you going to be in L.A.?" Andy directed the question to all three of them.

"We're here till Janis finishes recording her new album," Niall answered. "End of March, at the earliest."

"Great. I'm going to proposition you. You guys," he specified. They might have both looked alarmed. "I know for a fact I am not the only person who saw 'Lawrence of Arabia' and immediately went looking for O'Toole-Sharif slashfic, because if I were there would not be so much of it. And here it's standing right in front of me." Janis snorted. Geoffrey laughed. Niall blushed. "Okay, so at least half of you are not appalled by that idea."

"I have another idea," Geoffrey said, hand on Niall's back. "If you're serious."

"Oh, I am serious."

Geoffrey glanced at Niall. "The Tempest." He gave it a moment to see if Andy clicked on it.

No doubt about it. Andy said gleefully, "Oh my God Prospero and Ariel, I am there for that. Let's set something up. But shit, we have to mingle. Thanks for coming tonight."

"Good to see you, Janis," Victor said. He'd been standing there watching Andy, in a way that told Niall they were not bound for a party of anything but the most private sort. "Call me, we'll do dinner." Niall and Geoffrey shook hands with Andy and Victor again, then began moving toward the front of the theater where they'd last seen Valerie.

Janis followed a moment later. "How did you like those tattoos?" she said. "The thought of getting one makes me cringe."

Niall felt the same. "The art can be beautiful. How it's delivered, ugh."

Geoffrey laughed again. He'd briefly considered getting one. "I hope they didn't mind me staring. At first I thought they were identical." Both men had what amounted to an abbreviated necklace of ink, ornate but delicate, scrolling from the hollow of the throat up across the collarbones. Andy's centered on a capital letter V; Victor's, on a capital A. "The design gave me an idea."

"Oh did it?" Niall noticed his tone, something between mischief and intention. "You'd subject yourself to that?"

"Perhaps I'd try it in henna. See how you like it." He was almost laughing again because he knew the idea was outrageous. "So where are we bound?"

"We," Niall said, a bit smug because he knew Janis and Geoffrey would both be delighted, "are bound for a private milonga at a dance studio in West Hollywood. The choreographers teach there, apparently half the dancers in the film train there. Where Tomás works, darling," he said to Janis.

"Fan-fucking-tastic. If I finally get to see you dance with Geoffrey, that shit is going on Facebook."

She did get to see them dance. Niall hadn't really submitted to lessons, but he'd watched the others dance enough, and listened to enough tango music, that he could fake it. And because they were surrounded by experienced professional and semi-pro dancers, he found himself dancing with others almost at once. Men and women, all impossible to refuse, all generous with advice. He stood aside after an hour, watching Janis with Geoffrey. Though they all felt this to be a safe place, the two of them were in Public Mode: obviously good friends, but not obviously lovers. Niall took a few pictures with his phone. Janis had posted a few he'd taken of them dancing at the flat, but she looked spectacular tonight and he wanted the world to see.

"I beg your pardon," said an English voice behind him. Niall turned, surprised. "My name's Mary Warner." A tall black woman offered her hand.

Niall took it and kissed it, with a little bow because she looked like a queen. She was delighted. "Niall Phelps. Lovely to meet you."

"I couldn't help noticing you," she said, "you're so like my husband. I don't believe you've met?" Niall shook his head. "Come and see." Mary led him through the crowded room to a group of four men standing in a corner. One was another dark-eyed ginger. He was an inch taller than Niall and more massive, with a two-foot tail of wavy red hair. "Darling, look. This is Niall Phelps."

"Red Warner." The big man held out a hand; Niall shook it; they regarded each other for a moment before both grinning. "This is Sam, his husband Mateo, and our friend Vince."

Niall said, "I recognize you. You were all in the film tonight. Well done."

"Thanks," said the one he thought was Vince. "Nice to meet you. Mateo and I were about to hit the floor again."

"Don't let me keep you."

"Dance with me," Mateo said to Sam. "Nice to meet you, Niall." Vince offered a hand to Mary, leaving Niall and Red together.

"I might recognize you too," Niall said. "Are you an actor?"

Red nodded. "Used to specialize in fight choreography, stunts, and weapons work. Then a thing happened with our friend Tanith, and my career took off."

"Tanith Salazar, the director of the movie? We met tonight. My employer Janis – that lady in violet – is a friend of Valerie Benton, she introduced us."

"We know Valerie too. I worked on a play with Tanith six years ago, a musical. Valerie ran the whole music side of things for the production. Is Janis here in town to work?"

"To rehearse and record a new album. I'm her tour manager and general factotum. And have very little to do with myself until we begin properly planning a new tour." He had an idea. "As you're a weapons expert, perhaps you could tell me. Is there such a thing as a fencing club in Los Angeles? We're staying out in Glendale."

Red looked surprised. "There is. But I've got this thing." He made a face. "Not exactly fencing though."

"What thing?"

"There's a company that wants to pay me to do a limited web series with broadswords. Basic techniques for handling and sparring, basic fight choreography, and a demo fight. Six short videos for YouTube. There's a guy I used to work with at Renaissance festivals, but he's over on the East Coast now. Have you ever handled one of those?"

"No. A fake once, for a student play, never left my belt. My club in London only goes up to sabre." Niall was interested though. He had even less to do in L.A. than he'd had in London. "I'm not averse to learning. You did say it's basics?"

"I did. It would be great for me. You're so close to my height. Marco, he was in the movie? He wanted to do it, but he's going back to Mexico in January for his job."

Niall saw Mary headed toward them, with a 'meaning to dance with my husband' look about her. "Well, let's get your number, then. I'll work out with Janis when she does and doesn't need me, and I'll call you. Right?"

"Great." They exchanged contact information. "Hi beautiful." Red slid his arm around his wife.

"I'll take him now, thanks," Mary told Niall, and left him laughing.

He turned to survey the room, looking for Janis and Geoffrey. They were dancing together again, or still. Then Tomás – one of the movie's stars, and the pianist for the cast album - cut in for a dance with Janis. Niall could tell that she immediately started chattering, probably about the music they'd start working on together very soon. He saw Geoffrey look around and thought, *Now, if ever*. He crossed the room, sliding his arm around Geoffrey from behind with as much confidence as his nerves permitted. "My dance, angel eyes?"

"God, yes." Geoffrey turned into his embrace, left hand going behind Niall's neck, right hand into Niall's offered left, and face turning toward Niall's. Close enough that his forehead contacted Niall's cheek and their bodies touched from chest to thigh.

"Crikey," Niall said softly after a minute or two. "No wonder."

"No wonder what?"

"No wonder you fell for her."

"I was half there already, because you love her." Geoffrey's voice was very quiet. They were so close, no one could possibly overhear. "And because she's wonderful."

"Yes she is. So are you." Niall knew that his tango was still elementary. It probably always would be. But Geoffrey seemed perfectly content to remain in his arms until, much later, Janis found them.

"I have taken pictures that will make people cry, especially if they've seen the DHS post. Now my feet are killing me. We could do this again sometime." She said it hopefully.

"We could," Niall said, standing sufficiently away from Geoffrey that they could compose themselves for departure. "What's the time?"

"A little past one o'clock. I texted Mom and Dad on the way over here so they'd know we'd be late. I'll summon up our chariot." She wandered away, texting, somehow not colliding with any of the dancers still on the floor. Niall and Geoffrey located a few people they wanted to thank, or say good night to, or exchange numbers with. Then they located Janis' coat, bundled her into it, and went to meet their driver.

"You know," she said, on their way over the Hollywood Hills, "I haven't driven myself anywhere since a year ago August. I should probably get out in the car and see if I remember how."

"We all should," Geoffrey said. "I haven't driven in America for years. Though I didn't foresee the actual need while we're here, one doesn't care to admit incompetence."

Niall hadn't driven for as long as Janis. "And if you truly mean to take up surfing, you'll need a way to get to the ocean. Janis, is there one of your parents' cars that they won't mind us using? Given the potential for disaster."

Janis snickered. "Mom's car. She wants a new one." She leaned against Niall and said, "You want to close the window?" He didn't say anything, merely pressed the button to secure their privacy. "Thanks." She kissed him, in their usual manner. Then she tugged Geoffrey closer and kissed him, in *their* usual manner. "Seeing you guys dance was so goddamn sexy."

Geoffrey kissed her again, quite thoroughly. Then he moved to the other end of the L-shaped seat, put a hand on Niall's thigh, and kissed him even more thoroughly. "I've been wishing for that for hours. You two beauties."

"Speak for yourself," Janis said. "Niall, I had to actively defend his virtue." Geoffrey laughed.

"Funny," Niall said, smiling, "I could have sworn everyone there was coupled."

"Well, they were. But didn't it sound good?"

"It sounded marvelous." Geoffrey moved again, inserting himself between Janis and Niall. "If you weren't in this smashing gown, I'd be inclined to attempt your virtue right now."

"If I weren't in this smashing gown, I'd be inclined to let you." There was some more kissing. "Okay, you know, there is a lot to be said for letting someone else drive."

They were still snickering, trying to be quiet, when they let themselves into the house in Glendale. The driver had been just as such a driver should be: either truly oblivious, or doing a good impression. Janis and her smashing gown were only slightly disheveled. Niall and Geoffrey were thoroughly so. Once they all did a bare minimum of washing-up and landed in bed, Janis said, "Okay. Watching that was fucking killing me. I do not want to be rude and demanding, but help. Please. If you can," she said, sounding slightly cranky, because Geoffrey and Niall had brought each other off in the limousine not very long ago.

"Oh darling, I can manage." Geoffrey was amused. "Let's have you." He bore her down against the pillows, kissing her with enthusiasm. Then he kissed his way down her body until she could only reach his hair. "There you are."

"Jesus," she said, her voice soft and tight. "God, that mouth of yours." Niall knew all about that mouth.

He'd been in it less than thirty minutes before, just after Geoffrey had been in his. As usual, the sight, sound and scent of their love play made his body forget all about recent activity and clamor for more. By the time Janis started to whimper, he was close to climax. Then Geoffrey moved up again, mounting her, drinking in the sounds she made as she contracted against him, throat working with a stifled cry of his own a moment later.

"Christ." Niall took a minute to catch his breath. "I always scoffed at live sex shows. I thought, that would never work for me. How wrong I was." Geoffrey laughed into the pillow.

By the week after Tanith's movie premiere, all five residents of the Glendale house were sufficiently comfortable that Niall and Janis, or Niall and Geoffrey, or Geoffrey and Janis, reverted to their habitually-frequent touches and kisses. Ed and Deborah seemed reassured by it, as if this open and easy affection meant 'love' to them as well. Which made sense, Niall realized; Janis had to have learned it from someone. He'd long since extended a degree of physical affection to Deborah himself. And before long he was aware that Geoffrey did too, most often when he was in the kitchen with their hostess, who was teaching him how to do things other than bake bread. She managed to ask him why that was his principal (not to say only) culinary accomplishment without sounding too skeptical.

"I never had the chance," he said. "Wasn't allowed the kitchen at my parents' house. Learned how to assemble a breakfast when I was with friends. I began with bread because of Janis."

Deborah snorted. "My daughter has always contended that bread and cheese and wine is as good a dinner as anyone needs. Do you get her to eat a salad once in a while?"

"We order in," he said cheerfully, "and she's hungry."

"I heard that," Janis said from the next room. "And just for that, I'm dropping a spoiler about your porn project with Andy."

"Their what?!" Deborah was laughing.

"It isn't porn," Geoffrey said. He was smiling, but was not about to admit that Andy had already emailed them to request feedback on makeup, costume, and degree of nudity. "Mr. Martin said at the premiere that he wanted to take our picture. We'd had an idea about 'The Tempest.' And he liked the idea, so we sent him the bits of text we're particularly inspired by. He says he hasn't time to touch it till after he and Victor are done with the movie tour, toward the beginning of March, but it's the first thing he wants to do then. So I'll schedule my research jaunts around that."

Janis had come into the kitchen. "Weren't you and Niall going to run over to Mammoth?"

"Yes, sometime next month. I'm told the snow won't be at its best then, but we'll go to suss it out. I might put together a spec article for one of the magazines I write for, tell them I can go back later for peak-season destination data and some pictures. But in any case, I'm thinking of using that area in one of the new books, and I've never been there. Two trips will help me get the feel of it."

"I've never been there either," said Janis, showing no sign of wishing she had. "You can tell me if there's any reason for me to go. Where is Niall, anyway?"

"He's down in the gym." Janis and Deborah looked at each other, then back at Geoffrey, clearly stifling laughter. "Yes, all right, Andy did warn us the clothes might come off."

Janis went back to the study after a while. Geoffrey and Deborah tidied up the kitchen. Then she suggested a cup of tea, and set a hand on his arm. "I know you want to go write. I wanted to check in with you about the whole airport thing. See if you needed to talk about it."

He gazed at her, astonished. Everyone else seemed to think it was over and done with. He'd thought so, himself, for the most part. Aside from the thing he'd started to write in their journal and then moved to a different document because it grew too long, too dark, too hateful. That wasn't how he wanted his loves to see him. Wasn't, really, how he wanted to see himself. He blew out a breath. "I'd love a cup of tea, and I do need to talk about it."

"All right." She turned away. Until the tea was ready they didn't speak. "So how do you like L.A.? You've been here before."

"Only passing through. Everyone we've met has been terrific."

"There are a lot of annoying things about Los Angeles," she said, sitting at the table. "But it is one of the most diverse cities in the world, which makes it tough for people to stay in that 'everyone different is bad' place. Outside L.A., there's plenty of that in California. I haven't spent enough time in San Francisco or San Diego to guess how they are."

"Those are the cities I was in before. I was going out to Joshua Tree, the Salton Sea. Yosemite and

Lassen." Geoffrey leaned against the counter, sipping tea. "You've some of the best parks in the world."

"If they survive this administration. Anyway. I hear from Janis, who's heard it from Niall, that you really are a world traveler. And not the stay-in-hotels kind of traveler. You've been some sketchy places, I'm guessing."

He smiled. "Very much so."

"What's the most scared you've ever been?"

He didn't have to think about it for long; he'd already written it down. "The most physically frightened would have been in Africa. There was some kind of riot. By the time I got any kind of story about it, so much time had passed that I had to assume the story was largely fiction. I know more than a dozen people died."

"But that wasn't a personal threat."

"No more than crossing paths with a lion. It was simply a danger that arises that must be faced and, one hopes, escaped." He waited, but there wasn't another question. Only Deborah's kind eyes and her patience. "It's no wonder Janis is the way she is," he said. "You and Ed, you're magnificent." She smiled. "Yes, then. I've been to Palestine, Chechnya, Afghanistan. I've seen children killed by soldiers, soldiers who are children. The most threatened I've ever felt is in bloody America."

"I'd be feeling kind of bitter," she suggested.

"I am. I don't like it, I've never been conscious of that before. It's just so sodding *stupid*. With all the resources your government commands, twelve separate armed services and a military budget greater than those of the next seven highest-spending countries combined, the best they can do is harass *me*?

108

Put children in cages? Deport college students, or National Guardsmen? It's disgusting." He stopped and took a breath.

"Yes, it is. My personal feeling is that there is so much back-room bullshit happening to keep that military budget where it is, they are constantly looking for the next threat. Trying to create an atmosphere of paranoia, so that people will think, oh we need all this." She shook her head. "I try not to think about it much. It's in the category of problems I can't solve, except to vote for secession if it comes on the ballot."

Geoffrey smiled at that. "Will it?"

"Maybe. Anyway. Thanks for telling me that."

"Thanks for asking." He finished his tea, rinsed his cup, kissed her cheek, and went to write.

They had another late-night conversation, the three of them, a few days later. All of them had been voracious since the premiere and the milonga. Going out to a couple more dances had kept them even more than ordinarily inclined to handle each other. That night Janis, already satisfied, watched while Geoffrey brought Niall off. "There," he said. "Now a man can get some rest." Niall was still not really thinking, but he frowned a little.

Even though Geoffrey's voice held a smile, Janis asked, "Are we abusing this situation? We are, huh. We need to lay off you for a while."

"Oh no, sweetheart. That's not what I meant. I'm loving this. I've never been such a shameless trollop."

"Are you sure it's not too much?" Niall had caught up with the conversation. "I've only now realized you've never said no to me. Barely even 'not just now.' There must have been times you'd rather be left alone."

Geoffrey propped himself up so he could see both of them, in the light from a candle Janis had lit. "Truly, my loves. I don't *want* to say no. I really love both of you." They both murmured the same back to him. "I'm not a one or the other person, it's always been both, and only once before has that worked in the context of a real relationship. Even then it wasn't like this. This is different. This is perfect. It's what I've always wanted." Now that he said it, he realized it was true. Sex was only part of it. Friendship, and everything else they had, so much more. "Look. It's not as though you're chasing me through the house day and night." Janis snorted. "You might have noticed I'm the one starting things half the time."

"Well okay, yeah."

"Was there ever a time you were disinclined?" Niall was sitting up now himself.

Never with you. Geoffrey leaned on his shoulder. "I've been disinclined many times. There was a year when I didn't see men at all."

"Had something happened?" Niall glanced over at Janis. She was frowning.

"Something might have. I went to a club, a place I'd been told the men were … more mature. Not out for an anonymous fuck. More sure of what they wanted, and that being apt to include a public life. Dinners, the theatre. I found it not as advertised." He paused, remembering. "Most of the young men there were like me."

"Darling, no one on earth's like you." Niall kissed his cheek.

Geoffrey laughed under his breath. "Well, the older men there, let's say I received some propositions that shocked me. It wasn't a straight club, if you know what I mean. It was bondage and discipline and the like. Not at all up my street, and I had words with the person who recommended it to me. He ought to have known better. The whole thing put me right off for a good while. It was like being hunted. I couldn't stop seeing that look in men's eyes, after, even when I'd no cause to think they would want those things."

"Ick," Janis said. "I had a boyfriend way back who wanted to play around with a little bondage. I was up for it up to a point. Then I had a full-on panic attack."

"What did he do?"

"Panicked worse than me. It was so ridiculous, after the fact. I was like, untie me right now motherfucker, I will fucking kill you, you sick bastard, get me out of here." She snickered. "Honestly I'm pretty sure he was more traumatized than I was." She scooted up to kiss Geoffrey, then lay back down. "Niall and I know what to do with ourselves if we need to, honey. Do not hesitate to say no."

"I promise," he said, thinking *never*.

Chapter 6

Deborah laid on a fine dinner for Christmas Eve. They were all relaxed, well into a second bottle of exceptional California cabernet. Geoffrey watched Ed look around the table, almost as if he were deciding whether it was time for some announcement, or perhaps some inquiry. There had been few of those. So he wasn't surprised when Deborah then said, apropos of not much, "Geoffrey, we've heard so much about you." He couldn't help but notice the slight stress on the word 'about,' or that she glanced quickly at Janis before looking back at him.

"I know, I'm sorry." She laughed, as intended. Geoffrey went on to answer the unspoken request, that they should hear *from* him. "The moment they walked into my cousin's restaurant I was conquered. I'd followed Janis and her music for years, I'd been to her concert at Cambridge. And then Niall ... well, you might imagine he's difficult to resist. I didn't even try."

Deborah laughed into her wine glass. "I showed his picture to a friend not long ago. He said some very bad words when I told him Niall was about to get married." Niall, Janis, and Ed all laughed. "Like, *all* the bad words. Something about, why the hell did you show this to me, that's just mean. Could I ask you something?"

"Anything," he said, trying not to be nervous. The relationship was, after all, an established thing.

"Have you ever had a relationship like this before?"

Ah, he thought, relieved. Niall and Janis knew the answer, but not the details. This was a good time,

112

especially in view of their recent conversation. "I have. After university. My first real love affair was at university." He glanced over at Niall, who read the look with typical accuracy and reached for the wine bottle, emptying it into various glasses and then sitting back, apparently relaxed. Geoffrey knew that Ed and Deborah were aware of Niall's history. They'd known him for years, after all. To share his own was only fair. "That first affair was rainbows and flowers and heart-shaped boxes for the better part of a year. It was the first love for him too. We were both in love. Then we were, gradually but in hindsight unmistakably, no longer both in love." He stressed the 'both.' "Broken dates. Calls that weren't returned. Arguments. Eventually quite a lot of tears, and finally an admission that there was someone else." It didn't hurt anymore. Geoffrey suspected the others could all hear that in his voice. He'd long since worked it out in a novel – one he had written but not published – and in some poetry that only his mother had seen. "It was two years later that I met a young married couple who were in an adventurous phase. We were all attracted to each other. And that again lasted the better part of a year. Then they decided they wanted to have a child, and the young lady decided that meant they should be a couple again. We weren't in love." Another glance around to gather reactions. Geoffrey took a sip of wine. "We were friends. So when they said, thanks, we'll carry on from here, I said, thanks to you too, it's been lovely, and went about my life. A year and a half ago the husband called me." A reaction from Niall. "He wondered if we could see each other, and not down the pub." Ed laughed, then made an apologetic movement. Geoffrey gave him a quick smile. "Quite. So we met, and he was by himself. I asked why. He said his wife was content. It would be the two of us.

But she mustn't know." Janis hissed a little. "And I said, my dear man, that's not how I operate. I wish you well, but no. So we parted. I've no idea what he's done." There was one thing left to say. "I liked being their lover. I didn't want to be his mistress."

They all were quiet for a few minutes. Everyone seemed to be thinking. Wine glasses were emptied, the table was cleared. Then Deborah offered to make coffee. Geoffrey went with her to lend a hand. "You look so young," she said, "it's hard to remember you're a full-grown man with life experience and more than your share of brains. Apologies in advance if we're ever off-key with you."

"You and Ed have both been incredibly kind and welcoming. This situation is tricky, we're all too well aware."

"We want Janis to be happy. This is the happiest we've ever seen her. Therefore, we are adjusting our view of what's possible." She patted his shoulder. "There's something we should tell you, too. Let's take this to the study." He helped her transfer the coffee things to the big room with the baby grand. Janis was already sitting on the bench, tinkering with the keyboard. Niall and Ed were standing by the wall of books, records, and music scores. They each had a brandy in hand. "Oh, more drinking?"

Ed saluted Deborah with his glass. "I thought there was something we should tell Niall and Geoffrey."

"You read my mind."

Niall saw Janis's face change. She didn't look fearful or upset. She looked relieved. He thought, *we're about to hear what happened to her brother*. All he knew was that he'd died. Respecting her reticence

114

– her right to privacy – he had not gone looking for details, not even after they'd known each other in every sense. Geoffrey brought two cups of coffee, and they sat down next to each other in a pair of club chairs. "This is where I had my breakdown," Niall said softly, "where Janis started me on the road back to life. And where Ed and Deborah welcomed me into theirs. It's a bit sacred, this room." Geoffrey reached for his hand.

They all sat and listened to Janis play for a while. Christmas carols. Never a whole song, merely a verse or a chorus here and there, in between sips of coffee. Ed finished his brandy long before Niall did. Eventually Janis stopped playing with an air of finality, and took her cup to a chair next to her mother. "That's my cue." Ed set his cup down. "We have personal reasons for being inclined to like you guys, reasons that go beyond the fact that Janis loves you. We had a son. You'll know that. He died. You'll know that too. Here's what happened." He took a moment, and a breath. "He was twenty-one and in college. He had a boyfriend. They were fairly serious, but not in a this-is-forever way. Derek told us that. It was an exclusive thing, though. The boyfriend, Kyle, he wasn't a bad guy. But he could be rough. We had some arguments with Derek about it. He said, don't worry, it's consensual, we have a safe word. We didn't ask for details because, in the end, we trusted him. But something went wrong." Another breath, this one a bit shaky. Deborah stood up and went over to him, leaning over the back of his chair with her arms crossed over his chest. She kissed his cheek. "Thanks honey. Anyway Kyle called us, he was distraught. He said there's been an accident, I called 911. The police are here, they've taken Derek to the hospital, I'm so

115

sorry. A terrible, terrible night." Ed and Deborah leaned their heads against each other for a moment. Niall and Geoffrey were still holding hands. Janis was huddled in her chair, crying silently. Ed inhaled, exhaled, inhaled again. "They charged Kyle with manslaughter, but it was eventually ruled an accidental death. He was able to finish college, after a while. He's a social worker now. We do not keep in touch, exactly, but we're aware of each other. I think Janis has spoken with him."

"A couple of times," she said, sniffling. She shook herself, stood up, and went over to sit on Niall's lap.

He wrapped his arms around her. "All right, sweetheart?"

She sighed and nodded. "He was my big brother. And he was such a jerk sometimes, but I loved him. He had such plans. He used to fight with Dad all the time because Dad wanted him to be a musician and Derek was all, Dad, no." Ed almost laughed. "He had talent but he didn't have that ambition. He wanted to be a pilot, he wanted to fly planes."

"He could have done it, too," Deborah said. "He was as smart as Janis. Anyway. There you go. We lost Derek, and then Janis brought us Niall, and now we have two sons." Niall and Geoffrey both reacted, an involuntary movement and then a glance at each other with glistening eyes.

There was a quiet chime from the brass clock on top of the bookcase. Niall looked up at it. "And it's midnight. Happy Christmas."

It was Geoffrey who stood, went to Deborah, and hugged her. Then they pulled Ed up from his chair and hugged him too. A moment later Niall and Janis

116

were in the mix. All five stood for a few minutes with their arms around each other, saying nothing, simply allowing the mortar of their new connection to set.

Over the next week, Ed started work on a score for a cable movie. Janis took her turn in the study, communing with the songs she would be working on with Tomás and Isabelle, the cellist. Deborah continued teaching Geoffrey to cook; Niall found himself in the kitchen much of the time, watching them, enjoying their banter and their results.

Ed and Deborah were invited to a New Year's Eve party by a friend, and Janis had a separate invitation from Valerie. Niall and Geoffrey were content to stay home. By eight o'clock, they had the big house to themselves. "It's almost like our night in Oxford, isn't it," Niall said.

"Except with ten times the space and a well-stocked refrigerator." They finished clearing up from their dinner. Geoffrey handed his husband a glass of champagne and they went through to the den. "How are you liking California this time?"

"It's a completely different experience." Niall sipped champagne, thinking about the other years he'd stayed in Glendale. "The first time was three years ago. Janis went to see Stefan for a couple of days. The rest of the time we were all here together. The year after, she saw him again, and they had a terrible row. About me. Then she came back and found me in the garden and told me everything they'd said, and I was horrified."

"Why?" Geoffrey was half-laughing because the horror clearly didn't derive from fright.

"She told him about our self-comforting ways." Geoffrey laughed out loud. Niall shook his head, still disbelieving it. "He knew we kissed each other, because of all the pictures that were posted. But she told him we slept together sometimes, and that other things happened sometimes."

"And then you had that conversation." Geoffrey slid down on the couch and leaned close, resting his head on Niall's shoulder. "You said you loved each other. And wished for a third person."

"Did she tell you that before it turned up in our journal?" The journal that now lived in their bedroom. Niall finished his champagne and set aside the glass. He began running his fingers through Geoffrey's hair.

"Yes, she did. Then last year, you were with your parents in England and she had that disastrous visit."

"I couldn't believe he was so obtuse. Not to know how hurt she would be, that he went to someone else's concert when he wouldn't go to hers." If there was anything Niall truly disliked about Stefan, it was that. He couldn't blame the other man for being jealous of Niall's relationship with Janis, or for missing her when she was away. Though his way of expressing that was frequently inappropriate (or flatly offensive). "What were you doing last New Year's?"

"We had a family party. I was leaving the next day for a trip. I told you I went to Petra. Wanted to see it for myself while I still could, before there's another war there."

"Bound to be one, isn't there. That hellish mess in Syria." They were both quiet for a moment. "Well, my darling. Where in the world have you *not* been? Where would you go next?"

Geoffrey laughed. "So many places. I've not been to South America at all. So I hope the record company

118

will send Janis there." Another quiet moment. "And you? Where would you go?"

"Wherever you are." Niall turned his head. Geoffrey was looking up at him. Niall let his hand slide out of his husband's hair, down his neck, lightly cupping his jaw to turn his face up for a kiss. After a few minutes he drew away enough to say, "If you are ever in doubt about my love for you, you needn't be."

"I never could be." Geoffrey shifted, sitting up so he could go for another kiss. "You show me every day. You tell me with every word. You give me such a wealth of love. I feel whatever I give you couldn't be a tenth of it."

"You give me everything, sweetheart. Everything I ever needed." More kisses. "Everything I ever wanted. Everything I ever dreamed." Geoffrey's breath caught, and he pressed his wet face to Niall's. "Darling." A fierce embrace, and yet more kisses. "I love you."

"I love you." Geoffrey wiped away tears. "My God, what great good I must have accomplished in a past life, in order to deserve this."

"You deserve it on your own account, you peerless creature. I can't imagine you've ever done anyone harm in the whole of your existence."

"I try to walk lightly. As you do."

Niall moved his head, a gentle negative. "I am a getter of things done. Occasionally I tread on people. You walk in beauty."

"You tread on toads like that TV presenter," Geoffrey pointed out after another kiss. Niall huffed out a laugh, almost grateful for a turn back to humor. "Did I tell you what my current hero is up to?"

"I don't believe so." Niall settled himself comfortably in the corner of the couch, stretched out so Geoffrey could recline against him. "Is this one misbehaving?"

"Oh yes, but perfectly so." Geoffrey started to tell Niall what he was writing.

January 2019

Before she got properly down to work with Tomás and Isabelle, Janis had to meet with her manager Randa. She and Niall spent a couple of days organizing their notes for the new album and the wished-for new tour. Niall went with her to Century City for the meeting. "People make this frightful drive every day," he said with a sort of horrified admiration. "*Twice* a day."

"Thousands of them," she agreed, sounding quite annoyingly cheerful. No doubt because she wasn't behind the wheel.

"They're all mad," he muttered. "Next time, Randa can bloody well come to you."

Meanwhile, Geoffrey was taking advantage of a day alone to go and see a henna artist. He hadn't forgotten the design inspired by Andy and Victor's new tattoos. He suspected that after a day battling traffic and dealing with a lawyer – even one thoroughly on their side, like Randa – Niall and Janis would be inclined to be entertained. If the design worked at all. If not, he hoped there would be a way to remove it promptly. He'd talked to the artist ahead of time, the only one of several he'd called who seemed to have a sense of humor. When he told her what he wanted, she made a stifled noise that he was fairly certain was a laugh. She told him where to go, how long it would take, and what she would charge. All three were acceptable.

So not too long after Niall and Janis left, Geoffrey was half-naked, kneeling on a massage chair, having the back half of the design applied while the front half dried. The artist was humming to herself. "Have you ever done something like this before?"

She said, "No, but I'd like to put it in my book if you don't mind. I don't know what it means and I don't want to know but everybody could do their own thing with it. Where did you get the idea?" He told her about Andy and Victor. "Oh my God I saw that movie! A friend of mine is a dancer and said, I have to see this, will you go with me."

"Did you like it?"

"I really did. Never even heard of Argentine tango before, had you?"

"Oh yes. I like to dance."

It sounded like she muttered, "Figures." Geoffrey smiled to himself.

When the henna application was finished, he had another hour to wait before he could drive back to Ed and Deborah's house. Ed had assured him that he needn't hurry back with the car. Geoffrey thought his hosts might well appreciate having everyone out of the house for a while. "Is there a coffee shop nearby, one that has WiFi?" he asked the artist.

"I have WiFi," she said. "I have another client coming in half an hour, that job'll probably take an hour. And then I have to go out to do this birthday party. You're welcome to hang out here till then."

"Thank you. I will, then, and give this time to properly set. Wouldn't want it smudged when my husband sees it." He saw her register that, the swift disappointment, the equally swift acceptance. She'd had the same reaction to his wedding ring. "You're very kind," he said, and went to her waiting area (that was, her kitchen) to open his laptop and write for a while.

He was home before Niall and Janis, as he'd hoped, gym pants still slung low around his hips. Once the household was together again, he tried not to be obvious about avoiding the back of the couch, or of the chairs in the dining room and then the study. He spent more time on his feet than usual. Niall suspected something; at first, he seemed concerned. Geoffrey gave him a 'don't worry' signal, suppressing a smile, and Niall's face cleared. Janis was at the piano. Ed and Deborah were talking in the corner. Geoffrey went out after a while, to remove the henna paste as instructed and have a look at the results in the big bathroom mirror. He might have laughed out loud. There was a tap on the door. "What are you about, angel eyes?"

"Go to the bedroom and I'll show you."

Niall heard the stifled laughter. It made him smile. He wasn't sure if Geoffrey's mischief – whatever it was – was meant to seduce, but he certainly hoped so. The past two nights, he and Janis had both been up late working. He went down to the bedroom and switched on a lamp, had a seat on the bed, and waited. Geoffrey came in a minute later, closing the door behind him. He was wearing his bathrobe. "You remember Andy and Victor's tattoos?"

"Oh yes. I remember you said they gave you an idea. What have you done?"

"Henna. Found an artist not far from here. I think she did a cracking job." He stood there a moment, admiring his husband. "She fancied me."

Niall made a *pfft* sound. "Who wouldn't? Will you show me?" He watched while Geoffrey untied the belt of the robe and let it fall open. "Oh my." He swallowed. "Will you stand a bit closer, love?"

"For what purpose, sir?" Geoffrey was grinning. Niall's face was eloquent. "You wish to inspect it?"

"Very closely indeed." Geoffrey took a single step nearer. Niall leaned forward, trying to study the actual art and not its overall effect, which was tantalizing in the extreme. The henna design was a belt of complex loops and swirls, like a vine. It was almost perfectly symmetrical, draped between Geoffrey's hipbones, its lowest point a scant inch above the silky black hair of his groin. The design centered on what Niall realized was a letter, a capital J. He glanced up quickly and saw both laughter and love on his husband's face. Then Geoffrey turned around, letting the robe fall at his feet. "You wicked darling." Niall's voice had that low, caressing quality that never failed. It was like his hand on Geoffrey's skin: instant arousal. Then his hand *was* on Geoffrey's skin, a fingertip lightly brushing above the belt of henna drawn across the top of that already-irresistible arse. Again symmetrical, again complex, and centered on a capital N. Stupefyingly effective. He laughed under his breath. "Take a step back, would you, love?"

"What would my potent master?" Geoffrey's voice was trembling with both stifled laughter and onrushing lust. He took that step back.

"What's my pleasure?" Niall shifted forward on the edge of the bed and leaned in to press his lips to

123

that N, then above it, then below. Geoffrey's breath went out. He wanted Niall's hand. He took another step back, and there it was, brushing around the side of his hip to his erection, wrapping around it. Stroking, while Niall's mouth was on the curves of his arse. Geoffrey closed his eyes, lost in sensation. "There's my pleasure, you beauty. 'Hark what thou else shalt do me.' Turn around, and let me have you." Geoffrey turned around, almost losing his balance as his feet tangled in the fallen robe. Niall set a hand on each of his hips and put his mouth to that cock, exploring as if he'd never had it before and wanted never to forget it. Geoffrey made a muffled sound. "I'll have her part tonight, and then mine too. You make me greedy." Niall took all of him.

When Janis eventually came to bed, Geoffrey was sound asleep. Niall wasn't, quite. She said softly, "Looks like you had some fun tonight."

"You'll have yours in the morning, no doubt," Niall murmured. "Can you see?" He'd lit a candle, as one of them often did, because the room's lamps were too bright but there was no light from outside. He drew the sheet down carefully and glanced up at Janis.

She leaned in to see the henna design, bit her lip and smiled. "Let me guess what's on his back." Niall nodded. She got in bed, close to Geoffrey, trying not to wake him. Niall pulled up the sheet; Janis pulled up the quilt. "Good night, precious."

"Good night, love."

Work on building the music started in earnest the next day. Geoffrey was ready to do the physical research for one of his new heroes, so he went out to Malibu to see if he could connect with a surfing instructor. He returned to Glendale tired, delighted, and encrusted with sand and salt. "It's brilliant," he told the household at dinner. "Bloody hard work. And thank God they'd a wetsuit I could rent."

"I told you the water was cold," Niall said. "First time I stepped in it I thought *hell*, people never swim in that, it's like the Channel. But they do."

"They have to. It's a rule." Deborah was snickering. "Everybody in the water, at least once, or you can't claim to be a true Californian. So how many lessons are you going to do?"

Geoffrey swallowed a bite of his dinner. "As many as it takes. I've always liked swimming in the ocean."

"You like all kinds of horribly strenuous physical activity," Janis said, before apparently hearing herself and hastily changing the subject. "And speaking of which, Niall! What about this sword-fighting thing?"

Niall was stifling laughter. "I spoke with Mr. Warner and he said he's a new film shoot beginning in April but until then he's at liberty. Since I also appear to be thus, he agreed I could text him on the days Geoffrey goes out to Malibu. If those days are good, Geoffrey can drop me off in Van Nuys."

"The distances in California never fail to amaze me." Geoffrey looked around for more food. Deborah passed him the remains of the roast. "Thank you so much. Are you quite sure you don't mind us using your car?"

"Please," she said. "I think I put maybe a thousand miles on it last year. I was starting to get this vibe when I went into the garage, like, don't you love me anymore. Kind of creepy." Janis was giggling.

Geoffrey took Deborah at her word, and went out regularly. Even when he didn't have a lesson. It was the first time he'd spent on his own since his trip to the Hebrides, and it wasn't until he'd been going out for several days that he realized how tense he'd become. The house in Glendale wasn't as obviously a city house as their flat in London had been, and its grounds at least let him see the sky. But with five people in residence, one couldn't ever truly feel alone.

So the hour-long drive to Malibu, the two or three hours at the beach, an hour at a coffee shop to write about the day's experience, and then another hour (or more) home made for a calming, restorative block of almost-silence. Once home, there was the very necessary shower after a quick word with Deborah (and generally a snack). Two to three solid hours of writing saw him through to dinner, by which time he was looking forward to seeing and talking to everyone, instead of dreading it. He didn't question his own feelings, or worry about them. Wishing for solitude and the open air were part of his makeup, not a symptom of discontent.

On the days he deposited Niall in Van Nuys, the drive out was still most often silent; Niall was not at his best early in the morning. Geoffrey didn't stay out as long on those days. On his return he would generally find Niall and Red in the house, having a drink and talking of blades. Geoffrey continued to find the entire subject tantalizing, which meant on those days he and Niall often showered together. "One grows fond of American excess," Niall murmured once as they stood under the pair of ceiling-mounted showerheads, catching their breath. "When we have our own flat, we'll have a shower like this, shall we?"

"We most definitely shall," Geoffrey promised, and kissed him again. It was the first time Niall had mentioned having their own place someday. Geoffrey didn't examine it, simply stored it away for later. Everything was still so new.

Janis wanted him less, or at least less often. Almost never at night, unless he and Niall were up to something that she found stimulating. They fell into a routine of early-morning talk, cuddled together in bed, often kissing. When she did turn to him, it was as wonderful as ever. When she didn't – always leaving with a kiss and an 'I love you' – as often as not Geoffrey would turn to find Niall awake. "How are you," he asked one morning, "really?"

"How am I really," Niall said lazily. "Underemployed, battered by a movie star, and faced with you, you beauty, every morning? How should I be, but in bliss?" Geoffrey leaned in for a kiss. "I'm happy you like surfing. Happy you're taking yourself out. You were chafing a bit, weren't you, love?"

"A bit. That stretch since October, that's the longest I've gone without a solo trip for quite a while." He studied that much-loved face, those beautiful tiger eyes, that smiling mouth. He didn't have to say it wasn't the same. But in the moment, with Niall's body pressed to his, it didn't seem to matter.

Three weeks into building the music, Janis was past confusion and frustration, and well into excitement. She was chattering to her men and her mother in the kitchen one morning. "Never in my life," she said. "Never did I expect it to actually *work*. What I did with Stefan was so different. I mean, having him in the studio with me was never part of the plan."

"If you didn't expect it to work, why on earth did you want to do it?" Deborah sipped some coffee, eyebrows up.

"Because I don't know enough about tango! I needed people who had a clue. Tomás and Isabelle were both so good on the cast album for that movie. And you saw him in action." Ed and Deborah had both seen the film during its brief run at a nearby art house. "He's the real deal. But yeah, terrified, because his playing style's very different from mine, and then what the hell would we do about the vocals, and ugh." Janis slurped coffee.

Niall and Geoffrey were sitting in the breakfast nook, content to listen. Deborah said, "Your dad freaked out the first time he did a real collaboration too. It was kind of similar, though. He did a few things with limited input from other people, and then took a deep dive with a group."

"Why did he decide to work with the group? I feel like I should know, but I can't remember ever hearing this story." Janis sat beside Niall, looking at her mother expectantly.

"It was after his first Academy Award nomination, he had a little juice from that. At the same time, his first marriage was breaking up." Deborah glanced over at Niall and Geoffrey. "Because of me." They both stifled laughter. "So he was in a very confused emotional place."

"Sounds familiar. I had the whole neverending Stefan meltdown starting at the same time I was winning a Grammy."

"And then you were in the European tour, and you got hurt, and then, well."

"Yeah." Janis snorted. "Things happened. Maybe I'm just now feeling like I have the emotional bandwidth to work with other people. I mean really work. Because Stefan can diagnose problems like nobody else, but on the creativity side he's limited. Isabelle can do anything with that damned cello, and Tomás never stops having ideas."

"What's your favorite so far?"

"Honestly? 'Fool to Want You.' I did it on the very first album, and I liked it, but the way we're doing it this time is so different. Possibly unique."

"It may be." Deborah glanced at the men. "Have you let these two hear it yet?"

"Maybe today. We're definitely working that one today."

"Well, they're going to be here soon. You should go outside for a while before you lock yourself in the study for another however-many hours."

"Yeah, yeah. Anybody want to walk with me?"

"I will." Niall stood, and went to the kitchen door. He and Geoffrey exchanged a glance. Geoffrey had already had some private time with Janis, a quiet talk in the dining room after breakfast. They would connect later to catch each other up. "Ready?"

"I'm ready." Janis went outside with him. "So are you bored to sobs yet?"

"Perhaps I should be, but no. Geoffrey's been next thing to writing out loud of late. These new books will be brilliant. He's basing one of the love interests on me. A tour manager."

"And you get involved with some Jason Bourne type of guy?"

Niall laughed. "Something like that."

"So are you the one who surfs?"

"God, no. Nor do I fence. It appears I'm a borderline alcoholic who puts the hero's operation at risk, but of course he can't give me up." Niall made a queeny gesture and tossed his head, knowing it would make Janis laugh. "Anyway, I've the work with Red, and plenty to read, and I know once you finish this record my life's going to hell. So I'm enjoying my lazy days."

"And I can't turn the music off." Janis shook her head. "If I didn't have you two to help me switch gears, I don't know what I'd do."

"You're happy, then?" Niall glanced at her. They were walking slowly. Not for exercise so much as simply to be outside, strolling the path that wound through the back garden. "Our madness still makes you happy?"

"Niall." She reached for his hand. "You remember what I told Mom on the phone? I mean, I could add 'satisfied' since she's not listening." Niall laughed under his breath. "Aside from the fact that you both are totally adorable, and incredibly sweet to me, and take such good care of me? I absolutely *love* getting in bed with the two of you. It's all cuddle, all the time. If I'm horny Geoffrey's always willing to help me out. Of course, there have been plenty of times I'm not horny but then you two start something and it's like, me too." He laughed out loud. "But most of all, and best of all, it's that feeling of security. I know you love me, I know you both do. And I know you don't want to change me! Do you have any idea how unique that is in my experience?"

"Stefan wasn't the first?"

"Not even close. I actually can't think of a guy I was with who didn't want to change me. I was always too loud, too vulgar, too *loquacious*," she waited for applause, so Niall obliged, then took her hand again. "And too focused on my music. Every single guy was all, but what about me. And I was like, well, what

130

about you? You're a grown man, figure your shit out." Niall snorted. "I am not here to validate your dumb ass. Anyway, you and Geoffrey have figured your shit out."

"And you accept us too. You don't try to change us."

"Why the fuck would I? You're both perfect!" She squeezed his hand. Then, being Janis, she said, "I mean, now that I've had the Niall Dick Experience I can say that."

He stopped walking, wheezing with laughter. "God, Janis." He caught his breath. "That was a near-run thing."

"Eh. Whatever. It worked like a champ for me."

"For me too." He let go of her hand, but only to sling his arm around her shoulders. "I never thought it could make me feel so much closer to you, but it did."

"Yeah." They walked on. "Anyway, you and Geoffrey aren't going anywhere today, are you?"

"No, we're both home. If you'll let us hear something, we'd love to."

Geoffrey and Deborah were still in the kitchen, both watching through the window. "She's really happy," Deborah said. "I can't get over how happy she is. Janis is not one of those people who mopes, you know, she's always made the best of things. She's always social, she'll always talk, she's always funny. But too often it was like, let's laugh about this stupid thing so I don't have to cry. Thank you for that. I thank you and Niall, sincerely."

"We love her," he said. "Just as she is."

"I know. How much have you heard about Stefan?"

"Enough."

"I could write a book," Deborah said, voice full of remembered exasperation. "She used to say he was ninety percent great in person, and ninety percent a pain in the ass at a distance. They were apart more than they were together. It's kind of a miracle they lasted as long as they did."

"She says she thinks he really tried to love her."

"You shouldn't have to try." Deborah was certain of that. "You either do or you don't. How long was it before you knew, with Niall?"

"About an hour," he said honestly, smiling as she laughed. "I would have run away with him immediately. But I knew about Janis, how important she is to him. And how much she needs him to do what she does. That touring life, it's a bugger." Deborah snickered again. "It was such a relief to find that she and I attracted each other, that we liked each other. And then we danced together, and I knew it could work. She was brave enough to take the chance."

"She's a brave girl," Deborah agreed. "Does she ever lose her temper?"

Geoffrey could think of a few close calls. All related to outside factors, like the TV presenter in London, or the DHS. "Not quite. Her friend Bruno told me about Stefan, the last time they spoke on her tour. Stefan had called with a complaint, an hour before a concert. Bruno said she laid him waste." Deborah tried not to laugh again, and failed. "Niall and I, we each have a distinct relationship with her, you know. So if she's angry about something and one person can't help her work through it, the other person

132

generally can. And oftentimes what she's angry about has to do with us. She wants to protect us."

"I'll bet you let her, too."

Geoffrey smiled at her. "It's a way to love each other, isn't it? To smooth the path, to offer shelter. To do the thing the other person dislikes doing, so they don't have to, because you don't mind it. To answer the fan mail, as Niall does. Or to be elsewhere, so Janis can entertain someone she has to lie to." He gave Deborah a sideways glance. "She's a terrible liar."

"Oh my God, she totally is." Deborah sighed. "I wonder sometimes what would happen if she outed the three of you. Like, hi world, this is us. Would you mind?"

"I'd be honored." He was quiet for a moment. "It's not even a year yet. She may outgrow us. I hope she doesn't."

"Proceed as if she won't, I guess." She patted his hand. "I think you're all good for each other. I've never seen Niall this happy, either."

Chapter 7

Janis came to find them late in the afternoon, when she'd been working with Tomás and Isabelle for hours. "Got a minute?"

Geoffrey was writing; Niall was watching sword-fighting technique videos on his laptop. Both were willing to be interrupted. Niall set the laptop aside. "Is it a preview?"

"Yep. We're pretty much done with these three numbers." They followed her out. "Two of them are concert staples so I don't know if it was genius or insanity to do them again. Feel free to tell me what you think."

"After you've had a glass of wine," Niall suggested, and dodged a swat. When they got to the study, it was empty. The other musicians were obviously taking a break. "Working them to death, are you?"

"I told them to take an hour. Mom fed us, they went to do whatever. I, believe it or not, did some yoga."

Geoffrey's eyebrows shot up. "Did you really?"

"Yes, I did really."

"How's your neck? Do we need to get your therapist here?" One of the first things Niall had done after they were settled in Glendale was identify and engage a massage therapist willing to come to the house.

"She's coming tomorrow," Janis said. "I'm fine till then." She sat on her piano bench and let Geoffrey assess conditions around her neck and shoulders. "Satisfied?"

"You'll do." He kissed her cheek and surveyed the room. With two baby grand pianos, it no longer looked spacious. Each piano was littered with handwritten sheets of music. Another sheaf of music was on the standing rack next to Isabelle's cello. More pages were on the floor. He leafed through some of them. "It's the same pieces, is it? The ones you chose in December?"

"Yeah, the lawyers cleared all of them. We've done the arrangements, now it's working out the three voices." She waited, as if this were a test.

"You, and Tomás, and the cello?" Niall had suspected all along, from Janis' reaction to the movie's cast album.

She looked pleased. "See, you're smart, that's one of the reasons I like you so much. Yes. Isabelle's playing a harmony voice in almost everything but she's the main melody in a couple of them. 'Angel Eyes' and 'Wee Small Hours.' I'm doing enough of the lyric to let people who aren't superfans know what song it is, she's carrying it."

Niall knew better than to ask what they would be hearing that afternoon. Janis had her Making You Wait face on. He caught Geoffrey's eye and they went to arrange some chairs. The other musicians came in a few minutes later, followed by Deborah. Niall brought another chair over for her while everyone exchanged greetings, and then it was down to business.

The first song they played was 'I'm a Fool to Want You.' Geoffrey was thrilled at the way the tango arrangement worked with the melancholy lyric. Tomás and Janis traded lines; Isabelle wove a

135

haunting harmony alongside their voices. The next song was 'Bird on a Wire.' Of all the selections, Geoffrey had wondered how a tango arrangement could possibly work with this. But they'd emphasized the 6/8 time signature, making it close to a vals milonga. Janis sang, playing a simple accompaniment. Tomás played a more complex secondary theme. Isabelle this time played almost a descant. Geoffrey and Niall both applauded at the end of the song. Deborah sat silently, hands clasped.

"Okay, last one." Janis didn't look at them when she spoke. She didn't have her hands on the keyboard. The listeners understood when Isabelle began to play the primary melody of 'Angel Eyes.' Niall glanced at Geoffrey. They both knew why Janis had chosen to create a new version of this song. Janis came in with, again, a simple piano accent midway through the first verse; Tomás came in strong at the beginning of the second. The treatment was nothing like Janis' first big-band-adjacent arrangement of the song.

Niall had a thought that seemed ridiculous, and glanced at his husband again. Geoffrey murmured, "It sounds like sex, doesn't it?" Niall almost laughed; that was exactly his thought. He couldn't help wondering if Janis had told her collaborators about his pet name for Geoffrey. The music cycled through gradually-intensifying repetitions until it finally reached a peak. Then each instrument played a gradually-reducing cadenza, rolling down the keyboards and the strings to a rich and satisfied hum. Geoffrey leaned close to Niall and murmured, "I wonder if the others knew what they were doing?"

Niall turned his head and said, "Do you really think she could resist telling them?" Geoffrey put a hand over his mouth to stifle a laugh. Tomás was watching them, and he definitely looked amused.

Janis swiveled around on the piano bench, wearing an expression of such mischief that they both laughed out loud. "How'd you like that?"

Deborah said, "You're a troublemaker. And it's great. Still obviously the song. Ed's going to love it. All of them are great."

"Thanks." Janis looked pleased. "And thanks to Tomás and Isabelle, we are more than halfway ready for this craziness but now I will allow them to leave and get on with their lives." Isabelle was already putting her cello in its case. Niall offered to carry it out for her.

He took a moment outside to thank both musicians. "Janis hasn't been this excited about making a record for a long time. When do you go into the studio?"

Isabelle said, "March fourth. It seems like forever from now. Tomás has a few things he needs to take time for."

"Dance things," Tomás said. "I told Janis today."

"She's very likely scheming with Geoffrey as we speak, to go and see you. Give our regards to your lovely wife." There were handshakes and goodbyes. He watched them go, then went back inside to find that Janis was indeed scheming with Geoffrey.

"He's doing the Underground Cabaret with Vicky, the woman from the movie, right after they get back from Argentina." Janis was updating her calendar. "It's at that club in Hollywood where Victor did his shows. Jesus, that's five years ago!" She looked up. "So you guys have to figure out your trip, and get back here, because I want you to go with me to this thing."

Niall went into their temporary home office, the room adjacent to Janis' bedroom, before going to wash up for bed. He found a new email from Andy. The subject line was 'fun and games in Berlin' and the message was blank except for a link to a video. Geoffrey and Janis both heard him laughing and came into the room. "What've you got there," Janis said, leaning over. Niall re-started the video. "Oh my God. That is fantastic." It was Andy and Victor on stage, dancing to 'Mein Herr.' Andy was wearing a copy of Liza Minnelli's costume, complete with high heels. Niall laughed just as much the second time through.

Geoffrey was giggling too, but said, "Those legs!"

"I know!" Janis shook her head. "It's totally unfair. Would mine look like that if I were six feet tall? No, of course they wouldn't, because I sit on my ass all day."

"Your legs are just right." Geoffrey kissed her cheek.

"He *towers* over Mr. Garcia in those heels." Niall pressed 'play' again.

"Victor's five foot ten. Useful height for an actor." Janis reconsidered. "Well, he told me once they had to fake the heights when they had a guest star who was supposed to be his height and was shorter. Good thing that lead guy in the Countdown things is legit taller." Victor would begin shooting the third film in an action comedy series that spring. "Sweetie, how much of that is real tango?" She directed the question to Geoffrey.

138

"Not terribly much." They all snickered. "They dance wonderfully together, though. Let's go out again soon."

"When we get back from the mountains," Niall promised.

Geoffrey and Niall left for Mammoth Mountain two days later. Geoffrey wasn't sure how long he would want to stay for preliminary scouting; Niall promised Red he would be away a week or less. "I can come back by myself if you want to stay longer," he told Geoffrey, thinking *or if you want to be alone*. "Red says you'll love it, and not to miss June Lake." Geoffrey made a note on his list of things to see; some weren't open during the winter, but he wanted to get to as many as possible. They packed up, said their goodbyes, and were on the road – in Deborah's car - before noon.

"Janis appeared slightly forlorn when we drove out," Niall said as they merged onto the I-5 freeway. "Which exit is it?"

"That one. Highway Fourteen. Yes, poor darling, on her own for the first time since June. I'll miss her, too, but I've got you." He hesitated a moment. "And the truth is, some time with you alone is what I've been craving. I love Janis, and her parents are magnificent, but … perhaps you know what I mean."

"I do know what you mean." Niall felt the same. "We haven't been away together, ever. Ought we have done it earlier? This could be quite a test for us."

Geoffrey was smiling. "You can't truly think we won't get along."

Niall glanced over to confirm the smile he'd heard. He was smiling himself when he answered.

"Not truly. Oliver and I had a moment's fright when we went to the seaside the first time. He was a sun-worshipper, and I hid myself in the hotel like a vampire."

Geoffrey laughed. "You're a ginger! You burn if you walk past a window!"

"And I'll have to remember the sunscreen for myself now Deborah isn't on hand to do it for me. She said, up the mountain you'll burn much faster, don't forget or you'll be sorry."

"What did Oliver say about his lovely vampire?"

"He said, I should have thought of that. And I said, it gives us both time to re-charge, darling. Which is precisely what I believe you and I will find."

"You'll be re-charging in the bar, I expect."

"Too right. Straight on from here, is it?"

"For hours."

"Tell me a story." By the time they reached Bishop and took their second break, Geoffrey had spun a ripping yarn involving a red-headed vampire and a black-haired vampire hunter who fell in love, much to their mutual confusion. Niall had been giggling from the first reference to stakes. "My dear love, you should write that."

"I've absolutely zero notion how to approach the paranormal market. Or romantic comedy. Or paranormal erotic comedy, or whatever this mad thing would be."

"Write it and publish it and let the market sort itself out. Your contract doesn't prohibit you, does it?"

"No, it wouldn't be a conflict." They'd walked through the town to see what was on offer, settling on a Mexican restaurant for an early dinner. Niall was rolling his neck as they went in. Geoffrey glanced over and said, "Shall I drive the rest of the way?"

"Only if you've run out of story to tell me."

"I never seem to run out," Geoffrey said. "Perhaps because all these stories are about us."

"What an adventurous fictional life we lead, to be sure. Later on perhaps you'd like to essay that one scene?"

"Which scene would that be?"

Niall raised his eyebrows. "You might guess. I shan't tell you. We're about to order burritos and we mustn't shock the server." Geoffrey was giggling. Niall looked up with an innocent face. "Good afternoon. Coffee for me, please, and Negro Modelo for my husband." He ordered for both of them, then gazed at Geoffrey. "What a very naughty imagination you have."

Geoffrey sighed, settling down. "I imagine you'll get a neck massage before anything else tonight. You realize this trip is longer than driving from London to Yorkshire."

Niall shrugged, unconcerned. "But I've nothing at all to do once we're there. And I'm quite certain that should your excellent services be insufficient, I can find a proper massage therapist to see to me." He sipped some coffee. "Though I will concede that Deborah's car is bloody small for me, or I'm too tall for it."

"I'll drive on the way back, then." It seemed fair. "You can recline like a pasha and tell *me* a story."

"My dear sir, all of my stories are stolen from you." Niall thought for a minute; their food was delivered; he thought some more while they ate. "All right then. I believe I've identified some promising subject matter. I shall make some notes while we're up your effing mountain."

Two hours later they arrived in Mammoth Lakes. Easily locating a hotel with a bar and a vacancy, they checked in and went for a drink. Lingering in the bar, enjoying its fireplace, listening to the ambient music instead of speaking. After a while, Niall realized he was slightly nervous. Not so much as he'd been on his first night with Geoffrey, but definitely not serene. He couldn't tell if Geoffrey felt the same. Wasn't sure if he should say anything. *What's wrong with me*, he wondered, watching Geoffrey over the rim of his glass. He swallowed the last of his whisky and looked back at the fire.

Geoffrey glanced over at Niall, who was nearly frowning as he stared into the fireplace, humming along with the music. He held his empty glass by its rim, hand dangling from the end of the chair's arm. It was a pose that would read as 'relaxed' to anyone else. Geoffrey tossed back the rest of his own drink and looked around the bar. They were alone in the lounge area; only a few others, all men, were at the bar counter watching some sports event on TV. What Geoffrey wanted to do was go and sit on Niall's lap and ask him what was wrong. Then get his cock out and see to it in front of that fireplace. This was not that kind of bar. *Next time find a hotel room with its own fire*, he thought, almost laughing at himself. "How's your neck, darling," he asked softly. Niall turned his head as if startled. A moment later he set his glass aside and leaned forward, elbows on knees, still nearly frowning.

"My neck is stiff and my heart is troubled. I'm uneasy and I don't know why. It can't be only that we're here without Janis, can it?"

"Perhaps it can. Oxford was the last time we spent a night without her." They were both speaking very low. "And this is the sort of scene you've played with her much more often than with me." *Never*, he realized. The closest was their very first night.

Niall sat back with a sigh, shoving a hand through his hair, looking relieved. "Yes, all right. What would you like to do?"

Geoffrey's voice went even softer. "I'd like to kneel in front of you, get your cock in my mouth, and hear that sound you make when you come." Niall's head went back and his eyes closed for a moment. When he looked at Geoffrey again, it was with unmistakable intention. He didn't say anything, though, so Geoffrey added, "Shall we go to our room?"

"I believe we shall." Niall's voice was slightly hoarse. Again Geoffrey was reminded of their first night. He stood up and went to the bar to request their bill. By the time he was signing the receipt, Niall was standing by the entrance. They went outside and walked, shivering, across the parking lot to their hotel. The town was nearly silent. The sky was clear, a deep purplish black with a soul-stirring swath of stars. "One doesn't see this sky in Los Angeles," Niall said when they stood outside the door to their room. "Or in London. Let's look at it for a moment." He pulled Geoffrey into his arms, back to front, and they stood gazing up until they were thoroughly chilled. Then they went inside. Niall double-locked the door. Without discussion they stripped, washed up, and got in bed, shoving all the covers down to the foot.

143

Geoffrey delivered the promised neck rub for a while, then pushed Niall onto his back and knelt astride his hips. Niall gazed up at him, faintly smiling. "What's your pleasure, my beauty?"

"The same," Geoffrey said. "The same as yours, the same as ever. To love you."

"Then love me."

"Forever." Geoffrey set his hands down above Niall's shoulders, bent for a kiss, felt his husband's arms wrap around his back and pull him down.

They woke sometime deep in the night, shivering because the covers were half off the bed and neither of them had remembered to turn up the room's heater. Geoffrey saw to the sheet and quilts while Niall attended to the heater. There was a trace of light in the room from a streetlamp outside. "I glow in the dark," Niall observed. "Like a vampire, indeed." He got back in bed beside Geoffrey, pressed close and set his teeth against Geoffrey's neck. He lavished attention on that sensitive skin for long minutes of kissing, tasting, and gently biting, until they were both rampantly erect and panting for more. "How shall I have you now?"

"I don't know. I can't think." The first time, Geoffrey had his way with Niall, who'd returned the favor with his hand while kissing Geoffrey into oblivion.

"I shan't take you tonight," Niall murmured against his skin. "Nor tomorrow. Not till we feel we'll die without it." He reached for the lube. "Between your legs, darling. I'll have you thus, and kiss you."

"Yes."

"Then I'll have you in my mouth."

"If I don't spend from your words alone. Your voice. Niall." Geoffrey arched his neck, pressing his head into the pillow as Niall slid his cock between Geoffrey's thighs. His weight was comfort, and delight, and possession. The pressure and the movement had them both breathing hard. Niall's mouth was open against Geoffrey's. Geoffrey held him tight with one arm, straining against him, the other arm wrapped around Niall's head. He made an animal sound when he felt Niall's rhythm change.

Niall kissed him hard, making that sound deep in his throat as he climaxed. Then he pulled away almost roughly, saying "Now." Geoffrey reached for him, getting only a handful of hair as Niall got his mouth around Geoffrey's cock. He was so close already, it was over in seconds. After a moment Niall let go of him and said, "Christ, you *delicious* creature. Shall I ever have enough of you?"

"I hope not," Geoffrey said, still breathless.

It was more of the same, though never exactly the same, every night. Geoffrey went out on his expeditions, leaving Niall to contentedly wander the town, both – as they discovered upon reconnection - walking for miles without speaking to a soul. They each had text conversations going with Janis, who complained of abandonment while raving about her music. Niall also wrote to Janis, out of the blue because it was a sudden realization, *He needs more space*

Her reply came after Niall was in the room, before Geoffrey returned: *What about you?*

Hello darling. Hope the work today was good

It was fine what the fuck is going on there

He huffed out a laugh. *Lovely mountain if that's one's cup of tea. G is like a sea lion that's been kept on land a day too long and finally chucked back in the water*

Are we handling him wrong? So to speak

I don't think so darling, this is new to all of us and we've to adjust as we go. Perhaps we should have sought a how-to manual. Niall sometimes wondered how many people ever contemplated such an arrangement, much less attempted it.

You're okay though? You haven't had to live with me during this development stage

I'm well. I'm the hound by the fire aren't I?

Ugh not sure I like that. Waiting for people to throw you a bone?

No no no darling not what I meant at all. I meant I've my work and I do it at need, but otherwise content at home. A walk in the garden will suffice me. He's like a lurcher, coursing about the countryside, sleeping under hedgerows and happy with it

Problem?

Niall didn't know. He hoped not. *I can't leash him, can I? I can only trust he'll always want to come back to the fireside with me eventually*

I don't give him much. What should I do?

Darling, you give us the fireside. You ARE the fire. Coming back to me is always coming back to you. Niall hoped she knew how true that was.

I am going to save this exchange because my whole life happens between my head and my hands and I need to remember yours doesn't and definitely his doesn't. When you see him tonight tell him I miss you both and love you both

I will. I love you too and I know he does. Give our regards to your parents

Will do. See you soon. They signed off. Niall set down the phone and went to gaze out the window at the darkening sky.

They found a hotel room with its own fireplace on the third day, and moved there. Niall went to a liquor store for their own bottle of Scotch. He told Geoffrey, "I hardly need go out at all. If the views were not so inspiring, I probably shouldn't. Tell me about what you've been seeing."

So Geoffrey did, showing Niall photos he'd taken. "I'm quite liking this place," he said. "Some of the trails are very wild. The skiing must be good later in the season. March, I think. I'll have to come back and see. Will you want to?"

"I'll come with you and see you settled in. By March Janis will be in the studio, I'll have some work to do." Niall didn't want to say 'by then you might be happier without me.' They left it there, at any rate, because there was the whisky, the fire, and takeout from one of the local restaurants. Geoffrey showed no sign of wishing he were alone, then or later.

He was loving his days in the open air. The scent of the trees, the bitter cold, the delightful dearth of humanity. Returning to Niall after a day in the snow was sheer joy. Having only one person to be civil to, instead of four. And that person the one whose touch he always craved. Their nights of lovemaking were nothing short of spectacular, but as the days went by Geoffrey wanted more. *I am a trollop*, he thought, laughing at himself. Spent, satisfied and yet malcontent. At dinner on their fifth day, he told Niall he thought he'd done as much as he could by way of research until more of the mountain opened up. "We could go back to Los Angeles tomorrow, or the next day."

"All right. Tell me in the morning if you're ready. Either way." Niall was affecting to study the menu. "What have you to tell me today?" He set down the menu, reached for his wineglass, and took a sip.

Geoffrey said pleasantly, "If you don't get in me tonight I shall divorce you." Niall nearly did a spit take. He set his glass down hastily, coughed, wiped the back of his hand across his mouth while his tiger eyes laughed into Geoffrey's.

"I'll answer thy pleasure, my light spirit." Judging it safe, Niall took another cautious sip of wine.

Satisfied – or at least looking forward to satisfaction – Geoffrey addressed his own glass. "Rather a dark one, with all this time outdoors."

"Oh, not at all. Light, because easy to get off your feet." Geoffrey laughed. Niall leaned close and spoke low. "The way you yield to me is a constant delight."

God, that voice. "You'd best turn the subject, my love, else I shall have you back at our room instantly, and unfed."

"Very well." Niall looked around for the server, because he was hungry. "We'll order to go."

They decided to stay one more night, so that Geoffrey could write up a proposal for an article, and finish some notes for his novel. "I ought to have done this last night," he told Niall at midday, when he was mostly finished. "We could have gone back today."

148

"I'm content," Niall said. He was still in bed, next to Geoffrey, one hand in that glossy black hair and the other holding his e-reader. "And as I recall, you had rather different ideas last night."

Geoffrey laughed under his breath. "Indeed I did."

"Besides, I shouldn't want you to drive all that way so soon after receiving me." Niall stroked his hand down Geoffrey's neck. "I wasn't gentle with you this time."

"You weren't rough. You did what I wanted." Geoffrey knew that Niall sometimes underestimated him, even after all this time, and after so many uninhibited encounters. Only in the sense of physical strength. Niall had never done Geoffrey harm. Nothing close to it. He turned his head; they stared at each other for a moment. "Niall, my dear love. I am only three inches shorter than you, and only twenty pounds lighter. If I ever wanted you off me, believe me, you'd be off."

"You're so lissome," Niall said, almost apologetically. "Oliver was a rugged sort of bloke, you know. It's really only when I see you next to other men, or with Janis, that I think, blimey, he's full sized." Geoffrey laughed. "I look in your eyes and all I can think is how perfect, how beautiful, mustn't harm him."

"You're not precisely elephantine," Geoffrey pointed out. "A sabre, not a claymore." It was Niall's turn to laugh. Geoffrey set his laptop aside. "Kiss me, love. Only kiss me." Of course, after a while, it wasn't only kisses. When Geoffrey opened his eyes, sighing, he realized that the room was dark. "Darling, if we mean to dine, we'd best be getting dressed."

149

"And dine we must. I'm famished."

They unwound themselves from each other, tumbled out of bed, and staggered to the shower. As they left the room a half hour later, Geoffrey said, "Do you ever wonder if we've done the right thing? Because I don't."

Niall glanced over at him. He knew Geoffrey meant the entire 'thing,' the ménage plus the marriage. Neither of them knew of anyone else who'd tried anything remotely similar. But then, it wasn't the kind of thing one spoke of. "Does it ever work out in fiction?"

"I've not seen it much. When I have, it generally ends at sex. It doesn't proceed to actually having lives together, what happens when everyone's working. How to bring outside friends and family in, how to have a normal life. Never to openness, except in paranormals. Apparently if your household is composed of unreal creatures, a challenging relationship is less difficult to imagine." They were walking up the street to the restaurant nearest their hotel. The night was again crisply cold, and clear.

"I've never been happier," Niall said truthfully. "I do wonder how long we can keep it to ourselves."

"Quite a few people know." Geoffrey thought for a minute. The restaurant was in sight. There was something he needed to say. He said it clearly and quietly. "If Janis ever decided she was done with me, I would stay with you."

"Darling!" Niall stopped walking and stared at him, astonished.

Geoffrey touched his face. "I would miss her terribly. I would miss having a woman. But I truly couldn't do without you." Niall kissed him. "Always

150

you. And only you." More kisses, an embrace, and then a moment with their hands on each other's faces, staring into each other's eyes. "I love you."

"I love you. But darling, we have approximately forty minutes before that restaurant will heave us out." Geoffrey laughed, even as he realized that Niall hadn't said he would stay. *But he married me*, Geoffrey thought, *and he needn't have, and that means something,* as Niall slung an arm over his shoulders and they walked on.

February 2019

Back in Glendale, Geoffrey and Niall both made a point of spending quality time with Janis, even though she was neck-deep in music. "This is the stage when you've generally been with Stefan, since I've known you," Niall observed. He'd dragged her out of the study after Tomás and Isabelle were gone for the day, bundled her into a jacket and taken her outside. "Have you always been this possessed?"

"Kind of, yeah." She leaned against him and he put his arm around her. "But it was different. Stefan would listen to what I'd done, make a suggestion here and there. Sometimes even play it for me. But there was never a question of him writing something that I would then play, if that makes sense. I never asked and he never offered. Tomás has written huge chunks of stuff. I don't think he even realizes what he's doing sometimes. He's like, what about this, and it's this three-minute fantasia. I asked him what it was like when he worked in that piano bar, in Las Vegas. He said the management wanted a certain number of pieces per hour, they all had to be recognizable. He couldn't invent much, so he never really tried. He put his creativity into dancing, when he could."

"Will you use it? The material from Tomás."

"Oh yeah. But not in huge chunks. Because my audience wants a recognizable song, too. We're putting that big 'Un Beso' treatment on, but everything else is pretty lean. I told Tomás he should give himself some more time for composition. He frowned at me and said this isn't composition. I wanted to smack him." Niall snorted. Janis gave him a sideways look. "How are you guys doing?"

"We're in love." He said it lightly. "And you?" This time the question was about their personal life. He could tell she understood.

"Still in love. With both of you." They walked on for a minute. "How often do you, like, go all the way? I don't see it much."

Niall suppressed a smile. He knew Janis had been surprised by the frequency of their sexual encounters, but also by their nature. "We're not hiding it. Perhaps once in twenty."

"Jesus! Really? I always thought that was the main event." Niall was grinning now. Janis swatted him. "I mean, I expected to see it more. You fuck a lot."

He laughed out loud. "We're still new. Perhaps in time we'll see each other and think, eh, not today. Tomorrow will do. Next week." Janis giggled. "But that mouth of his."

"Oh my God, I know."

"That, though." He glanced over and saw she understood. "It doesn't lend itself to complete spontaneity in the way our other frolics do. One doesn't go from that to other things without due care."

152

"Yeah. I've always appreciated that. We do an awful lot of laundry as it is." He laughed again. "Okay, is it just me or is it fricking cold out here?"

"Such a delicate flower. In you go." They turned back to the house.

Chapter 8

One week after their return from the Sierra, Geoffrey found Niall in the garden and said, "I've lost the full week on these contracted novels because I was engaged with the damned vampire." Niall was laughing. "That story you told on the way back, where on earth did you get that? I've stolen the whole of it."

"I had days to think, didn't I? And it didn't have to make sense. You're the writer, I knew you'd fix it. All I wanted to do was make you laugh." Niall's story hadn't been 'once upon a time.' He'd taken inspiration from Geoffrey's comment that all the stories were about the two of them. His was a first-person tale of romantic confusion and sexual misconduct, as if he were the vampire doing filthy things to the completely-receptive vampire hunter.

"Nearly ran off the bloody road once or twice, as you well know, you madman. At any rate, enough of it's on the page that now I can get on with my real business. And I'll be going back to Malibu tomorrow."

"Then I'll check in with Mr. Warner and see if he's free to bash me about again." Niall was looking forward to it. The sword training was an excellent workout. His teacher also had an impressive store of British obscenity thanks to his wife. It was really quite like the fencing club.

"We've also to answer Mr. Martin concerning this photo shoot of his."

"Indeed we must." After considerable discussion, they decided to put themselves in Andy's experienced hands. They said yes to costume, yes to makeup, and yes to all but explicit nudity.

Andy sent them an email in return, a few days later, at a time when he really should have been asleep given that he and Victor were in Japan.

Hi guys,

First of all I promise we'll delete anything you hate. I have a friend working on some costume pieces and will get a makeup person lined up as soon as we confirm the date. Attached is a thing I mocked up from an old shoot to show you what the finished images might be like.

Now, to be perfectly clear I want to hang these, so if you don't want them seen tell me now.

I want to do fifteen images. One of each of you alone, and then thirteen together based on the lines you gave me. I'm going to tweak the order a little, alternating, starting with Prospero. Ariel solo at the very beginning and Prospero solo at the end. And I swear to God I don't know what you were thinking when you chose all these lines, because those last two of Prospero's are not addressed to Ariel in the play as I'm sure you know, but OMG PERFECT I CAN'T WAIT. These are going to be sexy.

With makeup etc it's going to take all day. Victor and I will feed you when we're done. By the way I am now planning to use one or more from this series to pitch some other people I know on doing other Shakespeare stuff so I can do a full show, probably toward the end of this year, or whenever I can get my shit together. Anyway thanks, it's a fun thing to occupy my brain with while I'm jet-lagged.

See you fairly soon – Andy

Niall opened the attached image and said, "Blimey!"

"What is it, love?" Geoffrey leaned over to see. "That's never what he proposes. How's he done that?"

"Special effects, I reckon. It's beautiful though, isn't it?" The richly-colored image showed Sam Lee - one of the men they'd met at the milonga and several times since, a slender dark-skinned man with long hair and a scarred face - on his knees with his head thrown back. They could see that he'd been on a stage, but instead of a set the background was filled in with semi-transparent layers suggesting ruined walls, naked trees, and clouds passing over a full moon. Across the bottom in a stylish font ran the legend 'désespéré.' "He does look desperate. I suppose Andy means to label our images with the bits from the play. What do you think?"

"Not my area of expertise, but if he makes us look like that I'll be happy. And of course he's welcome to make them public. Agreed?"

"Agreed." Niall sent back a note to that effect, then studied his husband for a moment. "You're sure you don't mind all this 'master' rubbish?"

"You are my most potent master." Geoffrey leaned in for a lingering kiss. "And as thou love me, I shall answer thy pleasure."

"My God, do I love you, you perfect beauty." They lost track of time for a while.

"Oh excuse me." It was Deborah, sounding equal parts touched and amused. "I didn't mean to interrupt."

Niall knew he was blushing as he hastily let go of Geoffrey. "Quite all right."

"I came looking for you because Ed's finished part of his thing and wondered if you'd like to hear it."

"We'd love to." Geoffrey stood up, angled slightly away from Deborah because he hadn't settled down quite yet, and gave Niall a hand. *In the nick of time*, he thought. The sunroom wasn't the place to indulge. At least, not in the middle of the day. Niall collected the laptop, holding it not too obviously in front of him, and they followed Deborah back to the study.

"Hi guys." Ed was standing by the piano stretching his back. "It's nice of you to tolerate all the noise around here."

"We like it," Geoffrey said. "Else we'd have gone mental last summer at the flat. Your daughter never stops. If she isn't playing or singing or doing exercises, she's listening to someone else's music. And that parlor wasn't soundproofed." They took seats.

Ed and Deborah were both laughing. "Okay, good point. So this is for a cable movie about a shipwreck." Ed sat down on the bench and began to play. Thirty minutes later Niall and Geoffrey applauded. Ed looked gratified. "It'll be orchestrated, of course, but at least it's done."

"It's easy to see where Janis got that particular talent," Niall said. "I've always enjoyed your music."

"A lot of people don't get it when he plays it like that." Deborah had remained standing by the piano. She stroked back Ed's wiry gray hair. "All those short pieces, a lot of people don't understand how they relate."

157

"As it happens, Geoffrey and I were just talking about 'The Tempest.' Perhaps I had that in mind," Niall said. Then Deborah asked about the play, which led to a few hints about their photo project with Andy. They were all still in the study talking Shakespeare and arguing about the best film adaptations when Janis got home from her afternoon meeting with Valerie.

"We are rocking and rolling," she said. "How's your thing coming, Dad?"

"We've just heard it," Niall said. "It's brilliant. You're on schedule for recording?"

"Valerie watched the practice videos we took last week and had some suggestions. When Tomás gets back from Buenos Aires and done with his dance thing here, we'll work them all through and then we'll be ready. We're going to try doing a live master take, the way Valerie and Tanith did for the movie. She thinks we could release some of the studio videos if we get through the damn things without screwing up." She went to the drinks cabinet and poured herself a whisky. "Anybody else want one of these?" Receiving several votes in favor, she distributed more glasses. "I am so excited. Dad, thanks so much for setting up the two pianos. Mom and Dad, thanks so much for letting us land on you and fuck up your life." She swallowed some whisky.

Deborah was laughing. "You did not fuck up our life. We love having you all here. So a master take and then go back and take your time with each one?"

"Yeah. Valerie says, send the master take to the company and get them excited about a tour, they can start working on it while we're still laying down the album with the other musicians. What's new with my boys?"

158

"We're off to do battle with sea and sword tomorrow," Geoffrey said. "Leaving early. We'll be knackered when we get home." For a moment he thought Janis might actually say 'then I'd better get some use out of you tonight' but she managed not to.

Deborah might have heard the ghost of it anyway. "Oookay. Well, let's see about some dinner." She went out, carrying her whisky, followed by Geoffrey. Niall heard them giggling in the hall a moment later.

All five of them decided to go down to the Hollywood nightclub called Chrome for the Underground Cabaret show. The title was 'Overboard,' and all of the music had to do with water. Tomás danced Argentine tango, with his movie co-star Vicky, to Madonna's 'Swim.' Geoffrey was ravished. Janis swooned. Deborah gave Ed a look that threatened dance lessons, and Niall fortified himself with the evening's signature cocktail, a water-clear vanilla martini with a sugar-and-salt rim. "That's shockingly good," he said, setting his second empty glass down on their table.

Janis agreed. She'd had a pair of them too. "Is it my imagination or are they playing tango nuevo?"

"They are," Geoffrey said. "At a guess, because so many people involved with the movie are here. Would you care to dance?"

"I would love to dance." She took his offered hand and stood up.

Niall said, "Damn." Deborah glanced over, eyebrows up in a question. "I meant to ask him to dance."

"I have a feeling you'll get another chance." She consulted Ed. "I think we have an hour before my prince turns into a pumpkin."

159

"You know I'm no good at late nights anymore," Ed said, offering a hand. Deborah took it; he kissed hers. "I would ask you to dance if I had half a clue."

"I have that much," Niall said. "Deborah? Would you do me the honor?" She looked so excited he was glad he'd asked. And the floor was so crowded that nobody would be able to tell if he did something wrong. He quite enjoyed himself for two songs, then three. Then there was a tap on his shoulder, and Geoffrey cut in. Niall danced with Janis for a while. "Happy, my love?"

"So happy." She leaned her forehead against his jaw and sighed. They ended up staying considerably longer than an hour, because the music continued to be danceable and they didn't have to drive themselves home. When the evening's limousine finally dropped them off at close to two in the morning, all five were well-flown on salted vanilla cocktails, and four of them on dancing. Ed waved goodnight to his daughter and her men, steering Deborah down the hall to their suite. "Okay," Janis said with a yawn. "Me first. If I'm asleep when you come in, don't wake me up."

Niall said, "Yes dear." Janis snorted, patted his chest somewhat randomly, and took a few steps toward the bathroom. Then she stopped, bent down and took off her shoes, and re-started. Niall picked up the abandoned shoes with the hand that wasn't holding Geoffrey's. "With me, darling?"

"Always. You'll dance with me again soon, won't you?" Niall stopped inside the bedroom door, tossed Janis' shoes in a corner, and kissed his husband. They were almost dancing when Janis came in.

The broadsword project was advancing. Red had long since gone beyond basics; he hadn't asked if Niall was ready, simply made the judgement for himself. With the end of the month looming, Niall meant to ask if they would start taping soon.

On his way to Malibu, Geoffrey dropped Niall off as usual. He took a moment to check for messages before going up to the Warners' house. He'd thought he heard a buzz from the phone in his gym bag on the way from Glendale to Van Nuys. It might have been from Janis, but it wasn't; it was from his father. Getting a text from his dad wasn't the usual. Hoping it wasn't bad news, he opened it up and read: *Guess who's master brewer now, son.* "What?!" he said out loud, instantly calling back. His father picked up right away. "When were you after that? It's brilliant!"

John Phelps laughed at the other end. "Been working my way through it, haven't I? Completed the examinations not too long ago. That porter? My name's on the label!"

"Dad! You clever old badger!" Nothing but laughter – almost giggles – at the other end. "I couldn't be more proud if I'd done it myself. What's Mum say?"

"Oh, she's rung up all her friends, hasn't she, dropping it into conversation, oh did I mention." John laughed some more, but fondly. "Silly girl."

"It's really brilliant, Dad. Well done. You'll have some of that famous porter laid by, will you, for the next time I can visit?"

"Already done. What're you about today?"

"Imminently to be bashed about by a movie star, he's teaching me a broadsword fight."

"You're mad." Niall laughed. His father added, "Mind he doesn't lop your head off."

"Blunt weapons, Dad. At worst he'll break my neck."

"Oh that's all right then. Get on with it. Give our regards to Janis and your Geoffrey."

"And a kiss to Mum. Bye Dad." He put the phone away, and turned to the house with a smile. Red was standing in the doorway, a sword resting against each shoulder. "Good morning sir. I've barely recovered from your last onslaught. What's to do today?"

"Today," Red said, "we tape."

"What, all of it?"

"No." He was smiling as he came out. "Need to come inside for a minute? Okay. Here's yours. Here's mine. Protective gear coming up." He went back in the house, returning quickly with a bag in one hand and a tripod in the other. He set up the tripod, mounted a camera, and said, "Ready?"

Niall really wasn't; his inclination to ask had been more due to an imminent need to be available for Janis. "Ready," he lied, and saw Red suppress a smile.

"You can say anything you want, it can be edited, but there are a few things I need to say."

"I'll follow your lead."

Red started the camera and stepped into its field, taking his weapon in his hand and resting it on his shoulder again. "Hi, I'm Red Warner and I'm here to introduce you to basic skills with the broadsword. Assisting me is Niall Phelps, a former member of the Oxford University Dramatic Society and an experienced fencer." He angled his body so the camera would capture Niall, standing behind him. He tried to look like a serious swordsman, listening attentively to a short speech about safety. He kept his face still with an effort when Red turned the blade and pulled the edge across the inside of his opposite forearm; it left a thin pink line. "No problem, right?" Red casually rotated his wrist. The blade swung in a circle and crashed down on a two-inch-thick oak branch on the ground, splintering and crushing the wood. "It won't slice your arm off, but it will break it. These are seriously dangerous weapons even without an edge. Do not use one of these with a partner unless you are trained, or supervised, or both. Do not spar without having a charged phone and a first-aid kit on hand. Now to the safety gear." He set the weapon aside and went to Niall, narrating the process as they both put on padded tunics, neck protectors, arm guards, and greaves. Then they went through the basic moves: the lunge, feint, remise, and flick; then parry, riposte, circle parry, and disengage. After four minutes of slow-motion demonstration, Niall stepped out of frame. Red stopped talking twenty seconds later and turned off the camera. "Good job," he said. "Considering how short a time you've been training, great job."

"I'd like to see it," Niall said. "I've no idea what that must look like."

"Come on inside. We need to hydrate." Red looked barely warmed up. Niall helped him gather up the gear and they went inside. After about a liter of water apiece, Red connected the camera to his flatscreen and played the video.

Niall was surprised. "I don't look nearly as bad as I thought I must."

"You've got a very sound stance and footwork. We're well matched for height and reach. Next time we'll do some of the things the viewers really want to see, turning, the overhead stuff, you know." He mimed whipping a sword in a circle around his head.

They'd done plenty of that in practice, but he still asked. "I trust you don't mean we'll tape that."

Red laughed. "Yeah, I do." He regarded Niall thoughtfully. "When we get to the demo fight, would you be up for doing it in character?"

"What character?"

"Macbeth and Macduff."

Niall thought about it for five seconds. "Well you'd have to be Macduff, because any fool can see you'd have my head off at a stroke in a real fight." At six foot three, Red was on the Captain America – Thor spectrum. He outweighed Niall by thirty pounds, considerable for the one-inch height difference.

"That's fine. I like winning." Niall snorted. "And I've always wanted to do that scene. Your voice is perfect for it."

"Oh aye? 'I bear a charmed life, which must not yield to one of woman born.'" Niall gave it some Scots. Red was grinning. "I'm not from Scotland, you know. Only a good mimic."

"Well, I'm from Ventura, so you're still way ahead of me." Red tried the accent himself.

"Passable." Niall raised his eyebrows skeptically, which got the intended laugh. "If we're meaning to do this, we'll need to rehearse it with the dialogue. I've never played the part. Haven't acted in eighteen years."

"I've never done the play at all. This will be fun."

"It is fun. It's good to do something so," he searched for the word, "uncivilized."

Red laughed again. "I'm lucky, I get to be uncivilized for a living. There were years when every part I did carried some kind of weapon. We're made for violence, let's face it."

Niall stood up, suddenly restless, and paced. "What do you think of my husband?" It was out of nowhere, maybe prompted by that word: violence. Knowing how very safe - how *tame* - Geoffrey's life had become.

"We haven't talked much," Red said. "Everything okay with you?"

"No. The love is there," he said, turning to make eye contact. "But we're in a hothouse, and he's stifling. He spent a decade traveling the world, and the past nine months he's been tied to -" he nearly said 'us' "tied to me. He's burning off some of his frustration at the beach, but it's not the same. I'm half inclined to send him away."

"Before he bolts?"

"Exactly." Niall stopped pacing. "I'm sorry, this is none of your concern."

"Well, it's good for me to know if there's something on your mind before we put a full-power fight together."

The dry tone fetched a smile. "He'll be here soon, no doubt. Next month he's off to the mountains again. If I'm lucky, he'll come back."

The video series proceeded quickly. Niall was amazed to find that their weeks of lessons had actually produced, in him, a credible sword handler. He was thoroughly enjoying it. Geoffrey, meanwhile, achieved an acceptable level of surfing proficiency for his purposes, and switched to rock climbing. On the days Niall was meeting with Red, Geoffrey stayed in Van Nuys to observe instead of going on to the beach. He was there when they taped the fifth episode, the second covering fight choreography. Red addressed the camera on the subject of armor. "We'll be presenting this fight in the context of Shakespeare's 'Macbeth.' The play was set in the time of King Edward the Confessor, in the eleventh century. Fighting men didn't wear armor as we think of it now. Most likely, they would have worn a mail hauberk, a long shirt made of woven metal that covered the head and neck like a hoodie. Men fighting with swords would also have carried a shield, which might have been fixed to the arm. For this demonstration fight, Niall and I won't be wearing hauberks, and we won't carry shields. When you design your own fights, decide for yourselves if you are going for historical accuracy or for maximum flash, which is what we're doing here." He smiled at the camera.

Niall put in, "And do be mindful that the less you have between you and the blade, the more likely you are to get hurt." He displayed his right upper arm, bearing a dark bruise.

"Yeah. Sorry about that." Red made a 'what can you do' face.

Behind the camera, Geoffrey stifled a laugh. "These are going to be a massive hit," he said once they were finished and the camera was off. "You both look splendid." He took some pictures with his phone, getting Red's permission to post them. Janis had things to say, when she managed to get her head out of the piano.

The next week, when Red told Niall that they were ready to tape the last episode – the Macbeth fight – Geoffrey said, "Do you mean to do it here?" They all looked around the yard. The big oak tree had served to frame the other videos, but it was clearly in a semi-urban yard. A street and other houses were visible, and the rumble of traffic always evident. "It's only I had an idea."

"What's the idea?" Red was open to suggestions.

"Point Dume." He could see from Red's face that the idea of taping on the clifftop, with the ocean behind them, met with complete approval. "Could you get permission?"

"I'll take care of it. I've got a friend on the inside. Niall, how early could you get here?"

Instantly understanding, Niall gave Geoffrey a hateful look, which made him laugh. "We could be here by five if absolutely necessary."

"Six will be fine. It should still be nice and gray out there at seven. Two days from now?" Niall nodded, resigned. "Be ready to hike."

Two days later, Geoffrey and Niall pulled into the driveway at the Warner house when it was still barely light. The door opened; Red invited them in for coffee. "We'll head out in about fifteen minutes. Mary's getting ready for a shoot. I'll be right back." Red's wife, trained as a dancer, was now also an actor with a thriving career. Within twenty minutes the three men squeezed into Deborah's car - with blades, camera, costume, and miscellaneous gear – and headed for Malibu. Geoffrey was driving, as a sort of apology to Niall for precipitating this much-too-early excursion. Ironically, the traffic was (for L.A.) negligible. When they arrived at the park the gate was still closed. They left the car on the side of the road, where a few others signaled the presence of early surfers or hikers. Each shouldered some gear, and they began the walk down to the end of the beach and then up the bluff.

"It's a little wet out here," Red observed. "Careful on this slope."

"Just like bloody Scotland," Niall said. "Remember Aberdeen, pet?"

"Ah yes, hypothermia in August." Geoffrey would have liked to hold hands, but they all were scrambling a bit. When they stepped up onto the clifftop, the wind that had been nudging at them all the way felt much stronger. He was glad for his North Face jacket, and repentant because he knew what Niall would be wearing. "Darling, I do beg your pardon."

Niall turned his face into the wind, eyes narrowed, and took a deep breath. "Actually, I quite like it. Feels like home."

"We'll need to mark this through." Red was pacing, finding the flattest, smoothest place to run the fight. "The footing is as good as our yard, but the wind needs to be accounted for."

"Let's have at each other, then." They unpacked the blades while Geoffrey set up the camera where Red suggested. Once he was satisfied that they could manage the wind, he and Niall took off their outer layers. By prearrangement, they both wore brown jeans, flexible hiking boots, and slim-fitting insulating vests. Now they put on sleeveless quilted linen tunics. Red's was painted with a woad-blue design, and Niall's with blood-red.

Geoffrey helped them both put on the leather forearm guards Red had packed. "Pity to cover those tattoos." Red had four bands of ink on his left arm.

The topmost was still exposed. "These leathers are marvelous, where on earth did you get them?"

"Straight from the Warner family workshop. I made a living in props for a while."

"Well done you." Red snorted, adjusting his wireless microphone. Geoffrey did the same for Niall, then stepped back to admire his husband. He was unsmiling, eyes still narrowed against the wind, hair blowing. Geoffrey took a picture or five with his phone. "Darling, you can't imagine how breathtaking you are." Niall gave him a distracted kiss, then concentrated on his thoughts, sword now in hand. Geoffrey took one more picture, remembered to take a few shots of Red as well, then put his phone away and went to the video camera. "Ready at your command."

Red strolled over to the area he'd selected. "In frame? Good. We'll do it twice if we can, okay?"

"Right." Niall joined him. He watched Red cue Geoffrey, then raise his blade. Niall turned his back to Red, holding his blade away from his body, point down. He took two steps away.

Then, "'Turn, hell-hound, turn!'" Red roared. Niall pivoted and struck first, swinging his blade up and over.

The swords clashed together and Niall spat, "'Of all men else I have avoided thee, but get thee back; my soul is too much charged with blood of thine already.'"

Advancing, metal singing as the blades circled, Red said, "'I have no words, my voice is in my sword; thou bloodier villain than terms can give thee out!'" Then the fight was on in earnest, lines gasped or shouted as they went on.

Geoffrey watched, breathless, moved almost to tears by the beauty of the fight. *It shouldn't be beautiful, it's so dangerous, they're mad*. But those two russet heads – Niall's hair short and sleek, Red's in a braid halfway down his back – stood out gorgeously against the stone-gray ocean and pearl-gray sky behind them. The two tall, strong men moved like dancers, except for the unmistakable shock when they absorbed the force of a blow.

Then it was Macbeth's last speech, and Niall gathered himself for his final charge. "'Lay on, Macduff, and damned be him that first cries, hold, enough!'"

The rehearsed end of the fight had Niall knocked to his knees by a brutal chop at his blade. He held it up to guard his head, then made the well-planned 'mistake' of lunging toward Red, half-rising. As his blade advanced, Red's came up, he spun, and lunged. Niall angled his body, threw his head back, and fell. From the camera's point of view, it appeared that Red's blade had gone straight into his chest. They held their end position for a few seconds. Then Red said, "Cut." Geoffrey pressed the camera's power button with a shaking hand. He only took a breath when Red held out a hand and Niall took it, letting the big actor pull him to his feet. "Fucking great, Niall." Red slapped him on the back, not too hard. "Seriously great. Could you go again?"

"In a minute." Niall was panting. Even Red was out of breath. All three of them became aware of applause. They looked around and saw a few hikers had joined them on the clifftop, drawn by the clamor of the weapons as much as by the voices.

"Hi," Red said. "We'll be done here soon, going to run it once more. Can I ask you to please stay well away from this area? These things are kind of mean when they're off the leash." There were nods and murmurs, the bystanders backed off, and Red went with Niall to get a drink of water. "I'll probably do some autographs when we're finished," he said quietly. "You can come with, they're going to want pictures, or you can hang back here with Geoffrey. Your choice."

"We'll see if I can walk and talk at the end of the next." Niall drank water like he'd been in the desert. They both stretched for a couple of minutes, checked in with themselves and with each other, and nodded. "Back in a minute," Niall said to Geoffrey, leaning in for a quick kiss. "To thy instrument, my spirit."

"I'll to *thy* instrument, my king," Geoffrey said in an undertone. Niall heard him. He was smiling as he walked with Red to the fight area. They took their positions; Red cued Geoffrey; Niall turned away in preparation, and they did it all again. It was even better this time. Niall remembered to let his shoulders sag and arms collapse away from the force of Red's final blow, his sword hand opening. Geoffrey, more composed, thought *zoom* and did that, framing the shot on Niall's empty hand with the sword's grip beside it in the foreground. In the background was Red's blade, apparently embedded in Niall's body, ascending to his merciless fist. It seemed they held the position for a long time. Then, "Cut," and Red stepped back, offering his hand to Niall again. They were both winded, both grinning.

"I took a liberty," Geoffrey said when they joined him. He ran the recording back to show the last twenty seconds. "It was such a striking – if you'll forgive the term – composition."

"That's terrific." Red was staring at the final image. "This whole thing was terrific. Thanks for the suggestion." He raised his head, took note of the

171

larger crowd of spectators, and laid his sword in its carry bag. Then he said, "Gotta go do my thing. Niall, get into something warm."

"What about you?"

Red smiled and walked off toward the spectators. "Do you want to go meet the public, darling?" Geoffrey was holding a clean, dry thermal shirt in one hand and a towel in the other. Niall shook his head. He got the leathers off, then the tunic and vest. Geoffrey toweled him dry, then handed him the thermal shirt.

"Thanks for that," Niall said, shivering a little. He reached for his own North Face jacket. "How did it look?"

"I would venture to say it's the best broadsword fight I've ever seen." Niall glanced over; they'd watched plenty of historical dramas lately, with several excellent sword fights. If Geoffrey said 'best' it must have been at least passable. As if he'd read Niall's mind he made an impatient face and said, "See for yourself, you daft bugger." Niall bent to the camera and watched the video. At the end he stood back, frowning a little. "What?"

"I'm reminded of something." Geoffrey raised his eyebrows in inquiry. "Of the fight described in that Ngaio Marsh book, the one about Macbeth. The last one."

"Oh! 'Light Thickens.' It does come to mind, doesn't it? D'you suppose he's read it?"

"Wouldn't be surprised. Well. Not bad, eh?"

"Not bad." Geoffrey rolled his eyes. "Daft." The two of them began packing away all the gear. Geoffrey kept Red's towel, shirt, and jacket out for him. He was still busy with the crowd. Once he'd been identified, everyone – even those who hadn't recognized him - wanted a word or a selfie or an autograph. It was almost nine o'clock by the time they finally escaped down the path to the beach.

"Hungry now," Red said as they got into the car. "Around the point to Paradise Cove?"

"Direct me, if you please." Geoffrey followed instructions and they got to the restaurant, not far away, without incident. By the time they'd eaten – quite impressively – and wallowed in coffee, they'd watched both videos twice. Geoffrey glanced up at Niall; he had another idea, but before he inserted himself any further into this project, he wanted to see if Niall had the same one.

Apparently Niall had. "Red, you know we're staying with Ed Vaughn, the composer. I've an idea he might be willing to score this for you and your backer. Shall I ask him?"

"The second one." Red nodded. "That would be great. I think they were planning to use some generic bagpipey thing." Geoffrey shuddered. Red laughed. "Yeah. Real music would be better. I'll send you the recording later."

"I assure you it won't leave our household." Niall knew he would never hear the end of it if Janis didn't get a sneak preview.

She and Deborah both swooned over the video. Deborah peppered Niall with questions about how exactly he and Red had managed not to kill each other. Geoffrey wrote a new fantasy in the journal having to do with a knight, his lady, and his squire.

Not too surprisingly, Ed was delighted to be asked for the music, and turned around the four-minute score in a week. Red delivered the video to his backer, and a few days later it went live. Niall sent a link to Andy.

Andy's reply text read: *Will you stop?! You're fucking killing me. That PG-13 video had some X-rated consequences*

Niall replied *Yes I'm aware*

LOL I'm totes screencapping that shit and putting it in my Shakespeare show. Tell Red. What a beast

He is indeed. I haven't been this fit since ever

Well, good job getting ready for our shoot. Have you and G worked out anything you want to do for those lines?

We have but unfortunately it's all X-rated

OMG ROFLMAO Never mind, we brainstormed it. See you soon Prospero. Niall put away the phone, still grinning.

Part III

Chapter 9
March 2019

Niall looked at himself in the full-length mirror, thought *we're both mad*, and turned away shaking his head. "What?" Geoffrey was smiling at him. "You're stupendous. You'd be cast instantly, whether you knew the text or not."

"Well, that's what *I* think," Andy said. He was in his home studio's office area, doing something on his laptop, as he had been the entire time the makeup artist was working on Niall and Geoffrey. "Though I've never tried out for anything with 'Shakespeare' in the casting notice, unless you count 'Kiss Me, Kate,' so what do I know."

The makeup artist had done very little with Geoffrey's face. Or at least, very little that was obvious, except for his eyes. A subtle facial makeup made him appear younger, or perhaps ageless; his hair was in a state of studied disarray, as if wind-blown. His eyes were framed with false eyelashes made of iridescent black feathers.

The Ariel costume consisted of a dance belt covered by a short one-shouldered toga made of sheer fabric, cloud-gray printed randomly with metallic gold. He wore no jewelry except his wedding ring, but his fingernails were painted gold and the backs of his hands and forearms were decorated with gold leaf. Geoffrey loved it.

So did Niall. He was glad of his own confining dance belt, especially given his suspicion that Andy's direction would have him in very close contact with

175

Geoffrey throughout the day. And he had to admit the artist's work was effective. The facial makeup was as subtle, in its way, as Geoffrey's: a matter of slightly greying the skin around his eyes, suggesting lines around his mouth and on his forehead. His eyebrows were enhanced with rusty-gray filaments, which were also glued into his hair.

Where Niall thought Andy had asked for 'wizard' came across with his eyes and hands. His eyelids were darkened with grayish purple and weighted with gray false eyelashes. At the base of the lashes was a startling dash of iridescent peacock-blue liner. The effect was a sort of fierce fatigue. Maria had also applied fake fingernails, iridescent golden-gray and pointed. "I suppose if I must look aged, this is the ageing I'd choose."

Andy said, "It's fantastic. You're all done, Maria?"

"I'm done," said the artist. "Everything you need to remove the makeup is in the bathroom. Stuff to touch-up after lunch, and if you need to re-set some of that gold leaf, that stuff is in there too."

"Thanks. Send me your big fat bill."

"Will do, Mr. Martin." Maria collected her gear and let herself out.

Andy studied Niall. "So you get where I was going with that? There's only context clues to how old Prospero would be. Miranda's fifteen or whatever, but he was already Duke of Milan so he's probably at least forty. Which, to us, is not old. I was going with, betrayal, shipwreck, isolation, a lot of rage, and dealing with magic."

"Magic is exhausting," Niall agreed, as if he knew. Geoffrey snickered.

"Right! So let's do these solo portraits first. Into your robe, Prospero." He'd already put on the heavy jewelry – rings, bracelets, and a necklace – from the box marked 'Niall.' The unbelted robe was floor-length, pale oyster-grey velvet on a base fabric of iridescent crimson, decorated on all its edges with arcane symbols drawn in many colors. Niall loved that too. It was perfect with his coloring, heavy yet soft to the touch. He went obediently into position. Andy's set for the photo session consisted solely of a wide sheet of watery-gray backdrop behind a massive throne-like chair that looked as though it were made of dragon bones. It was painted dark red and festooned with what Niall fancifully thought of as sea-wrack: weedy clumps tangled with pearls, shells, and driftwood. Hauling it up the stairs to the studio must have been a beastly chore.

Geoffrey watched for the twenty minutes it took for Andy to be satisfied. Then it was his turn. He couldn't tell how Andy was framing the shots, but the positions he was asked for were interesting. "Have you ever done any modeling?" Andy asked after ten minutes.

"No."

"What a waste." Niall snorted. Andy sent him a laughing look, and kept taking pictures. He went longer with Geoffrey, thirty minutes in all. "Niall, can I get you back for a minute?"

"Certainly."

"Help me turn this goddamned thing around." The two of them turned the chair so that its back was to the camera. "Okay. Now, your back to me, hands on the sides of the chair, on the back, yeah. Fingers down with some tension as if you're pulling some of your power from it. Looking over your right shoulder.

Eyes down. Perfect. Stay there. Geoffrey, onto the seat of the chair, standing up, looking down at him. This is Prospero's first line, you're like are we done now? But you don't really want to be done. And he really doesn't want you to be done. You're about to touch his left shoulder. Perfect." He gave them several more directions for the line, slight variations. Then, "Okay, Ariel's first line. Leaning left to make eye contact, Prospero looking up. God, I hate you both, you're so gorgeous. Hold it."

They took breaks after every hour. Niall and Geoffrey both found the process unexpectedly tiring. Niall thought that might derive at least in part from the erotic nature of the storyline for the shoot, and the necessity of restraint. Having Geoffrey wrapped in his arms beneath the robe, and not being free to do any of the myriad things it occurred to him to do, was hilariously frustrating for them both. He couldn't even say what he wanted to say; that would make it worse.

When they'd finished the first six lines, Andy said, "Let's stop for a while. I'm going to go over to the house. I'll send Consuelo over with some lunch for you. Once she is gone you will have exactly half an hour in private. You can get out of those dance belts but do not mess up your makeup."

They both laughed. Geoffrey asked, "What are *you* going to do?"

"I am going to have lunch, write a dirty text to my husband, and stretch. Not necessarily in that order. See you in a bit."

Geoffrey and Niall looked at each other and seemed to tacitly agree that they should wait until Consuelo had come and gone before even discussing how to use their private half hour. They got out of the dance belts with a sigh of relief. Each had a good scratch and a trip to the loo, putting on cotton boxers for decency. Then lunch was delivered. They thanked Andy's housekeeper, helped themselves to water from the studio's mini-fridge, and ate without haste. They kept their hands to themselves.

"We've only fifteen minutes," Geoffrey observed. "Shall we risk destroying the artistic effects, or shall we bide our time?"

"The rest are going to be worse, I suspect. Shall we have a wager?"

"On the climax? Surely that's 'potent master.' We'll look back on this and say I never knew I had that much willpower." Niall laughed. Though it was quite the opposite of what he wanted to do, Geoffrey said, "Let's bide."

"Agreed. Perhaps he'll have mercy and give us another half hour before dinner." Niall came close – not too close – and murmured, "Though fifteen minutes would more than suffice."

"Christ, Niall, when you speak to me like that *five* would suffice." Oh, how he wanted a kiss. But he knew it wouldn't end there. "Thank you for not speaking after 'Be subject to no sight.' It was a sweet torture, being so close to you. Your harness barely contained you." He had pressed his arse against it, heard Niall's stifled protest – almost a laugh – and seen the laugh in Andy's eyes too.

"Hell and the devil, *must* you say that? How am I meant to put the bloody thing back on, in this condition?" Niall went to stretch on the other side of the room.

By the end of the shoot they were worn out, thrilled, and desperate for each other. "I have a feeling I shall want

179

'Was't well done?' printed up as wallpaper," Niall said when they were alone again, promised a full hour – should they require it – of privacy before joining Andy and Victor for dinner. "If it's anything like as beautiful as I expect." Andy had taken several variations. They all involved Niall seated on the throne, slumped at an angle, with Geoffrey curled on his lap. Geoffrey's toga was off and Niall's robe used only as a drape across their hips.

In the moment Niall thought he would most like to see for the next fifty years, Geoffrey's face was pressed to Niall's bare chest but turned up in profile, with eyes half-closed. Andy hadn't asked Niall to put a hand on Geoffrey, but he hadn't been able to resist. Jeweled fingers caressingly on throat and jaw, his own head lowered as if for a fond, post-coital kiss. He was quite proud of the fact that he hadn't, in fact, gone for that very much desired kiss.

"That on one wall. 'Remember I have done thee worthy service' on another. You realize we shall have to acquire a flat."

"Janis will buy one for us." They both snickered. "Once she sees these photos. Yes, 'Remember' will be a stunner too." In that one, the throne had been turned to an angle. Niall was again seated, Geoffrey behind and above the chair thanks to built-in footholds. He bent over, head close to Niall's as if whispering in his ear, using his upstage hand to pull Niall's head back, exposing his throat. They'd both wondered at the direction, but after trying it in front of the mirror during their lunch break had looked at each other and said, simultaneously, "Crikey."

They finished taking off their makeup. The costumes had come off immediately, then Niall's fake fingernails. "I like this gold," Geoffrey remarked. "I'm leaving it on for Janis to see."

"I like it too." Niall turned, admiring Geoffrey's naked body. "How much time have we?"

Geoffrey tipped his head back, eyes half closing, lips parting. "How much do we need?"

"None." Niall went after the kiss they'd both been craving all day. "Christ, this day, have I *ever* wanted you more." He had Geoffrey's back to the wall, they had their hands on each other, kissing as if they'd been separated for weeks. They were both as fully aroused as if they'd spent an hour in foreplay. "You'd spend for me here and now, wouldn't you, you beauty."

"I would," Geoffrey said, breathless. "One more word and I will." He didn't get that word. What he got was Niall's hands on his thigh and his arse, and Niall's mouth on his cock. "God!" Niall made a sound, a hungry sort of growl that meant 'now, yes, give it to me,' and a scant minute later Geoffrey did. His hand was tangled in Niall's enhanced hair. After a moment he caught his breath enough to say, "Out into the light, my wizard." Niall climbed up his body, kissing him again before taking the few steps out of the bathroom. "You glorious, matchless treasure."

"How will you have me?" Niall was half out of his mind. "Will you give me your mouth, that perfect mouth. Before I die of wanting you."

Geoffrey kissed him again. There was no bed in the studio. Nothing like one. He went back into the bathroom for towels and threw them on the studio floor. "Recline, my king." Niall went to the floor in something close to a collapse. When Geoffrey touched him his knees came up and he made another animal

181

sound. Geoffrey knelt on the second towel and bent forward between Niall's legs, getting his mouth full. After that day of kisses and touches promised or implied and never achieved, Geoffrey would have taken hours for this. Only minutes were required. When they were both catching their breath again, Geoffrey looked at his gold-painted hands on Niall's white skin, framing his groin, and said, "This is a picture I'd like to have."

Niall lifted his head enough to see. He laughed. "My wicked darling. You can see that picture any day." He put his head down again.

Geoffrey stood up, went to find his phone, and then knelt by Niall's head. "I'll have this, then." He put his left hand on Niall's, interlacing their fingers, and took a picture showing both wedding rings and the swath of gold on his skin. He displayed it for Niall. "I'll send that to my mother."

Niall pulled him down for one more kiss. The studio floor wasn't a remotely comfortable place to recline. With Geoffrey's lovely mouth against his, he didn't care. But after the day they'd had, too many more kisses would have been ill-advised. So he reluctantly let go, allowing Geoffrey to help him up. "And now we'll dress, and have dinner. Perhaps you'll let me see how Janis likes you thus, you golden idol." They put themselves in order. Geoffrey touched up the adhesive to the gold leaf. Before leaving the studio, Niall found the script that Andy had left by his laptop and tucked it in his pocket.

When he showed the script to Janis later, she said, "Most literate porno ever?" and he laughed for a solid minute.

Prospero: Thy charge exactly is perform'd

Ariel: I come to answer thy best pleasure

Prospero: Be subject to no sight but thine and mine

Ariel: Let me remember thee what thou hast promised

Prospero: What is't thou canst demand?

Ariel: Remember I have done thee worthy service

Prospero: Hark what thou else shalt do me

Ariel: Thy thoughts I cleave to. What's your pleasure?

Prospero: (Do you love me?) Dearly my delicate Ariel

Ariel: What would my potent master? Here I am

Prospero: Our revels now are ended

Ariel: Was't well done?

Prospero: This rough magic I here abjure

The month of March was blocked out for recording. Janis, Tomás and Isabelle were scheduled to be in the studio with Valerie four days a week. First to rehearse the entire set, to get accustomed to the space and to the pianos. Then to record the three-instrument master take, which they accomplished in one day. After that, they began working through the thirteen-song set list with additional musicians. Niall was there for at least part of every day, handling Janis' correspondence as usual, serving as the middleman between her and her manager Randa or between her and the record company, and dealing with the inevitable schedule changes.

Geoffrey worked on his writing in Glendale, and planned his solo trip back to Mammoth. They went up together again; Niall stayed one night. Then Geoffrey was on his own. If not for their previous excursion, he would have thought this was a perfect scenario. The weather was ideal for all kinds of outdoor activities; the snow was spectacular; the food was good, the hotel was comfortable, and he was writing well. And being alone, truly alone, with no one to acknowledge or speak to beyond a text unless and until he chose to, let him feel he could truly breathe for the first time in weeks. *I love them*, he thought, *but God it's good to be away.*

All the same, the nighttime made him more than a little lonely. He'd never been lonely on a research trip before, not even the one to Wales after they'd met. Because then he hadn't known how nearly perfect life with Niall and Janis would be. At the time, he hadn't quite dared to think he might live with them. He certainly hadn't thought through what that would mean; he'd never lived with a lover before. Now he lay alone in his room remembering his trip with Niall in January. The knowledge that the others were equally bereft was rather the reverse of comfort. The single night before Niall left him was, in retrospect, like waving a slab of bacon in front of a hungry dog.

But he was there to work, he reminded himself, and so work he did. He made great progress. He flung himself down and across the mountain in various ways, ending each day chilled and tired and wanting nothing more than a good meal and his bed.

Toward the end of the week, the temperature rose. The trouble with a mild, sunny day on a mountaintop was its effect on the snow. Geoffrey looked out at the sparkling slope, wondered for a moment about his planned excursion, and – as usual – decided to go out. It was too beautiful, and he couldn't reasonably stretch the trip much longer. Once more into the forest, and then he could bear the thought of

Glendale. After breakfast, he assembled his day pack with his customary care, strapped on his avalanche transceiver, sent a text to Niall and Janis to tell them he was off for a hike but would check in later, and went out into the crisp clear air.

He met up with a couple he recognized from the hotel. They were all going the same way. It was an easy path, no climbing required; popular with the mountain's visitors, and one Geoffrey had already written of for his article proposal. Today he wasn't even carrying his camera. This was just for fun.

He chatted with the couple for about a half hour as they walked, leaving the groomed area behind. They were retirees, regular visitors, and this was a favorite trail; they knew it by name as well as by its number on the trail map. After another half an hour he outdistanced them, giving them a wave the last time he turned to check their location. A few more minutes and he could neither see nor hear any other humans. Only the birds, distant vehicles, and the slow drip of water from snow melting in the sun.

Until he heard the snow break and thought *Hell*. It was such a subtle sound. Surely he'd imagined it. But no, there was the following sound, more like a gust of wind than anything else, only there was no wind. He knew there was no point in trying to run; he was as apt to run into the avalanche as away from it. *I'm sorry Niall, my darling love, let this not be the last time I think of you.* He turned back the way he'd come, the way he thought was 'away,' walking quickly but calmly and breathing deep, trying to hyper-oxygenate. Mentally reviewing the survival tips he'd studied.

In a moment he could hear a rumble, and the snap of breaking wood. Then there was a wind, icy cold, air pushed downslope by the wall of snow that picked him up a second later and tossed him down the mountain.

He hit something hard, felt the shock of bones breaking, and silently cursed every subsequent impact. Tried to swim through the snow, tried to keep his hands in front of his face, tried to keep breathing. He rolled – perhaps in the air, he'd absolutely no sense of orientation – and then was caught once more and pushed bumpily along until he came to rest. *I'm alive*, he thought cautiously. Aside from that, the situation was not promising.

He couldn't move his legs, and his body was screaming with pain. He centered his breath until he could distinguish between pain in his leg and in his side. *Face too, curse it.* He thought nothing there was broken, though there was blood in his mouth. All his teeth were present and accounted for. *Ribs and leg. Survivable.* Definitely tricky for digging himself out. Right ribs. His right arm seemed to be tied to his side; he knew it couldn't be, hoped it wasn't broken too, no point in speculating. He couldn't tell if both bones of his right shin were broken. Best assume they were. *How long.* He didn't think he'd blacked out, but had no sense of how much time might have passed. *Eighteen minutes to asphyxia. Must try to dig.* He could just move his left hand, presently under – behind? – his body and with a distressing lack of sensation. *It's only cold.* He didn't otherwise feel cold, but knew that was deceptive. He could still die if he wasn't found. Would, most likely, die. The thought was almost abstract. No chance of reaching the whistle lying snugly and uselessly in a zipped pocket.

He tried drawing breath to call out and immediately cancelled the attempt. *Bloody ribs.*

On a new attempt, the left leg was functional. He kicked hard a few times, trying to get a sense of which way was 'up.' The snow seemed marginally less hard-packed above him; he was able to get some play in the knee. *Right then. Dig.* The left hand simply had to work. He rotated it and felt his mittened fingers snag on the webbing of his pack. The shovel, there. Its modest digging end, he could pull it through. One hand was better than none. The shovel, leagues better than a hand. He could get a grip on the handle now. *Faster, the snow is settling.* Scoop, rotate, push. Packing the snow away from him. Trusting that 'up' was truly 'up.'

He kept at it, working up toward his face and then away. If it wasn't the right direction, he wouldn't live long enough to be disappointed. He couldn't hear anything except the muted scrape of the tool on the snow. He knew there were regular patrols but had no idea what the rescue response time might actually be, hadn't done even that bit of safety review this morning. Feeling warm and sleepy now, the most dangerous possible time. Thank God he'd the transceiver. He'd confirmed it was set to transmit, before leaving the other hikers. They'd been kind, maybe even concerned that he was going further out of the groomed area. They would remember him, where he'd been, where he was bound. Geoffrey took a moment to give thanks to those people, for not being the type of people who fled a dark-skinned foreigner who needed a shave.

He was still stubbornly, if ever more slowly, working away when he heard voices. Focused on scoop-rotate-push, the sounds didn't register at first.

Then they did, and he instinctively tried again to call out. *Fuck,* he thought stringently, holding his breath for a second against the stabbing pain. *Do not puncture anything you sodding splintery pieces of rubbish.*

Then he realized what hearing them meant. He was near the surface. One more effort. He shoved hard with his left foot, levered his body up into the narrow channel he'd created, grunted at the new pain in his side, and the snow broke away above him. A patch of sky. *Jesus Christ.* Air rushed in. He breathed deep, mindless of the pain, clarity returning to his thoughts and hope to his heart.

He pushed the bright-red blade of the shovel up above the snow. Now he could wait. He heard helicopter rotors, the voices, someone addressing a search dog. *Good dog,* he thought gratefully, *I'm here. Find me.* It might have been an hour before they found him; it might have been ten minutes. He could see the patch of sky dimming, but not yet dark. The voices were nearer now. He sucked in more air and tried to wave the shovel's blade. Someone said, "What was that?" He did it again. The voices definitely approaching. The crunch of steps. Then he could hear the dog panting, and knew he was going to live.

Once found, he was soon freed, and being assessed. The searchers had their protocol. Out from under the snow, he could breathe more normally, and speak. He responded as needed. In due course he was strapped to a stretcher and the searchers carried him out. The eastern slope was entirely in shadow, though the sky was still light. It was then he began to shiver.

It was twilight by the time they reached the hospital, the pain in his leg had gone from 'bloody awful' to 'cut it off now,' and he was lightheaded from hunger despite the survival beverage given him by the searchers. Once delivered to the nursing staff, he was rapidly undressed, warmed up, and – after a somewhat cursory initial examination – fed. The small emergency unit had more urgent cases. There were two others found after the avalanche, one a child; plus they were looking after a skier who'd gone into a tree and had severe injuries. He was being stabilized for transport via helicopter to a larger hospital. Geoffrey was content to wait. He'd been given painkillers that had a sedative effect. When at length it occurred to him that he hadn't checked in with Niall and Janis, that they would be worried, he realized he didn't know where his clothes and gear had got to.

It took forever to get a nurse's attention. She told him he'd have to wait. That his x-ray would be back soon, and then a doctor would see him. He said, "Where's my phone? I need to call my husband."

She checked his chart and frowned. "Hold on." Then she left the room, and he didn't see her again for an hour. When he did, he asked again for his phone, but the nurse was with the doctor this time, and that woman looked like she'd been awake for three days. She wanted to get his leg in a cast and go home.

"Yes, I understand. But my husband was expecting a call. He'll be worried. He knew I was going out today." The doctor and nurse both made pacifying noises and went away again. Another hour. Geoffrey was beginning to wonder if he were really in a hospital at all, or in some kind of Kafka-esque nightmare. Then two different nurses came in, telling him there had been a shift change and they'd take care of him now. His ribs were strapped, a temporary measure. His leg was tended to. He was offered more food, water, a remote for the TV in his room. No one knew anything about his phone. *Niall is thinking of me*, he told himself, knowing it was true. *He'll come.* The nurse gave him more painkillers. He gave up and went to sleep.

Janis and Niall got home from their day at the recording studio only slightly concerned by the lack of a text from Geoffrey. They didn't begin to worry until after dark. Deborah was frowning at the clock in the kitchen when they went in to see if she wanted help with dinner. "No, I'm good," she said. "Maybe you should get online and see if there was anything funky up in the mountains today." They wheeled around as one and went to their home office.

Niall was having the worst kind of thoughts now, and kicking himself for not checking earlier. As if she'd read his mind, Janis said, "If something happened, knowing earlier probably wouldn't have been helpful. Let's find out." She set her hand on his shoulder.

He typed 'mammoth mountain today' in the search bar, and said, "Fuck!" He almost never used the word. There were four active stories, all with the word 'avalanche' in the title.

"Oh Jesus. Breathe, honey."

Niall needed the reminder. He clicked on each story in turn. They all said the same things: three people missing, search underway. They were all time-stamped hours earlier. "Why don't they have updates?" he said helplessly.

"Because they don't have you running the show. Listen to me." She turned his task chair away from the desk and bent to look in his eyes. "Believe that he's okay. We will figure it out. We will get there as soon as we can. And we will probably find out he was in a coffee shop having completely lost track of time while he wrote another epic piece of vampire porn." She tipped her forehead against his.

Niall didn't move for a second. Then he stood up, moving into her, and put his arms around her. He kissed the side of her face, then her mouth. "I'll believe he's okay. I love you."

"I love you too. Let's have dinner, we need to eat. Then we'll call the hotel. If they don't know anything we'll call the hospital. We'll keep calling until somebody fucking knows something."

"All right." They hugged each other for a minute. Then they went to join Ed and Deborah.

Niall was grateful for Janis and her parents, but by the time they went to bed he was ready to scream. He couldn't concentrate, kept losing the thread of conversation, could barely eat. He knew Janis was every bit as worried as he was. She took a sleep aid, and told him to do the same. He didn't want to. Whatever was happening with Geoffrey – whatever had happened *to* him – Niall felt being awake might somehow keep their connection open. He knew it made no sense. But it was bad enough being awake, being able to shut down the worst imaginings, to run through the litany of non-disastrous reasons they might not have heard from their love. He knew from experience that the dreams would be worse.

Chapter 10

The next day was a genuine nightmare. Geoffrey woke at six o'clock hungry, restless, hurting, and irritated. He wanted his phone. He wanted to talk to Niall, of whose presence he had dreamed with such clarity that waking to an empty room nearly brought him to tears. The nursing staff gave him a trip to the loo, breakfast, assurances, and more painkillers, but no phone and no answers as to where it was. Instead, three hours later, the first uniformed investigator walked into the room. Geoffrey immediately knew what was about to happen.

The entire day, with a few breaks enforced by the nurses, was a recurring loop of his encounter with DHS coming into the country. Over and over, with different officers from different departments. The same questions, the same answers. "What the hell is it you think I've done?" he finally asked – possibly demanded – when yet another new person came into the room. This one was wearing a nondescript navy suit and looked tired. Geoffrey knew that he himself looked much worse. The mirror in the bathroom showed overlong hair, a week's beard, and bruises worthy of a prize fight. "Why can't I call my husband? I am here on a valid visa. My husband has a work visa, he's working in Los Angeles. I've answered all these questions all day long and everything I've said is verifiable. It's been twenty-four hours since I was brought here, and this is fucking ridiculous!" It was the first time he'd lost his temper. Now he held his breath.

The man stared at him for a few seconds. His face gave nothing away. "Don't go anywhere." He turned toward the door.

Geoffrey said furiously, "How in hell would I?" The man in the navy suit didn't answer, simply left the room. "Fucking bloody bollocking *shit*!" It hurt. He closed his eyes and tried, for the millionth time that day, to regulate his breathing. There was a tap on the door. "Yes, what is it." He assumed it would be another of the questioners, so no doubt he sounded snappy.

Instead the door opened for a nurse he hadn't seen. "Mr. Anand, right?"

"Yes."

"I've been off the past two days. I was just in the hall. Did you say you've been here since yesterday and haven't been able to call your husband?"

"That's right."

"Where's your phone?"

"I don't bloody *know*. No one would tell me. I'm assuming that the effing Nazis have it."

She muttered something that sounded a lot like 'fuck.' "Use mine." She pulled one out of her pocket and offered it to him.

He was shaking now from reaction, and from fear that the man in the suit would come back and stop him. "Thank you." He hurriedly dialed, had to correct a number, tapped the button to send the call.

It rang twice. Then, "Hello?" Niall's beloved voice, sounding raw.

"Darling. It's Geoffrey. I'm all right."

"Thank Christ! We've been so worried! What's going on?"

"It's bloody New York all over again. I don't know what the hell they want with me. Everyone from the dog-catcher to the FBI has been in here." Trying for lightness.

193

"Where are you?"

"I'm in hospital. Here in Mammoth Lakes. Avalanche, did you see?"

"Yes, we saw, we've been frantic since last night."

"I'm sorry, love. I've broken a leg and some ribs, can't get about on my own, and all my gear's been sequestered. Can you come?" Couldn't keep the tremor from his voice.

Niall heard it. "Need you ask? We'll be there as soon as we possibly can be. We've spent the day phoning every effing person in that foul little town trying to find out what happened to you."

"I love you. Tell Janis I love her. Come soon. I have to get off the phone. I love you."

"I love you too. We both love you. We're on our way."

Niall stayed on the line for a moment more, but the call had ended. He dropped his head into his hands, trying without success not to cry. He felt Janis' hand in his hair. After a moment he said, sniffing, "How can we get there, when can we get there, and can we drop a bloody bomb on it as we leave it?"

Then he had her on his lap, in his arms. "Jesus, what a relief," she said after a while. She got a hand free to wipe her face.

"He said, tell Janis I love her."

"How did he sound?"

"Frightened." They looked at each other. Niall said, "I'm feeling somewhat violent." He knew Janis would take this to mean 'feeling like reducing someone to their component parts.'

"Me too. Guess we shouldn't make any phone calls for a few minutes. The airline people might not appreciate the amount of 'fuck you' I am one wrong word from spewing."

The man in the suit didn't come back. No one did, except nurses. Dinner, the loo, the TV. Geoffrey was beginning to think he ought to have lost his temper much earlier. Having spoken to Niall was such a relief he couldn't even worry about what might come the next day. When they gave him another dose of the sedative painkillers, he took them.

He woke again at six o'clock, and the day began exactly as the day before. At nine o'clock, instead of a resumption of interrogations, a hospital orderly came in with his day pack and what remained of his clothes. He set the phone on the side table, within reach. "Are you serious," Geoffrey said with disbelief. "All of that, and it's over without a word?" The orderly affected not to know what he meant. Everyone must know. Geoffrey was, if possible, even angrier. He picked up the phone. Of course, the battery was dead, and the charger was back in his room at the hotel. *If it hasn't been confiscated with my laptop*, he thought with sudden alarm. But surely not.

Then it was noon, and he heard them. Janis and Niall, talking to the nurses down the hall. Niall quite firmly stating that Janis absolutely *would* be allowed to see the patient. Oh, the glory of that voice. And oh, the delight of Janis quite firmly stating that anyone who got in her way would be sued.

A nurse he'd seen before opened the door, looking not at all cowed and in fact as if she might laugh. Janis and Niall walked in past her. Geoffrey

195

said, "You'll forgive me if I'm seeing you with Dyrnwyn in your hand."

"Please tell me there's someone I'm allowed to smite," Niall said, bending to kiss him. Janis was holding his hand. They both exclaimed over the bruises on his face, on his right arm. They were both careful of his ribs. It was intensely frustrating.

"Bugger these ribs," he said eventually, after kissing both of them as solidly as he could. "When can I get out of here?"

"Now," said Niall, but of course it wasn't that simple. There was an immense amount of paperwork, ostensibly having to do with Geoffrey's travel insurance. There was Janis, very close to losing her temper while assuring the hospital administrator that yes, the bill would be paid as soon as it had been thoroughly reviewed, since according to the doctor they'd spoken to Mr. Anand should not have had to spend even one night in the hospital. And that no, Mr. Anand would certainly not be spending another night there.

It would have been funny if he weren't suddenly feeling so tired. He looked at Niall, sitting next to the bed and holding his hand. "I never realized how exhausting tension is. I slept eight hours but it feels as though I didn't sleep at all. How are you, darling?"

"I'm well," Niall said, "now that I have you before my eyes and your hand in mine. We should have come yesterday. We'll be out of this soon. Here, the last nurse left these. You'll want them once we start moving." He handed over another dose of the magic pills. Geoffrey couldn't see a single reason not to take them, so he did.

Geoffrey had no idea what time it was, or how much time had passed, the next time he woke. It was surprising to feel so disoriented. He hadn't been knocked out, hadn't been given anesthesia. Maybe it was simply the sense of being flung off his proper path for a period of time. First by the snow, and then by the events at the hospital.

He remembered being moved to the hotel. A different room, on the first floor. The room was dark except for a candle on the bureau. He turned his head and saw Niall, slumped in an uncomfortable-looking chair beside the bed. His legs were stretched out; one elbow was on the arm of the chair; his head rested on his hand. Geoffrey started to say something and couldn't. Cleared his throat and tried again. "Darling."

Niall looked over and sat up. "There you are."

"Why are you in that ghastly chair?"

"Because you have broken bones and I don't want to hurt you."

But I want you. "They're all on one side." They stared at each other. Niall looked like he hadn't slept for days. Geoffrey put up a hand to confirm his own still-unshaven state, and was reminded of the bruises. *I must look a fright.* "Is Janis here?"

"She's in the lounge. There was a piano. It's just down the hall. Do you want me to fetch her?"

"Is she playing?"

"Very likely."

"Could you open the door? Perhaps we could hear her." Niall did, and they could. "I don't suppose I'm allowed Scotch."

Niall almost laughed. "It's been sufficiently long that I believe you could responsibly choose between the hospital's drug or nature's."

"Nature's, then. After you prop open the door with that chair, and before you lie down with me." *And kiss me.*

"Do you want the loo?"

"Not now." Geoffrey hitched himself up, carefully. His ribs protested and he silently told them to piss off. He watched Niall move the chair, watched him go across the room to the desk and pour two glasses of whisky. The neck of the bottle rattled slightly against the lip of the second glass. *Poor darling.* "I'm sorry it took so long to reach you."

The whisky bottle hit the desktop hard. "For Christ's sake, Geoffrey, it wasn't your fault. We should have come yesterday." Niall took a moment, settling his breathing, before he picked up the glasses and brought them to the bed. He handed one to Geoffrey, tapped his against it, and they both drank. Then he sighed, climbed onto the bed, and arranged himself next to his husband. And, finally, leaned over for a kiss. Too light, too brief. "I'll hurt your mouth."

"The devil you will." The cut on his lip stung from the whisky. Geoffrey would have borne a great deal more pain to make up their deficit of kisses. He got his free arm around Niall's neck, and didn't let him pull away. "Kiss me again. I love you."

"I love you." More kisses, deep lingering kisses that felt like heaven. After a while Geoffrey let Niall sit back. He had another sip of whisky, staring at his husband. The bruises were frightful; Geoffrey's right eye had a patch of blood in the white. His expression said only 'I wish you could hug me.' Niall wished that very strongly. "May we never again live through such an ordeal. The charge nurse said she'd never seen anything like it, all those officers. And that business with your phone. When the call came in, of course I didn't recognize the number. If I hadn't been in such a panic about you, I might not have answered."

"She was livid. We talked after. A good friend of hers was deported last year. She'd heard me ask why I couldn't call you. She said, where's your phone, and I told her I didn't know, and she said, use mine. She was *furious*. She was wonderful." Geoffrey was smiling. He drank some more whisky. With the light contact of Niall's body against his, he felt infinitely better. "She stood with her back against the door till I was done talking to you. They never came again, though."

"All the nurses were up in arms. To be fair, I doubt the officers were out of order. They had their brief. It was the brief that's a load of shite." Niall studied Geoffrey for a moment. "When I first saw your face I wanted my bloody sword back."

Geoffrey smiled. "Nobody hit me except Mammoth."

"Bitch." They both snickered, though Geoffrey not for long. "Don't laugh, you have broken ribs."

"Don't make me laugh, then." They were quiet for a minute. Geoffrey tuned in to the music from the bar. Janis was playing 'Un Beso.' He wondered if there were people out there listening.

Niall might have read his mind. He said, "When I left her there were a few dozen people packed into the lounge. Shouldn't wonder if there's a mob now."

"Go and see. Tell her I'm all right. Will she come in here with us?"

"No, she's the room next door. She said, the bed is too small and he's broken, so one at a time, and you first."

"It's a king," Geoffrey said. "Tell the silly darling to come in here. I want her. And you. I want you both.

199

But tell her to play as long as she needs to, I like to hear it."

"All right, love." Niall kissed him again, tossed back the last of his whisky, and went out. He left the door propped open by the chair. Geoffrey listened. There was a pause at the end of 'Un Beso.' *They're talking*. The piano started again, and he really did want to laugh. She was playing 'Angel Eyes.' Then he heard her sing. *Christ, don't cry*. He managed to settle himself down before Niall returned. "It's packed full out there. She says she'll come in later, and she loves you."

"Good. I'll have the loo now, I believe."

"So you can listen in comfort?" Niall gave him a hand shifting to the edge of the bed. "That leg might complain when you go vertical."

"Bugger the leg." It truly didn't hurt much. He remembered the doctor saying it was a clean break. More luck.

Niall gave him one of the forearm crutches upon demand, then watched him stand up, ready to offer support. "Do you really propose to hop over there, or will you accept the wheelchair? I can't think your ribs will approve of hopping."

Geoffrey blew out a cautious breath, frustrated. "They won't. Ah, I suppose it's the sodding chair, then." The leg was complaining. Another glass of whisky ought to settle it.

Niall tried not to laugh as he brought the wheelchair around. It was obvious Geoffrey was going to be a difficult patient. He insisted on standing up for his pee, washed his hands and face, rinsed his mouth and swore floridly at the blood in the basin, then grumblingly accepted assistance back into the wheelchair, demanding more whisky. "Are you always like this when you're unwell?"

"Like what? Stroppy?"

Niall laughed out loud. He was still smiling when Geoffrey was comfortably back in bed, and when he brought refilled glasses over. He arranged himself on Geoffrey's uninjured side, this time with his arm around his husband's shoulders. A kiss on the cheek, then, "Yes, stroppy."

Geoffrey was smiling into his glass. "Made you laugh, though." They were quiet then, listening. Janis began to play a very familiar song.

They could barely hear her say, "If you know this, sing along with me on the chorus. My friend who got hurt in the avalanche is listening." She started to sing 'Hallelujah.' On the chorus, many voices joined in. Geoffrey closed his eyes, trying to manage his breath as tears started. Niall hugged him gently. She sang all the verses. Every time there were more voices with her in the chorus. After the seventh, Niall pressed his own face to Geoffrey's. They were both crying.

When they settled themselves Janis had changed to a different song, without singing, something quiet. It must have been very late. "Don't tell her I cried," Geoffrey said. "She'll worry about my ribs."

"I do too. Will you lie down?"

"Yes." Geoffrey wriggled himself down to flat, swore at the fresh objection from his ribs, accepted another kiss or ten from Niall. "I love you."

"I love you too. Go to sleep. She'll be here soon."

The next morning was a symphony of complaint from the broken bones. Geoffrey suffered another wheelchair visit to the bathroom, accepted a dose of prescription painkillers, listened to Janis rant about the investigators while they ate a very fine breakfast delivered from a local restaurant, and eventually allowed Niall to strip him bare and wheel him straight into the shower. "The disabled room," he said disgustedly. "I wonder how many skiers per year land here."

"I'm told they have more than one room like this," Niall said, scrubbing his back. "You're still beautiful with that beard."

"Shall I keep it?"

"Not forever." Niall could tell Geoffrey was mastering the art of laughing without hurting his ribs. "Perhaps we'll have you barbered before we go back to Los Angeles."

"When can that be?"

"I'll have to send Janis home tomorrow. The doctor said those ribs would be barely knitting in a week to ten days. She didn't want you risking a long drive, much less a flight, before then. Oh, don't sigh, stroppy." Niall rinsed his hair. "Christ, I'm as wet as you are."

"Should have stripped off before you wheeled me in."

"Indeed I should. Next time." Niall transferred his attentions to Geoffrey's front. This took some ingenuity in view of the wheelchair and the propped-up leg, which wasn't supposed to get wet. "Bloody cast." Then: "You're *joking*."

"When have you ever known me not to spring to your touch?" Geoffrey's voice trembled with laughter.

Niall looked up, exasperated. "Not a bloody chance. Not today."

"But you're right there," Geoffrey said reasonably.

"Geoffrey! You have five broken bones!"

"Tomorrow?"

"For Christ's sake, look at these bloody bruises!" All down Geoffrey's right side. Niall was deeply grateful whatever he'd hit so hard, he'd only hit it once.

They heard Janis through the half-open door. "What the hell is going on in there?"

"This little tart! I'll have you in cold water," Niall warned.

Geoffrey was trying very hard not to giggle. "Don't say you'll have me, you vicious tease."

Janis poked her head through the gap and surveyed the scenery. "You have got to be kidding. What kind of drugs did they give you?"

Once some order was restored, the three of them discussed how to proceed. Janis reluctantly agreed to return to Los Angeles, and the recording studio, the next day. Three days' schedule-shifting was as much as the studio could accommodate. Niall spoke to the hotel management about their room, and was assured that they could stay in it for up to two weeks. Then they went through all of Geoffrey's gear to make sure everything was accounted for. "I wasn't sure if they'd done anything with my laptop," he said. "Or my camera. But it seems nothing was molested."

"I was wondering if, after they had your ID, they would have seen anything about that bullshit in New York." Janis was angry all over again about that. "I mean, they'd be able to check in like ten seconds that you're with us."

"I really haven't any idea. Information was only going one way. I keep having to remind myself that it was only one day. Felt much longer."

"To us, too. Neither of us even knew there was an avalanche until we got home that night, Mom and Dad weren't online at all so they didn't know. Then, you know, it was midnight and we're all obsessively checking the internet, and Niall called the hotel and they only knew that you weren't in your room. It was awful."

"We didn't know if it was better to wait for word, or to come straight here." Niall shivered at the memory of that horrible uncertainty. "We rang the hotel again in the morning, then the hospital. Janis cancelled their session for that day. The news was updated, it said all three caught in the slide were found, no one died. But we knew you would have called us if you could, so maybe you weren't one of those caught. We were online looking for a flight when you called. We should have come first thing in the morning."

"And that stupid airport," Janis said. "It was like oops, nope, no flights till tomorrow. Niall is right."

"Darlings, none of this is any fault of yours. And you came to me like a pair of avenging angels. I'm so grateful."

Niall took his hand. "It was such a relief to see you. Have you spoken to your parents?"

"Hell! No, I haven't. They'll have been expecting to hear from me. I don't suppose the avalanche made the news over there, or I'd've had a message from them." Geoffrey's phone was on the side table. He composed a text; it was too late in the day to call. At least they'd get the message in the morning. He sent it off, set the phone down, then had a thought. "You recall that pornographer who wanted an interview?"

Niall's eyebrows went up. "Have you heard from him again?"

"Yes, an email last month. I sent back a noncommittal answer. But perhaps it wouldn't be the worst idea to do a bit of press. Even that sort of press."

Janis was doubtful. "What were his emails like?"

"Funny. Sharp. He does publish interviews regularly, I've read several. They're not all about what positions people like best. I believe Playboy is his model. And his subscribers … well, there's a good chance some of them might buy my books."

"I'm not averse," Niall said. "You know how to manage a conversation. Janis?"

She looked surprised. "It's not really any of my business, is it?"

Geoffrey shook his head. "Of course it is. The world may not know the precise nature of our relationship, but it certainly knows we have one. I don't want to do anything you'd dislike."

She stood up, came over to the bed, and kissed him. "I would not dislike it. I trust you. Maybe you can air out this whole getting-profiled thing."

"Maybe so. All right then. I'll call him tomorrow. And now perhaps you and my husband could go to dinner and relax."

"What about you?"

"I've a mind to write for a while." He was actually desperate to be left alone, which was the last thing he would have expected. Niall may have guessed. He helped Geoffrey back into the wheelchair so he could get around as needed. Then he and Janis took themselves off. Geoffrey thought about pouring himself a drink, remembered the time he'd last taken a painkiller, and settled for water. He opened the laptop and read over his last few thousand words until new ones began to come to him. He was still working when the others returned. His greeting was brief and distracted.

"Here darling." Niall set a takeout container down on the desk. "We'll go next door. Give us a bell if you want anything."

"Thank you, sweetheart." Geoffrey accepted a kiss and kept working.

Niall and Janis retreated to the adjacent room and stared at each other for a moment. "He's okay," Janis said, but it sounded like a question.

Niall nodded. "He is. I suspect it's only now sinking in. Near-death experience. No one here who loved him. He was very moved last night, by your music. So was I." She stepped close and hugged him. He sighed, then gave her a kiss. They sat down on the room's little couch. "And of course he's still on deadline. The publisher wanted synopses of all three books by the end of this week. So he's a legitimate need to concentrate."

"He was making good progress though, right?"

"Oh, very good. He's been writing like a fury in L.A. With all his time alone up here he's bound to be well along." Niall picked up her hand and kissed it. "As you are. I'm sorry for the delay this week."

"Not your fault. We had some wiggle room. We can, you know, not try every single experimental idea we have while in the expensively-reserved studio."

206

Niall snorted. Janis was smiling. "Those two are great to work with. The other musicians have good ideas too. It's going to be *such* a different album."

"Nervous?"

"A little. I mean, it's still standards, mostly. It's still me singing and playing, mostly. But the flavor. If I were the person waiting for a scoop of Janis Vaughn that tasted like vanilla, you know, and then picked up this thing and it's all, like, mango?"

"Mango tango." They both snickered. "Your other records are not vanilla."

"I like to think of them as caramel. Milk chocolate. Maybe rum raisin. Not too challenging but not boring."

"Definitely not boring, love."

"Do you think we should sleep in here?"

"No." He was certain of that. "We'll give him till eleven, and then go in. There's time for a movie, if you like."

"Yeah. Let's see what's on." Niall picked up the remote and activated the TV. Janis leaned against him; he put his arm around her shoulder. She spotted something on the menu. "That one." The movie was 'Cliffhanger.'

Niall started laughing. "Are you serious?" He felt her nod and selected the movie.

When they went back to Geoffrey's room later, he was leaning back in the wheelchair, stretching his hands. The laptop was closed. "Hello loves. Thank you for the dinner."

"You're welcome." Niall studied him; he looked more relaxed, less frustrated, more like himself. "Anything you need?"

"A bit of help transferring up to the bed, if you would."

"Of course I would." Niall was already adept at this maneuver. "You know getting you in bed is one of my favorite things." Geoffrey took advantage of their proximity to get a kiss. "Good thing I did that training with Red, isn't it?"

"My mighty king. Janis, darling, did you know your 'Hallelujah' singalong is on the internet?"

"Oh yeah? I'll check it out in the morning." She got into bed beside him and leaned in to kiss him. "This beard, honey. No." He was doing that laugh-without-laughing thing. "Your poor face. But promise the beard will not come back to Los Angeles."

"I promise. Kiss me again anyway." Once Janis and Niall were both in bed, Geoffrey said, "One thing more, loves. Stop castigating yourselves about not being here the morning after. It wouldn't have been any use, it might have made things worse with all those investigators, and it was good for me to get angry. I've realized in New York, and most of yesterday, I was doing the compliant, submissive colonial thing that I've always hated. As soon as I pushed back, literally the first time I did, it stopped. So I needed that day. I'm only sorry you had such a wretched one yourselves."

Janis kissed his cheek. "It was wretched. Don't be in any more avalanches."

"I'll do my best. Niall?"

"Yes, love."

"Will you state for the record that none of this was your fault?"

Niall laughed under his breath. "Take it as read. Good night, sweetheart."

Everything was slightly better the next morning. Geoffrey alleged that kissing had helped his cut lip to heal; Janis suggested good food, plenty of rest, and regular applications of Vaseline might have more to do with it. They had another excellent breakfast before she had to go and pack her overnight bag. She returned to Geoffrey's room ready for the airport. "But I don't have to leave for another half hour."

"Then let me apologize," Geoffrey said. He was in bed again, with a cup of coffee to his right and Niall to his left. "To both of you."

Niall frowned. "What on earth for?"

He had to say it. He'd thought it through for an hour before they woke, when he was lying there feeling helpless and knowing it was all his own fault. Desperately grateful and yet resentful, because he had to say something he'd never dreamed of saying. This wasn't as trivial as losing mobile signal and choosing not to use a land line. He still wasn't clear on why he'd so blithely walked into danger, but walk he had. "For putting you through that. I knew the conditions were dodgy. It's one thing to risk myself when it's only me. It's not only me anymore, and I won't forget that again."

"It's never been only you," Janis said after a moment. "Your family would be devastated if anything happened to you."

"They would be hurt," he said. "Not devastated." The implication was clear.

Niall didn't miss it. "I would have been. Never having had this would have been difficult, but manageable. Doing without it now, well." He shook his head.

209

"And so I'm sorry." Geoffrey took his hand. "Janis, Niall, my loves. I promise. I'll always adore wild places, but I won't put myself in harm's way again if I can help it." He hoped they couldn't hear how little he wanted to make that promise. If they could, he hoped they could tell he meant it.

Janis leaned over to kiss him, then Niall, then Geoffrey again. She sat on the edge of the bed. "I appreciate that. When I woke up the morning after and the bed was empty and there still wasn't a message, I started to think, what if this is it?"

"Oh, darling."

"Then Niall came in and he could tell I didn't get anything, and I could tell he didn't get anything. It was like all the air got sucked out of the room for a minute. I had this crazy thought, if he breaks Niall's heart, I'm going to kill him." Niall coughed out a laugh. Janis said, "It was bad. So thank you for not breaking our hearts."

"I'm so sorry."

"It still wasn't your fault. Mostly," she said. She patted his thigh. "Heal fast, sweetheart."

"I'll do my best." Another round of kisses, but no goodbyes. Instead he said, "See you soon." Niall walked Janis out to the waiting taxi. Geoffrey stared at the ceiling, conscious as never before of the commitment he'd made and what it truly meant. *This much love is not to be trifled with*, he thought. He wouldn't forget the lesson. And he'd find some other way to be free.

Niall returned with fresh coffee for both of them, reminding Geoffrey to call his mother, who'd texted to say *You and those blasted mountains, this is why I tell you to write poetry*. Their conversation was long, affectionate, and restorative. He promised her a new poem. After that, Geoffrey contacted the operator of the gay porn site. The call was answered with a cheery "What's up?"

"Well you'd know, wouldn't you?" Geoffrey said. "Hello Reggie. This is Geoffrey Anand."

"Geoffrey! To what do I owe the pleasure?"

"I wondered if you'd still be interested in hearing from me for your site."

"Would I be *interested*? Did I see your masterpiece of a husband dissect that loathsome toad on Channel Four? Did I see that picture from the plane? Did I see you dancing me to bloody heartbreak? Interested!" The faintly-Cockney voice was loaded with outraged humor. "May I turn on my recorder this instant?"

"If you like." Geoffrey was smiling. "Tell me when you're ready."

"I'm always ready, my dove, why d'you think I'm in this line of work."

Geoffrey blew out a breath. "Don't make me laugh, it hurts. First let me send you a link." His laptop was lying beside him on the bed. He had the swordfight video queued and ready; he copied the link and sent the email as he heard a sound of assent from Reggie. Then a mutter, and then the music and the voices from the video.

Then, "Bleeding hell," Reggie said devoutly. "Well that's proof of life. That's properly tented me trousers, that has. Tell me what's what. Why can't you laugh?"

"Before I tell you that, let's get this video out of the way. Niall asked the other bloke, that's the American

211

actor Red Warner, about a fencing club while we're here in California. Red had been asked to do this broadsword series. That video was the last of six."

"Not much doubt why you married him, as I'll tell anyone who asks. All right, now you've ruined me for all others, what have you to say? How go the new novels?"

"They go swimmingly. Or rather surfingly, rappellingly, and snowingly." Geoffrey told a snickering Reggie about the three books he was working on in parallel, with just enough detail to tease a reader's interest. "I'm told my last is doing well in paperback."

"And where are you now?"

"I'm flat on my back in a hotel bed in Mammoth Lakes, with a broken leg and three broken ribs." That was a slight exaggeration; he was sitting up.

"What the hell have you done?!"

"The mountain had a go at me. Avalanche. Lucky to be alive," he said seriously. "I'd gone out for a hike, had the proper gear, people knew where I was going. In fact I'd walked out with a couple from the hotel, had been within sight of them minutes before I heard the snow break."

"What does it sound like?"

"Whumph!"

Reggie whistled. "How long did it take to reach you?"

"Long enough to know it was coming straight for me."

"How long till you were found?"

"They tell me it was only two hours. I was never unconscious. It felt like weeks. The snow picked me up and threw me about two hundred yards down the mountain. Couldn't get to my whistle, and couldn't draw breath enough to call out."

"Were you buried, then?"

"I was."

"Hell!"

"That's one of many words that crossed my mind. I had enough play with my left leg and arm to get to my shovel and, obviously, took the right direction. Broke through and got some air. I don't like to say just in time as I don't know how long it took, but let's say it felt rather like coming up from a long dive. Then my transceiver was on, and the crews here know what they're about."

"Blimey! Well, I'm glad you're all right, and that's a fact. How long till you're back on your feet?"

"I can manage to hop about with crutches already, though only a step or two. Bloody painful with these ribs, and the doctor says the more I move around the less happy with me she'll be. So I'm rather laid up for three or four weeks."

"Your husband's there with you?" Reggie sounded certain of it.

"He is. They were in Los Angeles, Ms. Vaughn's been in the recording studio. They didn't hear from me as expected, and then still not the next day. A nurse here let me borrow her phone to call them, and they were both here the following morning."

"Where was your phone?" Sharp interest now.

Geoffrey had expected it. "I have it back now. It was taken by some investigators here." He told Reggie about the relays of officers and officials, from so many different departments.

213

Reggie said incredulously, "What the bleeding hell. Did they think you set it off?"

"Well, you know how people joke. I've since heard someone said something about how easy it would be to start an avalanche. Someone else said they'd seen me. Described me, you know."

"As the popular idea of a miscreant no doubt. All white around there, is it?" Geoffrey knew from the website that Reggie was black himself.

"Not as solidly as you would expect. But my hair's a bit long, I hadn't shaved since Niall left me here to go back to L.A., I'm clearly a foreigner, and nobody knew me. I fit the profile." He knew his voice was cool; he'd practiced keeping it so. "At any rate, there's apparently a protocol, which is if someone makes comments of a certain nature, certain departments are activated to investigate. It's like being in an airport and making a joke about a bomb."

"Bloody stupid."

"They've cause for caution. September eleven is nearly twenty years ago but no one's forgotten."

"Effing paranoiacs won't let them. Meanwhile their homegrown nutters keep massacring students." A heavy and impatient sigh. "So, Mr. Phelps arrived and sorted things out?"

"He and Ms. Vaughn. She was threatening lawsuits up and down the ranks. Niall sent her home to L.A. this morning so she can get back to work on this record. He's still here with me."

Reggie said approvingly, "As he should be. What will he do with himself while you're out of action?" The tone was slightly suggestive.

Geoffrey lobbed it right back. "We can still entertain each other." He hummed a little bit of a tune,

214

Monty Python's 'Sit on my face.' Reggie was howling. Geoffrey was trying not to laugh along with him, because it hurt.

"You're a classic, you are." Reggie giggled a little more. "Are you going to write a book about this misadventure? It's happened to you twice this trip, hasn't it?"

"Being profiled?" Geoffrey had, of course, considered it. "I don't know that my story alone is enough for a book."

"Must be legions of others with similar stories. But I mustn't keep you, you've bones to knit. If you should ever care to write a little something that might entertain my subscribers, a letter perhaps, call me instantly."

"Perhaps I will. Not every inspiration belongs in a book." Geoffrey was smiling; he knew the kind of letter Reggie meant.

"You can always compile them later. Reserve your rights, lad. I'm off now. I'll send you the transcript to approve, shall I?"

"Thanks Reggie, it's been a pleasure." They ended the call and Geoffrey relaxed against the stack of pillows, looking over at Niall. "He'll boost that video, you can rely on it."

"I'd better not end up being hounded by film producers. I've quite enough to do, thank you." Niall leaned over for a kiss. "Sit on your face, is it?" Geoffrey again tried not to laugh. "Perhaps we'll give that another day or two." Another kiss. "I love you so."

"I love you too."

Chapter 11

Geoffrey was still taking painkillers, but they didn't reliably keep him asleep. So he found himself awake, sometime deep in the night, and the room was so quiet he couldn't help but hear Niall breathing. *Not breathing*, he thought with a sort of horror, *he's crying.* Crying together was one thing; crying alone in the night something entirely different, and very much worse. He stretched out a hand until he could reach his husband. "Sweetheart," he said softly, "are you all right?"

"Oh." Niall sniffed. "I'm sorry, did I wake you?"

"No, these drugs are shite, that's all. Will you kiss me, love?"

Niall took an audible breath and sniffed again. "Of course." He put a hand on Geoffrey's arm and followed it back to his body, then brushed lightly across his chest and up his neck to his face. Their lips met. His tasted of salt. "I love you."

"I love you."

"Ought I have left you alone this evening? You seemed so frustrated." Geoffrey thought *shit*, because he had been. He'd been snappy, monosyllabic. An ungrateful shit. He might have been better left alone. He couldn't think of an answer. After a moment Niall said, "Do you want me to go? Would you rather have a nurse?"

"No!" The only possible answer, the only true answer. "I'm so sorry, Niall, darling, no. Please stay. It's only I can't walk, and I can't breathe, and it's my own sodding fault. I'm so furious with myself. And I'm furious that this thing I've always loved is a thing

216

I can't do without worrying you. And Janis," he added. It was clearly an afterthought, but she wasn't there and Niall wouldn't tell her.

Niall gave that a moment. "You can do every part of it that doesn't involve sauntering along under a slide hazard." His voice sounded normal now. Not amused, but normal. "Fair enough?"

"More than fair," Geoffrey said, because it was. "I'm so sorry. I'm truly grateful you're here."

A sound from Niall, equal parts impatience and embarrassment. "It was a bad moment, that's all. You know what we thought when we saw 'avalanche' in the headline. We thought we'd lost you. For twenty-four hours."

All he could do was apologize again. "I'm sorry."

"Sshh. You didn't set the effing thing going. The Gestapo were to blame for you not contacting us. You've already apologized for putting yourself in harm's way." Another quiet moment. "You were frightened, in hospital. Did it seem they might never stop?"

"It did, it was so *stupid*. All those questions, over and over. I'll never write an interrogation the same way again."

Niall huffed out a laugh. "Were you frightened before?"

"In the snow?" Geoffrey realized with some surprise that he hadn't been. Awash with emotion, yes, but not with terror. He tried to think of a way to explain that.

Niall didn't give him time. "Were you frightened of dying?"

"I didn't have time to be. I was busy." That got more of a laugh, and another kiss. Geoffrey had a handful of Niall's hair now, holding him close for more kisses. "I

217

love you so much. Christ, I wish I could make love to you right now."

"As do I. However, as you've so recently admitted, you can't breathe."

"You could toss yourself off," Geoffrey suggested, smiling. "I'd like to hear that."

"What a depraved young man you are," Niall said silkily. Then, with audible regret, "No, I shall wait until we can do that together, or better yet to each other."

"Till I'm out of that sodding chair. Not a minute longer."

Niall made an unconvinced sound, but he kissed Geoffrey again, and this time he was smiling.

Two days later, right on schedule, Geoffrey sent off the synopses to his publisher with a request to tell him which book they wanted first. He also sent a brief summary of the international team of investigators he'd invented, in order to free his heroes from verifiable procedural necessities. In reviewing other series in the genre, he'd found that a very common device, which made perfect sense. It would give him a way to add new heroes without over-explaining their context each time, to create connections between the books, and to provide another marketing hook for the publisher. Niall approved of the strategy. "I like a tied-together series myself. The only author I can think of who wrote brilliant books time after time that *weren't* connected, is Dick Francis. Did you add an avalanche?"

"Couldn't waste the experience, could I? My mountaineering hero has a narrow escape. No broken bones."

"Which love interest is that?"

"I don't know if I should tell you. Since you've so resolutely denied me spousal comforts."

Niall gave him a look. It hadn't been even a week. "If you did not wince every time you draw breath, perhaps I should be less careful of you."

Geoffrey relented. "It was beastly of the mountain to break me high and low, wasn't it? If it were you, I shouldn't risk it either. So I forgive you. And I'll tell you my snowbound hero, he's the one investigating a drug dealer, is involved with the private pilot."

"Very good. Which has the fictional me?"

"The fellow investigating insider trading. And the gent inside the human smuggling ring is involved with the itinerant photographer."

"Have you based that on our friend Mr. Martin?"

"Stolen his description down to his toenails." Niall laughed. They'd actually seen Andy's toenails, since he was barefoot in the studio during their shoot. "And his love of fine wine."

Niall was still smiling. "Who would have guessed Janis had a rival in that regard. Is there anything you need now, for these projects?"

"Not a thing. All the essential research is done, I know where the plots are going, and I seem to have given each hero what he wants."

"No squid?"

"Nary a tentacle. Then I've sent off a proposal for an article, which in view of recent events has a very different focus from that previously envisioned. It was more the 'best places to drink in Mammoth' type of article. Now it's 'winter safety.' I've established my bona fides. The searchers said they wouldn't have found me without the transceiver, not before dark." The others they'd found had been on the opposite side of the slide, another hundred yards downslope.

"We'll not think about that. I heard from Janis today."

"She texted me too. She said, fix those ribs immediately, everything's going to shit without Niall."

"That's approximately what she said to me. Why can't anyone else in L.A. organize anything. I told her not to be feeble. Don't laugh!"

"Don't make me laugh!"

They left Mammoth nine days after the avalanche, which seemed to Niall precipitate, but to Geoffrey long overdue. The amount of work he'd achieved was set against his confinement. "This sodding wheelchair," he said as he watched, unable to contribute, while Niall packed the rented car.

"Another two weeks or you'll rue those ribs."

"I know, I know." The forearm crutches were slightly less impossible than under-the-arm crutches would have been, but the ribs still argued against their use for more than a step or two. Geoffrey had many times wished that the broken ribs could have been on the opposite side from the broken leg. "At least in Glendale I'll be able to go outside. Thank God for Deborah and her garden paths."

"And you'll have the freedom of the house. She swears the chair will go anywhere."

"Except into the shower. Bloody cast."

"Yes, stroppy. In you go." The transfer into the car was not as smooth as the transfer in or out of bed, but it was achieved. Niall folded the wheelchair and jammed it behind the front seats. "Let's away."

The drive home was uneventful. Geoffrey had his camera out, since he knew he'd be the passenger all the way. The eastern slopes of the Sierra were spectacular. He took pictures whenever he had a good angle. "I'm not sorry I came," he said approximately halfway back. "I've done good work."

"It wasn't the carefree jaunt you envisioned. Had you enough time away, before everything landed on you?"

Geoffrey winced. They both knew this trip had been every bit as much about his need for space as about the need for research. They hadn't discussed how he was meaning to cope back in Glendale, with no freedom of movement for weeks to come. "It would have been enough," he said finally, even though he wasn't certain that was true.

Niall kept his voice neutral. "Have you heard back from the publisher?"

"Not yet." Geoffrey checked his phone just in case. "Oh. Here's a new text from Janis. She says Randa called her up. There's been chatter about her nights in Mammoth. Someone claimed that we all slept together." They glanced at each other. "Randa wants to know if she wants to make a statement."

"Nothing more?"

"No." They both thought about it for a few seconds. "Of course it's true. Whether she confirms or denies, there'll be more questions."

Niall wasn't sure he knew what Janis would rather do. "Could you ask her if she's responded?"

Geoffrey sent a reply text. They were quiet for a while, both pondering the possible consequences if the chatter became a major story. "How major could it be?" Geoffrey said, thinking out loud. "Is her audience one that would be repulsed by the idea, or tantalized? If she's able to keep them guessing – neither confirm nor deny – will people be more interested in her as an artist, or less?"

"I really couldn't say," Niall admitted after a minute. "The social media engagement has always indicated a certain laissez-faire attitude. But we all know that social media does not reflect a true cross-section of a given audience. Her music has, until now, been pitched to the more conservative listener."

"But conservative tastes in music don't necessarily reflect conservative ideology." They lapsed into silence again. There was no way to know. Finally Geoffrey's phone buzzed again. "There she is. She says she asked Randa what benefit there would be in making a statement. Randa said none, other than appearing responsive, unless the statement included a confirmation or denial."

"Spectacularly unhelpful. Anything else?"

"Janis told Randa to see if the record company had a preference. Her own inclination was to not respond."

"Is that what she says?" Niall knew he sounded amused. He rather doubted those were Janis' words.

"No. She says 'not that it's any of their fucking business either.'" Niall laughed. Geoffrey sent a reply: *It never is, darling. Sorry if we've put you in an awkward position*

Janis texted back immediately: *Those are my favorite kind*

Geoffrey read both texts to Niall. They were still snickering when they pulled off in Lancaster for a snack.

It was Niall's suggestion that they should have Geoffrey sleep on the pull-out couch in the home office until he could do without the wheelchair. Janis' queen bed was manageable when they could all wriggle around, but getting in and out of it with broken ribs (and the awkward cast) seemed an unnecessary chore. "On the couch itself," Geoffrey said after due consideration. "It'll leave space to maneuver the sodding chair."

"You always call it that," Niall said, amused.

"And I always will. You'll still kiss me goodnight, I trust?"

"I shall very likely sleep beside you on the floor like a faithful dog." He didn't, of course, though perhaps only because Janis, Deborah, and Geoffrey wouldn't hear of it.

That first night back was exhausting. Deborah and Ed quite naturally wanted to hear the whole story. Janis wanted to hear everything that had happened since she'd left. Niall was trying to make sure Geoffrey had plenty to eat and wasn't overdoing, and by the end of the evening Geoffrey was desperately glad to escape to his temporary bedroom. He told himself sternly, *You've chosen this and now you must deal with it. That's what commitment is. Grow up.* It would be all right. He could get himself on and off the couch, to and from the wheelchair, as long as he didn't try to rise to his full height. Eleven days more, eleven nights alone, and he'd be rid of the wretched thing. By that time surely he'd come to some conclusion about how to be free without hurting the others. Or himself.

223

"So basically," Janis told them the next day, "Randa kinda sorta asked if it was true, and I said don't ask the question if you're afraid of the answer, and she turned slightly green and said she wasn't asking."

"Should I go to the next meeting, then?" Niall had been working with Randa for years, but he wouldn't have said he knew her well.

"Yes, please. She likes you. It's not our situation she's afraid of, it's how to articulate a response. Plausible deniability is best." She shrugged, looked away, then added, "Plus, you ask the questions I forget to ask, you remember everything, I need you. This is your show. You ran Europe perfectly, Randa and the company know it, you are not optional." Janis looked scared now.

Niall patted her gently. "All right. You know I'll go wherever you need me to go, and happy to do it."

"Thank you." She shook herself, then hugged him. "Geoffrey, are you huggable yet?"

He was standing, leaning on the wall, left arm propped on a crutch. "Darling, of course. Left arm over my right shoulder, please." It was so much better than no hug at all, especially when she lifted her face and he could kiss her. "Regrets, love?"

She must have known what he meant. "Not for a second." She held on for a minute. "Have you lost weight?"

"No idea. I'll get into your father's gym once I'm walking."

"Maybe you should go see what Mom's doing in the kitchen." Janis kissed him again and let him go.

224

Niall lent a hand as he lowered himself into the wheelchair.

When Geoffrey went to find Deborah, she was simmering a giant pot of stock made with the carcass of the Thanksgiving smoked turkey. She told him she would make soup to feed his bones. "And in the meantime, there's smoked turkey mac 'n' cheese in the oven for lunch. I forgot there was so much meat in the freezer."

"It sounds delicious, my dear. I'm sorry to put you to so much trouble." He was watching her tidy up. It was a task he would have liked to help with.

She turned around to look at him. "It's no trouble. You know I like to cook. And I want you out of that chair, it bothers me."

"It bothers me, too. It won't be long." He spared another curse for his ribs. If they hadn't broken, he'd never have needed the sodding chair. "I'm sorry I put you all to such trouble."

Deborah turned again. Geoffrey knew she understood he wasn't talking about trivia like meals. "Janis and Niall were as close to frantic as I ever want to see them."

"I've apologized to them, and I will to you. There was a risk, and I put myself in front of it. I won't do that again."

"That whole stupid phone thing, though. You'd have been through to us before bedtime if that hadn't happened, right?"

He nodded. That, like the avalanche itself, wasn't his fault. The fact remained that the avalanche could have killed him. If his head had struck whatever broke his leg, if he'd sustained any one of many equally possible, more dreadful injuries. "I've received an

225

apology from the hospital administration. Couched in the very vaguest of terms."

"Weasely, you mean."

He snickered. "Yes. Distinctly ferret-like." Deborah laughed. "Poor buggers, can you imagine being in that position? Forced to act as part of the police state? Violating the state's own laws on patient confidentiality because of gossip. I don't blame them. Especially since one of their own helped me get a line out. I should have made more of a fuss earlier."

"Oh well." She sighed. "You're safe now, and the worst of it was over in a day. So where are you on the books? Did you get caught up?" Geoffrey accepted the change of subject with relief, and started telling her about the directions his heroes were taking.

Niall and Janis met with Randa two days later. She made no reference to the chatter from Mammoth, other than to show Janis a draft statement confirming her travel to and from the resort town due to Geoffrey's injuries. "I thought it might be good to remind people what's important about that trip," she said. "You were there because your friend was hurt. He could have died. You gave what amounted to a free concert that close to a hundred people heard. Did you know the hotel bar made so much money they made a donation to the Eastern Sierra Avalanche Center? We can link this to that unauthorized video that we have not pulled down, the 'Hallelujah' thing." She watched Janis and Niall consult with a silent look. "Is that workable?"

"That's fine," Janis said. "Thanks. So we're close to done in the recording studio. What does the company say about releasing a couple of the videos from the master take?"

"They're gung ho. You've always had great response to the informal videos, and these would be different versions from what's going on the album." They discussed who would be assigned to produce the videos for release, and then moved on to a proposed 'sneak preview' concert. "You guys are here till June, right?"

"At least," Niall said. "We'll be applying to extend Geoffrey's visa. If the extension isn't granted, though, we'll all be going back to England."

"So it runs out in June? We'd have to do this preview no later than the end of May. Damn." Randa chewed a fingernail. "Let me see what I can do. What's the smallest venue you'd accept?"

"I don't give a shit about the venue. Oh wait!" Janis suddenly looked excited. "Could we do it at Chrome?"

"Oh, that's brilliant," Niall said. "It's a terrific venue for music. But you wouldn't be able to use the baby grand pianos, they'd never go down the stairs."

"No. They have an antique upright, Tomás told me about it. He says it's gorgeous, he played it when his wife did her set last fall."

"Okay," Randa said. "Would you need another acoustic piano, or could you use a digital?"

"If you used a digital," Niall said to Janis, "there might be room on the stage to feature a dancer or two. I'd say Tomás but he'll be playing. Surely he'd know someone."

"God I love that idea. I wish we could get Andy and Victor. Victor's going to be away on location."

"Let's see if we can get the venue. Then we'll confirm Tomás and Isabelle, figure out the instruments, and then worry about dancers."

"It will have to be super hush-hush," Randa warned, "right up to the day. Unless you want to make it a benefit and charge an obscene amount of money for tickets."

"I suck at hush-hush." Janis shrugged. "So let's make it a benefit. Who gets the money?" It was a rhetorical question. Randa and Niall let her think. "I know. The ACLU." She gave Niall a sideways look. He nodded.

Randa sighed. "Could you not do something warm and fuzzy like breast cancer research?"

"Randa. How long have we been working together? Am I remotely fuzzy?"

"Not remotely. Okay. I'll get on this and let you know ASAP."

If one could be said to be walking on tiptoe when actually in a wheelchair, Geoffrey might have thought of it that way. He was careful, he was quiet, he was losing his mind. And he couldn't complain, because it was all his own fault. His progress anywhere was slow. A jaunt around the garden on his own was beyond him. Going out with someone else was better than nothing, but everyone was so solicitous he wanted to scream.

Niall and Janis were still in the throes of recording. Deborah and Ed went about their business. They all convened for dinner every day. Geoffrey pretended more of an interest in their doings than he actually had, felt like a prick for pretending, and then was all the more fed up for feeling like he had to pretend.

He was working more or less constantly, because he couldn't do anything else. In the moments when he wasn't thinking about one of the three books – he continued to work on all of them in parallel while he waited to hear from his publisher – he kept thinking about why he, of all people, with as much experience as he had, would have strolled out into the path of an avalanche.

Of course he couldn't have known it *would* happen. He'd been out in far worse conditions and come home safely. But he certainly had known it *could* happen, and out he'd gone as if it didn't matter. As if he didn't care. Failing to get to the bottom of why was nearly as troubling as the consequences.

A week after their return to Glendale and sixteen days after the avalanche, he was in the kitchen getting himself a cup of coffee – at least he could manage that, thanks to the low counter where Deborah kept the coffee things – when she came in behind him and said, "What's the matter with Niall?"

Geoffrey set down his mug with a startled click and swiveled around to face her. "What do you mean?"

"Geoffrey, you know I'm extremely fond of you, but he is acting like a man who's facing a very unwanted divorce. So what the hell." Her expression was serious. Geoffrey's might have been astounded. Hers eased. "Is he not talking to you?"

He shook his head. "Not about anything except the record, and my effing ribs, and this blasted leg, and this sodding wheelchair. Really? Has he said something to you?"

She pulled one of the kitchen chairs over and sat down beside him. "He has said one thing. I asked him if he was having trouble sleeping, because he looked so tired, and he said he missed you. Then he blurted out that he keeps having these moments of blinding fear that you'll leave as soon as you can. And then he tried to make that sound like it was only a joke, but his hands were shaking."

"Bleeding hell," Geoffrey said blankly. "I'd no idea. Of course I don't want to leave him. To leave them. I want to get out of this frigging chair, and up on my feet, and out into the world again. But not *away*." They stared at each other for a moment. "What about Janis?"

"I don't think she's noticed, to be honest. She is deep in this record. But one day she's going to come to the surface and wonder why her best friend is miserable again."

A stream of the most vile obscenities he knew was running through Geoffrey's head. He had no idea what to do, or even what to say, so he opted for unvarnished truth. "Deborah, I told Niall in January that if Janis ever decided she was through with me, with this thing we have, that I would stay with him. That he was the one for me. I love her, but he is all in all." *And he didn't say the same.* He realized it still hurt.

"Then why is he so scared?"

"Could it be because of all this?" He gestured to the broken leg, the wheelchair, and by implication the entire avalanche scenario. "Because I was fool enough to let this happen? Could he think I *wanted* something like this to happen?"

"People think some funny things when they're afraid of losing someone." She studied him for a moment. "Why were you out there?"

230

"I don't *know*."

Some kind of comprehension seemed to be dawning. Deborah said, slowly, as if feeling her way, "Geoffrey, when is the last time you were prevented from doing what you wanted to do? In a serious way?"

"Never. I've been cautioned, berated, lamented, persuaded, and roundly cursed, but never prevented."

"But since this. Since you and Niall and Janis. Have you chosen not to do things you would ordinarily have done, because of the relationship." It wasn't even a question, but Geoffrey nodded confirmation. "Okay. That's normal. Everyone does that when they're in a relationship. Is it possible that, knowing you were due to come home, you just ... hit the wall? That you deliberately did something reckless because you knew, once you were back here, you were going to be hemming yourself in again?"

"Shit," he said sincerely, memory instantly flooding with a fact pattern supporting that conclusion. Not only in this relationship, but in others.

Deborah almost smiled. "The thing is, Derek told me once that his biggest problem with us was that we never gave him anything to rebel against."

It all made sense now. "Neither of them has ever asked me not to do something. I volunteered for this, for Christ's sake. But there's nobody to talk to about it, except you. Thank you," he added. "There are others who know, of course, but we've thought it's better for everyone if the public face is me married to Niall who works for Janis. It's easier for people to understand, to relate to." He came very close to saying 'sometimes I wonder if the marriage is more for Janis than for Niall.' The second it crossed his mind he realized he'd been burying that sickening thought for weeks.

"Right. I get it. You could have tried to pull that here, too. Obviously the sleeping arrangements would have had to be different." Another long look. "I think that's it, honey. You've changed your whole life for a relationship you can't acknowledge. Even though you love them both – which by the way I believe you sincerely do – that's difficult. But sweetie, they *know*. They understand. It's the same for them."

"I know." Geoffrey shoved a hand through his hair. "Maybe I've felt that since they were already in it, they haven't given up so much." He felt awful, saying that. Acknowledging that he felt he had given up anything, let alone 'so much.' But Deborah's face didn't change.

She nodded. "They haven't. They were in the weeds. They didn't know what to do. And then there was you, and you made this possible. You have a lot of power here."

"I don't want power."

"I know. It's just one more weight for you to bear."

He almost cried then. It took a moment to steady himself. "I need to think. About what to tell him."

She patted his shoulder. "You want a ride back to the office?"

"Yes please. Thank you, pet. What would I do without you?" He let her roll him down the hall. She kissed his cheek and patted him again before she went away. Then he reconsidered, and wheeled himself first to the washroom and then into the bedroom for the journal laptop. He typed out the entire conversation, as completely as he could remember it. He included

232

his recollection of similar idiocies past, left out his unspoken fears. At the end he wrote AND I SHALL NOT LEAVE YOU, BECAUSE I LOVE YOU WITH ALL MY HEART AND TO MY LAST BREATH.

He left the laptop on the bed where they would have to see it, and (he hoped) deduce there was something new. After that, exhausted, he went back to the office, levered himself onto the couch, and went to sleep.

When he woke up, it was dark. The only light was from the nightlight plugged into the power socket by the door. He was vaguely hungry. But he didn't move, because Niall was sitting on the floor beside the couch, his head pillowed on one arm beside Geoffrey's thigh, his other hand resting on Geoffrey's undamaged ribs. "Niall," he said very softly. He didn't know if it was the touch that woke him, or if perhaps Niall had been there for some time. If he were asleep, then Geoffrey would try for the same. If not, he desperately wanted a kiss.

Niall lifted his head. They gazed at each other for a minute. "Hello love. Have I made a sufficient fool of myself?"

"My God, Niall, would you please, *please* kiss me?"

Whether it was due to Deborah's excellent soup, his own tendency to heal fast, or sheer bloody-mindedness, Geoffrey was out of the wheelchair three weeks to the day from the avalanche. His leg was still in a cast, his ribs were barely knit, his doctor disapproved; but he could manage the house on crutches and was determined to do so. "It's better for me," he told Niall, impatiently, when misgivings were expressed. "I'll recover my strength faster. And I want you."

Niall blinked. "For what purpose?"

"For every purpose, you ninny. Have you noticed I can laugh?"

"I have, yes. Though I notice your laugh is yet restrained." Niall tipped his head to one side, studying his husband, suppressing a smile. They were in the sunroom, early in the day. He had to leave soon with Janis; there was certainly no time to indulge in spousal comforts beyond a kiss. That, however, he couldn't resist. Geoffrey's response was, as it had been for some time, reassuringly vigorous. "Do not wander," he warned. "Deborah's your monitor. I know perfectly well you're not meant to stress those ribs for another three weeks."

"The bare minimum, I promise. But I cannot manage another day without your touch." He didn't mean to sound so desperate. He lowered his voice and spoke with his face against Niall's. "I've survived my own. So I'll survive yours." The very thought of it – combined with that kiss - had him hard; he was close enough to Niall to confirm an equivalent response.

"Then I'll have you on your back before day's end, my beauty." Niall kissed him again. "Shall I save all of this for you?" One hand on Geoffrey's waist, urging their hips together, braced to take his weight.

Geoffrey let his body rest against Niall's, meeting him for another starved kiss. "I'll have you in my mouth, my king," he said when Niall eventually raised his head, and watched the reaction – the flush, the darkening eyes, the parted lips – with delight. "Shall we wager?"

"Who goes first?" Niall stood away half an arm's length, steadying Geoffrey. "I'll be above, with you in mine. Perhaps a race, rather than a wager." They smiled at each other.

234

"What's the prize?"

"If you win, I'll allow you Janis tomorrow."

Geoffrey laughed, with restraint. "You'll *allow* me, you tyrant. And is winning to come first or second?"

"I'll decide that later," Niall said loftily. "Perhaps I shan't wish to allow you Janis tomorrow."

"Greedy. Go see to her record. I love you."

"I love you. On your balance?"

"I'm well." Niall kissed him again, briefly; adjusted himself, with a rueful glance; and left the sunroom. Geoffrey stood there alone for a minute, recovering his composure, inclined to laugh. *Didn't think he'd surrender so easily*, he thought. *He must be desperate too.*

So it proved, ten hours later. "I believe that was a photo finish, sir," Niall said, after a minute to recover. "Since we have no stewards to decide the result, shall we go again?"

"As soon as possible." Geoffrey didn't even try not to laugh. "Christ, I've missed you."

"And I you." Hugs were still cautious, but Niall could – and did – kiss Geoffrey as much and as hard as he wanted, until they were both ready to go again. The next time they lay gasping, he managed, "Surely two photo finishes in a row is some kind of record. Shall we go for three?" They were still giggling when Janis came into the room.

A great deal of creative work was accomplished by month's end. Janis and her team wrapped the recording session. Valerie sent a segment of the master video to Andy for his feedback regarding an album cover photo. He sent back a design showing

235

two baby grand pianos nestled together, shot from above with a cello lying across their narrow ends like a bridge. His email suggested he extract some images of the musicians from the master, for liner-notes photos. Janis liked the idea and nobody else objected; it would save them all time and keep the images consistent with the clips that were being prepared for release.

Reggie the pornographer sent a well-edited transcript of his phone interview with Geoffrey. Everyone in the Vaughn household read and approved it. Geoffrey sent his permission to publish promptly, and provided (upon request) a selfie he'd taken on the day of the interview. Reggie sent back a text: *One trusts you no longer look as though you've been flattened by a mountain*

Geoffrey replied: *The leg is a bastard. The face is recovered*

Thank God, the world needs that face. And does Macbeth sit on it?

My dear man, you'll have to buy me a drink before I answer that sort of question

Ring me when in London, I'll stand you a round of cocktails. And possibly a cockstand

Geoffrey giggled and showed the exchange to Niall. "He's making a pass."

"So he is." Niall gave the phone a narrow-eyed look. "If you would, sir." Geoffrey handed over the phone. Niall wrote *Mr. Galant, if in fact that is your name, which I take leave to doubt, please refrain from propositioning my husband. There are penalties for that here at Dunsinane. Yrs, the Thane*

Bring that sword of yours and you can exact any penalty you like, my juicy russet

236

Niall and Geoffrey both laughed out loud. "He's not shy, is he?" Geoffrey took the phone again. "Shall we have a drink with him?"

"In a very public place," Niall said. "Cheeky."

Geoffrey wrote once more: *London this year depends on my visa status. If extended, we'll go straight to tour from L.A. Must regretfully advise any future rendezvous will be well chaperoned. Yrs G. Anand*

In other words 'hands off.' Well you can't blame a fellow for trying. I shall follow your movements as the tides the moon. Yrs R. Galant p.s. tell your red king that IS my real name, cynical bugger, thx for intvw & will launch with fanfare

The first result of the interview was an email from Geoffrey's publisher with cautious approval. The caution was jettisoned when, by the following week, the post was flooded with comments. Nearly all were positive, and many begged for more detail on the forthcoming books. Sales of Geoffrey's last e-book and its paperback counterpart shot up. The week after that, the publisher sent their preference for order of publication. "They want the mountaineer first," Geoffrey told the household over dinner. "And since the article's been accepted, that's the snow forgiven."

Deborah sipped some wine. "How long do you get to finish the book?"

"They want it in June. I'll be poor company till it's done, I'm afraid."

"You're never poor company," Janis said. "Oh my God I just realized I'm on vacation until the tour starts."

Ed gave her a look. Janis wasn't a person who really took vacations. "What are you going to do with yourself?"

"No clue. Keep the new material in practice, I guess. Niall's going to be busy. Geoffrey's going to be busy. What the hell did I do before I was the tour monster?"

"You were a teacher," her father reminded her. "A good one. But that might be difficult to manage now. I was wondering," he said, and stopped. Deborah set her hand on his.

Niall and Geoffrey both focused in, because Ed very rarely left a sentence unfinished. Janis was also on alert. "What?"

"I had this idea," he said, almost diffidently. "One keyboard, four hands."

"Dad! You want me to *write* with you?! Holy shit!" Janis hurtled around the table, flung her arms around her father, and kissed his cheek. He was laughing with tears in his eyes. "You liked my variations that much?"

"You're so good. Could be fun?"

"Oh my God. So much fun. I love you."

"I love you too, honey."

238

Chapter 12
April 2019

"The great thing about this is that we get to decide where to go," Janis said, looking at the world map pinned to a cork board on the office wall. "And the bad thing is we have to decide where to go."

Niall nodded thoughtfully. Videos extracted from the master take would be released in May. The record company was planning to release the new album in June. A tour would, ideally, begin no later than September. Their proposed itinerary should be set as soon as possible. "You could wait till next year," he suggested. "See how the record does."

"Yeah, but I don't want to. I miss it."

They stared at the map for another minute. "The other problem is how to perform these pieces. Is it at all workable to take Tomás and Isabelle with us?"

Janis sighed. "It really isn't. They're both married with kids, they've both toured before, Tomás told me never again."

"Then you have to consider guest artists. Which means working with strangers at each concert."

"Gaahh."

"Or backing tracks." She made a face. Niall said, "Yes, I know. But the cost would be much lower. Your product could be very consistent, and you'd be promoting exactly the music that's on the record, with Tomás and Isabelle. You could still add solo pieces to the set list and play them entirely live."

Janis thought about it for a minute. Niall knew she'd been worrying about this aspect ever since deciding to collaborate. "If I want to do the whole set live, and I don't want to fuck around with guest artists, then I have to do whole new arrangements, basically." He nodded, encouraging her to talk this through. "I could see getting a decent pianist and a cellist to play what we've written. If we add another singer it's getting super complicated." Another pause for thought. "Dad said he liked Tomás for the record but he doesn't think that voice is essential for live performance. The cello he thought was key."

"The cello could play the Tomás melodies," Niall suggested. "Would you have to do much with the arrangements?"

"Not a lot," she admitted. "I could do smaller venues." It sounded like a question. The European tour had gone into some large concert halls. Niall knew that Janis preferred smaller, more intimate settings. "How many potentials do you have?"

"Easily thirty without North America." He'd begun assembling his list months ago.

"Holy shit. Thirty weeks?" They needed time to travel, time to get acquainted with the venues and guest artists, time to rehearse for each appearance.

"At least."

"Starting in South America." Janis was definite about that. She wanted to begin in Buenos Aires. "Literally around the world?"

"Begin in Argentina. Two concerts in Buenos Aires, six more on the continent, then to Mexico City." He tapped likely destinations on the map. "Across the Pacific to Australia and New Zealand. Japan and Hong Kong. Mumbai. Cape Town. Up into Europe, eleven dates there from Istanbul to Barcelona. End with four or five dates in the U.K. London,

Edinburgh, Dublin, perhaps Cardiff; and toss a coin for Cambridge or Oxford."

"Wow, Niall. What happens if you can't get a venue that makes sense for the itinerary?"

He shrugged. "We drop the city. Most of Europe you've done before, you know the audience is there, and there are countless good venues. I believe I should spend the next week doing nothing but setting a tentative calendar and making preliminary contacts. We might be able to announce the tour schedule at the same time the record is released."

"I would love that. The record company would love that. But then we need to come back to North America, I haven't toured here for two years."

"You could easily do thirty dates on this continent."

"Ugh, no, I hate most of it."

Niall laughed. "Ten? Bigger venues?"

"Yeah, maybe." She was staring at him now. "Your life is going to be a shitshow if you're wrangling guest artists *and* venues *and* travel. For the three of us. Do we need to get you an assistant?" Neither of them said the next obvious thing: adding another person to the road show meant a much higher probability of accidentally outing themselves.

Geoffrey finally spoke. He'd been sitting on the couch, listening, absorbing the scope of the project and falling in love with both of them all over again. "I could help." They both turned to look at him. "I've been thinking about the visa situation, and the public perception issue. If I worked for you too, darling, might it be simpler?" He directed the question to Janis and saw her instantly understand. "Pay me a token. Enough to make it a legal engagement. I can handle the travel end, I've a decade of experience and five languages. I'll have Spanish by the time we go."

"Too smart for your own good," she said. "What about your writing?"

"From the moment we're at the hotel to the moment we leave it, my time is my own."

"Are you sure, love?" Niall was feeling something between concern and relief. Perhaps a combination of the two. Running an operation of this complexity on his own had been a daunting prospect. "You are under contract, after all."

"The first two books will be delivered before we leave," Geoffrey said with confidence. "The last isn't due till December." Niall still looked concerned. "Sweetheart, I'm going with you anyway. Don't you think I'd like to be of some use?"

"Oh, you're going to be of use," Janis said. Geoffrey snickered. "I personally would like to say thank you, and you're hired, and I will get my lawyer on the engagement thing. Or Niall will." Niall made a sound of protest. "Okay, okay, I will. Aside from that, let me know when I need to do something other than rewrite these arrangements."

"You need to kiss me," Geoffrey said. She went over to the couch and did that. "Once more, with feeling, if you please." Janis laughed and complied. "Thank you. Would you send my husband this way now?"

It might have been coincidence that landed Niall and Geoffrey in their washroom not much later. Might have been, but wasn't. Geoffrey had opened the door and was getting a grip on his crutches when he looked up to see Niall leaning against the door frame. "Hello darling. I'll be out momentarily."

"No you won't." Niall stepped in, closed the door and locked it. "I've a sudden need, and not for the loo."

"Oh?" Geoffrey let the crutches fall and put both hands on the vanity for balance. He needed it; he was swamped with desire at the expression on his husband's face. "Blast. Will I need those?"

"I don't believe so." Body contact, and that mouth against the skin of his neck, and that voice vibrating through him like the avalanche. Geoffrey shivered. Niall said, "How is it that a single kiss can put all business but one entirely from my mind?" He was pushing Geoffrey's gym pants down, hands roaming front and back. Their eyes met in the mirror. "I tried to work. All I could think of was you."

Geoffrey let his weight go back onto Niall's chest, turning his head for a kiss. "How shall I serve you, my king."

"By letting me see your pleasure." Niall had Geoffrey in his hand, stroking. His other hand holding Geoffrey to him by the shoulder. "Give me your mouth. Your kiss."

The support, the control, the kiss. Niall lifted his head for a moment. They were both flushed and hot-eyed in the mirror. "God," Geoffrey breathed. "Will you not let me touch you?"

"Not yet. Oh, you beauty, look at you." Another kiss, deep and slow while Niall's hand worked its magic. Geoffrey had one hand on Niall's thigh, the other on Niall's wrist. He wanted to wrap that arm around Niall's neck and couldn't. *Sodding ribs*, he thought hazily, as Niall murmured, "Shall I speak thy pleasure?"

"Niall. I love you."

"You lovely creature. You fill my hand so perfectly. You sigh, thus. You shudder. Yes, that sound, like the beginning of a word. Christ, the scent of you. Will you now, you'll give it to me, there, my love, *now*." Niall kissed him again.

Geoffrey lay against his chest for another minute, breathless, gaze locked with Niall's in the mirror. "Jesus."

"I shall never have enough of you," Niall said conversationally. "It's clear to me now."

"You want me." That was obvious; Niall was rampant against Geoffrey's arse.

"Always. And I'll not be taking you, because the way I feel I'd break the rest of your ribs." A slight smile.

"Will you let me serve you as you've just served me?" Geoffrey turned himself around, pivoting on his good foot, deliberately not pulling up his gym pants, and undid Niall's jeans. He leaned against the vanity now. "God almighty, look at you. My tiger." That beautiful cock against his own belly, in his hand. Niall's mouth on his again, and then his breath in Geoffrey's hair. "Soon, sweetheart, I'll spread for you and you'll work us both to screaming. Won't you? But I'll bite the pillow, and you'll bite your lip, because to be quiet makes that tension so ravishing, doesn't it love, as you're quiet now." Niall had his head on Geoffrey's shoulder and both hands on the vanity, bracketing Geoffrey's hips. There was barely space between them for Geoffrey's hand to work. "You'll ravish me, and I'll spend to your hand, and you'll come with your teeth in my neck, Christ! Yes, like that." Niall was shuddering, gasping, spent. They stood there without moving for a minute more. Then kissed, washed their hands, and tidied themselves. When at length they left the washroom, they heard Ed and Deborah and Janis down in the study.

Niall followed Geoffrey's slow progress down the hall, gaze on the trace left by his mouth. Before they reached the study he said, "I've marked you."

Geoffrey smiled. "I meant you to."

Niall sent the proposed tour schedule to Randa, and Janis sent the new employment agreements, before the end of the week. The next phase was negotiating with the record company about backing, and possibly seeking a sponsor. But they all took a day off to go down to West L.A.; Andy had written to remind Niall and Geoffrey that the 'Tempest' photo shoot was ready for review.

He greeted them outside, stared at the crutches, and said, "In the house." He pointed them at the door and then went up into the studio. By the time they were inside he was back with a big laptop. They all sat down at the dining table. "I wanted to get you in here because my life got complicated again. I want to hang this in June and show it for a couple of weekends before I have to fuck off to Michigan for this movie shoot with Victor. It was going to be May but I'm doing a thing."

Janis said, "What thing?"

"A dance thing. I did this interview soliciting a dance partner and actually got one. We're doing a performance at Chrome next month. So I'm getting flogged through this routine every other day till then. Now. Why is Ariel temporarily flightless?"

Geoffrey told Andy all about the avalanche while he gave them coffee. Then he asked about Janis and her upcoming album, and that led to Niall giving a status report on the tour plans. Andy wanted to know when they would be back in Los Angeles. Janis said, "If this whole thing comes off, maybe next summer. Or next fall. Not soon, anyway. I'd like to stay in England for a while again once we wrap the U.K. I'm going to buy a place there." Niall and Geoffrey glanced at each other, startled; this was news to them.

"Excellent," Andy said. "Let's get comfortable and look at some pictures. These guys are so goddamned hot together, I can't stand it." When he opened the file, they were surprised to see so many images. He set the display to slideshow mode without comment. It seemed the camera had been firing almost continuously as they went in and out of requested positions. "The camera sees more than I do," he said after a while, noticing their surprise. "Sometimes it's the transition that produces the perfect image. Or a movement the subject makes based on their own response to what's happening. Like 'this rough magic,' the one I flagged. I don't think this can be improved on, personally, but there's a ton of shots for that line so tell me what you think." He stopped the slideshow and selected an image for full-screen display.

"Holy fuck," Janis said. "What's the line again?"

"'This rough magic I here abjure,'" Niall said after clearing his throat. "In the play, it's Prospero giving up magic, and the rule of his island, to return to his place in the world." That was definitely not the subtext of the image.

Geoffrey was seated on the floor, right leg folded and left knee up. Niall reclined over that right leg, supported by Geoffrey's right arm. Geoffrey's left arm was draped over his raised knee. They both appeared to be nude. The wizard's robe was wound minimally across Niall's hips. Their heads were turned toward each other. Niall's eyes were nearly closed; his expression spoke of exhausted satisfaction. Geoffrey's gaze, equally satisfied but full of power, was directed at the camera.

Janis said, "The ring. He has your ring now." One of Prospero's ornaments was on Ariel's left hand.

"I directed that. I didn't direct Geoffrey to look at the camera." Andy was smiling.

"It's like Prospero gave his magic to Ariel. I need to see this whole thing again now that I know what the punchline is. My dad needs to see this. This is a fucking concert, right here."

Geoffrey couldn't remember why he'd looked at the camera at all, let alone in such a way. "I had no idea. Was that something my brain stem retrieved from your earlier direction?"

Andy made a *pfft* sound. "I don't know how, because I didn't know any of this shit was going to happen. But once you see this, you see the whole shoot leading up to it. Feeding into it. Ariel conquering. It's such a fucking cliffhanger."

"Yes! Exactly!" Janis was excited. "Is he going to keep Prospero, is he going to let him go, is he going to love him, is he going to kill him."

"Is he going to clap him up in a cloven pine," Niall said. "My God."

Janis said, "What were you thinking, Geoffrey? Where did that look come from?"

"I don't recall. I might have been thinking, we're nearly done, thank God, we can get out of these dance belts and have at each other." Everyone else laughed. "But also, I think, I did feel powerful. The gold, and

247

that ring. I felt *armored*. And Niall's position was so abandoned."

Niall said, "You remember, love, a time when you suggested you might amend the text."

"I do."

"I think we have."

"Frankly, the whole rest of the play is a waste of time," Janis said. Niall and Geoffrey both made sounds of laughing protest. "I need a piano and I need it now."

"Possess thyself in patience," Geoffrey said. "We need to see Andy's fifteen. If you've chosen this one," he said to their host, "I'm quite sure the rest will tell the story perfectly."

"Okay, well." Andy seemed almost embarrassed. "The truth is I had the other fourteen selected and then fell over this one and thought goddammit, because it totally does change the story. I have to go back through. Do you want to do that now? I could open a bottle. I don't have to dance any more today."

"I want to see," Janis said. "And I want a drink."

Niall gave Andy a semi-apologetic look. "It appears opening a bottle is in order."

Andy made to stand up. "In the fridge. Only be a minute."

"I'll fetch it," Geoffrey said. He went to the kitchen, selected a bottle of champagne, opened it. Took down glasses from the rack over the counter, and commenced service while listening to Andy talk through the solo portraits. *What would Reggie say*, he thought, and almost laughed again. He took a glass to Janis. Without even looking at the screen, he said, "Andy, the Prospero solo simply must be the nude one. You're hanging it as the conclusion, yes? Stripped bare, foundered, wrecked. But not without hope." Niall was looking at him with eyebrows up.

"Wait a minute. There was a nude one? How did I miss that?" Janis sounded annoyed. All the men laughed.

"I wasn't nude," Niall said. "It's implied. And there's more than one, so perhaps the writer could deliver unto us some fizz, and then I'll be soothed for this disastrous turn of events." Geoffrey brought him a glass, kissed him, stroked a hand through his hair and went for the next glass.

"This one." Andy sounded certain. Geoffrey set down the glass. The image was Niall on the floor, bare except for jewelry and the robe across his hips. Twisted away from his folded legs, propped on his hands. His head hung low but he looked up at the camera with a slight smile and narrowed eyes. The expression that said 'I'll have you.'

"Yes. That one." Geoffrey went back for his own glass, not even minding the awkwardness of the crutch. "I like that look."

"Honey, everyone on planet Earth is going to like that look." Andy drank half of his champagne. "Okay. Back to the beginning."

May 2019

Niall was frowning as he listened to the person on the phone. He gave Geoffrey a sideways glance before he spoke. "I'm not sure I understand you. I'm not an actor. No, intentionally." He laughed. "Oh, I see. Red told me he knew you, that you'd worked together many times. He sent you that link? All right. Well I have plenty to say on that subject. You're certain they'd care to hear it from me? Ah. Soon, yes. Janis is preparing to launch the new tour, we haven't heard yet if Geoffrey's visa will be extended, and if not we'll need to get back to England. Yes, we'll all go, from here it's mine to manage. That'll do. All right. See you then." He disconnected and looked at Geoffrey. "That was Tanith Salazar. Red gave her my number. She's teaching a senior seminar in the drama department at this university, and wants me to come in and tell people why it's all right not to be an actor."

Geoffrey laughed for half a minute. Once he recovered, he said, "You're to be an example of the brilliant amateur?"

"More a cautionary tale, I believe. You know I've had casting agents up my arse ever since that effing video went up. No one seems to believe me when I say I don't want to be an actor."

Geoffrey stretched luxuriously, knowing Niall was watching. The call had come in at a perfect time: after satisfaction. "Everyone here wants to be in the movies."

"It's a wretched existence, they're all mad." Niall was smiling, as much from the flattering phone call as from the sight of Geoffrey's healthy body and the memory of their recent activity. "If you feel as well as you look, perhaps we should see if Janis wants to go dancing."

"Darling, Janis *always* wants to go dancing." Geoffrey swung his legs off the bed and stood up. The still-healing bones acknowledged his weight with the merest sigh of protest. "I am not ready to run," he admitted. "But to dance? I should have to feel a great deal worse to say no."

"Then I'll go find her. You can have the shower first." Niall had finished dressing. He came over for a quick kiss. "She may want you later."

"I hope she does." They'd been engaging in certain activities for weeks, but with a considerable degree of care. Only today had Geoffrey felt it safe to kneel. Now he reconsidered. "Actually, love, if you don't mind?"

Niall turned away from the door. "What is it?"

"If she's free, I suspect I'm more able now than I will be after dancing." The thought of it had him readying again.

Niall noticed; he crossed the room, bent his head to kiss the side of Geoffrey's neck, and brushed his fingers down that bare body. Filled his hand for a lingering moment. "Able, is it? I've half a mind to deprive her for another day. Do tell her that, would you?" He kissed Geoffrey's mouth, then reluctantly backed away. "You stunner. When you can bear my weight I shall *plow* you." He watched Geoffrey's reaction, shook off his own response – enough, at least, to proceed through the house – and left the room.

Geoffrey slung on his robe, went to freshen up, and was back in the bedroom a few minutes later. If Janis wasn't engaged on the piano, he suspected she would join him soon. And so it proved. He was stretching, thinking indiscriminately lustful thoughts, when she entered. "Hi cutie. Niall said you might have something for me." She closed the door. He lay back on the bed, letting the robe fall open. "Oh. That's very nice." Geoffrey laughed. Janis tore her clothes off and joined him within seconds, going for a kiss, letting him roll her over.

He had one hand between her legs. "Janis, darling. Did Niall say we might go dancing tonight?"

"He might have. God, keep doing that."

251

He kissed her again. "I want to do more. I didn't want to get to the end of today without doing more. I've missed you." He was moving against her slickness. "You've missed me too."

"Oh God Geoffrey. That thing we did the other day worked pretty well but – *Jesus*."

"I like you on top," he said against her neck. "I like you any way I can have you. But I've missed this." He sank into her, heard her breath go out, watched her head go back, and noted that his injuries had very little to say about it. Janis hooked a leg over his hip and pressed up against him, matching his rhythm. "You priceless beauty." He kissed her again. "I love you."

"I love you too. Geoffrey, holy shit, *oh*," she curled up against him. "Fuck!" Her pulse sent him over too. She was still holding him tight as they both relaxed. "That was too fast."

He laughed. "Tomorrow. We'll see how long we can last tomorrow." They lay together for a few minutes, talking and kissing. Then Janis sat up. "What's the time?"

"Time for me to go finish the email I was in the middle of writing." She patted his thigh. "Stop giggling. Niall had that look, you know the one. The one that says if you don't go get yours, I'll have mine again. I mean, there was clearly not a moment to lose."

Geoffrey was still giggling. "I've quite thoroughly debauched the pair of you, haven't I?"

"Yes! Yes you have. Thanks for that." She kissed him again, got dressed, and went out. Geoffrey put himself together and went to shower. It was so unspeakably good to be out of the cast, off the

252

crutches. So good to be able to walk freely in the garden, and to drive. Each week since he'd left the wheelchair, there had been greater freedom. And since that talk with Deborah, and the ensuing hour-long talk with Niall, so much greater understanding. Geoffrey supposed that was, after all, why talk therapy so often worked: merely articulating the problem helped to point either to a solution or to the fact that nothing really needed to be done. That time – as it proved in their case – was the best remedy. He'd written blisteringly of the second profiling experience, decided not to let it trouble him further, and gone on to write a truly filthy letter for Reggie. He shared that with Niall, who laughed and suggested that they act it out. Someday soon, they would. And someday soon, the time would be right to ask Niall about those buried fears. But for tonight, there was tango.

Niall asked Geoffrey to come with him to the university, to speak to Tanith's students. Geoffrey was doubtful. "Won't I be a distraction?"

"No doubt they won't have seen anyone as lovely as you before, but they'd better learn to cope. In any event it's for me. My nerves, darling."

"You're daft, darling. But if you want me, you'll have me. As ever." Niall seized him and kissed him. Geoffrey was laughing. "Madman."

"Mad about you. I give thanks for you daily, you know that." Niall still had a hand in Geoffrey's hair. He stroked it down his neck, down his back, and to his waist. Then he stood back a little, letting that hand trail forward over the ribs that had been broken and now were whole again. "I re-live that day we didn't hear from you. Those terrible twenty-four hours. I never thought I could be more frightened than I was

253

watching Oliver die." His voice was shaky. "But there it is, every hour without word was such a torture."

Geoffrey set his hands on Niall's face. They all knew it would be a while before those memories faded. "My precious love. It was a dreadful day for all of us. I've no desire to be parted from you, ever. So I promise. My future travels will be conducted with all possible attention to safety. Hearing the snow, all I could think was, will I ever see him again." Niall tipped his forehead against Geoffrey's. "I love her too, you know that. But it was you on my mind when I thought it might be over."

"And that is why," Niall said, "I need you for this ridiculous seminar." Geoffrey smiled, kissed him, and nodded.

Looking around the room, Niall knew he'd been right to bring Geoffrey. Tanith was sitting at the other end of the long table. In between them were a dozen very young-looking seniors, all hoping to hear that there was life beyond college dramatics. Or perhaps they were hoping to hear that it was all right to continue dreaming. Niall turned his head for a moment, finding Geoffrey in a chair off to the side of the room. He held a notepad and a pen. Niall had no doubt that something about this scene would make its way into a fiction. "Good afternoon," he said. "Has Ms. Salazar told you why I'm here?" There was a murmur of assent. "Why d'you suppose she asked me, in particular?" An exchange of confused looks. No one seemed brave enough to venture a guess. "Tanith, if you would."

"I asked Mr. Phelps here today because he is a person who has some theatrical training and considerable theatrical talent, who has chosen a different path. You saw that video and a couple of you asked why he isn't a star. I thought his reasons might be illuminating for some of you. He is not here to talk you into anything, or out of anything. You think you're ready for the rejection, the insecurity, the poverty. You all know the odds against success as an actor. You've heard my story. Before you go out and start banging your heads against all those closed doors, I wanted you to hear another."

The wave of discouragement, defiance, and resentment was almost palpable. Niall made eye contact with Tanith, confirming that she'd felt it too. They almost smiled at each other. Then he shook his head slightly and said, "I was at university reading history. I am the first in my family to go to university, and so far still the only. I was recruited into the Oxford University Dramatic Society early on because I was tall and had a good voice. I also have a good memory, which for an actor is even more essential than the other things. What I don't have, and never had, is the desire for an actor's life. I was in it for the boys." Scattered laughter. "My first love was a professional actor, a member of the Royal Shakespeare Company. By the time we met I was already working as a tour manager. I'd drifted off the stage because what I really liked to do is manage things. I'm good at it. I was a decent actor," he added, forestalling the question he saw quivering on more than one student's tongue. "But there are countless decent actors. The hard truth is that there are many, many talented people in the world. You need talent, craft, connections, *and* desire. I didn't have the desire. Yes?"

"What was it like being with a professional actor?"

Niall thought, *Ah*. He'd hoped for that question, because he wanted Geoffrey to hear the answer. "It could be difficult. Oliver was one of those who can inhabit a role to such an extent that he seems a different person. That meant, for me, *living* with a different person. It's tremendously wearing. It was worst through rehearsals. Once a play was running, he was able to leave it at the theatre. And I wasn't in the sweat-box with him, so I could always breathe. I knew, you see, that this was his job. It was a thing he did, not a thing he was. And I wasn't living it with him, so I could get outside it, and wait for it to pass." There were some very thoughtful student faces. "I was nearly my best self with Oliver. But as much as I loved him, there was an element of self-defense. Not because of his personality. Because of his profession." A reaction from almost everyone. A mouth opened, then closed. "Yes?"

"You're married now." Eyes going to Geoffrey.

"Indeed I am. Mr. Anand is always himself, a self which happens to be perfect for me. And thus I am my best self with him."

"When did you know you'd rather be a tour manager?"

"After my very first gig. It was a weekend, taking an actor from London to Bath for a benefit. I had her itinerary, I knew where she needed to be and when, I knew what she needed at each end. I was given the means to provide what she needed, and I did it perfectly. She was appreciative because the last time she'd had a handler, he botched it entirely and she barely made the gig."

"What did you like so much about it?"

"There was nothing subjective about it. I had my brief. If I executed it well, she gave her performance, the hosting company was happy. She was happy. My employer was happy. And there was no one reviewing me to say, oh that bloody ginger's eyebrow was up when it should have been down." More, less tentative laughter. "Also, frankly, being out on the road, the opportunities for vice are legion." A solid laugh.

"What's the worst thing about what you do?"

Niall glanced at Geoffrey. "The worst thing is the travel, if you hate travel. I happen to like it. If you like it, the worst thing is trying to have a relationship. Until Oliver died, I only worked in the United Kingdom. The four countries together are smaller than California. I could be anywhere on a tour and still see him regularly. I could go to him, or he to me."

"Was he your husband?"

"He would have been, had it been legal. We were three months away from a license when he died." Another palpable wave, this one of sympathy. "And then I fled to America. For years I couldn't face the thought of another relationship. I could barely face the thought of living. But I had a friend, and she pulled me through. Now I work for her, and we're about to go out on what may be the longest tour yet. This time I'll have Mr. Anand with me." Again he glanced over at Geoffrey, whose gaze was like a tow-rope of braided love. Niall took a deep breath and returned his own gaze to the group of students.

He didn't know what they could possibly be getting out of this, but until Tanith gave him a sign that he was off track, he'd continue. "My employer gave me permission to tell you this. She was in a long-distance relationship for years. She only saw him during the summers, or for a day or two over a holiday break. He was jealous of her friendship with me. She told him, for everything but a hug, there's a battery-powered alternative." All the girls in the room laughed, including Tanith. "But when you want a hug, you want a bloody *hug*." Another solid laugh from everyone. "It has to come from another human being. I can't emphasize enough the importance of touch. Why do you think so many entertainers' relationships break up? It's not for lack of love. It's loneliness. It's being apart. It's being *away*." A few of the students shifted uneasily. "Yes?"

"Do you think infidelity starts there?"

"Some people aren't built for fidelity. Others simply don't care for it. So not always, but often. I haven't had that experience myself but I've spoken with many, many artists whose careers required extensive travel and whose progress was littered with the corpses of failed relationships." Some people wanted to laugh, he could tell, but it would have been the kind of laugh that goes with feeling sick. "Plenty of other professionals too. The same problem exists for ships' pilots or diplomats or soldiers."

"What do you do if there's no one to touch?"

"You go slowly mental, and perhaps you drink too much, until you find someone who doesn't disgust you, and then you fall into bed together." More laughter, mixed with sounds of disbelief and disagreement. "Or perhaps you're one of the bright ones, and you go find a dance class."

"Tanith said that!"

"She's a teacher for a reason, you know." Niall checked in with her. It appeared he had permission to wind things up. "How many of you here are uncoupled? Raise your hands." Half of the students put their hands up. "When's the last time someone hugged you? Someone not your mother." There were

258

mumbled responses ranging from 'a month' to 'last summer' to 'can't remember.' Niall gave Geoffrey an incredulous look. *These poor bastards are doomed.* "Well, get on with it!"

All the students were staring at him, clearly startled, not sure if he'd meant what they thought he meant. Tanith said impatiently, "You idiots have known each other for four years. Get up off your asses and let's see some hugging." There was laughter, and heads were shaking 'no,' but everyone stood up, and everyone started hugging. There were soft words, some more laughter, and then a stifled sob. Three people started crying. Niall stood up and went to Geoffrey. They sidled down toward Tanith, who was also standing. "Can you believe these kids?" she said softly. The students were milling around, looking for someone new to hug. No one was left alone. "This is great."

"Is this what you wanted?"

"I didn't even know what I fucking wanted. I was hoping something about your experience would help them get a sense of what the acting life can mean. I think I got exactly what I wanted."

"And all this from a clifftop frolic in Malibu?"

She looked up at him. "Do you think Red Warner would trust his million-dollar neck to just anybody? Mr. Anand, thanks for coming with Niall today." They shook hands. "I hear you had a close call."

"A close encounter of the snowy kind. I was very lucky."

"I also hear the clifftop frolic was your idea."

"Well, I'd seen the fight, you understand. They were so," he searched for the word, "so *grand*. It wanted a grand setting. I'd been out there often, learning to surf."

"It was a great idea. The second I saw that video I thought, well, Red's finally going to get the sword and sorcery epic I've been promising him for years, and I'm not going to have to write it, so yay." Geoffrey laughed. Tanith was smiling.

The students were still hugging, talking, and in one case crying. Geoffrey asked, "What is your next project?"

"Not a hundred percent sure yet. I'm working on a stage thing for the summer, a dance concert, not much of a script. We'll probably film it because we can – I've got all these GoPros now – but there may be an actual movie in it at some point. Anyway, I'd better shovel these guys out, there's another seminar in half an hour. Thanks, Niall. Give my regards to Janis."

"It was a pleasure, truly, and we will." They said their goodbyes and worked their way out of the room. Niall was holding Geoffrey's hand. When they were out of the building and heading for the car he said, "Have I mentioned how deeply grateful I am that you'll be on tour with us?"

"Once or twice. Have I mentioned how much I'm looking forward to it?"

"Once or twice." They looked at each other, both smiling. Niall unlocked the car. "What adventures we've had. Have you written any new filth for your mate Reggie?"

They got into the car. "As a matter of fact I have. Buy me a drink and I might let you read it."

"If I buy you a bottle, will you let me act it out with you?" A decidedly wicked look from Niall as he started the engine.

Geoffrey pretended to consider it. "This scene might not go for less than Macallan 25."

260

"Extortionist." Niall pulled out his phone.

"Do you need directions back to Glendale?"

Niall gave him a look. "No. I'm after directions to the nearest source of Macallan 25." Geoffrey was still laughing when they exited the parking lot.

He was more serious later, when he invited Niall to go for a stroll in the back garden after dinner. They each took a modest glass of Scotch with them. "This is an exceptional tipple," Niall remarked after a few minutes of silence. "Well worth the extortionate price, particularly in view of certain promises."

"Indeed." Geoffrey walked on. He could tell from Niall's voice that he was relaxed. "Did you mean to tell those students so much about Oliver?"

Niall gave him a sharp and cognizant glance. "I did. Tanith didn't provide me much guidance, only a vague request for a reality check. I couldn't speak to having been a professional actor. What I could speak to was the charge that profession laid on our relationship."

"I had the sense that they had all thought, more or less deeply, of how they personally would deal with the trials of the acting life. And after you spoke, that they hadn't at all considered how everyone else in their lives would deal with it."

"Precisely. They are young, and therefore egomaniacs. Amplify that with ambition. I suspected none of them had given a thought to the effects on their future partners. I don't know that they fully understood me. But clearly you did."

"I'm quite a few years in advance." They were still strolling. "It meant a lot, you saying that your relationship with Oliver wasn't perfect. That you

261

loved him anyway, and to a degree in spite of his approach to his profession."

"Mind you, I don't know that his approach was a conscious choice. It may have been simply how his talent manifested. And he was talented. As you are," Niall added. "The way you can write amazes me. It pours out of you sometimes. But you share it, so beautifully. You can talk about it, and even invite us to participate. You make it fun for all of us."

"All the same, I do need a great deal of time to myself. There's time when I'm unsocial, or silent. There will be times when I'm away." Geoffrey stopped walking. They stared at each other for a minute. "Do you truly think I'm perfect for you?"

Niall took his free hand and led him over to the garden bench. "Sit with me, darling." He took a moment to savor the last mouthful of Scotch, then set the glass under the bench. "Yes. For the past eleven months we have been in an extraordinary situation, facing extraordinary challenges. For not a single second of that time have you been less than perfect." He leaned in for a kiss, wiped away a tear. "My love. You have made possible a life that I thought could never be. And you've done it with such grace, such generosity. Such good humor. Janis and I have asked of you a staggering level of commitment, and you have not faltered for a single second." Geoffrey set his own empty glass on the ground and put his arms around Niall. They held each other tight. "It's possible that these past eleven months have been the most difficult we'll ever have. Having got through this, I doubt the next ten years will seem a challenge at all." He drew back enough to study Geoffrey for a moment. "Have you been in doubt?"

"It's only I've never been perfect for anyone before. And in January," he began, then stopped.

Niall thought back. *Hell.* "In January you said you would stay with me." He kissed Geoffrey's forehead. "And I, being thick as two planks, didn't say the same. Well I'll say it now. Mr. Anand, you are my true love, and should our lady ever suggest that either of us were no longer essential to her happiness, you would still be essential to mine. This marriage ring," he kissed Geoffrey's hand, "is for you and me, darling. The two of us. Forever." He rested his cheek against his husband's hair, tears stinging his own eyes as he listened to the shaky breaths against his chest. After a while, when those breaths evened out, he said, "Only do simply *say* when you need to be alone, won't you? This business of burying yourself in a thousand cubic yards of snow was a bit extreme."

Geoffrey coughed out a laugh, sniffed, and said, "Once the tour begins I'll have plenty of time alone, won't I?"

"Not alone, sweetheart, actually. Never alone. But left in peace, yes."

"Can I tell you a secret." Geoffrey's voice was barely audible, a murmur directed to Niall's collarbone.

"You can tell me anything."

"I know. That's one of the reasons I love you. Don't tell Janis." He moved away enough to make eye contact. "Promise."

Niall was only mildly concerned. "I promise."

Geoffrey leaned in again, so no one else could possibly hear, and not even Sherlock Holmes could have read his lips. "I can't bloody wait to have two bedrooms again." He tucked his face into the curve of

Niall's neck and smiled at the silent laughter that went on for the next minute.

"And a king bed," Niall said when he could. "The parents required no adjustment at all compared with that queen. I've been tempted to kick that effing footboard across the room more than once."

"You nearly have," Geoffrey pointed out. "I shall make that a non-negotiable requirement when I do the bookings. Connecting rooms, yes?"

"Wherever possible." Niall waited to see if there were any further specifications. After a moment, "Is this the entirety of your demands? Because if so I have one of my own."

"What's your pleasure, my king."

"What I require of you, my spirit, is that you instantly and without reserve confess to any discontent. If I found you had gone without something you need in order to accommodate me or Janis, a great deal of my pleasure would be void. I told you once that her well-being is essential to my own happiness. So is yours, and as noted previously, it is you who are my husband. If a time comes when I must choose, I'll choose you." It was a realization slow to arrive, but Niall was content with it. He and Janis had both healed, grown so much stronger, in the past year. Neither of them would break now.

Geoffrey took a moment to compose himself again. "All I really need is a quiet room from time to time, Janis, and you. You most of all."

"Am I then also perfect for you?"

Geoffrey lifted his head, laid a hand lightly on Niall's face, and kissed him with a degree of fervor that seemed to answer 'yes.' When they separated they were both breathing hard. "From the first, in

264

every way." Another kiss. "I could not have committed myself to this had you not been so exactly what I wanted, and proved so exactly what I needed." Yet more kisses. "I shall write you a sonnet. A book of sonnets, each devoted to one of your perfections. My God, how I love you."

"I love you." Quite some time passed before they separated again. "This bench does not conduce to amorous embraces." Niall shifted.

Geoffrey laughed and sat back. "Let's go in. I believe I owe you a spot of role-playing. You'll find the part no challenge. I based it on you, after all."

Part IV

Chapter 13
May 2019

Niall woke to soft voices at dawn, as he often did. He woke slowly, which was less common. He lay with his back to Geoffrey's, drowsily half-listening, and only gradually realized that he wasn't hearing the usual pillow talk.

"Are you sure you're okay with this?" Janis, and not in the tone that meant some proposed molestation.

"Darling, I'm madly excited about it. I've never been to South America at all. To think that I'll go with you and Niall on such a grand adventure, it's marvelous."

"You're going to be working, though."

A short pause, mostly likely for a kiss. "Sweetheart, I'm always working. I know it doesn't look like much sometimes." Janis laughed under her breath. "There is literally nothing different about this from one of my usual research trips, aside from the length of it and the fact I'm booking three tickets and two rooms instead of one and one."

"Okay." Another pause. "Okay. What about Niall."

"You can't be serious. He adores you."

"I know. I feel like I've dragged him all over everywhere and I can't believe he's not tired of it."

Niall kept his breath quiet and slow with difficulty. Janis clearly wanted Geoffrey's reassurance in this moment, not his. *Tell her what I told you, angel eyes.* "Do you know what he told me, love?"

"What."

266

"He told me that meeting you was the best thing that ever happened to him."

"Oh." Pleased. "Wait." Worried. "What about you? He's insanely in love with you. How can –"

"Sshh, hush, darling. He said meeting me was, quote, the best thing that ever happened to *us*."

"Oh." Another pause. "It really was. Mmm. Uh wait, nope." A giggle. "No, I have to get up. Really. Geoffrey I have to go pee, don't make me laugh." Niall heard her get out of bed, still giggling, obviously trying to stifle it. The rustle of the robe, footsteps toward the door. He watched through his eyelashes as she went out.

"How much of that did you hear?" Geoffrey sounded amused.

Niall rolled over and smiled at him. "From just before 'madly excited.' It was rather a different madly excited from the usual. What gave me away?"

"A certain rigidity, rather different from the usual, at the notion you might be tired of traveling with Janis."

"She's worn out," Niall said. "This record took it out of her, and all the business. I'm almost glad we haven't heard about your visa. I think a couple of months to ourselves in London would do her a world of good. And I'd like to see people before we're on the move for eight months."

"As would I. Shall we pounce on her when she comes in? We need to hear about this idea of buying a place, too." Janis hadn't mentioned it after their day with Andy, and they'd both had enough else to do that they hadn't brought it up.

"You realize there's not a snowball's chance she'd let us contribute." Niall hitched himself up and

267

leaned against the headboard. For once Geoffrey's soft eyes and warm body weren't tempting him past the point of talk. "You could hear her to Land's End when I suggested paying rent last year. It was oh no, I have to have a place, there are things I want and I can afford them, it doesn't cost me a dime extra to have you, on and bloody on."

Geoffrey laughed. He leaned over and kissed Niall's bare thigh, then sat up himself. "Sometime today I have a new scene to show you. But we'll talk to Janis now. Kiss me though." Niall touched his face, rubbed his knuckles across his stubble, and kissed him. "I love you."

"I love you. Thank you for telling her that."

"It's true all around, isn't it? Meeting the two of you was the best thing that ever happened to me." Another kiss. They were sitting quietly, holding hands, when Janis came in. "See who woke up."

"Hi Niall. You look like you have something to say." She sat cross-legged on the end of the bed.

"I wondered if I could beg a favor."

Janis looked surprised. "Anything. Of course."

"I know there's still a chance Geoffrey's visa extension could come through. But would you mind going back to England next month anyway? I'd like to see my family before we're off around the world."

"Sure! Sure, no problem." She looked relieved. Niall decided he'd pitched it right. She was worried he wasn't getting enough out of their situation, so let her think this was only for him.

"Excellent. Thank you so much. We'll set it up. Then I thought I'd ask you about this notion of buying a place. You haven't mentioned it since we were with Andy."

"Oh yeah. I kind of wanted to keep it on the down low until I had a better sense of the possibility. I'd been thinking about it for a while because of you two. England's your home, you have important people there. It's great you like my parents, but I like yours too and we all need time with our people. The thing is, that place we lived last year? It was such a great location. The right amount of space, with the piano, walking distance to everything we needed. Anyway, I contacted the agent about getting it again sometime, and he wrote back to say it was on the market. And since then we've been going back and forth because I don't know the first fucking thing about buying property in England and he doesn't know the first fucking thing about Americans, and long story short nothing's really happened because we're clueless."

"Sounds like a question for a banker," Geoffrey said. "I know one or two of those."

She stared at him for a second. "For fuck's sake." Both men laughed. "Why do I ever not ask you guys about stuff? Between you, you basically know everything. Or you know somebody else who knows everything. Whatever, yeah. Could you throw the question at your dad, or your brother, or both of them?"

"I could, and I will. Right after breakfast. For which I am now hungry."

"Me too." Janis crawled up on hands and knees to kiss each man. "I love you guys. What else do we have to do today?"

"We have some business to attend to," Niall said. "I believe you have an appointment with your father in the study." They all got out of bed to start the day.

Geoffrey's actual work for the tour wouldn't begin until the backing and sponsorship were contracted, and the venues confirmed. He was nearly done with the first novel, thought he'd wait until they were in London before he went all-in on the second, and therefore spent some time thinking about things between him and Niall and Janis.

They were all still using the journal. Janis had written, most recently, a rather hilarious summary of her reactions to the 'Tempest' photos. Niall had contributed a list of the twenty most unpredictably awful touring failures he'd witnessed. Geoffrey added a comment to that: 'Only witnessed?' Niall then added a reply comment: 'I shall never admit to anything that might alter your perception of my perfection.' After which Geoffrey had to go find him and prove that nothing ever could. He also added a sonnet he'd written for Niall. Someone left a cryptic comment on that; it was only 'OMG,' so it had to have been Janis.

When he thought about things unsaid, he realized there was a topic they'd left unexplored for many months. It was something he'd examined on his own, because he was the only one of the three who seemed to have had this thought in the beginning. In view of their upcoming life change – he couldn't think of the world tour in any other way – he thought it should be addressed. So on a day when Janis and Niall were in Century City arguing with Randa about the details of the sneak-preview benefit concert, Geoffrey took the journal laptop out into the garden and wrote.

> Once upon a time I thought it would be lovely to have a child. Since then I've spoken at length with my brother, and learned things that nearly broke my heart. I'd no idea, simply none, that he and Parris came so close to disaster. Wellington told me that

they were all right after the first child. Exhausted, confused, and not as they were before, but all right. After the second, Parris was terribly ill for months. Dangerously depressed. They moved to her parents' house, she saw a counselor, and gradually they found a new way to be. Even less as they were before, but together, and moving forward. Parris went back to work, and was happier. They hired a nanny when they moved to their own flat. Wellington told me, we never knew this would so change us. It changed us in ways we couldn't have imagined, let alone predicted. We will never be the same. A child is not a pet. It's a unique person, and every day is a new decision to get wrong, or something new that must be done and may be done wrong. Each decision, each action, is so terrifyingly consequential. He says, we can hardly remember each other sometimes. They see a counselor now together, not because of depression, but for a quiet hour to speak with each other. To find each other again. When I thought of having a child, I never thought of these things. I realized I did think of a child as a sort of pet, something that would add to our household but not really change it. I don't want to change it. I don't want to give up travel. I don't want to be in a position where I cannot – literally cannot – say 'sorry love I'm writing.' I don't, frankly, want to have to put on clothes to go from bedroom to kitchen, or to cease misuse of the dining table. What we have is extraordinary and wonderful and I wouldn't change it for the world.

For a couple of days there were no new entries. Geoffrey suspected Niall and Janis had both read his, and supposed they were thinking about it. Then a note appeared that made him laugh so much that Deborah asked him what on earth had happened. He said, "I'm sorry, pet, I can't tell you or I'll be instantly throttled." She made an oh-I-see face, stifled a laugh, and invited him to the kitchen for a snack. The note was:

> OMG that dining-table thing every time we're sitting there with Mom and Dad I think IF THEY ONLY KNEW. And then I think OMG WHAT IF THEY DO.

After sending another 'letter from the road' to Reggie, which resulted in another flirty exchange, Geoffrey had an idea that he took to Janis and Niall. "You haven't done an interview since last fall. There's so much news. Has Randa tried to set anything up?"

Janis shook her head. "We're assuming there will be press at the sneak preview, and I'll do some follow-up after that. It'll all have to do with the album and the tour. I told her I'm walking out if there's a single question about you and me and Niall in Mammoth."

"The questions about your personal life won't stop," Niall said. "Your posts get a lot of attention."

"Yeah." She made an 'eh' face. "I am not scared of this, you know that. I love you and I love our life and eventually it'll blow open. Probably because I say or do something indiscreet, because you two are like clams. I'm okay with that if you are. I just don't want to deal with it right now. In L.A."

"What would you think," Geoffrey said slowly, "of speaking with our friend the pornographer. Not to blow it open, as you say. Simply to address our household arrangements in a way that will satisfy most people. Tell them our roles in your business."

"But not in my life?" Janis seemed unconvinced. She quoted the movie 'Silk Stockings.' "There's absolutely no truth to the rumors, we're just good friends?"

"Mr. Galant is sharp," Niall said. "And he's half in love with Geoffrey, which makes him perceptive. It's my sense that he values the connection. That being taken seriously, by Geoffrey, has secured us his loyalty. Should you also choose to trust him, I believe that loyalty would extend to you as well."

"Should we advertise the album on his site?" She was half-smiling now. "I mean, it is pretty sexy music."

"Yes it is. Particularly 'Angel Eyes.'" Geoffrey took her hand. "Only if you think it's wise. You saw the transcript he provided for my interview." It hadn't been solely a transcript. Reggie had provided a concise introduction with Geoffrey's biography and publishing history, as well as a conclusion linking to news coverage of the avalanche.

"He's impressively literate for a pornographer." Niall snorted. Janis nudged him. "Well, but seriously."

"Have you read 'Othello'?" It sounded like such a non sequitur that she blinked. Niall said, "The part where Iago is describing the fictitious scene in which Cassio caresses him as if he were Desdemona?"

"Oh! Oh yeah. I remember thinking, uh, what?" Geoffrey laughed. "But then I was so full of rage about the storyline that I was like, no, fuck you." Janis stood up and went to refill her coffee cup. "You want? Okay. I have to play for a while. I will talk to your guy. You two definitely have to be on the call so you can drag me back on track if I start to go off the rails."

Geoffrey left it for a day, so they'd all have time to consider it. Then he checked in again, and when the answer was still 'let's go ahead,' he sent a text to Reggie: *Mr. Galant, Ms. Vaughn & Co. will be returning to London next month. The new record will launch while we're there, and some press will be required. We wondered if you'd like to get in first.* He was certain that Reggie would read some amusing innuendo in the last sentence.

He wasn't disappointed: *I'd like to get in first, last, and in any position. When and where?*

Perhaps by telephone? J appreciated how you handled mine. Another opening. He couldn't seem to help himself.

You merciless bastard I've spilt my tea laughing. Does your red king know how you toy with me?

It entertains him

Christ he's even worse than you, then. Yes by all means and in all seriousness would be pleased to speak with Ms. V & Co at your convenience, might I hope we'll have a link to her new record?

We'll even pay for an advert

It's the least you can bloody do. 'Handled mine' indeed. If wishing made it so! They set up a mutually-agreeable time, and Geoffrey disconnected, smiling. He had no intention of ever following through on this flirtation, and he was sure Reggie (and Niall) knew it, but he couldn't deny it was fun.

They made the call from the home office, to have the map, venue list, and other tour-related material directly in front of them. Reggie picked up immediately. "Well, Mr. Anand, what have you to say for yourself? That last letter's blown the top off."

"There's something very inspiring about California," Geoffrey said, smiling. "We're on speaker here. How goes the business?"

"I have taken some measures to dignify my mode of conveyance of filth," Reggie said grandly. "Next time you visit the site, you'll see. So far, no cries of outrage from the seekers of filth."

"Well done. Shall we begin?"

"And on goes the recorder. Ms. Vaughn, thank you so much for agreeing to this interview. You are the first female person to so honor me."

"Hi Reggie. I've been enjoying your back and forth with Geoffrey." She bit her lip, knowing what was about to happen.

"Oh Christ, not you too." Niall and Geoffrey laughed. "It stands to reason, doesn't it. Very well. Let the record show that Mr. Anand is a member – oh *hell* can't even say that can I? – never mind. This household wants looking into. Ms. Vaughn, I see from your social media that you've traveled with Mr. Phelps for a good many years. Would you tell my readers a bit about that?"

"Certainly." Janis went into the story. Reggie prompted her with questions from time to time; Niall inserted a comment here and there. "And then, when we were in London a year ago, Niall met Geoffrey."

"Ah yes. And in very short order, much to the dismay of single gentlemen everywhere, they were married. How's that affected you?"

"Geoffrey is a great addition to the household. Because he's self-employed, he's able to work around our schedules and manage things we can't. And because he is very kind, he's willing. For the new tour, he'll be acting as my travel coordinator. Niall is going to be up to his neck in venues and guest artists."

"Lucky artists," Reggie said, predictably. "You'll have other musicians on stage? Tell me about this record." So she did, and he asked intelligent questions. When she expressed appreciation, he said, "I petitioned your record company for a copy of the index. You've recorded some of these songs before. What made you go back to them?"

"Tango," she said. "I got obsessed with it after meeting Geoffrey. I mean, I've always kind of loved it, but he knows how to dance. He's been teaching me. He's even managed to get Niall dancing once or twice."

"So I've seen. How else do you keep fit?"

It was a tangent, but Janis went with it. "I started doing yoga two years ago on my doctor's recommendation. All the travel, and all the time at the piano, were kind of wreaking havoc with my back. Then last year there was that accident on the road to Liverpool, and my neck's never been quite the same."

"Still get massage, do you?"

"Regularly. We found a great therapist here and I have one or two I can call in England. If I get too gnarly, Geoffrey has good hands."

Reggie snorted out a laugh. "As I'm sure Mr. Phelps can confirm. The three of you are a menace. So, only yoga?"

"I hate to exercise," Janis confessed. "I've been gym-averse my whole life. Niall is athletic, but Geoffrey is an athlete. He does yoga every day, and he nags me all the time, and I actually am in better shape than I was two years ago."

"You're quite a lovely shape if you don't mind my saying so."

"Reggie, you can say so any time." She was pleased.

"I can and I will. Now, I spoke with Mr. Anand earlier this year when he'd just had a very narrow escape. You went up the mountain with Mr. Phelps after. What was that like?"

"I was ready to burn the place to the ground. We didn't know what had happened for twenty-four hours. We didn't hear from Geoffrey, we couldn't get through to him, we were both frantic. He is essential to Niall, and that means he's essential to me." Janis left it at that. Niall was holding her hand.

Reggie didn't pursue it. He said, "You've permitted a video to stay online. You were playing and singing, quite beautifully I might add, in the hotel bar. That song means something to you?"

"I think it means something to everyone who plays it. It's not a song of praise, exactly. For me, I guess," Janis paused for a second. "You know what, it is. It's praise, and thanksgiving, and acceptance. It's here I am, and here you are, and there we were, and it's okay. We're doing our best, hallelujah."

"Will you play it on tour? In that way?"

Janis looked at Niall and Geoffrey, and seemed to make up her mind. "I hadn't planned to, but now I think we will. It was kind of profound having the audience sing like that."

"Lovely. I shall make a point of attending your concert in London, and croak along with you. So when does this world tour of yours commence?"

"September. I'm terrified and excited, we're going places I've never been. Actually places none of us have ever been."

"Sounds quite the adventure. I trust you'll have a smashing time, and a brilliant success with it." He wrapped it up then. "And that's the recorder off. I'll send you the transcript. May I ask a question off the record?"

"Okay," Janis said cautiously.

"Thank you. I know what *I'd* do for fun with Messieurs Phelps and Anand in the house. How do you manage?"

"For everything except a hug," she said, "there's a battery-powered alternative." They all listened to Reggie laugh. "Time to get back to the piano. Thanks, Mr. Galant."

"And thanks to the three of you." He disconnected.

Niall said, "I think that went quite well. He could have pursued the personal angle, and didn't."

"Not because he isn't interested," Geoffrey said. "I shouldn't be surprised if he's figured it out."

"Maybe I shouldn't have said the thing about good hands." Janis made an 'eek' face, then shrugged. "But it's a porn site! I couldn't resist."

Niall leaned against her shoulder. "I expect the average reader will see it in context, and giggle, and dismiss it. Now off with you to the study, you've a piano waiting."

"The depth of her creativity never ceases to amaze me," Niall remarked. He was standing at the wall of windows in the sunroom, looking out into the back garden on yet another bright and beautiful California morning. Geoffrey was on the floor – terrazzo, but covered with two kilim rugs - stretching. "What did you think of the piece she and Ed have made?"

"I love it. It's like the Goldberg Variations, only in tango."

Niall laughed softly. "Yes, exactly. To think that five years ago I wouldn't have known what the Goldberg Variations were."

"Your musical schooling was of a different nature. As was mine." Geoffrey never knew if it was that comment that set Niall humming, or if he might have anyway. It was that sort of morning. Ed and Deborah were in their private den, Janis was – as far as they knew – in the study or in the home office. A peaceful, quiet interlude after breakfast, one of the many pleasures of their stay in Glendale.

The song he was humming – nearly singing - was familiar. Geoffrey didn't say anything. He liked to hear it. Niall never made much of it; he was shy of compliments about his voice, in every context other than lovemaking. Geoffrey was turned away, bending over the recently-healed leg, when he heard a second voice. "'That's the time you miss her most of all,'" she sang softly. Geoffrey looked behind him; Janis had her arms around Niall, her cheek against his back.

"You've rumbled me, my love," he said lightly.

"Niall. Have I or have I not spent my entire life marinating in music." He made a sound of assent. "The likelihood that someone with your vocal qualities cannot sing is roughly the same as the likelihood that George Clooney is not attractive." Niall laughed. So did Geoffrey, half a room away.

Niall said, "It's a mental thing. If I don't want to be an actor, how much less do I want to be a singer?"

"Which has always been blazingly obvious to me, which is why I have never pestered you about it." Janis slid around to his front and lifted her face for a

279

kiss. "I was coming in to see if I could pester Geoffrey about writing something, and then I heard you. I promise I won't pester you. Just, you know, for the record," she paused, glancing at Geoffrey and then back at Niall. "You singing to me would be on a par with that other thing you did once." Niall kissed her again, apparently speechless.

Geoffrey was sitting up now, his back resting against the loveseat and legs folded, absently pressing a thumb into the tight connective tissue above his right ankle. Thinking, *if anything could make him do it, that would.* "What is it you had in mind, darling?"

"That sonnet. I'm assuming it's not the only one you've written." He shook his head. "Other poetry? You said you'd written some."

"Quite a lot, growing up and at university. Here and there since, mostly for my mother. I like it for working out emotional drama. Never published, much of it's personal, or too angstily adolescent."

"Have you ever written a song?"

"Not as such," he said slowly, starting to see what she was getting at. "Have you a mind to compose one?"

"That photo shoot. I said it should be a concert. Mom and Dad are going to go with us when Andy gets it up on the wall. I told Dad what I thought, and he said, you should write it. And then I was like, eek, because I've never done that before, and then I thought, but what if it's songs, the kind of songs I've been doing forever. New songs." She looked excited and terrified.

Geoffrey was getting interested. "Music first, or lyrics?"

"I don't have the first fucking clue." Janis went over to the loveseat, sat down and said, "Have you ever looked at the structure of a pop song?"

280

Geoffrey swiveled around, resting his elbows on the seat and looking up at her. "Not with any sort of analytical intention. Would you like me to?"

"Only if you're interested. There are other people I could take this to. You're busy already."

"No, I'm interested. The first book is practically finished. I won't start seriously on the next until we're in London. We've loads of time. You could be working these up while we're on tour. Will you have an instrument?"

"I've never traveled with one before. But things are happening in here." She did a wind-up thing with her hand, beside her head. "New things. I think maybe our situation has unlocked me. Being so safe and supported." Geoffrey stretched out a hand and patted her thigh. She put her hand on his. "Dad said, I always thought you had some original things to say when the time was right. Maybe it is."

"You know I've a tendency to be flowery."

"You and the redhead both. You're like a master class in how to speak English. But your books aren't like that. You can say a lot in not many words. That's what a song needs." They stared at each other for a minute. "Maybe I'll take along the tabletop keyboard." Her digital piano with eighty-eight weighted keys, stored in the garage since she'd moved out of her solo apartment before launching her first out-of-state tour. She'd written in the journal about how odd it was to be away at first, to not have that particular, constant companion. "Another thing for you guys to wrestle with."

"It's only luggage," Niall said. "You've a proper case for it, I imagine."

"Oh yeah. So what do you think?" Looking at Geoffrey.

"Songs about the pictures? Is that what you mean?" Because he could already feel the words coming. "All fifteen?"

Janis huffed out a breath, eyes bright. "Wouldn't it be awesome?"

Chapter 14

Once the seed was planted, Geoffrey could hardly wait to see it grow. He talked to Niall, then sent a text to Andy: *Dear Maestro, Ms. Vaughn has a notion to write some songs about those pictures and approached me for lyrics. Might I come by and have a look at the fifteen again?*

Andy wrote back promptly: *Absolutely. Any day after 14:00. Niall & Janis welcome too if they're free*

A date and time were settled. Niall organized a morning meeting with Randa on the same day, Geoffrey dug out the miniature voice recorder he'd barely used on this trip, and they went back to West L.A. The business meeting was accomplished without trauma. They arrived at the Faux Chateau (Andy and Victor's name for their house) a few minutes after two o'clock.

Andy was pleased to see Geoffrey without his crutches. "I thought I was going to need some myself for a minute there. This dance piece is kicking my ass. Or actually, my partner is. He does some dance rehab shit, therapy, right? And he's all, sir, you need to work out more. Sir, plié more so you can jump higher. Sir, get some physical therapy on that ankle. I'm like, what the fuck did I get myself into."

"We're really looking forward to it," Janis said. "I'm doing a thing at Chrome the week after. Did Valerie tip you?"

"No, so she's in trouble. Tanith did. Victor and I already have our tickets. If the damned producers won't let him off the leash two weeks in a row I'll drag along a friend. Did you get dancers?"

"How did you know we were thinking about dancers?"

He shrugged. "Tango. You know."

Janis made a yeah-I-know face. "The tall blond guy and his wife, from the movie. Mike and Paula. They're doing three numbers with us. They told us they know a couple who did the original-length 'Un Beso' and mentioned it to them, but when they heard eight minutes they were like thank you and goodnight." Andy giggled. Janis grinned at him. "So then I said well could Sandesh and Tasha do their thing on the part they know, and Mike and Paula do the new part, so it looks like that's happening. Tanith said we could borrow some of her cameras and tape the whole show, super excited."

"Oh, that's a great idea. Well listen, I've got coffee, champagne, or The Prisoner. Who's the designated driver?"

"That's me," Geoffrey said. "I believe these two would adore a glass of The Prisoner."

"Indeed we would." Niall offered to open and serve while Andy got the others situated.

"I'm done processing," he said. "They've gone out for printing and mounting. But if you don't mind, I want to save the final images for the show. So this is the original fifteen shots."

Geoffrey nodded. "That's fine. I only wanted to see them again and make some notes as to what I think they express, and how they make me feel."

"Are we allowed to talk?"

He looked at Janis, amused. "Why do you think I brought the recorder?"

For the next week and a half, Niall was almost fully-employed setting up venues for the tour; Janis was completely employed rehearsing for the concert at Chrome; and Geoffrey was wallowing in lyrics. He read articles about songwriting, found some analyses, even found a movie called 'Music & Lyrics' and watched it twice. The lyrical structure forced him to a concision he'd never had to cope with. Even a sonnet, with its precisely defined sequence, was easier. For a couple of the images, he ended up writing sonnets out of sheer frustration, and then picked them apart. He kept all his notes for each one, not knowing how Janis might be able to use any of the material. He asked if she wanted to see any of it as he built it and she said, "Not right now. Still stuck in tangoland." He nodded and carried on.

"What are you doing?" Deborah asked finally, finding him once more at the kitchen table glaring at his laptop. "That is not your writing-a-novel face." He laughed and leaned back. "But you're writing." It was almost a question.

"A project for your daughter. Something new for both of us." Deborah's eyebrows shot up. "I don't think she's ready to talk about it yet," Geoffrey added apologetically. "I hope before we leave you. Certainly before we're off on tour."

She sat down beside him. "We're really going to miss you. It's been fantastic having you all here for so long."

"You'll be glad to have your privacy back."

"Privacy is overrated. A little bit goes a long way." Geoffrey made a sound of assent. "Janis told us this property deal is going forward. You'll be back in England next summer too?"

"For two or three months, from the end of the tour. Then I think she'd like to come here again. There may be something new to work on with Valerie. And she's loved being here. All of us have." They regarded each other for a moment. "Employing me will make our cover story stronger." Deborah laughed. "If it breaks, though, will you and Ed be all right?"

"Oh, honey. We couldn't care less. You're not breaking any laws that I know of, you're not hurting anybody, there's not even any kids to be confused about it. We were a little nervous at first. Only because it's kind of out there, and we couldn't begin to guess how it would go."

"Nor could we. It's a matter of faith, isn't it?"

"Faith, and commitment." She studied him. "Before you all come to stay again, we should get a king bed in there." Geoffrey laughed.

A message rolled in from Reggie Galant as the five of them were getting ready to go down to Hollywood for Andy's performance: *Mr. Anand, transcript for Ms. V tomorrow. It may interest you to know that I'm buried in letters from people who've been profiled. They've been coming since your interview but it doesn't bloody stop. Have you the faintest desire to speak with any of these dark and stormies?*

Geoffrey had, of course, even though he felt fully occupied. He wrote back: *Mr. Galant, always delightful to hear from you. I trust my letters from the road have met with your approval*

You bloody well know they have as I've published every one to howls of ecstasy. I trust the revenue has met with your approval

286

Quite so. As to other travelers' letters, I'm deeply interested but also at the moment short of time. I propose to set up a mailbox for these communications. We could advise your readers to that effect? Full discretion, etc is assured and patience requested as I mustn't commence another book-length project until I've satisfied my contract

That'll do. Send me the address once established, I'll handle you from there. A moment later: *Would of course be delighted to handle you from here if that would help satisfy anything*

Geoffrey laughed, as he always did, and wrote back *I was thinking 'wait for it'*

THAT'S ALL I'M BLOODY DOING

Niall, of course, heard Geoffrey giggling and came to find him. As soon as he saw the phone he knew who it was. "Is your pornographer at it again?"

"He's not *my* pornographer."

"He'd like to be. Get your tie on, we must be off." Niall leaned in for a kiss and took the phone with him as he went out. He wrote *Mr. Galant, if we promise to help you find one of your own will you cease and desist? Yrs, N. Phelps*

The reply came back: *No*

Niall laughed, as he always did.

The nightclub was absolutely packed. The word had gotten out not only that a celebrity was performing, but that his nationally-famous husband was in attendance. Niall and Ed exchanged a glance as they were all ushered into the club past a mob of press. Niall thought Ed's face said 'thank God for limousines;' they'd been decanted mere feet from the

287

entrance. Janis was recognized, and waved to the crowd before they went in.

Andy's performance was to be the closing number in a theatrical dance showcase. It wasn't much like the show that the Vaughn family had seen in February; there was no through-story or theme. Many of the performers were billed as students, performing thesis or competition pieces. The only familiar faces in the first half were those of Sam Lee and his husband Mateo, who'd both danced in Tanith's film. They opened the show with a paso doble to music from the movie 'Strictly Ballroom.'

During intermission, Deborah said, "This thing Andy's doing. We saw the ballet a million years ago when it was here in L.A. Have you seen it?"

"The Bourne 'Swan Lake'? Yes, in England. Both of us have," Geoffrey added. "I thought it such an interesting treatment of the story. A tremendous lot of acting required."

"Oh, I know. It could go wrong so easily."

Niall said, "There was so much confusion at first. Some people couldn't be convinced it wasn't a sexual thing."

"I don't know how you could miss it," Deborah said, making a face. "I mean, clearly the prince doesn't want to, you know, sleep with the swan. He wants to *be* the swan. Free to fly."

"Exactly."

"And the swan is like, you know what, I'll help you, you can fly with me. I cried at the end," she confessed. "Didn't I?"

"Yes, you did, Mom." Janis was clearly enjoying the night off. "I wonder if there's going to be dancing after the show this time. I wore my good shoes just in case."

"I noticed," Geoffrey said, smiling. The closer they got to her concert, the harder it was for her to stay away from the piano. He was glad she didn't seem to miss it tonight. "How did you like the opening number?"

"I love those guys! Now I want to watch 'Strictly Ballroom' again. Man, what I wouldn't give to work on a movie with Baz Luhrmann. His music person is a genius."

Ed was shaking his head. "You're going to need to stay put for a while if you want to work on a film."

"Maybe after this tour. The world, some time in England, some dates in the U.S. and then camp here again for a while." She glanced at her men.

Niall knew why. They were all still, after nearly a year, inventing this relationship day by day. But still, after nearly a year, it seemed to be working. "One thing at a time, my dear."

The second half was enjoyable, but all of them were mostly concerned with Andy's number. They could see his husband Victor up front, with a young woman in a fabulous dress who appeared – judging from the proposal they all thought they'd witnessed - to be newly engaged to the man dancing with Andy. Finally it was time.

The stage went black after the penultimate performance. Scrims were rolled in from the sides. Andy and his partner Zach took their positions in the dark. Then the stage was lit, not with a spotlight but with dim, blue-tinted overhead light and a projection onto the scrims. It was a full moon over leafless trees, water in the distance, and ornate pillars on the sides –

very much like the set shown in the filmed version of the ballet. At the bottom of the rear panel was the suggestion of a drift of sleeping swans. Andy and Zach held their positions for a minute, waiting out the applause, before the stage manager cued their music. Geoffrey drew in a breath and reached for Niall's hand. Neither of them moved again until the end. Then they were on their feet with everyone else, the room exploding with applause, whistles, and cheers.

Andy had exited the stage leaving Zach alone. Now he came back on and both men advanced for a bow. And another. Andy was grinning at Victor, down front and on his feet with a 'Bravo.' Zach was smiling at his young lady.

"Wow," said Janis, her father, and her mother. Deborah wiped her face. Geoffrey did the same. Niall and Ed exchanged another speechless look. They were all well accustomed to seeing remarkable performances. There was something about this one that clutched at Niall's heart. It might have been knowing that Andy was a dozen years older than himself, and had given up the stage for a long time. It might have been knowing about the younger man, who'd never even met Andy before saying 'I'll be your prince,' and who'd worked tirelessly to make it so. It might have been simply the powerful beauty of the dancing.

Eventually Andy and Zach left the stage, though the applause continued even after the curtain was down. "He probably wants to get out of those swan pants," Ed remarked. Deborah laughed. "Who could use another drink?" House music had started. Not all tango this time, though tango was there; also waltz, and some easy-tempo jazz standards. After they were served, they were all quiet for a while. Possibly processing what they'd seen, possibly remembering that in a week they would all be back here for Janis' concert. Once that was over, the time to part was drawing near. Perhaps not surprisingly, Ed made no objection to staying for an hour, then two, so his wife and daughter could dance with Niall and Geoffrey. They all had a chance to speak with Andy and Victor, and to meet (and congratulate) Zach the prince and his fiancée Karen. It was long past midnight before they finally made their way upstairs and into the waiting limousine.

The interview transcript arrived the next day, as promised. The entire household reviewed it, as before. And as before, they all approved. "Have you seen the site now?" Geoffrey asked Niall, after Janis sent a text with permission to launch. "It's completely different."

"I haven't. I've all the stimulation I require here at hand. So to speak."

"Let's have a look, it's bookmarked now I'm doing so much business with Reggie." *Every phrase sounds a double entendre*, he realized. "But I've been working, so I haven't seen it all." They were in the home office; there was no chance of embarrassing Deborah or Ed. He opened the tab and turned the laptop so Niall could see too.

"Well, that's … completely different," Niall agreed. Where the homepage had previously been a mosaic of brightly-colored and variously-explicit tiles to click, under a screamingly obvious banner, it was now a tasteful magazine cover laid out in bronze and gray. The site name, AT YOUR SERVICE, appeared at the top with a subtitle of 'entertainment for the gentleman's gentleman' below. At left on the main page was a table of contents with interviews, entertainment reviews, essays and letters listed above a line discreetly offering 'the art of love.' All that text floated above a subtle sepia-tone image of a nude man. On the right were advertisements and links to photo essays or videos. No one would be in any doubt as to the subject matter, thanks to suggestive or cheeky labels, but nothing was explicit. "What's that?" Niall indicated the 'art of love' link. Geoffrey clicked it. "I'll be damned."

Geoffrey scrolled through slowly. It was a page offering original paintings and limited-edition prints, mostly but not entirely nudes, most erotic but none explicit. All featured men, singly or in pairs. Quite a few were by R. Galant. "Of all things. Our Reggie's been hiding his light."

"Those were never on offer before, were they?" Niall hadn't spent much time on the site.

"Not to my knowledge. I wonder what led him to offer them now." They glanced at each other. "He's a devil of a painter."

"The best of this lot, and none are less than good. There's a bit of Sargent to him, isn't there?" Seized by impulse, Niall stroked his hand through Geoffrey's hair. "Shall we have your portrait done?"

Geoffrey glanced over. "Mine alone? Never. Oh *Niall*." A sudden notion made him turn. Niall's hand stayed on his shoulder. "Together, in our morning coats. Suggestively at dawn. Strolling down the platform at Oxford. Wouldn't it be grand?" They grinned at each other.

"It would be grand." Niall leaned in for a kiss. "Let's see the rest, then you can sound him out." When they clicked through to the interviews link, and then to Geoffrey's, they found links to his own books and to his 'letters from the road,' but no other explicit content. "This is brilliant. Is every subject's page like this?" They explored a few and found it was so. "If Mr. Galant is not quite careful, he'll find he's gone into legitimate journalism."

Geoffrey laughed under his breath. "It's a vast improvement. I shouldn't fear giving this link to my parents. Though I would have to warn them off the letters."

"Indeed you would. And I've business, so I'll leave you to commissioning the maestro." Another kiss, and then Niall went to find Janis. Geoffrey woke up his phone and sent a text: *Mr. Galant, the Thane and I have just reviewed your excellently redesigned site. Your artwork is exquisite. What are your terms for a portrait?*

The reply was considerably delayed. Geoffrey was well into some writing work when a return text lit up his phone: *Are you serious?* Geoffrey picked up the phone again and dialed. Reggie answered immediately. "Don't be cruel, lad, I can take a bit of teasing but some things are close to my heart."

"Quite serious," Geoffrey said. "We were looking at the site together and had the thought simultaneously. Of course, Mr. Phelps mentioned a portrait of me alone." He tsked.

"If you'd let me paint you in the nude I'd do your portrait for nothing. That's either of you, mind. Both together might be more than even I could survive. When are you back in England?"

"Next month."

"And have you a particular scene in mind? Obviously I do, but 'portrait' suggests something one's parents might hang over the mantel."

Geoffrey laughed. "We married in morning coats. Wore them back to London from Oxford the next day. You're familiar with the station there?"

"I am, and can be more so. Swab me decks and shiver me timbers." Reggie blew out a breath. "My hands are literally shaking, lad."

"Get that out of your system, sir. I'll consider your offer and ring you once we're in London." Geoffrey knew at least two people who'd like a painting of himself in the nude. It seemed a very small price to pay for a wedding portrait. That had been, after all, the best morning of his entire life. Which, given the array of dazzling mornings he'd had in the past year, was saying something. "And congratulations on the site. It really does look splendid."

"Thanks. Tell your friends." Reggie disconnected without another word. Geoffrey went back to work. The book due next month was already longer than requested; he might have to cut something. But between the action scenes and the development of the romance he'd been having such fun with it that he decided to send it no matter what, and have the publisher sort it out. *Let that editor earn his keep*, he thought, and kept writing.

Geoffrey had also continued working on the 'Tempest' lyrics, finally had a set he was satisfied with, and was perishing to give them to Janis. But she was in the last frenzy of preparation for her concert; he didn't want to break her concentration. Instead, desperate for feedback, he took them to Deborah, who always seemed interested in his writing process, and Niall, who was temporarily at a standstill in the tour preparation.

"These may not make a great deal of sense out of context," Geoffrey told Deborah. "I've written them for Janis. They are based on the fifteen photographs Andy will be showing next month, from our session in March."

"And those were based on, or inspired by, 'The Tempest,' right?" She waited for his confirming nod. "Well, if you think I can get it without the images, lay it on me."

Niall said, "I think the key is to have in mind that the story of the photographs is a passionate love affair between Prospero and Ariel." His glance at Geoffrey was amused.

"Oh. That, yeah, that'll help." Deborah was sitting beside Niall at the kitchen table. Both of them looked at Geoffrey expectantly. He set down the laptop, with the document live on screen, and waited. As soon as she saw the structure of the first lyric, she said, "Oh! They're songs? You're writing songs?" She sounded excited. "Janis is going to write songs?" It was as though she couldn't quite believe it.

"Well, we're meaning to try," Geoffrey said, hoping he hadn't overstepped. He was trusting that a woman willing to tell her parents she was in a three-way relationship might also be willing to share an embryonic writing project. "It's a new thing for both of us."

"Sshh," she said, reading. Niall was reading along with her. He, of course, had the photographs in mind, as well as their discussions both times they'd seen the images. They seemed to be reading at the same pace. At the end of the fifteen pages, Deborah clicked back up to the top and read them all again. Then she sat back and stared at Geoffrey. "Have you written songs before?"

"No," he said cautiously.

"Well, they scan perfectly as I'm sure you know. I'm reading five of these in three-quarter time and the rest in standard. Some of my all-time favorite pop songs are in three-quarter time. And I'm sure since you can dance you know all about waltz timing. Anyway, the language is eloquent, and elegant, but spare. Nicely done. I think she'll really like them. I really like them," she added.

Geoffrey didn't even try to hide his relief. "Thank you."

"I like them too," said Niall. "They work as poetry. If Janis can set them to music, she may have a new record here."

"And if she purely despises them, I have about three other versions of each one," Geoffrey said. "I've a whole new appreciation for songwriters now. Writing the novel has been a relief. Thank you both so much for taking the time."

"If you've a moment to spare yourself?" Niall was giving him that look. "A question's arisen in the home office." Geoffrey was not in much doubt what sort of question, and probably Deborah wasn't either. She might have been snickering as he and Niall left the kitchen.

A few minutes later, "Was that the question, my king?"

"Indeed it was," Niall murmured against his neck. "Your answer pleases me."

Geoffrey unbuttoned his shirt, then his jeans. "So I see. How shall I love thee?" His face against Niall's chest, mouth on his skin.

"In every way you ever have, my beauty. How do you find such words?" Niall's hands on Geoffrey's face.

An ardent kiss. "I look at you."

296

On the night of the concert, Janis and Niall went ahead to Hollywood, to have an hour with Tomás and Isabelle and then a moment to speak with the dancers. Geoffrey drove Ed and Deborah. They were all dressed to impress, knowing that there would be a mob of press again. Geoffrey wore his white dinner jacket, Ed was in black tie, and Deborah wore a tango-inspired dress of black lace over peacock-blue satin. They arrived a half-hour before showtime. Ed spoke to reporters outside the nightclub for a few minutes. Geoffrey stood aside with Deborah, politely brushing off questions directed his way.

On their way in, Deborah said, "Is Niall the official representative?"

Geoffrey gave her a laughing glance. "Not precisely. Tonight's affair has two purposes. None of those questions had to do with either."

"Good point." She patted his arm. "I'm a little excited."

"I know you are." Janis hadn't done a concert in California for a long time. The benefit tickets had sold out, advance reviews of the album were good, and the tour's countdown clock was up and running. If the audience response tonight was good, and if there was at least one decent video clip to post, the prospects for the world tour were excellent. "She couldn't have done it without you," Geoffrey told Deborah. "None of this, without you and Ed. She loves you very much."

"Oh." Deborah pinched the bridge of her nose as they found their seats, reserved up front again. "Don't make this mascara run."

"Apologies, my dear." He kissed her hand and signaled a passing server. Ed joined them a moment later. They had time for a drink, then to visit the loo, and to find some friends in the audience and make 'we'll talk later' gestures before the house lights dimmed. Geoffrey missed Niall, told himself *don't be ridiculous*, and went right on missing him.

Janis opened with 'Bird on a Wire,' a song she hadn't recorded before. All three musicians were loosely grouped upstage right. The antique upright piano and Tomás were at an angle facing upstage center; Janis at her digital piano was positioned to see Tomás, and the audience. Isabelle was stationed between them. Mike and Paula, the featured dancers, were downstage left under a subtle spotlight. It was simple but effective staging.

They played straight through, without intermission. With the eight-minute fantasia on 'Un Beso' to close, the set ran almost seventy minutes. The audience didn't seem to think that was enough. Demands for an encore brought the musicians back for a quick discussion. They had, of course, prepared for this eventuality. After a few words, including an invitation to sing along on the chorus, Janis began to play 'Hallelujah.'

During the first verse, the dancers returned to the stage, gathering behind the pianos. Unexpectedly, Niall came with them. *You're never going to sing*, Geoffrey thought delightedly. But he was. Janis was smiling. Ed and Deborah were singing along, he could hear Andy close by, and by the seventh chorus the nightclub sounded like a cathedral. When the musicians finally wound it up, the applause felt like an earthquake. Or an avalanche. Deborah had a cocktail napkin up to her face, cursing her mascara. Ed was rubbing her back. The curtain fell. Geoffrey twisted around to see what was happening behind them. A lot of people standing and still applauding, quite a few people hugging, and more than one crying. He got his phone out and took some pictures.

After a few minutes, house music started and the servers began to circulate again. Geoffrey was standing, waiting for Niall and Janis. Andy – dressed exactly as he had been for the movie premiere in December, and sporting a rather promising week's growth of beard - found him first. "That was quite a show," he said. "Victor is mad as hell that he couldn't be here."

"We're sorry to miss seeing him. The movie shoot's going well?"

"Oh, it's going great. They're having a blast. He and his co-stars wrote the treatment back when we were in Miami, the script is really funny, and they're doing this action scene on this horrible bridge that's going to scare people to death. Did you see the other two?"

Geoffrey was glad he could say, "We did. Niall and Janis knew you of course, they'd seen the first one already, but we all watched the first two last fall. He's a brilliant actor, isn't he? What he does in the 'Countdown' films is completely different from Tanith's film."

Andy looked pleased at the compliment to Victor. "He kept trying to throw me at the Carlos Gardel part. Some nonsense about our singing voices."

"Oh, but it was perfectly cast," Geoffrey said. "His voice was distinct from the rest of you."

"That is exactly what I told him, about a hundred times. So thanks. And hey, I got the prints in, and 'A Tempest' is going to totally fucking kill. I was going to do it over a couple weekends at home, you know, but it's too

299

good if I do say so myself, so it's going into this little gallery on Wilshire that happened to have two weeks open." Andy dug a card out of his jacket pocket and handed it to Geoffrey. "What's up with the lyrics project? Have you had time to work on that?"

"I'm finished," Geoffrey said, though with a questioning note in his voice. "Janis hasn't seen them yet, she's been too much involved with this concert. Soon. Deborah and Niall say they're good."

"You're going to let me see them, right?" Andy was smiling. "I'll be at this gallery thing on opening night. Let me know if you can be there. Oh hi Niall. Where's Janis?"

"She's been accosted by fans," Niall indicated a knot of chattering people near the stage steps, then shook hands with Andy. "She'll be joining us momentarily. Did you enjoy the show?"

"Loved it! Loved the arrangements, great performance, and of course with the dancing," Andy kissed his fingers dramatically. "I was just telling your husband, 'A Tempest' is going in a real gallery. I still want to use those in a bigger show later, is that still okay?"

"Of course." Niall had his arm around Geoffrey now. "Will you sell prints?"

"Not this time. I expect much wailing and gnashing of teeth over that." He shrugged, superbly indifferent to lost sales. "And now I'm going to circulate, see if I can work my way over to her ladyship. See you soon, right?"

"Right." Niall and Geoffrey watched him go. "Well darling?"

"It was brilliant. I wished I could have heard you singing." Geoffrey was smiling. "Janis could."

"One of these days I expect I'll sing for her properly. And for you." Niall kissed him. "Mike and Tasha are quite good singers. Paula and Sandesh did us all a favor and faked it." Geoffrey laughed. "The dancing, how'd it look?"

"Oh, it was lovely. Not at all distracting. Come and see Ed and Deborah. She's been in floods."

Chapter 15

Geoffrey took Ed and Deborah home an hour after curtain. The concert event was due to shut down at midnight, but Niall and Janis were very much later getting home. When they eventually crept in, Geoffrey had been asleep for hours. There was giggling, and a stifled oath when Niall knocked into the footboard. Janis crawled into bed and almost instantly went to sleep. Niall sat on the edge and put a hand on Geoffrey with less than his customary precision. "Where've you been," Geoffrey said, amused and drowsy. "Painting the town?"

"One might say." Niall leaned down to kiss him. "Sorry to wake you. Mmm, you're warm." Another kiss. "I'll stop."

"You taste of whisky. Don't stop." Geoffrey wound an arm around his neck and pulled him down.

"It's no more than you deserve," he said, eight hours later, when Niall was sitting beside him on the loveseat in the sunroom. Squinting at the window, clutching a mug of coffee, and bitching wholeheartedly about his headache. "And you oughtn't've driven home in that condition." Geoffrey had actually been a little horrified to realize that they must have. In the wee hours, with Niall's body against his, the thought hadn't occurred.

"I know. It wasn't very far."

"Not very far! It's a dozen miles of effing Los Angeles!"

"No no no, God, keep your voice down, I pray you. We weren't in Hollywood. We were lured up to a

302

local tavern, not two miles from here and no traffic at that hour. But you're right, and I apologize, and it shan't happen again."

"Should have sent you with a driver," Geoffrey said, stroking a hand through Niall's hair. "I should have guessed Janis would be in a mood to celebrate."

"So should I." Niall turned his head to kiss Geoffrey's wrist. "Bloody good show, all the same."

"Indeed. Is our beauty still sleeping?"

"I'll be amazed if we see her before dinnertime." They both snickered. Niall put his head back, cursed his height, accepted a pillow from Geoffrey, and closed his eyes. "Aspirin. Vitamin C. Water. More coffee."

"And some food."

"Ugh."

Geoffrey stifled a laugh. "Is this incapacity what I have to look forward to, at forty?"

Niall opened one eye to glare at him. "I seem to recall being perfectly capable not many hours ago."

"Ah, but that was before the toxins had fully, shall we say, penetrated."

"Christ, it's no wonder Reggie likes talking to you." They both giggled. "I'll go for some bread and butter. Presently." It was all Niall could contemplate eating.

Geoffrey kissed his cheek. "I'll serve you, my master. Since you served me so well in the night." He made a move to stand.

Niall caught his wrist before he could rise to go. "Geoffrey."

It was so uncommon to hear his actual name, rather than some endearment, that Geoffrey was startled. "Yes, darling?"

Niall turned his head to make eye contact, hand still wrapped loosely around Geoffrey's wrist. "Do you know how wonderful it was to know you were there last night? To know you'll be there every time now, when she performs? I might have survived, if you hadn't wanted to tour with us. But I would have missed you so."

"Niall. My dear love." Geoffrey kissed him. "I miss you when you're in a different room." Niall laughed shakily. "I never want to miss you again. I'll be with you every minute I possibly can be."

"And I with you."

"Now let me feed you so you'll be capable again soon." Another kiss, and then to the kitchen, where he was surprised to find Janis – pale and hollow-eyed, but upright and smiling – talking to Deborah. "Good morning. I'll admit I didn't expect to see you before midafternoon."

"Had to get up to pee, nobody was in bed with me, so I shuffled out here for coffee." Deborah was laughing. "Sorry Mom. My filter's been dissolved by alcohol. I'm too old for that shit."

"The secret is one glass of water for every cocktail, no more than one cocktail per hour, and food of an equivalent volume at least once per two hours of drinking." Deborah sipped coffee, looking innocent. "You forget we survived the seventies."

"One cocktail per hour?! How did you get any drinking done?"

"Or two glasses of wine."

"Oh, okay." Deborah was laughing again. Janis drank some coffee. "Where's Niall?"

"Incapacitated in the sunroom. I'm here to fetch him some fuel." Geoffrey sliced bread, lavishly buttered it, poured a glass of orange juice, and put it all on a tray. Then he noticed that Janis looked interested, so he repeated the program for her. "You were truly wonderful last night."

"Thanks. And thanks," she said, with her mouth full of bread. He kissed her anyway, then took the tray back to the sunroom.

"Our lady is awake and talking," he said, setting the tray on the side table. "Round one for you. Perhaps you'll manage an egg later." Niall made a doubtful sound and reached for the bread.

It was late afternoon before Geoffrey thought Janis might be up to analyzing his lyrics. He wouldn't have asked, if he hadn't wanted to give them to Andy as soon as possible. The more he read them himself, the more he thought *they should be seen with the photographs*, but without Janis' approval he wouldn't suggest it. He asked her, somewhat tentatively, after she joined him and Niall in the sunroom. She looked at him with such an astounded expression that he didn't know what to do. "Are you serious?" she said after a long pause. "You've already finished them?"

Oh, he thought, relieved. "The first five were a bugger, but then I found my way with it. I think," he added. "Niall and Deborah thought they were good."

"I know why you didn't show me first, so I forgive you for not showing me first. Show me right now. Please." He thought she might have been laughing if not for the hangover. Judging from a post she'd made well after midnight, that hangover was thoroughly earned. Geoffrey went to fetch the laptop. He opened the document and handed her the machine without comment, then got down on the floor to stretch. It seemed a long time before Janis set the laptop aside and said, "Come hug me."

He was happy to. "Are they what you wanted?"

"Squeeze in here with us." It was tight, but they could all fit on the loveseat. "You sweet adorable genius. I can hear the music already. This is going to be awesome."

"Don't start working on them yet," Niall said. "Not till we get to London. There's too much else to do."

"Gaahh, bossy, whatever. Okay. Not till London. Are you going to send them to Andy?"

"I thought I might. You wouldn't mind?"

"Geoffrey." She gave him a look. "Those are your work. Your property. Your copyright, whatever else gets done with them. You know about that shit. You do whatever the fuck you want with them, except give them to another musician. Okay?"

"All right," he said, laughing, and kissed her cheek. Then he picked up the laptop, printed the document to PDF, and sent it to Andy. "Off they go. I've no idea if he has any use for them, but he did ask. Could I interest either of you in a game of Scrabble? Janis?" She indicated agreement.

"I'll play too," said Niall. "Must test my capabilities." Janis gave him a narrow-eyed look, possibly because his tone promised other experiments. "Darling, such a minatory glance."

"Ooh, good word. How do you spell that?"

A reply email came back in an hour, just before they went to help Deborah with dinner. It appeared Andy was completely in favor of Geoffrey's notion concerning the lyrics, and not at all concerned about the gallery.

306

Dear Geoffrey,

Thanks for sending the OMG GORGEOUS POETRY to go with these photographs. I'm assuming that's what 'perhaps for the gallery?' meant. Those people will be bitching because they'll have to rearrange things, oh well, sucks to be them.

By the way I saw a post from some shady dive last night, am guessing the artist and manager are a little under the weather today. My personal favorite remedy is champagne.

Talk to you soon – Andy

Over the next week, Niall worked with Randa and her team to choose and extract video from the sneak-preview concert. They both thought it might be worth releasing the whole thing at some point, but for the moment they selected a few clips to post on Facebook. Geoffrey provided his pictures of the crowd reaction to 'Hallelujah,' and Janis wrote a few posts raving about Tomás and Isabelle, about the dancers, about Chrome, about Tanith for her help with the video. There were links to Tanith's movie – now available on DVD – and its soundtrack, to a classical album Isabelle had played on, and to dance performances featuring Tomás or Mike and Paula. "There," Janis said, reviewing the engagement. "People are looking at that shit. They're talking about it. And only one undignified picture in the whole batch, which as usual is my own fault."

"Dignity," Niall said, "is overrated." She gave him a look; both of them remembered all too well her ex-boyfriend Stefan's consistent disapproval of her 'inappropriate' social media content. "That said, I should rather not see any further photos of myself with my head on a bar." Geoffrey, on the couch in the home office, stifled a laugh. "Yes, darling, I realize it's my own fault. Now that I'm facing my fifth decade I'd prefer to be more intentional about my lack of dignity. How goes the mountaineer?"

"He's won," Geoffrey said with satisfaction. "Drug dealer in custody, community free of evildoers, and about to fly off for a weekend's frolic with the pilot."

"You'll let me read that, I trust," Niall said. "To help you … verify." They both laughed at Janis' elaborate eye-roll.

Geoffrey was sufficiently interested in Niall's verification that he spent the afternoon writing the frolic, and then excused them both from the usual post-dinner gathering in the study. "Fastest three thousand words on record, I believe," he told Niall when they were in bed together. "Do read carefully."

Niall was already reading. He glanced over, smiling. "You must know that I race through your love scenes at a breathless pace. Then read them again, and again, imagining that you've imagined them for the two of us."

"Always." Geoffrey put a hand on Niall's arm, preventing him from setting down the laptop. "Not yet, sir. You've not finished."

"Tyrant." Niall turned his attention back to the text. "Oh really. Oh *indeed*." Geoffrey was giggling. Niall scrolled back to the top of the new section and read it again. "You've left a bit to the imagination here."

"I'm quite certain you'll fill in as needed."

"You *wicked* darling." Niall set the laptop down. This time Geoffrey didn't stop him. "Fill in, shall I? Is

308

that what you want now?" Niall's hand in Geoffrey's hair as he went for a kiss, then bore him down. Their bodies pressed together. "Does writing these things excite you?"

"As reading them excites you." More kisses, legs entangled, then an impatient kick at the footboard. Geoffrey laughed against Niall's throat. "Diagonally, then, sir." They both moved, so Niall could stretch out. Geoffrey on top now, kissing Niall everywhere. Then he knelt astride Niall's hips, propped himself on one hand, and brought their erections together in the other.

"God almighty, how that looks," Niall said, voice low, his own hands brushing lightly up and down the insides of Geoffrey's thighs. "How you look. Will you finish us thus?"

"Is that what you want?" Geoffrey stroked them both. "We know this works. We needn't verify."

"Oh, I think we do. Need that. Kiss me. Give me that mouth."

"I'll kiss you. After." He knew what would happen now. Niall would talk. *Give me that voice.*

He wasn't disappointed. "Christ, you torturer. Was there ever a more perfect mouth. And you deny me, you heartless beauty. If you come first I'll have you bent over that footboard, begging."

That did it. "Jesus!" Geoffrey lost his grip on Niall, moving hard against his own hand.

Niall surged up, one arm pressing Geoffrey close, holding his breath, absorbing that pulse and fighting back his own. Then he turned that yielding body, and a moment later had his hand between his husband's legs. "Ask for it."

"God, Niall, give it to me. Give me that cock. I almost had you."

Niall laughed softly, lube on his fingers now. Caressing, stroking, pushing. "How much do I love you?"

"As much as I love you. Niall, *please*." Bent over the footboard, begging, as predicted. Eyes closed, mouth smiling, panting.

"Please what?"

"In me, now, oh my *Christ*, yes." The footboard creaked rhythmically as Geoffrey braced himself to take Niall's thrusts.

"I'll have that bastard off yet," Niall said with satisfaction a few minutes later. Geoffrey, face down on the bed under Niall's full weight, had just enough breath to laugh.

Geoffrey told Janis the next morning, as Niall lay mostly-asleep beside them, and she laughed. "You know you could just unscrew it."

"Unscrewing is the opposite of what we do here," Geoffrey pointed out. "Don't you prefer this?"

She had a leg hooked over his hip and an arm around his neck, the other hand on the back of his thigh. "I do prefer screwing," she said, breathless. "I've had quite enough of unscrewing. Oh fuck, yes, this is better."

Later that day, Geoffrey was on the couch in the home office and saw Deborah go by with something in her hand. He was online doing research, and didn't think anything of it until he heard strange noises from the bedroom. He set down the laptop and went to see what was happening. She was on the floor at the end of the bed, doing something with the tool, but looked up at him. "You know you guys could have done this back in December."

310

"Done what?"

She held up the tool. "Screwdriver. Good for taking things apart."

"What did Janis tell you?"

"She said, that precious idiot has been hating the footboard all this time and didn't want to complain." She was giggling. "I *knew* he was too tall for this bed. Oh my God. And now you're almost out of here." The footboard came free; Geoffrey caught it.

"It honestly never occurred to me to ask. Thank you." He gave her a kiss. "Where would you like this?"

"Oh, out in the garage is fine. Then come and have a cookie with me."

June 2019

It was another limousine ride to West L.A. for the opening night of 'A Tempest.' Niall and Geoffrey were profoundly nervous about walking into a room full of people there to see pictures of them nearly naked. Ed and Deborah knew them both well enough to say the right sort of reassuring things. Janis made fun of them the entire way. The combined approaches worked well enough that when they went through the door they were not immediately looking for the exit. Someone handed them glasses of champagne, and they followed the familiar voice to find Andy. "Oh my," Niall said under his breath as they approached. "I do hope he keeps the beard for this new movie." Geoffrey snickered.

"And here are the stars," Andy said, smiling. "Do you want to say anything to people? Yeah, thought maybe not. Take it easy. Ed, Deborah, good to see you." He shook their hands. "Janis, lovely as always." He kissed her cheek. "I'm so glad I got in here.

Victor's been sending insane suggestions about which Shakespeare characters we can play, I need to get to Michigan and straighten him out." He walked them all around, deflecting or managing all inquiries, introducing Niall and Geoffrey to a few people. Before long they were more at ease.

They picked up one of the gallery's brochures for the show, then went around once more. "I'm glad we did this," Geoffrey said softly. "Do you still think of wallpaper?"

"I'd wallpaper the world with these photos," Niall said. "When he's ready to sell prints, which should we have for your parents?"

"Oh goodness." They shared a glance, half-laughing. "Perhaps 'Let me remember thee what thou hast promised.' And for yours?"

"Oh, I think 'Thy charge exactly is perform'd,' don't you?"

"You're only in profile," Geoffrey protested. "Though I note fully clothed there."

"They've seen my face for forty years. I like the composition. And the way I don't seem certain you'll stay. And the way you reach out to me, as if to reassure me." They gazed at each other for a moment, then realized people were listening. Niall said, to the listeners, "Mr. Martin's work is quite extraordinary, isn't it?" as if he and Geoffrey hadn't had anything to do with it. They escaped during the ensuing burst of conversation, sought more champagne, and eventually fetched up beside Ed and Deborah again.

"Have you a favorite?" Geoffrey asked, smiling. "Before we flee to dinner?"

"I like 'Let me remember thee,'" Deborah said. "It's edging toward dangerous, not as dangerous as

312

'Remember I have done thee worthy service.' Kind of a reminder that Ariel has his own power even though Prospero's nominally in charge. He's the one who raises the tempest, really." She glanced at Geoffrey. "Of course I got half of that from your lyric. If I were looking at these gorgeous pictures without the words, I would have thought, he's not fully convinced yet."

"Convinced of what?" Ed said.

"Convinced that he's earned his freedom. That he deserves it. Or maybe that he wants it. Look at his face." She gestured toward the photo. Geoffrey glanced at Niall again. The chosen image had a quality of supplication, as if Ariel begged a word of love from Prospero. In the preceding image for 'Be subject to no sight' he'd been wrapped in Prospero's arms beneath the robe. In the following, 'What is't thou canst demand,' Prospero stood with his back to Ariel as if impatient or dismissive, one hand on the throne. His eyes, and the accompanying lyric, hinted that he couldn't bear to hear Ariel ask to go. On its own 'Let me remember thee' seemed to show Ariel at his weakest. With the lyric, the subtext of 'I serve by consent, and you'd best respect that' became clear.

"It's the one I want for my parents," Geoffrey told Deborah. "They know Niall, they know how we are together." *They know everything*, he thought and didn't say. "They'll appreciate the image on its own, but especially with the lyric. My mother always did want me to write more poetry."

"It's good you wrote these." Ed made an apologetic face. "Janis told me about this story you all got going through the pictures, and I have to admit I wouldn't get it without the words. I would have just thought, sexy pictures." Deborah laughed. "I can't wait to hear what she does with the music."

"Nor can I," Niall said. "But she's forbidden to work on it until we're in London."

Their leavetaking was prolonged and emotional. Ed and Deborah knew that Janis wouldn't be back in Los Angeles for over a year. They seemed almost as sad to see Niall and Geoffrey go. "God," Janis said in the limousine on the way to the airport. "That was epic." She wiped her face again.

"Yes it was." Niall had his arm around Geoffrey. "Your parents are outstanding human beings."

"Yes! Yes they are. I hit the jackpot in the parents lottery. How're you doing over there, sweetheart."

"I'm sorry we're going," Geoffrey said. "But I'll be glad to be home for a while. There's so much to talk about with my family."

"Do they know about the stuff you're sending Reggie?" Janis sounded amused. Her mother had discovered it, swore that Ed hadn't, and had spent more than one morning giggling with Janis over the 'letters from the road.'

"Christ, I hope not. There's an open and honest relationship, and then there's my son who's writing pornography. Even if it is behind a pay wall."

"Their son with a first from Cambridge, who's writing pornography," Niall said. "And your publisher?"

"Well," Geoffrey said, as seriously as possible, "it's cross-promotion, isn't it?" Janis laughed. "They did express concern that the new novel should be no more explicit than my last. Fortunately, as you well know, it is. I sent it off last night." Geoffrey looked around Niall at Janis. "Just before bedtime."

"Ah, I see." No doubt she did. Geoffrey had read through the book after dinner, the book closed with a love scene, and in consequence he and Janis had shared one of their own. "Which one are you doing next?"

"The climber with the saucy tour manager."

Niall kissed his cheek. "However will you make insider trading thrilling?"

"Do you doubt me?" Geoffrey's tone was wounded. Niall laughed. "Perhaps I'll write something while we're in the air. You can tell me if it's sufficiently thrilling."

"Do not do that," Janis said. "Not unless I can read it too."

Chapter 16

The flat seemed the same as when they'd left. The piano, the beds, the other furnishings: all as they'd been before. Spotlessly clean, with fresh linens and everything they needed to settle in and survive their first few days. A note from the domestic – the same person engaged by the agent the previous year – lay on the kitchen table when they arrived, requesting to be notified of any desired alteration to the service schedule. Within two days, Niall had Janis' work schedule organized, Geoffrey had the marketing done and bread in the oven, and Janis was in the parlor, working on the piano.

Her revised arrangements for the 'Tango à Trois' set list had been completed, printed, and sent off to the venue managements. Niall would be in communication with them all, reviewing and in some cases interviewing guest musicians. The South America dates seemed very close. They were all excited.

And as much as they'd all liked staying with Ed and Deborah, it was pure joy having complete privacy again. They were blessed with warm weather, and took advantage of it to roam naked, or nearly so, through the flat. All that nudity had unsurprising results. The dining table would have blushed, if it could have.

Niall came home from the fencing club one day, tired and inclined to nap, to silence. He knew Janis hadn't planned to go out; wasn't sure of Geoffrey's intentions; shrugged to himself and started through to his room. Then he heard Janis say, "Is that you, Niall?"

"None other. Were you expecting someone else?"

Laughter, two voices. "Could you do us a favor?"

He changed direction. Leaning on the kitchen door frame, he said, "Coffee, tea, or that ripping zinfandel?" Listened to a brief discussion, ending with more laughter and the expected reply. "In a moment, loves." He continued through to his bedroom, stripped off his clothes, and slung on the lightweight cotton haori he'd found in Los Angeles. It was sufficient covering to feel clothed, without feeling confined. Then he went to the kitchen, opened the wine, and carried the bottle to Janis' bedroom with three glasses. She and Geoffrey were sitting up against the headboard, a sheet pulled up to their laps, otherwise naked. "You look like honeymooners," he remarked, setting down the glasses and pouring the wine. When they each had a glass, there were clinked rims, approving sips, and happy sighs. Niall sat cross-legged on the foot of the bed.

"You look like the last samurai," Geoffrey said, eyeing him with interest. "Had your mates at the club anything to say about your Macbeth?" He knew that the video series with Red had been quite a hit in the U.K. Reggie had begged him to write a 'letter from the road' having to do with the erotic consequences of non-euphemistic swordplay, and linked the series to it.

"A bit." That was an understatement; Niall had been mobbed by junior fencers, more sedately congratulated by his older acquaintances. "A theatre company wants me for the part. There was a letter at the club." Janis was making Interested Face. "And no, I shan't be accepting the role. I still don't want to be an actor. Besides, we've far too much to do, and they aren't staging it till October."

"You're not even going to talk to them?" Janis seemed disappointed.

"You could train another actor for them," Geoffrey suggested. "You'd have time for that, wouldn't you? Teach them the fight as you and Red did it?" Niall looked undecided. "Well, don't give them a flat refusal till you've thought about it. If they've an adequate rehearsal space, they might open it to the public. You know the small companies are always desperate for cash."

"I wonder if Red could come over," Janis said. "Didn't Mary say she hadn't been home for years? When was his movie shoot finished?"

"This month." Niall stared at both of them for a moment, surprised to find he didn't remotely loathe the idea. Geoffrey had that warm expression, the one that said 'you can do anything' and also 'please do it to me.' Niall smiled suddenly. "Yes, all right, I'll have a word with him. If he and Mary can come over, we'll find them a place to stay near here, and then I'll contact the company. Satisfied?"

"Not entirely," Geoffrey said, "but perhaps after I've finished this excellent wine we could see about that." They talked for a while, contemplated a second glass and decided to save it for dinner, discussed what dinner should be.

Then Janis got out of bed, leaned over to kiss Geoffrey, and said, "I am going to play for a while. You two can entertain yourselves, I'm sure."

Niall set down his empty glass on the nearest available surface and stretched out on his back in the space vacated by Janis. "Thought I might have a nap." A glance up at Geoffrey, who was looking not at Niall's face but at his body, nearly bare as the haori fell away.

They heard a snort from Janis, the rustle of her summer robe, and then soft footsteps leaving the room.

"Choirs of angels, you're a lovely creature," Geoffrey said softly.

"You quote me now?"

"I remember every devastating thing you say to me." Geoffrey leaned over for a kiss, setting a hand on Niall's chest, brushing it down to his hip. Sweeping lightly down across the tops of his thighs, then up and around. Watching, from the corner of his eye, the predictable and irresistible results. Circling closer and closer to the erection that rose to his touch. "Every devastating thing you do," he added, trailing kisses down Niall's throat. "My God, Reggie would set the world on fire to see you thus."

Niall laughed, breathless, as Geoffrey's hand closed around him. Then it was another kiss, deep and lingering and passionate, with Geoffrey's bare body pressed to his. Moving against each other with growing urgency, until he was half out of his mind. He wrapped an arm around his husband and hauled him out of bed, stumbling a few steps, pressing him to the wall.

Geoffrey braced himself, feet apart, eyes closed. Listening to the nightstand drawer open and close, waiting for the touch he wanted. A senseless sound escaped him when Niall's hand went between his legs, lightly caressing at first, then more strongly to ready him. "Kiss me," he managed, turning his head. Niall did, his other hand on Geoffrey's face, breath quickening as he engaged. "Yes. More. Niall." Geoffrey let his head rest against Niall's shoulder, face turned toward his, pushing back against his thrusts.

Niall lost track of time, lost track of his hands, lost all capacity for self-control. When he came to himself he said, "Geoffrey." His mouth was on that sleek trapezius and his teeth had been set quite firmly in it. "Christ."

"Mmm." Geoffrey was trembling, his own quiescent cock in Niall's wet hand. "My tiger."

Niall disengaged. They both made a sound. "Are you all right." His legs were shaky, and his voice slightly so.

"I'm well."

"Let's get you off your feet." Niall moved him to the bed, laid him down, kissed his bruised shoulder. Stroked a hand down his back and staggered to the washroom. Geoffrey heard water running and thought *always such care of me*, eyes closed to savor the feeling of having been so possessed. Niall was there a minute later with soft words, more kisses, gentle hands, and a robe laid over him to keep him warm. Then lying down beside him with an arm across his back. They gazed at each other for a minute. "I feel such a brute sometimes."

"You know you don't hurt me. You know I like it. You feel how I like it." Geoffrey smiled. "My potent master."

Niall blew out a breath, half-laughing. "Potent, is it. I give thanks you're a strong man."

"Strong enough to take you. Never doubt it. Never hesitate," Geoffrey added. "I take what I need, whether time or silence or distance. I serve by consent."

It was a current that had run through the entire relationship without open acknowledgement for perhaps a day too long. A truth that, thanks to Deborah, they had all now articulated and accepted. And a reality made explicit – if only to them – in Geoffrey's lyrics.

"Unless and until one of us is sufficiently old and decrepit that such frolics are medically prohibited," Niall said lightly, and kissed his nose. Geoffrey laughed. "I still don't quite believe you let me have you so soon after the bloody avalanche."

"Soon! It was six weeks!"

"Yes, and your leg still in a cast."

"It itched like the devil. I was never so glad to feel the sun on my skin." Geoffrey's right shin was still somewhat paler than his left. "You didn't let me fall. You never would."

"I'll always catch you. Thank God I didn't have to, I was afraid enough for your ribs as it was."

"Didn't stop you, though."

"No, it didn't," Niall agreed smugly, and they both laughed again.

Janis was regularly practicing her set for the upcoming tour, but she was also at work on the Tempest lyrics. Geoffrey sat in the parlor, working on his novel, less than half-listening most of the time. The process wasn't music, precisely; it was phrases, chords, a good deal of scribbling on staff paper, and continual muttering. He found it no more distracting than her playing the previous summer. "I can't believe you can write while I'm doing this," she said one day, after a long session. She stood up and paced, stretching her hands, rolling her neck. "It's driving me crazy and I don't have to listen to it."

Geoffrey smiled at her. "If you'd asked me thirteen months ago, could I write while someone practiced the piano, I'd've said no. Funny what's pleasant when you love someone."

"You sweetie." She came over to kiss him, then wandered away again. "Massage guy is coming later. Should I stretch before or after?"

"Both," he said. "You know, I think why it's not distracting is it's like a different language. There's that Chinese restaurant I like to go to, everyone chattering away at the tops of their voices, but it doesn't get in my way at all."

"And then you bring home lemon chicken and make the rest of us happy. I'm getting into my yoga pants." She left the room for a while. Geoffrey got on with the scene he was writing. The tour manager had – perhaps inevitably – taken on some of Niall's characteristics. The book's hero, however, was nothing like himself, which presented certain difficulties. In a sense, Geoffrey was making his own true love fall in love with someone else. It was oddly unsettling, but it was working. He gave the hero some of the dash he'd seen in Oliver Dunn's filmed performances, a physical similarity, and a tendency to disappear into his work. He knew Niall (who now routinely read his drafts) had noticed, though it was acknowledged with nothing more than one of those thoughtful glances.

Geoffrey finished the scene, was well ahead of his target word count for the day, and was therefore on the floor stretching when Janis returned to join him. They were still there when Niall got home from a meeting, bearing takeout from a favorite Italian restaurant. "Hello loves," he said, leaning into the parlor. "Ready for your massage, Janis?"

"Is he here?" She got her feet under her and stood up.

"Momentarily." Niall gave her a kiss as she passed him on her way to the powder room. "Darling, can you manage for the time it'll take me to go for wine?"

Geoffrey was also on his feet. "Or I could go. I haven't been out today."

"Then off with you." Another kiss as one of his loves passed by, this one with a quick catch of their hands. "That Brunello she likes, if you would."

"Naturally." Geoffrey was smiling as he went to fetch his shoes, keys, and wallet. He passed the massage therapist coming up the street, nodded a greeting, and recognized a stringer for one of the entertainment news sites. Another nodded greeting, but no pause; he wanted to dispatch his errand and get home again.

The stringer was still there as he returned with two bottles of wine. Geoffrey suppressed a sigh, and gave in to her urgent but tentative gesture. "Mr. Anand. Thank you for stopping. Rumor has it the American actor Red Warner and his wife are coming to London to work with your husband. Is that true?"

Geoffrey was surprised. "Where'd you hear that?"

She looked shifty. "Sources."

Probably the letting agent for that flat we found them, he thought, amused. "Well yes, it's true. Mr. Warner and Mr. Phelps will be helping a theatre company put together a sword fight."

Her eyes went wide. "Like the one in that video?"

"If possible."

"For the same play?" She sounded truly excited. "Oh, our readers would love to know more. When it's to be, whether the rehearsals might be open?"

323

Geoffrey knew that the company would jump at the chance of early publicity. He also knew that Red was well able to handle himself, even with the British tabloid press, and that Niall was perfectly capable of unleashing the bastard if necessary. Would probably enjoy it, in fact. So he told the stringer the name of the company, and the name of their contact there; accepted her gushing thanks; and strolled off home. With that slight delay, it was only a half-hour more before they were sitting down to their dinner.

"Ugh," Janis said some time later. "Why did I eat all that tiramisu."

"Because you like it," Niall said, amused. "Shall we to Regent's Park for a walk?"

"Not a bad idea. I'll stretch again after. I will," she said to Geoffrey, who looked unconvinced. "And then I will play one thing from the tour set, and then I will go to bed and dream of Italy." It was an excellent plan, and one that altered only slightly. She virtuously stretched (as did Niall, in response to Geoffrey's murmured 'unless you want a cramp later'), then had a glass of water, and then returned to the parlor. She started to play the twelfth song from the set, not singing.

Geoffrey was on the couch again, relaxed, half-watching, half-listening. Niall was beside him, and then he wasn't. He stood behind Janis, one hand on her shoulder and the other stroking back her hair. She leaned against him, her hands still on the piano keys but no longer playing. "I love this song," she said.

"So do I," said Niall. "'Promise me you'll remember this love together today.'" He sang it, soft and low. Janis caught her breath. Niall sat beside her on the bench, still singing, his back to the keyboard and shoulder against hers. "'We may not have tomorrow, it's not for us to say.'" He reached out a hand. Geoffrey stood up and went to them. Then it was Niall singing to Janis with their heads close together, one of his hands on Geoffrey's waist and the other on Janis' thigh. Geoffrey with his hands in their hair, and Janis starting to play again, an unadorned arrangement, in a different key for Niall's deeper voice. Tears on her face. "'Promise me you'll remember how good we are,'" he finished, an eternity later.

Then he pulled Geoffrey down onto his lap and they were all in a tangle, crying together, until the piano bench gave an ominous creak. Janis sniffled, said, "It's not the ménage-rated bench," and kissed Niall. They all stood up then, for another hug and more kisses. "I love you," she said to both of them. "No matter what, I will never not love you."

"I love you," they both said to her, and to each other.

Then Niall repeated, "No matter what." All of them seemed to take a breath, as if they all knew what he meant.

"Things might change," Janis said. "Once we're back from this tour. We'll see how we go."

Geoffrey kissed her cheek, still wet with tears. "And till then let's love each other."

Janis nodded, swallowing. "I will never forget that. Not ever." She wiped her face. "You know when I tell Valerie about that she's going to say, did you tape it, and I'm going to have to tell her no, and she's going to be on my case till the end of time because she's been after me for fucking *years* to make you sing." Niall was laughing silently. "Would you give me some goddamned warning next time?"

"I didn't know you were going to play that," he pointed out, which of course didn't answer the question.

Janis tried to glare at him. It didn't quite come across. "I will play it for you any goddamn day. Would you ever sing it again?"

"Yes, love. Only for you. Both of you." He kissed each of them. "I might even submit to recording. Here, by ourselves. Not, absolutely not, in public. It's bad enough I've this effing swordfight to do all over again."

"Oh shut up. Geoffrey, don't you have anything to say?" He shook his head. "Can you believe he did that?" Another shake of the head. "Do you need some whisky?" A nod. "Yeah, me too."

They didn't talk about it that night, or the next. It wasn't until Janis was out at dinner with some new friends that Niall and Geoffrey addressed the notion of change. They walked down to a neighborhood restaurant, strolled home through a warm humid twilight, and went to their room with cups of tea. They sat on the bed, leaning against the headboard, still in their jeans and summer shirts. "She doesn't need me anymore," Niall said after a while. "Not the way she used to." No pain in his voice, only acceptance and affection.

"She still loves you."

"Oh, of course. We'll always love each other." He glanced at Geoffrey. "She had such a time of it with that pigheaded sod Stefan." Geoffrey laughed under his breath. "She said it was better than nothing. I always wondered."

"You had nothing, for a long time. Would a Stefan have been better?"

"Decidedly not." Niall sipped tea. "But then, I didn't have that pressure to deliver every year. A new album, readying the material. Having seen that first-hand, perhaps I can grasp it. To not do that alone. To have a person who truly understood it, and who also tried to love her."

Geoffrey set his cup aside. "He did at least try, you say."

"He didn't do as well on his best day as you on your worst." Niall leaned over for a kiss. "I suspect after next summer, we'll have the short tour in North America. And then I expect she'll stay with her parents again." Niall set down his cup.

"Will we stay with her?"

"I'm sure she'll give us the option." They gazed at each other for a moment. "We'll know, when it's time for us to go."

"I hope it may not be for a long time. Thank God I'll still have you." Geoffrey wrapped his arms around Niall. They held each other quietly. "Could you have imagined this, two years ago?"

Niall made a *pfft* sound. "Could you?" He tipped his head to see Geoffrey's face. "What were you up to, two years ago?"

A wicked sideways glance. Geoffrey thought quickly, retrieving a story ripe for embellishment of the filthiest kind. "I was in Dubai, being pursued by a sheikh."

"You never were." Niall leaned back, smiling. "Tell me that story."

July 2019

Niall brought in the package from Andy Martin saying, "Were we expecting something?"

"We weren't," Geoffrey said, examining it. "Shall we wait until Janis is here to open it?"

"Not bloody likely, it's our names on the label, isn't it?" Geoffrey snorted as Niall went for the scissors. It was open a moment later and they looked at the contents, then at each other, in stupefied silence. They'd guessed from the shape that the package contained a large-format book. They'd never have guessed it was a book of their 'Tempest' photo session.

They paged through it slowly, standing by the kitchen table because they didn't want to look away from the book until they'd seen it all, not even to sit down. Every image taken for every line, as well as for the individual portraits. An opening essay from Andy, a letter really, directed to them and thanking them for the inspiration. A brief credits page, thanking the costume designer, the jewelers, the makeup artist, and the builder of the dragon-bones throne. "Our friend Mr. Warner," Niall said. "A man of many talents." Then a section with the fifteen images that had been shown, each filling a facing page. On the page beside it, Geoffrey's lyric. And finally a section for each line, with the gallery image isolated beside it, and all the other images following.

"Only the two copies," Geoffrey said at last. "One for him, and one for us."

"He said he'd hang those again when he finished the rest of his Shakespeare things. Would he print a book then, for the general public? I know he's done a few." Niall made sure Geoffrey had a good grip on the book, and went to fetch them some coffee. "Let's sit. I can't decide if I want to write him an embarrassing love letter, or berate him for not warning us, or simply cry."

"Nor can I." Geoffrey sat down with the book cradled against his chest. "Everything I've ever felt for you is on these pages."

"Yes. That's it exactly." Niall brought the coffee and sat down across from him. "It's the most priceless artifact, and I would never have thought even to ask."

Geoffrey kept one arm wrapped over the book, holding his coffee cup with the other hand. He knew the book wasn't really warm, didn't truly have a beating heart. He couldn't let go of it. They sat in silence for a while. "We'll take it to your parents, shall we? Let them see it? And mine."

"Oh, of course." Niall set down his empty cup. "I never even told Mum and Dad we did that. I was going to wait until he was ready to release prints."

"I want to show Reggie," Geoffrey said suddenly. "May I? He worked in galleries before the site began to pay."

Niall leaned forward, instantly understanding. "A show here?"

"What if we could bring the Shakespeare show to London, when Andy's ready?"

"We might not even be here." They stared at each other for another minute. "Wouldn't that be grand?" Niall grinned. Geoffrey smiled at him over the rim of his cup, still clutching the book.

After a while, when he could let go of it (or when Niall pried it away from him to look at it again), Geoffrey went for his phone and sent a text inviting

Reggie to the flat: *Don't get excited but we've something to show you*

The reply was prompt: *And I'm not meant to be excited? You do realize you've had precisely the opposite effect. Is this to do with your portrait?*

Not this time, but we'll speak of that soon. They arranged a day and a time, and Geoffrey signed off. He and Niall prepared themselves (and the flat) for Janis to see the book. And then they sent a text to Andy: *Mr Martin we've received your gift. We are now making inquiries for a fireproof safe in which to keep this treasure. Words cannot express our thanks. We are in your debt. Yours sincerely, Niall & Geoffrey*

The reply came in overnight: *Other way around. I'm reading my way through the complete works while Victor and his gang do their thing on this ridiculous movie. Have already warned prospective subjects. Cannot fucking wait to get started, haven't felt like this about a photography project for three years. Will advise when it's close to done. Oh and here is Molly's face after stepping into Lake Superior.* He attached a photo of his dog, wearing an expression that clearly said 'shocked and betrayed.'

"I'll vouch for that," said Niall. "It's colder than the bloody Pacific."

Reggie came into the flat talking. "Your letters from the road, lad, are making me rich. Unbelievable demand for the ad space. It seems ages since we spoke; did you miss me?"

"My dear man, of course." They all shook hands. "Come in. Welcome to the London HQ. Janis wanted to put down some roots here, she had a chance to get this flat. It's a blessing for the two of us as we're off on a world tour in September. Coffee?"

"Ta. Oh, very nice." They were in the parlor. Reggie looked around with approval. "The piano came with the flat?"

"I think it's half the reason Janis wanted this place," Niall said. "That and Abbey Road. She's over there today. Have a seat. We'll have coffee and catch up, and then we'll show you something."

"Ah yes. The thing I'm not meant to be excited about. From which caution I've deduced I shan't be seeing either of you with your kit off."

"Well that isn't precisely the case." Niall laughed at the way Reggie's face lit up. "Not in the flesh, I hasten to add."

"Have you done some dirty pictures, my doves? Have I died and gone to heaven? Can I publish them?"

Geoffrey heard most of this from the kitchen. He was smiling as he brought in the coffee. "Calm yourself, Mr. Galant. We do not own the copyright, so any question of publication rests with the author. And these pictures aren't precisely dirty. But you were at Newcastle. I saw it in your bio." The bio that mentioned Reggie's degree show, among others.

"Bless my soul, someone on Earth has read it." Reggie sipped coffee. "What's that got to do with anything?"

"If you still ask once you've seen this, I wash my hands of you."

"I haven't been *in* your hands, you vicious sod. Well, then, tell me about this tour." He listened as Niall talked.

Geoffrey watched both of them, half-listening. Janis, of course, had loved the book. She was one hundred percent behind the notion of bringing Andy's Shakespeare show to London, whether they were there to see it or not. If it happened the following summer, though, they might … . Geoffrey realized that Niall had stopped talking and was giving him an inquiring look. "Is it time?"

"Yes, darling. Will you fetch it or shall I?"

"I will." He went out and down the hall to their bedroom, where the book currently reposed in the top drawer of the bureau. Before taking it out, he washed his hands. It didn't look the treasure it was, from the outside. A black hardcover book, with the title – 'A Tempest' – stamped in silver on the spine. Andy's signature, an illegible scrawl, stamped in silver on the front. Geoffrey couldn't help hugging it to his chest again as he went back through to the parlor. "Clean hands, Mr. Galant?"

"I've just washed." He sat there expectantly, not reaching for the book, as if he could tell how important it was to Geoffrey. "Will I look at it alone or will you sit with me?"

"Ordinarily," said Niall, "I shouldn't quite trust you in that proximity. However, in this case, an exception can be made." He moved over to the couch. Geoffrey sat down on Reggie's other side, and passed him the book.

Reggie read the opening letter. Made a pleased sound at the first gallery image, the Ariel solo. In the chosen image Geoffrey stood balanced on the balls of his feet, in profile, the filmy toga blending into the backdrop and the applied effects. One bare arm reached straight down, his gilded hand contacting the top of his bare thigh. The other arm reached up. His head was tipped back and his gaze directed at the lifted hand. He looked like a dancer, or as if he were about to take flight.

Then Reggie was silent, his progress slow, his attention absolute. When at last he closed the book, he passed it back to Geoffrey and then pressed his hands to his face. "Fuck. Me. Stupid. Is there the remotest chance this artist would bring these pictures to London for a show? Or send them?"

Niall and Geoffrey looked at each other across Reggie and smiled. "This artist," said Niall, "is not just any Andy Martin. He is the co-star of last winter's art-house hit 'The Ghost of Carlos Gardel,' had a long career on Broadway, and recently performed the prince and swan pas de deux from Bourne's 'Swan Lake' in Los Angeles, to swooning reviews. He is currently on the set of his husband Victor Garcia's feature film, in which he had a cameo."

Reggie dropped his hands, looking appalled. "An effing movie star? Christ on a plank, a sodding *movie star* made *those photographs*?"

"He's a bit talented," Geoffrey said, trying not to laugh.

"But look." Niall had some sympathy for Reggie. "Andy's told us he's planning a full-scale show based on Shakespeare. He asked if he could center it on this group of pictures and of course we said yes. He'll show it in Los Angeles first. We got to know him quite well."

"And?" Reggie stood up and turned, leaning against the piano where he could see both of them.

Geoffrey said, "There's a very good chance for a show here. Mr. Martin is, if possible, even less enthused by an actor's life than is my own husband. He is a dancer and an artist. He's brilliant. I think he'd like you." *As I do*, he thought but didn't say. He was confident Reggie knew.

"He can hate me as long as he'll let me hang that show. I can do it," Reggie added, pacing restlessly. "I've the connections. Not everyone in the art world minds how I make my living, and hardly anybody else even knows."

"Only your subscribers." Niall didn't think Andy would care.

"Those who read past 'click here for filth.' I don't know what to tell you." Reggie stood still. "You know how good that work is. Much as I'd like to publish it, it doesn't belong on my site. I'd never ask it of you, or of your friend. But if you could pass the word, that I'd mount a show for him here, I'd owe you."

"Certainly. We hoped you would." Geoffrey stood up. "And I'd disagree. Mr. Martin might think your art page a worthy avenue. I would." He was still holding the book – it seemed once he had it, he never wanted to let go of it – but offered his free hand.

Reggie shook it, glancing down at the book. "Tell you something else."

"What's that?"

"My greatest love and I weren't like that on our best day. I've a mind to do better. How does one begin?"

"Well," Niall said, "first of all you must have a set of requirements it is absolutely impossible for a single person to meet, and second of all you must walk into the least likely possible place at the most random possible time. Having done that, should the one other person there be willing to walk out with you, you must simply allow yourself to fall."

Reggie stared at him for a moment. "You don't ask much, do you?"

"If it's meant to be," Geoffrey said, "he'll catch you."

THE END

*The story of Janis & Niall begins in stand-alone
novella A SECRET CHORD, available at Amazon.
Thanks for reading!*

*****

About the Author

Alexandra Caluen lives in a small purple house with
her husband, a bottle of Laphroaig, a lot of books, and
nine pairs of ballroom shoes. She works in patent law
and has enough hair for three people.

www.thelastories.com